KAY JENNINGS

A PORT STIRLING MYSTERY: BOOK 8

HUNTER'S BOG

Copyright © 2024 by Kay Jennings

All rights reserved. No part of this publication may be reproduced, distributed, or transmitted in any form or by any means, including photocopying, recording, or other electronic or mechanical methods, without prior written permission of the publisher, except in the case of brief quotations embodied in critical reviews and certain other noncommercial uses permitted by copyright law.

Author's Note

No part of this story was created using artificial intelligence. The fun of producing a book — and, for me, that's certainly *not* the design, the formatting, or any of the technical parts — is the storytelling. Making it all up and seeing where your beloved characters take you this time. A fresh page every morning. A strong cup of coffee as I sit down to write. Knowing that I, and only I, am in charge of my work. Why would I let a machine take that away from me?

Hunter's Bog/Kay Jennings — 1st ed.

ISBN: (Hardcover edition): 979-8-9922798-1-8
ISBN: (Paperback edition): 979-8-9922798-0-1

Publisher's Note: *Hunter's Bog* is a work of fiction. The events and circumstances that occur within are a product of the author's imagination. While certain locales, including the title, may draw on real life, they are used fictitiously to add authenticity to the story. The cast of characters are fictitious and are not based on real people, businesses, or organizations.

Cover Design by Claire Brown
Interior Design by Steve Kuhn/Kuhn Design Group
Author Photo by Erica J. Mitchell

Printed and bound in the USA
First printing 2025
Published by Paris Communications
Portland, Oregon.

www.kayjenningsauthor.com

Reader Praise for A Port Stirling Mystery Series

This 5-star series is a must read—lots of twists and turns making the books hard to put down —Debra L. Jacklin

Bought for my mother-in-law in the U.K. who is a crime/thriller/who dunnit book snob :) She LOVED them. —Amelia Highfield

This book was gripping and hard to put down. It didn't feel like everything else you see out there, it felt very fresh. —Alicia Goeser

Jennings is a master at creating authentic, believable characters whom a reader can either fall in love with or absolutely detest. —HeyAnnisPoet

From the opening page to the final words, the author holds your interest completely. —Barbara Baker

I've read all of the books in the series, in order, and already am salivating for the next one. —James Duran

Highly recommended for fans of well-crafted, suspenseful mysteries. —Joanne Hurley

Great storyline from the first page on. Love this author. —Barbara Greene

Love the setting, characters and the twists and turns of this all-round good mystery series. Always building tension all the way to surprise endings. —Dorcas Herr

Love Kay Jennings ability to draw me in and make me feel like I am part of the team working on the case. —Betty Folmsbee

Best book I've read this year. I enjoyed it immensely and would recommend it to anyone interested in a well written and intense novel. —Al Lieteau

Other books by Kay Jennings:

Shallow Waters

Midnight Beach

Code: Tsunami

Dark Sand

Phantom Cove

Mourning Bay

Cold Rock Island

I find myself thinking about my two wonderful grandmothers these days, to whom I was close, and what I received from each.

*From Eula Mae McIntee,
I developed a love of art and gardening.*

*From Virgie Billings,
I acquired my business sense and a love of fashion.*

*Both women are responsible
for my fondness for tomato/mayo sandwiches.*

Both women showed me there is a bigger world out there than our little Oregon corner of it, and for that, I am most grateful.

This book is dedicated to them.

SPOILER ALERT!

If this is the first book in my Port Stirling Mystery series you've opened, and you think you might enjoy reading all of them, please set *Hunter's Bog* aside for now. This story draws heavily on earlier book villains and characters and will ruin the mysteries in my first seven books for you. Hunter's Bog will make more sense and be much more enjoyable if you've read the others first.

I mean it...set this book down now if you haven't read Shallow Waters, Midnight Beach, Code: Tsunami, Dark Sand, Phantom Cove, Mourning Bay, and Cold Rock Island!

HUNTER'S BOG

CHAPTER 1

Oregon State Penitentiary—April

The visitor turned off State St in Salem, Oregon, and drove up the tree-lined driveway to the Visiting Center. The tooth-rattling speed bumps leading to the parking lot added to the visitor's anxiety. The unmistakable eerie silence of the grounds was always unnerving.

Directly in front of the entrance, a three-story tower with wrap-around windows like an air traffic control tower intimidated the visitor. But the car was parked, and there was no turning back now.

The visitor had completed the application process last year and only needed to check-in at the reception desk on the right through the building's main entrance. The officer checked the visitor's ID and compared it to his computerized list of approved visitors. All belongings—car keys, cash, credit cards—except for ID, in this instance, a driver's license, were deposited in the lockers provided.

Shoes were removed to pass through the X-ray metal detector apparatus. *All clear.*

Down the ramp to the first set of barred, steel doors. Show ID and sign in. *All clear.*

At the second barred gate, ID was again produced, and the visitor's hand, at the request of a disembodied voice, passed through the opening in the dark, tinted window to receive a stamp on the hand. The visitor's ID would stay in this booth, in exchange for a visitor's badge to be clearly displayed.

A uniformed guard escorted the visitor to the main entrance; the adult in custody (AIC) would enter through a different door. In a previous visit, they had to meet in the basic visits room, which consisted of two chairs on the opposite side of a strong, tempered glass window, a phone on each side to communicate. The prisoner had been under disciplinary sanctions for some rules infraction — the visitor didn't know why, and never asked. *Didn't care.*

But this time, the visitor was escorted into the main visiting room, which was divided into two large sections, each section holding twenty-five tables with two chairs at each — one colored gray for the AIC, and one burgundy for the guest. The table and chairs reminded them of the kids' table during the holidays.

Thankfully, the room was sparsely populated today, and the visitor chose a table well away from the others. As much privacy as possible — difficult in this building — was needed for today's conversation.

The AIC was escorted to the table, and the two people sat facing each other. The prisoner smiled a timid smile.

The prisoner: "It's good to see you. You look good."

The visitor: "I don't have much time today."

The prisoner: "That's OK. I'm just glad to see you. It's been a while."

The visitor: "Yeah, this place gives me the creeps. Sorry."

The prisoner's mouth contorted into a sardonic smile. "It gives all of us the creeps."

The visitor: "I had to talk to you today."

The prisoner: "What's up?"

The visitor: "I'm getting low on money."

The prisoner shrugged: "Sell the house then."

The visitor: "And go where? I don't want to do that."

The prisoner: "Move into Matt Horning's house." A snarl. "I hear it's big enough for all of us."

The visitor: "I hate him. Him and his obnoxious wife. It's not fair. You and I are thinking alike, and it's why I'm here today. Here's my idea." The visitor leaned in closer to the prisoner, and whispered, "Could you help me work up a scheme to kidnap her and make him pay a fat ransom to get her back? Where we wouldn't get caught, of course."

The prisoner, wide-eyed, stared at the visitor for a long while. "Are you nuts?" The two sat and eyeballed each other. Then the prisoner whispered back, "Possible. Some of my colleagues in here might help. Let me noodle it. Are you sure you want to take on Horning?"

The visitor: "I can't think of another way out, can you? I have a life, too. Don't take too long. I'm in a hurry." The visitor stood and strode quickly out of the room.

CHAPTER 2

Scotland, Two Weeks Ago

Edinburgh Airport was a nightmare, but it would be much, much worse fourteen days from now.

Once Port Stirling Chief of Police Matt Horning and his wife, U.S. Special Agent Fern Byrne, got through Customs on this afternoon in late May and made their way to the small plane that would carry them to the Shetland Islands, life started being fun again.

Three months pregnant, Fern and Matt decided it was finally time to get out of Dodge and take their oft-postponed honeymoon…before she got too uncomfortable, and, in her words, 'fat and fatter'. They chose to travel to Scotland for two reasons: neither one of them had been there previously, and, most importantly, they hoped they would get far enough away from their jobs that they might actually get some time alone.

"They say 15 million people a year go through Edinburgh Airport," said Matt. "I think they are all here today."

"What a freakin' zoo," Fern agreed. "I thought we were never going to get through Customs. But I do feel safe, and I'm positive not a single terrorist survived that ordeal."

"You, of course, with your red hair, blend right in here. But the Customs folks weren't fond of me."

Fern laughed. "You did get the stare down. I didn't like being separated from you in that crowd, but I had to chuckle."

"Don't ever laugh in this building. It's not allowed."

"I'm going to pop in here"—she motioned at a women's restroom—"and have a quick pee before we get on the puddle-jumper plane—it might not have a bathroom," Fern said.

"OK, I'll wait right here."

She came out smiling. "There, that's better. This having to pee all the time is annoying as hell."

"It will be worth it six months from now," Matt grinned. "C'mon, let's see if the Shetland Islands are all they're cracked up to be."

He threw his backpack under the plane seat in front of him and helped Fern with hers. As they stepped out of the narrow aisle and took their seats, Matt smiled at the couple boarding behind them. They had been on their plane from Newark to Edinburgh, too, and he thought the woman looked vaguely familiar. Couldn't place her, though.

"Are you doing OK?" Matt asked his wife as she looked out the plane's small window, rubbing her neck.

"I'm doing great." She hugged his arm. "We're in Scotland! We actually made our getaway! I'm so excited to see the Shetland Islands. People I know who've been said it looks just like Port Stirling in places."

"Well, it may look similar, but there's no way it can be as beautiful as Port Stirling."

Fern consulted her travel journal, flipping a few pages. "There's a place called Eshaness that a friend told me is more dramatic for coastal cliff-top views than anything we've got at home."

Matt made a sound like 'humph' and said, "I'll be the judge of that. Are we going there?"

"Yeah. I thought we'd check in, walk down to Lerwick's main street, have dinner, and then go to bed early to rest up. I am a little tired after the long flights. I booked a local guide for tomorrow."

"What time are we meeting?" he asked. Fern had planned their entire trip, and Matt was just now learning about the schedule. *It was better this way,* he thought. He was just as excited as his wife to see all that Scotland had to offer, but Fern's attention to detail surpassed his. If left to his own devices, he would wander around and be happy, but he might end up with a crappy hotel and bad food. Fern would make sure that didn't happen. They were a great combo.

"Our guide is coming to our hotel at 11:00 a.m. tomorrow to pick us up. He'll do all the driving and show us the north part of the island. He lives up north and says it's the most beautiful. Then, the next day, we have a rental car, and we'll head out exploring on our own."

Matt looked at her and raised an eyebrow. "Who's going to drive on the left side of the road?"

"You are," she grinned. "It'll be a piece of cake."

The flight was one hour and twenty-five minutes on their Loganair turboprop and took them over the east coast of Scotland and a big expanse of the North Sea before landing at Sumburgh on the southern tip of Mainland Shetland. A waiting taxi drove them the roughly thirty-minute drive to Lerwick. Although the sky was leaden with dark clouds and a fine rain, it was about an hour before sunset, and the Hornings got both a good look at the landscape, and a non-stop narration from their driver, an enthusiastic, affable Shetlander.

He dropped them at the door of their accommodation, a small apartment on the second floor of a white-stone building on a short, narrow street of other two-story, old stone structures. Fern opened the rust-colored front door with the keypad code that was emailed to her when she booked. She'd chosen this place rather than a more traditional hotel because they wanted privacy—it was, after all, their honeymoon.

Matt took a deep breath as he hoisted their bags out of the taxi's trunk. *It smells like the sea*, he thought. *Like home, only older somehow.* The air was brisk, and he hoped the heat had been turned on in their place.

"Make sure you get everything out of the boot," the driver said. "I'd hate to have to put up your stuff on eBay." His eyes twinkled and his mouth turned up in a telling smile. "Your missus picked a good accommodation—this is one of Lerwick's best." He stuck out his hand to Matt. "I hope your stay on my island will be everything you want it to be." Matt thought he sounded confident that it would be. He set down one bag and shook the man's offered hand, hoping that everyone here would be as friendly.

"There's no elevator, hon," Fern announced as they stood in the black and white tiled foyer and looked up the two flights of stairs that doubled away from and then back to the front of the building. "Give me my wheelie."

"Nope. I'm the lugger of luggage on this trip. You can wear your backpack, but I'll get the rest." In truth, they'd decided to travel light on this trip because they would be moving around quite a bit. They each brought a small wheelie and a backpack, and their backpacks mostly contained just their personal laptops and toiletries for the trip here.

"I'm just pregnant, I'm not sick," Fern said. But she took off up the stairs because she knew it would be futile to argue with her own personal Sir Galahad. She waited for him at the top of the landing before she opened the door.

"Wow," she said, entering the space ahead of him.

"Wow is right," he agreed, setting down their suitcases in the small entry. It was just big enough for a three-foot wide bench, and two mounted coat hooks on opposite walls. The flooring here and throughout the apartment was a warm, blonde wood. It was as spotless as the rest of the place. A glass-paneled door to their left led into the main room at the front of the building overlooking the street they'd arrived on.

Two large windows looked across the street and let in what little daylight was left. At one end, there was a functional kitchen with a dorm-room refrigerator, sink, dishwasher, microwave, and small cooktop, and a compact eating table with two chairs. The other end of the good-sized room served as the sitting room — sofa in front of the windows, IKEA-looking small recliner, coffee table, and a TV against the internal wall.

A small bedroom with an even tinier closet (although, compared to their giant walk-in closet at home, any closet would seem tiny) was on the opposite side of the entry. A well-appointed — and large by European standards — bathroom was situated between the two areas.

"It's very Scandinavian, don't you think?" asked Fern, hugging him.

"Yep. Clean, light woods, and modern. Not what I expected. I thought it would be more English — heavier furniture, darker rooms, that kind of thing. This is gonna be real comfy, bride. Well done."

She laughed. "It's a good start. I'm not as sure about some of the other places we're staying in for the next two weeks. Let's drop our bags and go find some dinner. I'm starving."

They'd each brought a waterproof jacket, and it was a good thing—when they stepped out the building's door in the now-dark night, the rain pelted them. And the wind was blowing a little more than when they had arrived. They tied their hoods firmly under their chins and took off walking arm-in-arm down the wet sidewalk.

Fern had the map of central Lerwick memorized in her brain, and knew they wanted to turn left at the first corner, just two buildings up from theirs. Immediately, they were walking down a fairly steep hill which looked like it was about two city blocks long. "This will be fun coming back up," she said sarcastically.

"Aww, it's good for you and our baby—good exercise," Matt said. "It feels great to be out here. Get that airplane air out of our systems."

"If you say so," she said, just as a fat raindrop splatted on her cheek. She pulled her hood out more to cover her face. "We're not going far. There are three or four restaurants at the bottom of this hill, and Rick Steves likes them all." She pointed to the street they would intersect with. "That's the main road through the center of town. We'll go right and should come to the restaurants."

Sure enough, there was a pedestrian-only area that veered off at an angle from the main road, and it was filled with shops, three banks, and several small restaurants. One was a fish place that had a good rating, but it was boisterous tonight with a couple of loud groups. The other was a tiny French restaurant with only five tables, but it looked cozy and warm, and they chose it.

"I'm tired," Fern admitted. "We can do the noisy place tomorrow night once we've caught up on some sleep, OK?"

Matt smiled. "I'm not interested in loud tonight either. This little restaurant suits me fine."

They stepped up the big stone step, opened the door into the warm interior, and were greeted by a plump woman who, indeed, looked very French. She eyed them and said in heavily accented English, "It's quite late for dinner."

Fern eyed her right back and replied, "We just flew here from New Jersey, and I would've asked the pilot to fly faster if I could have. We're hungry."

The hostess laughed loudly with pure joy at Fern's remark and said, "Bonsoir, Americans! Come in." She indicated the table for two in the center of the close-packed room, and they obediently took their chairs.

Their hostess handed them menus and then turned to a man standing behind a partition with an open window. "My husband, Alain. He is your chef." Alain, who looked even more French than his wife, gave them a small wave and a broad smile before resuming his work.

"How does a French couple end up running a restaurant halfway to the Arctic Circle?" Matt asked in a friendly manner.

"Ooof, it is a long story," she said, dramatically brushing her forehead with the back of one hand. "I will tell you once you have some wine in front of you."

The Hornings settled in.

...

Yes, the weather was not ideal. Yes, the wind was relentless. Yes, they almost drove their rental car straight into another car in the first roundabout they had to negotiate. But also yes, the Shetland Islands were magical for Matt and Fern.

They toured in their guide's little car and saw sights which they'd never seen before. The cliffs of Eshaness from their ferocious heights and even more ferocious winds were as advertised. The Atlantic Ocean butted up against them repeatedly with violent waves, whose spray was sent hundreds of feet in the air and carried by the wind to wherever it damn well wanted to carry it.

Their first-day guide, Callum, had taught them how to exit the car when the winds were up. Only one car door at a time could be opened and then shut before the second door could be opened. Which made it tricky because Matt and Fern had to hold onto each other and Callum to keep from blowing away as they slowly progressed to the edge of the cliffs.

Callum was thrilled that they had caught Eshaness on "the best day possible!", and they could only assume that he was talking about the drama the nearly gale-force winds provided. They returned on their own the second day when the wind had subsided and reveled in having the entire bluff to themselves to take pictures and frolic without fear of being blown into the sea.

They ate haddock fish and chips that even the born-and-raised Oregonian, Fern, had to admit were hard to beat. There are more sheep than people on Shetland and choosing between the excellent seafood and equally excellent lamb was difficult.

Their Scandinavian apartment was a godsend, extremely comfortable with a hot shower and nice bed at the end of their sightseeing days. The mini fridge was perfect for storing yogurt and fruit so they could start out with a modest breakfast that would be gone in time to gorge on more fish and chips at lunch. They made love every day, Matt at first nervous about her condition and worried his bride wouldn't want to. Fern said, "I'm pregnant, I'm not dead. And I'm on my honeymoon. C'mon, cowboy."

Matt could not argue with that.

Fern would have stayed longer, as there were some places on her list they didn't have time for, but Matt was ready to get off the island and back to the mainland. In case they forgot they were on an island, one incident reminded them. Out of cash, they went to an ATM in the center of Lerwick to get money to pay their guide. Their card was accepted, but it wouldn't dispense any cash.

They tried another bank a block away. Same story. No cash. Callum said, "No problem. Try again in the morning and just leave it in an envelope with my name on it at this bank—I have an account here, and they'll take care of it." So, they went back the next morning, and, sure thing, the ATM worked, and they took cash into Callum's bank. Turns out, the teller told them, it had been too rough for the ferry from Aberdeen bringing cash and goods to sail yesterday, and the ATMs all ran out of money.

Outside the bank, their task finished, Matt said, "If you lived here, wouldn't you plan for that to happen occasionally, and have a stash of cash on hand at the banks?" He shook his head in disbelief, and Fern laughed at her logical American husband. *Looks like we're not moving to Shetland,* she thought.

"What if that wind kept up for a week?" he continued. "A month? What the hell would they do? And what about fresh produce? You know the bulk of it has to come from the mainland."

"Guess they'd survive on haddock and lamb," she noted. "And whisky."

CHAPTER 3

Flying out of Shetland's small but functional airport after four days in Lerwick, they headed to Aberdeen on the northeast coast of Scotland. The plan was to loop around through the Scottish Highlands for a week.

Matt, cop that he was, noticed the male half of the couple he'd seen twice before on the same plane with them again. He approached him in the waiting room at Sumburgh airport while Fern went to the ladies' room prior to boarding.

"Hey, are you following us?" Matt smiled in greeting.

"Looks that way, huh?" the man said, chuckling. "What'd you think of Shetland?"

"Awesome place to visit, wouldn't want to live there. You?"

"I probably liked it better than that," the man said. "There is something about the place that appeals to me. The isolation of it, I guess."

"What did your wife think? Where is she?" Matt looked around the waiting room.

The man said, "She got called back to the U.S. Had to leave early. I decided to carry on."

"That's a shame," Matt said. "My wife and I were just talking about the fact that neither of our bosses has called us with urgent news. It's a miracle," he laughed, throwing his hands up in the air and giving them a shake. "Name's Matt Horning."

The man didn't shake hands. "I'm John Smith."

"Really?" asked Matt.

"Really," said the man. "Me and about eight million other guys. I hope you and your wife have a nice vacation, and I'll probably see you around." He turned and went to the far corner of the waiting room, took a seat, and buried his nose in a paperback.

Guess we're done chatting, Matt thought.

• • •

They had an even smaller car in Aberdeen than their rental in Shetland, and it was a good thing.

"Could these roads be any narrower?" Matt exclaimed as they headed west on a road through the countryside. "No, they could not."

Fern, looking nervously out her passenger window at the low stone wall that ran alongside the road, said, "You've only got about four inches to spare over here, cowboy."

"What the hell am I supposed to do?" he yelled. "Hit the oncoming truck? I'll take my chances with the rock wall."

Their drive was gloriously beautiful, with sparkling rivers and forested landscape…until they met another vehicle. Then it was sheer terror as Matt squeezed them between the stone wall and the other vehicle. About the third panicky time, he said, "I'll get used to it. I will. Just don't talk when another car approaches, OK?"

"Yes, dear."

"And give me more notice when I have to make a turn."

"Yes, dear." Fern had a paper map open on her lap, plus the GPS to help them navigate.

"What happens next?" he asked.

"You just keep going on this road for about thirty kilometers—that's about eighteen miles. We're going to come to a small town called Ballater, and then you're going to make a right turn onto Bridge Rd and then Braemar Rd. I'll let you know when we're getting close to our destination. We're staying in a country house hotel for two nights while we tour this area. The royal castle, Balmoral, is just a few miles west. I thought we'd check in, drop our bags, and go there this afternoon. See if Charles is about. How does that sound?"

"Well, it's a sunny, nice day so we should get out. Walking around a castle sounds good to me. Is the King here?"

Fern laughed. "Why? Are you intending to meet him? I don't know where he is right now. But my guide book says if he's at Balmoral, we can't go in the castle, but we can walk anywhere on the grounds. It's about 50,000 acres, so that should do us for today. I'm sure our hotel can tell us."

"It's good to be king, I guess."

. . .

Oak Hillside Hotel was everything Fern had dreamed it would be and more. They'd missed the miniscule sign for it hidden in the trees and had to turn around and come back. The small driveway went sharply up from the road a few hundred yards before they rounded a tight corner and entered a small, graveled car park with room for only ten cars — and only if they were small cars.

It was a grand old house, three stories tall and appeared to have been built during the Victorian era. Mostly constructed of a warm stone that Matt and Fern would later learn was known as Cairngorm smoky quartz, it had ivy covering the entry and forest green trim around the gabled windows. On the far end, an obviously more recent one-story addition constructed of all glass, looked to house an elegant, conservatory restaurant.

Exiting the car, they turned their backs on the house to look out at the view from their perch above the Dee River Valley toward the Cairngorms.

Fern said, "Spectacular. Have I died and gone to heaven?"

Matt pinched her on the arm, and she flinched. "Nope. Alive and well."

Things got even better once they went inside to the lovely interior, and were greeted by a thin, chic, charming woman in her fifties.

"Hello. Welcome. I'm Catherine," she said. She stood from a small antique desk she'd been working at and came to the entry foyer. "You must be the Hornings."

"Yes, ma'am," Matt said.

"Please set your bags down and let me show you around. Would you like a bottle of water?"

"That would be nice," Fern said.

Catherine, wearing a mid-calf plaid skirt, white silk blouse, and pearls, returned with their water. "I won't keep you long and we'll get you settled in your room. We just find it's helpful if we show you the basics." She walked briskly to a small sitting room to the right of the entry.

"You are welcome to utilize any of the rooms on this ground floor. This is one sitting room, and there's another, slightly larger, further down this hall."

"I'll take this one," Matt smiled. It did have a masculine vibe to it. On his left was a good-sized, stone, wood-burning fireplace with an intricate carved-wood surround, flanked by two cognac-colored leather chairs, each with matching plaid pillows. A well-worn Oriental rug was in front of the fireplace, and it was anchored by a multi-legged, round wood table holding a large bronze tray with a floral arrangement. A floor-to-ceiling, multi-paned window was opposite the doorway they were standing in, and two small camel armchairs, with solid dark blue pillows, and a round mahogany table with a lamp between the chairs were the only other furniture in the room. Knotty pine wood floors added a country touch.

Catherine returned Matt's smile. Cryptically, she said, "We'll see about that."

The next room was larger and lighter, due to its corner positioning with a repeat of the large paned windows, but here, on two walls. Several different seating areas — two of them included sofas — allowed for small groups, while still providing corner armchairs with good reading lamps. The color scheme was light blue, ivory, and a gentle taupe. But the stunning thing about sitting room number two was beneath their feet.

"That is the most beautiful carpet I've ever seen," Fern exclaimed to Catherine, as she reached down to rub her hand across the plush carpet. It was pale blue with light brown and ivory stylized tree arms woven through it.

"It's lovely, isn't it?" Catherine agreed. "It's a bespoke carpet from one of the U.K.'s best manufacturers. The house burned badly several years ago, and we wanted something special for the carpets we had to replace."

The carpet continued into the all-glass conservatory restaurant, which was set for dinner. The seven tables—four seating foursomes, and three for couples or singles—were spaced discreetly apart from each other.

"This is where you'll have your breakfast and dinner each day of your stay. I thought you might like the table for two set in the far corner by the window. Does that work for you?"

Matt and Fern shared a smile before Fern replied, "Yes, that works for us. It's perfect. What time should we be here for dinner?"

"Well, that all depends on the next room I must show you," and Catherine took off at a fast clip back to the entry hall, and past it where she stepped down one step into a tiny room and said, "Mind your head. You're both taller than me."

As he entered the snug little bar enveloped in Scottish blue and white plaid wallpaper, Matt laughed. "OK, now I get it. *This* will be my room."

There was barely room for the three of them in the delightful space, furnished with only a six-foot long carved white wood bar topped with zinc, two small leather armchairs, and a very old-looking two-seater wooden church pew. Behind the bar, Matt noted the three shelves of bottles, mostly Scotch whiskies—about sixty different brands—with a few bottles of gin and vodka thrown in for good measure.

"Do we have a bartender?" he asked. "Is it you?"

Catherine laughed. "No, he's called Ian, and he's my husband. He runs this room, and I manage everything else."

"Typical," chuckled Fern. She winked at Catherine, who, to Fern's surprise, winked back.

"And what time does Ian show up?" Matt asked.

"Promptly at five o'clock. Most of our guests like to have a cocktail and then go in to dinner anytime between six-thirty and seven. Let's get you checked in now, and then you can head out to enjoy this beautiful sunshine."

"I don't want to leave this floor," Fern said.

Catherine laughed again. "When you see your room, I believe you will be just as happy."

Yep. Their room was above the entry on the first floor facing south and looked out to the most entrancing views of the river valley and the

Cairngorm hills beyond. The large master room was flooded with light and managed to be both elegant and comfortable.

Catherine briefly showed them how things worked and then bid them goodbye. "We shall see you later, and we're so happy you're staying with us."

When the door closed behind her, Matt grabbed Fern in a bear hug. He said, "You, wife, are a genius. How did you find this place?"

"It jumped out at me. I knew we wanted to stay somewhere in this area, and their website was so much better than everyone else's." She looked around the room and then ran to the bathroom, coming out with a broad smile.

"I'm never leaving this house," she said. "Seriously, I'm never leaving."

. . .

They hopped back in their small car, or as Matt was now calling it, 'the death trap', and drove to Balmoral Castle.

A couple of kilometers before they arrived at the Balmoral car park, Fern glanced in her passenger-side rearview mirror.

"That's the third time you've looked in your mirror in the past five minutes," Matt said. "What's going on?"

Fern glanced at the mirror again. "I'm not sure, but I've got a sense that the car behind us might be following us. It's been there for quite a while. Gets closer and then drops back."

"Well, there's not a lot of places to pass on this road, and I'm not going that slow. Could just be a coincidence."

She looked again. "I suppose. Guess we'll know when we turn into Balmoral."

Matt put on his turn signal and steered into the Balmoral parking lot. Fern twisted in her seat to watch behind them. The car kept going, and Fern could see the driver was a woman wearing a hat and huge sunglasses. "Odd," Fern said, as the woman gave their car a good stare as she continued on.

After parking in the car park and walking on the green bridge over the River Dee, they approached the gate to Balmoral. They were told by the lone female in a smart uniform that the King was currently in residence (!), so the castle was closed, but they were welcome to go anywhere they chose on the grounds. The long, winding walk through the forested approach to the castle was peaceful, with nothing except the sound of birds to disturb the serenity.

The castle came into view ahead of them, and it was a majestic sight. However, Matt's attention was diverted by a gravel road that took off through the trees on his left.

"Do those look like greenhouses to you?" he asked Fern, pointing to three structures barely visible at the end of the road. "Let's go down here and see what it is."

Fern followed her garden-loving husband as the short road curved around a huge tree. They came to an elaborately carved iron gate, but it stood open. "She told us to go anywhere, right?" he grinned. In they went.

"Holy crap — it's the king's kitchen garden! Get a look at this."

Fern followed Matt to the first greenhouse, where a roll-up garage door was open. Two people in jeans and sweatshirts sat talking at a makeshift card table desk covered with paper files. There were no other people in sight.

"Hello," Matt said. "Are we supposed to be in here?"

The man and woman smiled brightly at them, and in a friendly fashion she said, "Absolutely, sir. The garden is open to visitors, and we love having some company. Please feel welcome to take your time."

"So, we can just wander around?" Fern asked.

"Yes, the King loves to share his gardens. He's quite an avid gardener. Are you?"

"I'm the gardener in our family," Matt smiled. "I grew up on a ranch in Texas — that's in the U.S. — and I love to grow things, especially vegetables."

The workers smiled. "We know where Texas is," the man said shyly. "Is that where you live now?"

"No, we both live in Oregon, on the west coast above California," said Matt.

"Ahh, we know Oregon well. You are in the same garden zone as us!" the man exclaimed. "Whatever you see growing here" — he flung his arm over the garden — "you can successfully grow, too. Isn't it exciting?"

"That's what we've been thinking," Matt said. "The landscape here is similar to ours in Oregon, and the weather is, too. You get colder in the winter, I suspect, but we're certainly not afraid of rain."

Fern added, "And the people are all friendly and nice to be around, and we think that's true of Oregonians as well."

And, like gardeners everywhere across the globe, they babbled and gushed together about plants, immediately old friends.

Matt and Fern stayed for two hours, and only had time before sunset to do a quick walk-around of the castle, which was really beautiful. As they turned to walk back down the roadway, Fern took one last look over her shoulder and said, "I could live there."

"Of course you could; it's a castle." He laughed and grabbed her hand.

CHAPTER 4

Back at Oak Hillside, they barely had time to change their clothes before checking out the snug bar. Fern had rightly predicted that their casual pants and sweaters were not going to cut it during the dinner hours. She donned her black ponte dress—the only one she'd brought—and added the vintage diamond ring and subtle necklace that Matt bought her for her birthday. Matt managed his one dress shirt, neatly tucked into slacks.

"I'm not wearing a tie when I'm on the first vacation I've had in years," he announced, somewhat defiant.

"That's fine. You be you. You look very handsome." Fern suspected her husband would be the only man downstairs without a tie, but she didn't care.

Fern was right. The women all wore dresses or pretty silk blouses and skirts. The men, all ties and jackets. But because they were Americans and so very, very charming, Matt and Fern were warmly welcomed by the assembled guests, numbering about twenty.

And no one was more enamored of Matt than Ian, Catherine's husband and the bartending co-owner of the hotel. From the minute Matt ducked into the snug, he and Ian were best friends for life. Matt accepted him as his personal guide and savior to Scotch whisky, and the tall, debonair Scot enthusiastically obliged.

Most of the guests had gravitated to the two sitting rooms where Catherine was busy delivering drinks, leaving Matt and Fern as the only patrons in the snug. They stood at the small bar.

"Which of our whiskies have you tasted during your trip?" Ian asked.

Matt, embarrassed, said, "None, I'm afraid. We've just come from the Shetland Islands, and we were too busy sightseeing to drink much."

Ian waved his hand, as if pooh-poohing Matt's admission of guilt. "Shetland doesn't count anyway. They are more Norwegian up there than Scottish. Don't worry, mate, we'll get you on the straight and narrow."

"When we leave here, we'll do a driving tour along the whisky trail," Matt said, trying to get in Ian's good graces. "Where should we visit? And can I try some of the local whiskies?"

"Does the sun rise in the east?" Ian twinkled. He pulled out a map of the Highlands. "We're here," he pointed, "and here's where you will drive. First, I must give you a taste of our local." He turned to the shelves behind him and pulled down a squat, clear bottle with a black band and gold cap half-full of amber whisky. "And for you, Mrs. Horning?"

"I'm afraid I'll just have some orange juice, if you have it." She patted her barely visible stomach bump.

"Ah, drinking for two, are we? Orange juice, coming up." As he worked, he asked, "What do you two handsome Americans do at home?"

Fern said, "We're cops. Police."

Ian's eyebrows shot up. "Well then, I'd better mind my business."

The Hornings laughed. "We're on vacation," Matt clarified. "Our honeymoon, actually. We were married last year, but…"

"Circumstances prevailed," Fern finished his sentence. "We needed to get away from it all."

"You've come to the right place. Catherine and I will take good care of you," Ian said as she came into the snug to reload her drinks tray, "and point you in the right direction once you leave our house. How much time in the Highlands do you have?"

"We have to be back in Edinburgh for our flight home in six days," Fern answered. "We've booked a hotel for one night in Inverness, where we drop our rental car. Then, we have train reservations from there to Edinburgh, and then one night in Edinburgh the night before our flight. Other than that, we are as free as the birds and can go wherever you recommend."

"Excellent," Catherine said. "You must take the Whisky Trail and go north to Speyside—Ian will tell you where to visit. And then, continue on to the north. Cullen is nice, directly on the North Sea. From there, it's easy to travel to Inverness, or Nessy, as we call it. Where did you go this afternoon?"

"Balmoral Castle. The castle was closed because the King is at home, I guess, but we walked all around the grounds and spent most of our time in the kitchen garden, all alone except for two workers. My husband, the gardener, was in heaven."

Catherine nodded. "Yes, the King is officially 'at home' in Balmoral, but he's really at the cottage his grandmother gave him on the other side of the river—it's called Birkhall. He prefers it to the castle, and always stays there. It's lovely."

"Why do they close the castle then?" Matt asked. "If he's not really there?"

"Because he entertains there while he's in the area, and they don't like the masses traipsing through when company is coming. I believe tomorrow night the French ambassador is a guest and they're having a fancy dinner affair," Catherine said. "They will be picking some of the veg you saw today to serve the ambassador, I'm sure."

"It was amazing to us that we could just wander anywhere," Fern said. "And the estate grounds are so beautiful. We thought we'd go back in the morning and go for a run around some of the trails."

Catherine said quickly to Ian, "Two G&T's, two Balvenie 21's, please." Ian nodded and went to work, jotting down the order. "We're not joggers," she said to Fern, "but we do sneak over to Balmoral occasionally to hike the hill trails. You will enjoy it."

"Oh, good. In the afternoon, we're driving through Braemar and the Cairngorms, and, if we have enough time, make it to Blair Castle," Fern said. "We'll do our run as soon as we wake up, and then come back here to clean up and have breakfast. Does that sound OK?"

"Certainly. Blair Castle is a goodly drive, however. You'll want to leave here immediately after breakfast, so you can enjoy the drive and look around some."

"What's the weather forecast?" Matt asked.

Ian looked at his watch. "What time is it?" he said with a broad smile.

Catherine slapped him playfully on the arm. "He's toying with you. Just ignore him. Yes, our weather can change in a minute, but the morning is supposed to be just like today, sunny and mild. You'll want to start back through the highlands before it gets too late, though, in case the weather rolls in."

Ian placed the four drinks on Catherine's tray. She said to Fern, recognizing who was in charge of the social calendar, "What time will you be coming in for dinner?"

Fern looked to Matt. "About thirty minutes? Will that give you enough time to whisky?"

Matt smiled. "That will get me started on my education, yes."

Ian nodded sagely.

• • •

With the warmth from the mellow, delicious, local malt whisky Ian had served him, and the blushing glow from the candlelit dining room, Matt thought his pregnant wife had never looked more beautiful.

"Can we stop for just a moment and recognize how perfect our lives are?" he asked.

"Oh, please don't say that," she laughed. "The last time I even thought it, trouble ensued almost immediately. But, yes, we are so lucky, aren't we?"

"Especially to have found each other," Matt said, turning serious. "I can't imagine my life without you in it. And the baby on the way just puts the cherry on the cake…or whatever that cliché is."

"Is it icing on the cake, or cherry on the cake?"

"It's both, for me. Icing, cherry, whatever. I'm so happy right now."

"It's the whisky, honey," she said, smiling knowingly.

"I'm sorry you can't have any. This stuff is damn good. By the time we get home, I will know exactly what malt whiskies to buy. Excellent trip planning, my dear. Maybe we should retire now and spend our time travelling the world."

"Yeah, that would work," Fern said. She rolled her eyes. "I'd give you about one month, and then you'd be itching to get back to work. And, besides, Port Stirling would fall apart without you. It's probably already happening. Chaos everywhere since you left."

"I am somewhat surprised that no one has called me," he admitted.

"Yet," she said. "However, I did mention to your staff that it would be nice if no one called us." She smiled.

"I did, too," he grinned. "Maybe they actually got the message. For the record, it's even more surprising that Joe Phelps hasn't called you, don't you think?"

"My boss wished me a very happy honeymoon and told me to not think about work. I think he still feels guilty for pulling us home from Maui last year."

"He should, although, in hindsight, it was the correct call on Joe's part. If he hadn't, there might still be some very unsavory characters roaming around Chinook County instead of in the state pen where they belong."

Fern glanced around the room, taking it all in. "When we get back to our room tonight, I'm going to do some research on where we'll stay when we leave here. I only want to stay in country house hotels the rest of my life."

"You can take an hour on your laptop, and then I have other plans for you." He twirled a non-existent handlebar mustache, and Fern laughed and laughed.

• • •

Buck Bay, Oregon — early May

The woman recognized the man the minute she entered the dumpy café on the outskirts of Buck Bay because he looked like no one she'd ever seen before in this corner of Oregon. She approached him and said their pre-set greeting, "Have you had a nice trip from the east coast?"

The man stood and replied, "Very pleasant indeed." They shook hands and took their seats at the beat-up wooden table.

"Thank you for coming," she said.

"My pleasure. It sounds like an interesting project. Tell me more." He sat back and listened while she explained everything, stopping only when the waitress came by. She ordered coffee, he ordered tea.

"You will need a new identity, a passport, and boarding passes which I will provide," he said.

"Yes, but let me be clear; I am running the show. I only need you for logistics and the product," she said. "Am I clear?"

He smiled. "But of course, dear."

• • •

Oregon State Penitentiary — May

The visitor plonked down in the same burgundy chair for the fourth time, across from the prisoner.

"Are you ready?" the prisoner asked.

"Just about," the visitor answered. "Your 'colleague' in here proved to be even more helpful than you thought. His referral got in touch with me a week after we first talked, and I can report now that he's definitely the guy for the job. Gives me the fucking creeps."

"That's what you want, isn't it?" asked the prisoner.

Steely-eyed and clenched jaw, the visitor said, "Yes. It is precisely what I want."

"When and where did you meet with him?"

"Don't worry your pretty little head — I was careful. We met at a crappy diner on the outskirts of Buck Bay the first time. No one we know would ever go there. I wanted to meet in public, just in case he was a psycho."

"And is he?"

"Not really, no. He's on the edge, but not over it. Once I decided he was the guy for the job, we met a second time closer to home, but in an isolated location where no one would see or recognize me."

"You're sure?"

"Absolutely. We were quick and quiet. He seems efficient, and very experienced."

"You think you can pull this off? That it will work?" the prisoner asked. "How will you get out of the country when the deed is done? And what about the money?"

"I have a plan for every step, and he and I agree that it's doable. I can do this." The visitor paused. "I don't think you need to know the details now."

"What? You think I talk in my sleep or something?"

"You do," the visitor laughed, and stood to exit. "I'll let you know when we're leaving."

CHAPTER 5

Over the course of the next few days, Matt and Fern took a magical tour of the Scottish Highlands. Matt tasted whisky, and Fern enjoyed the educational aspect of the distillery tours, secretly making a list of her husband's favorite ones for upcoming gift giving. They poked around historic castles, dined well on the bounty of Scotland's land and sea, marveled at the rivers, lochs, and forests that reminded them of home, and enjoyed the quirkiness of the wonderful Scottish people they met. In general, the couple benefited from the advice of Catherine and Ian, and their Shetland guide, Callum, and really dug into the local scene.

Callum had told them about a hotel in Inverness — where they would spend their second-to-last night — that he always stayed in during his frequent trips to that city. Fern booked it, and they absolutely loved both the hotel and Inverness.

Their room, with its three tall sash windows, overlooked the wide, fast-flowing River Ness. Matt stood looking out while Fern unpacked some clothes and set up her toiletries, and he noticed the broad walkway that went in both directions alongside the river. She came to join him at the window.

"I'll bet we could run on the path to our left to the bridge you can see if you lean forward. Do you see it?" he asked.

Fern leaned close to the window. "Ooh, yes, what a graceful footbridge. Looks like there's a nice path on the other side of the river, too."

"Don't you think there is probably another bridge to our right, closer to the central part of town? I'm thinking we could make a loop and see a lot of Inverness while we run. What do you think?"

"Let's hurry and change and go for it," she said. "It looks like it's trying to cloud up."

"Wait a minute," Matt said, grabbing her arm. "There's that guy again." He pointed at a middle-aged man sitting on a bench overlooking the river about fifty yards downriver from their hotel.

Fern looked out the window. "What guy?"

"The guy on the bench. He was on our plane from Newark, and again at Shetland Airport. I talked to him. I think he's following us."

"And I think you're a cop," she said, smiling at him and rubbing his arm. "I haven't seen him before."

"You were in the bathroom at Shetland when he and I had a brief conversation. He was a little odd. I'm sure I don't recognize him, though, and he has a Scottish accent." He took another hard look at the man. "But, he doesn't look like a Scot, does he? More of an eastern Slavic look about him. Sort of a round face and bulbous nose. Strong jaw."

Fern looked again. "Well, I guess so, maybe Russian or Ukrainian? It's hard to tell from here." She started pulling on her running apparel. "I trust your people judgment, but hardly anyone knows we're in Scotland, much less that we're in this hotel. Only Callum, Catherine, Ian, and my mother—who I called last night—know we're here."

Matt laughed a snarky laugh. "There's probably about a thousand people in Port Stirling that know we're in Scotland by now. You know better than anyone how word travels around that town like wildfire."

Fern looked pensive. "I suppose word could've gotten out about our trip." She took another look at the man on the bench. "But I'm sure I've never seen that man before. Have you ever seen him in Port Stirling?"

Matt shook his head. "Nope, only on the flights and in Shetland. He was with a woman on the Newark flight, but he told me she had an emergency and had to leave Shetland. He decided to continue on."

"I'm guessing that a lot of American tourists go to both Shetland and Inverness. It's probably just a coincidence. There were some people from

Seattle on a group tour in our lobby here when we checked in. And I don't think they are following us."

"S'pose not," Matt admitted. "But if he's still there when we go out, I'm going to confront him."

The man on the bench was gone when Matt and Fern left for their run.

. . .

After their highly enjoyable sightseeing run, which did take them back across the river into the center of town on another bridge, Fern pulled out her phone from the small fanny pack she always wore when running. She wanted to know where the train station was, and to scope it out now, so they could make the most of their time tomorrow in Inverness before their train left at 3:30 p.m. She looked up from her map, and, shielding her eyes from the sun, peered ahead on the street they were on, High Street.

"The Tourist Center is just up there on the right after that big intersection. And, according to my map, we keep going that way to the train station, and it's not far. Let's go to the info center and make sure it's the train station we need tomorrow."

"Following you, oh great guide. But we'd better make it snappy; see those clouds? Looks like our sunshine might be taking a hike soon."

They found the train station easily, found a ticket kiosk, printed out their tickets using the confirmation code Fern had in her phone from when she booked the tickets yesterday, and were in and out of the station in ten minutes.

As they exited on to the street, Matt hailed a taxi to take them back to their hotel. It wasn't far in this compact, walkable city, but a booming clap of thunder, followed by dark, ominous clouds, and a sudden downpour, made the taxi decision an easy one.

"Aye, good choice, mate," said their driver. "Close the door."

. . .

They took a hot shower and dressed—more casually than at Oak Hillside—for dinner in their hotel dining room. It wasn't as fancy, but the food was very good. Matt had seared Shetland scallops, and Fern had pan-roasted North Sea cod.

"Eating this yummy fish without a glass of chilled Sancerre is almost a crime," Fern said wistfully.

"Your time will come soon, love," Matt said. He reached across the table and put his hand on top of hers. "I appreciate your sacrifice on behalf of our baby. Maybe I should give up whisky and beer until he's born. You know, in sympathy."

She laughed. "Not necessary. I'm tougher than that. And, how do you know it's a boy?"

"I just know. I don't care what sex it is, I truly don't, but I'm sure it's a boy. What shall we call him?"

"We've got plenty of time before we have to pick names, but if we're not going to learn the sex ahead of the birth, we'll want both boy and girl names ready to go. How about Harold Horning, and we could call him Hal, for short?"

"You've been in the U.K. too long," he laughed. "That's such a British-sounding name. I was thinking more along the lines of Dak Horning."

"Let me guess…as in Dak Prescott, the Cowboys quarterback? No, absolutely not. You named your pet seal, Roger, after Roger Staubach—you are not naming our child after another Cowboys QB."

"It's a cool name, you have to admit. Why don't you sleep on it?"

"I could sleep on it every night for the next five-and-a-half months, and I would still veto it. But I think it might be a boy, too, so we'll have to think on it. Let's get a baby book of names when we get home, and each come up with five possibilities. Won't that be fun?" Fern's eyes sparkled.

"The most fun ever," Matt agreed, squeezing her hand. "What are we doing tomorrow?"

"I hope this rainstorm passes tonight," she answered. The rain was running in rivulets down the restaurant's windows next to them. "The only thing I really care about is visiting Leakey's Bookshop. It's a world-famous bookstore. We walked close to it today. What about you? What do you want to see?"

"I thought it might be fun after breakfast to take one of those sight-seeing buses we saw today around the city. Since we don't have much time, I'd like to get a feel for the whole place."

"Great idea. So, then it's Edinburgh tomorrow night and then home."

"I'm ready to go home—you?" he asked.

"I guess. I do miss everyone, and I don't mind going back to work. It's only that it's been so nice having this time together, just the two of us."

"We don't have to lose that feeling when we get home, you know. Let's make sure we carve out time for us."

"It's easy to say that now," she smiled. "But our work is so demanding, you know what will happen the minute we set foot in Port Stirling."

Matt nodded. "We'll be busy. No doubt about it. But only we control our schedules. We have to set boundaries and stick to them. Yeah, Bill Abbott and Joe Phelps will have something to say about it, but they are both reasonable men who want us to succeed. We can negotiate with them."

"Agreed, but I'm sensitive about not letting our pregnancy be an excuse, for either one of us. I intend to keep doing my job as long as I can waddle around."

"You will never waddle. It's not in your nature."

"Maybe not," she grinned, "but I do think you need to be prepared for some level of waddling."

Matt rose in his chair, leaned across the table and kissed her. "Waddle all you want. You'll always be my love."

. . .

"I think it's tomorrow," the man said into the phone from an out-of-the-way corner in the Inverness train station. "They are boarding the Edinburgh direct train now, and I believe they will be on the 1:50 p.m. United flight from Edinburgh to Newark tomorrow. Are you in place?"

"Yes, I'm ready. Why don't you think they'll be on the 9:40 a.m. flight?"

"It's possible. But their pattern has been to not start early on this entire trip. I think it's more likely they'll have a leisurely night in Edinburgh and take their time tomorrow morning making their way to the airport."

"Do they have any idea they're being followed? How have you managed to not be seen?"

"I told you," he barked. "I'm good at my job. I had one dicey moment in Shetland, but I handled it. They aren't suspicious or acting like cops at all. Just a couple on vacation enjoying themselves."

"Perfect. They're relaxed and won't be expecting a thing."

"Do you have your disguise ready? You know the U.K. is loaded with security cameras. They're fucking everywhere on this island."

"So I've noticed. Yes, I have a subtle wig that looks nothing like my real hair and will cover part of my face. And I bought some local clothes so I'll look like a native. Even my brother wouldn't know me. Are you going to fly to Edinburgh tonight like we planned?"

"Yeah. I don't dare get on their train. Park at the Holyrood car park, and I'll call you when I'm getting close. Walk out on the path toward Hunter's Bog, and I'll meet you and take you to the place."

"Sounds good. I'll want to rehearse with you so we make sure we get this right. No slip ups."

"There won't be any slip ups. I've done this before, as you know. As long as you don't chicken out or do something stupid, by tomorrow night we'll have two million dollars to split."

"I like the way you think. And I'm not stupid. See you tonight."

...

On their last night in Scotland, Fern and Matt enjoyed the best Edinburgh had to offer. A fabulous dinner at an off-the-beaten-path restaurant that Catherine had recommended to them, after-dinner stroll on the Royal Mile, hitting a couple of the tasting rooms for Matt to get a last-minute whisky lesson, and finishing on a bench in Princes Street Gardens, soaking up the stars and fresh air on a beautiful night.

"Let's do this again," Matt said, taking Fern's hand in his. "It doesn't have to be Scotland, I mean, but take a vacation. This has been a new experience for me, and I've had the time of my life every single day."

"Me, too. I hope we haven't peaked as a couple."

He turned to look at her. "Why on earth would you say that? We're just getting started!"

"Hope so," she said quietly. "I never take anything for granted anymore. Not since you got shot. I realized that night that life can change in a heartbeat. I want us to maintain and build on our time together here, but what if things turn bad?"

"Are you worried about the baby? Because if you are, yes, it's going to change some things for us, but it doesn't have to change what we have together. I think it will make us even stronger. A kid that is half you and half me will be a spectacular human being, don't you think?"

She laughed. "No doubt about that. No, I'm not worried about the baby affecting our relationship, more about the world we're bringing it into. Our chosen professions keep showing us the evil that is present around us. Yeah, we've been able to put a dent in it, but will there always be wicked, vile people around us? What if our child is put in harm's way because of what you and I do?"

"Oh, sweetheart, you can't worry about that. We're going to be great parents—probably the best parents on the planet—and we will always take care of our children and put them first. Just like your parents and mine did. We've had excellent role models on how to raise a child, and we will ace it, too."

"Our parents didn't have people shooting at them," she noted, with a tinge of sadness.

Matt stood. "C'mon, let's get you to bed so we can get some serious ZZs under our belt for the trip home tomorrow. You need your rest."

They walked back to the hotel with their arms around each other, each unwilling to let go.

CHAPTER 6

Edinburgh Airport was again a nightmare.

"Thank goodness we got here early," Fern said. She looked around at the lengthy lines for check-in and shook her head. "I love the Scots, but they need to streamline their airport process."

"I'm with you. Look how easy the train was yesterday," Matt said. "Why can't they figure that out? Let's buy that Fast Track pass and get in the priority lane—what do you say?"

"Right behind you, cowboy."

"Ahh, headed home," the airport employee who stamped their pass said. "Did you enjoy your wee stay?" He smiled brightly at them, as if he truly cared that they had a good time in his country.

"We had a wonderful time here, and we love Scotland," Fern said. "A perfect vacation."

"Already planning a trip back," Matt added.

"That's what we like to hear. Sorry about the queues today."

"Yeah, is it always like this?" asked Matt.

"Pretty much, I'm afraid to say." He handed them their Fast Track passes and pointed to his left. "The Fast Track line starts over there."

Matt looked for the end of the line and groaned. Even the fast line would be painfully slow.

"Oh, dear," Fern said. "I think before we get in line, I should go use my favorite women's bathroom." She pointed behind them at the end of the concourse.

"Good idea. I'll go to that little shop around the corner from it and pick up some items for the long flight to Newark." He stared at the security line. "I swear if we come back here, I'm dying my hair red," Matt fumed.

Fern giggled at him. "Maybe it's your belt. I think that buckle causes the grief. You need to leave that one at home next time."

"I think those guys just don't like the looks of me. They're all smiley and lovey-dovey with you, and I get the stare and frown act. You probably look like their sister or wife. It's unfair, I tell you. But I'd smile at you, too, so there's that."

"I'm leaving my wheelie with you, and I'll be right back."

"Ok, and then we'll switch when you get back so I can go, too, before security and boarding."

She strode briskly down the concourse toward the familiar women's bathroom, about fifty yards away, not noticing the woman who fell into line immediately behind her.

・・・

What the hell is taking her so long? Matt thought. He checked his watch again. *Fifteen minutes. I know she's pregnant, but she never takes this long to pee.*

He paced around their suitcases and looked in the shop windows while he waited. He checked his watch again. *Twenty minutes.*

Matt dialed his wife's cell phone. Straight to voicemail. *OK, now I'm worried. What is she doing? Where is she?*

He took their wheelies, one in each hand, and moved close to the entrance of the women's restroom. He dialed her phone again and got as close to the restroom opening as he dared without looking like a pervert. He didn't hear it ringing, and, again, his call went straight to voicemail. *This is so unlike her. Maybe she's fainted?*

He turned to an elderly couple standing next to him and said, "I'm sorry to bother you, but could you watch these two suitcases for just a minute? I'm worried about my wife. She's been in the ladies' room for quite a while, and I want to check on her."

The man said, "Of course, young man. Go find your wife. We'll wait right here and protect your luggage."

Matt walked to the open entrance, cupped his hands around his mouth, and yelled, "Fern! Fern, are you in there? Please come out." He waited. *Nothing.* "Fern! Are you OK?" *Nothing.*

He stood at the entrance to the restroom and said loudly, "I apologize in advance, ladies, but I'm coming in to look for someone." He waited a couple of heartbeats, and then entered the restroom. He could only see four women in the brightly lit space, and none of them were Fern.

A pretty, heavily freckled woman adjusting her long red hair at the mirror turned to look at Matt, paused, and said, "Hi there. You can come look at me anytime in the bathroom."

"I'm sorry, ma'am, I like redheads, but I'm looking for a particular one right now — my wife. She's thirty-eight, tall, slender, chin-length red hair, your color, wearing black sweatpants, a white tee shirt, and a black zip-up hoodie. American. Have you seen her?"

"No, I'm afraid I haven't. Is she missing?"

"Not yet, but it's unusual for her to stay so long in here, and I'm worried about her," he explained. He turned quickly, and went stall-by-stall, looking in the empty ones, and peering under the door of those occupied, while yelling "Fern. Are you in here?" *Nothing.*

A woman at the far end of the large room changing a baby's diapers on a fold-down shelf, turned to Matt and said, "She was in here when I first came in, but she left."

"You're sure?"

"Yes, she was with another woman. She was American, too, I think. Older than your wife."

"Did my wife say anything? Did they talk?"

"I don't think so. I wasn't paying that much attention."

"Please think hard," he pleaded.

The young mother stood still for a minute, hand on her baby's stomach while the baby kicked its legs in the air, and it was clear to Matt she was trying to remember.

"I'm pretty sure they didn't talk, but they did leave together. Your wife looked different than when she first came in."

"How so? What do you mean?"

"Well, she was friendly when she came in. Smiled at me and the baby, you know?"

"That sounds like her," Matt said.

"But when they left, she was frowning and didn't look so hot."

"What? Was she sick?"

"I don't know. Maybe. She kind of slumped against the older woman. And then they left."

"Was the other woman holding on to my wife?"

"She might have been. Like holding her arm. It crossed my mind that your wife might be drunk. Sorry."

"No, you're very helpful. Can you tell me what the other woman looked like? You say she was older?"

"Not old, old, but older than your wife. Maybe fifty. She was shorter than your wife. And not as slim. Not fat, but pudgy, I would say."

"How much shorter?"

She thought. "Probably about five or six inches."

Matt said, "So she is about five feet three inches? Roughly?"

"Yes, that's about right. I'm five four, and she was shorter than me, but not by much."

"What race?" he asked. "White? Black?"

"White. Pale skin. Long black hair. She was also wearing a mask covering her nose and mouth, like she was afraid of catching something, you know?"

"What color was her mask?"

"Black. Sort of a medical looking one. Sturdy."

"You're doing great. What was she wearing? Quickly, please."

Sensing Matt's panic, the young mother said in a rush, "Tartan trousers, green and tan plaid, and a greenish jumper."

"Jumper?" he asked. "What's that?"

"Oh, right, American. Sweater. We call sweaters jumpers. She was carrying a big tweed top handle bag. Garish. Purple, blue, green, and busy."

Impulsively, Matt reached over and kissed the witness on her cheek.

"Thank you! Please give your name and contact information to a security guard before you leave the area. I think there are two of them just outside this door. We may need to talk to you further if we don't find my wife. You've been really helpful."

The woman nodded and said, "I hope you find her."

Matt ran out of the restroom and flashed his badge at the first security officer he saw. "You need to listen carefully to me," Matt said, talking fast but enunciating clearly. "My wife is missing. She went into that bathroom and a witness said she left with another woman. She's not answering her phone, and something is wrong. She's missing. You need to call your head of security—NOW—and lock down this airport."

"Are you sure she's not just left you, mate?" the guard said, smiling.

Matt grabbed him by the shirt. "Listen to me, MATE. I'm a police chief in America, and my wife is a special agent for the United States Department of State. I'm not messing around. This is serious business, and something has happened to her. You need to act now. Do you understand?" He grabbed the walkie-talkie off the guard's belt, held it up two inches in front of his face, and said, "Lock it down."

The guard paled and his hand shook as he took hold of the walkie-talkie. "Code 2," he shouted into it. "Code 2. Shut us down." A pause, and then to Matt he said, "What's the missing person look like? Your wife?"

Matt calmly took the walkie-talkie from his hand, and speaking clearly and slowly, he described Fern and gave the witness's account of the woman with her. "Did you get that? Please confirm."

The man on the other end said, "Confirmed. Please stand by," and then Matt heard the announcement over the loudspeakers. "Attention please. All exits in the airport are temporarily closed while we search for two women. Please stay in your current location, and if you see a woman matching either of the following descriptions, please notify the nearest guard. Thank you for your patience. This will be a brief disruption."

He read the women's descriptions, and Matt watched as people in the area looked around. There was no panic, and people seemed to be seriously looking for the missing women. While he waited, he nervously called Fern's phone again. *Nothing, straight to voicemail.*

In less than a minute, Matt and the guard were approached by two fast-moving uniformed men. The shorter of the two came up to the guard, stopping less than a foot in front of his face, and said, "What the bloody hell do you think you're doing?" And to Matt, "And who in the bloody hell are you?"

"To whom am I speaking?" Matt said coolly. He patted his agitated guard on the arm as if to say, 'I'll handle this.'

With more of a measured tone, the red-faced, stout officer said, "I'm Constable Charles Thistlewhite, and I'm in charge of airport security for the Department for Transport. Are you the American I spoke with?"

"Yes. Matt Horning. It's my wife who's missing. Thank you for taking quick action."

"It's an extreme measure certainly," the constable huffed, but he visibly tried to compose himself.

"I know my wife, and I know she's officially missing now. She would not have disappeared on her own accord. We are both police officers in the States, and there are lots of people who would want to harm both of us. People we've put in jail. Do you understand me?"

"Yes. We will find your wife, Mr. Horning. No harm will come to her while she's in our country."

Matt looked up in the corner by the womens' restroom and pointed. "Is that a closed-circuit television camera? CCTV?"

"It is," the constable said. "We have them throughout the airport." He spoke into his walkie-talkie. "Please collect all the CCTV footage for the past..." he paused and said to Matt, "When did you first notice she was missing?"

"It's been thirty minutes or so now. Have them collect for forty-five minutes, please."

The constable gave the order.

Matt ran his hands through his black curly hair, as he sought to regain his equilibrium and think like a cop. "Also, please ask everyone in the terminal to save any photos or videos on their personal phones that might show my wife and the other woman. Fern's height and her hair are distinctive, and she would stand out in the crowd. Do you have a special repository like a website, or email address where they can send them?" Matt asked.

"Yes, of course we do," Thistlewhite said. "Excellent idea." He spoke again into his walkie-talkie, and the message was relayed terminal wide. Again, Matt watched as several people in the immediate area looked at their phones.

"Also, you need to close off this restroom immediately," Matt said. "Lock it up tight. Do you have a forensics team on site here at the airport?"

"We have one forensic detective with a basic kit," the constable answered. He rubbed the stubble on his chin. "I'm not sure he's ever used it."

"No time like the present then. Let's get him and his kit to the women's restroom, and let him do his thing, OK? I realize that is a longshot, but you never know down the road if any fingerprints he can lift now might come in handy. Maybe a match in your national database."

Thistlewhite nodded in agreement.

"Do you want to adjourn to my office, Mr. Horning, while we wait to see if the lockdown produces results?"

Matt looked around frantically. "Let me go around this area one more time, and then I'll go with you. It's hard for me to consider leaving her."

Constable Thistlewhite placed his hand on Matt's shoulder and said, "I understand. Please, take your time and we'll go when you're ready. I'm sure someone will locate her any minute."

Matt made a large circle of the area, taking in all the shops, security line, and going in both restrooms again. *Nothing. It's like she's dropped off the planet.* He finally had to concede that Fern was gone.

CHAPTER 7

Constable Thistlewhite escorted Matt to a dark, windowless room that held large banks of TV screens, about fifty in all. A young woman in uniform unlocked the door for them and stepped aside.

"Don't just stand there, lassie," Thistlewhite barked at her, "make Mr. Horning a cup of tea."

"Yes, sir," she said, and turned to leave. Matt touched her on the arm, ignoring the constable, and said to her, "Please make yourself a cup, too, alright?"

She smiled shyly at him, and said, "Yes, sir, I will. Thank you."

Matt approached a console operator, who greeted him and said, "I'm sorry, sir. My name is Barry."

Matt shook hands with the round young man with longish hair and wire-rim glasses. "Hi, Barry. Can you pull up the cameras outside the women's restroom just outside the security area? That's where my wife disappeared."

"Yeah, I've got it cued up starting forty-five minutes before you called us."

"Good man," Matt said. Without waiting to be invited, he pulled out a chair next to Barry and sat down, pulling in closer to the screen in front of him. They watched the recording for a few minutes before the camera showed Fern walking in.

Matt yelled, "Stop! That's her," and Barry instantaneously hit pause. Matt half-rose out of his chair, leaned forward, and put his hand on Fern's image. Quietly, he said, "This is her. This is my wife." His chin dropped briefly to his chest. The room was completely silent.

Barry said in a barely audible voice, "She's very beautiful, Mr. Horning."

Matt, pale and still, stared at the screen. He replied, "Yes, and she is also smart and warm and loving. She's three-and-a-half months pregnant with our first child."

A gasp went up somewhere in the room. "We will get your child back," Constable Thistlewhite said, at Matt's side. "You can count on us; we know how to do our jobs."

"I want my *wife* back," he said through clenched teeth. "Nothing else matters right now."

"Yes. Yes. Of course," Thistlewhite corrected.

It was a good view of Fern, full face, and her clothing all mostly visible. "Take a snapshot of this frame and get it out to your entire law enforcement community as soon as possible," Matt instructed Barry. "That meet with your approval, Constable?"

"Yes. That's our protocol," Thistlewhite said. "If we can't stop her at the airport doors"—in his heart, the constable worried they were too late—"someone will see her. Edinburgh is a relatively small city, and we're a tight police community."

Matt continued to give directions, "Stay with this camera and let it run." Barry hit play. All eyes in the room were fixated on the one screen. About six minutes later, Fern and a woman appeared, coming out of the restroom door.

"Pause!" Matt shouted. He moved in until his face was just a few inches from the screen.

"Do you recognize the woman with your wife?" Thistlewhite asked.

Matt didn't immediately answer. He moved from side to side, backward and forward, checking the image from different angles. He considered his police training and tried to imagine the woman in question with a different hairdo, makeup, and clothing. But it was no good. With much of her face hidden behind the black face mask, only her white skin, and long black hair were visible. Matt agreed with the witness's description of her as pudgy.

"I don't believe I recognize her," he said finally, shaking his head. "Do any of you?" Matt looked from Barry to Constable Thistlewhite to the other officers now crowded into the claustrophobic room.

No one did. "But we can do a great deal analyzing this image," the constable told Matt. "If Police Scotland has had any dealings with this woman at all, we can track her down." Matt nodded mutely, and took his chair, while Thistlewhite spoke inaudibly to Barry.

Matt allowed the two of them to jot down some notes, and then said, "Barry, when you're ready, can you please advance the recording? In slow motion?"

Everyone took a seat, and Barry went back to work, hitting 'play'. Fern appeared unsteady on her feet, and as the witness in the restroom had indicated, seemed to be slumping against the unknown woman. The woman's left hand held firmly to Fern's arm, while her right arm was wrapped around Fern's waist. It looked to Matt as if the woman had a tight grip.

"The other woman seems to be holding up your wife," Thistlewhite noted. "Was she feeling well when she entered the restroom?"

"Yes, she was fine. We'd moved briskly through the concourse, and were getting ready to go through security," Matt answered, his voice hoarse with emotion. "She gets through quickly, and I always get stopped. We laughed about her red hair being useful in Scotland."

"She does look a wee bit like one of us. Keep going, Barry."

The recording advanced one frame at a time. After about five clips, Matt yelled "pause!" again. And, again, he lifted from his chair and moved in close to the screen. "There! Do you see that movement from my wife?"

Still slumped against the other woman, Fern briefly fluttered her eyes open, raised her head ever so slightly, and looked up at the camera. As she did so, she ran her hand weakly and fleetingly across her stomach. Before her arm dropped to her side, she made a slight motion with her hand — a sort of up and down, wavy gesture.

"It's a signal," Matt said. "She's telling me that she's somewhat conscious, and that our baby is OK. See that pat on her stomach. Don't you think?"

"I agree," said the constable. "But what does that maneuver with her hand mean?"

"I'm not sure," Matt said. "It looks like she's waving."

"Could it signify water? Like the waves on water?" Thistlewhite said.

"We live near the water in Oregon, on the Pacific Ocean."

"Could she be trying to tell you that it has something to do with your home?"

"That's it!" Matt exclaimed. "Something related to Port Stirling. Fern must know her abductor or recognize her somehow."

"Did you meet any women that your wife may have talked to on this trip?"

Matt thought. "There were really only two women we engaged with since we've been in Scotland. One owned a restaurant in Lerwick, and that was a brief talk over dinner. The other owns the country house hotel we spent several nights in near Balmoral. We did get to know her, but there's no way she could be involved. A lovely woman, very nice."

"Something to do with waves," Thistlewhite said. "Think more on that. But let's continue with the recording." He looked up at the monitor. "She's barely responsive, however. Look at her eyes. I realize the definition is grainy, but are her pupils constricted? Can you tell? I have to ask you, Mr. Horning, had Mrs. Horning been drinking today?"

Matt looked at his wristwatch and clicked on the calendar. "My wife has not had a drink for three months and sixteen days. Since the day we discovered she was pregnant." He looked at Thistlewhite. "You don't know her, and I don't expect you to understand, but Fern is the most alive, animated, efficient woman you'll ever meet. Even if she was dead-drunk, she would look and act more energetic than the woman you see here. It's clear to me, however, that she's been given something, somehow. Her pupils do look narrower."

On his own accord, Barry advanced the recording another frame. "Does it look like your wife is wheezing in this one?" he asked Matt.

Matt looked carefully. "Possibly. It's hard to tell."

"Does Mrs. Horning have a history of asthma or breathing issues?" Thistlewhite asked.

"No." Matt looked again. "She does appear to be laboring to breathe a bit."

"Oh, dear God," Thistlewhite whispered.

"What?" asked Matt frantically.

"Those are two symptoms of a nerve agent being introduced into her body."

Matt began to shake. "Why would you say that?" He spun in his chair and looked up at the constable's distressed face.

Thistlewhite placed his hand on Matt's shoulder for a second time. "Because we've had some experience with it here in the U.K. It's a tactic of Russians, primarily, to take out dissenters and Putin opponents."

"But my wife doesn't have anything to do with the Russians. Nothing at all."

"You mentioned she works for the Department of State. May I ask what her specific role is?"

Matt stared into Thistlewhite's eyes for a moment, thinking how to handle this question under these circumstances. "She's the west coast liaison, and works for a special department in Washington, D.C."

"What does she do on a daily basis?" the constable persisted.

"Fern makes sure that any foreigners doing business or visiting in our part of the United States are treated fairly and have what they need," Matt waffled.

"I see," Thistlewhite said. Matt thought he seemed satisfied with that answer, or, at least, unwilling to challenge him further.

"Has she been involved directly with any foreigners of late?"

"Only one," Matt said, "and he isn't really a foreigner. A man of Chinese descent, but has permanent resident status in the U.S. His name is Zhang Chen. My wife and I put him in prison last year. Drug smuggling, human trafficking, and attempted murder."

"He sounds like an enchanting person," Thistlewhite said. "To your knowledge, is he still in prison?"

"Yep. He'll be there for 25 years minimum."

"Are there any other criminals who might have a reason to dislike you and/or your wife?"

"Is the sky blue?" Matt answered ruefully. "Plenty, I'm afraid. It comes with the job, as you probably know."

"I do understand, that is why I asked the question. May I suggest that we continue to look at our CCTV until we lose sight of Mrs. Horning."

"Go, Barry," Matt answered.

The cameras picked up Fern and the woman, still glued together, as they made their way out of the area, down the escalator and into the central Arrivals terminal. Matt paced around the depressing room, following his beloved wife—clearly in distress—on successive CCTV cameras until they left through the door that the couple had entered earlier that afternoon.

The last clear shot of them was taken outside the terminal building, from the back. It appeared that they moved across the roadway toward the car park, but that's where the cameras lost them. Matt and the airport security folks slowly and methodically worked their way through every CCTV camera outside the terminal, but no luck.

Once Fern and the woman exited the airport terminal, they were not seen again.

CHAPTER 8

There was no way to sugarcoat it—Matt was distraught. He remained calm and tried his best to be professional, but he knew, better than anyone else in the room, what could happen to Fern. They needed to act quickly, and he needed all the help he could get.

"Thank you for your help, gentlemen and ladies," he said. "It looks like we've come to the end of the road on your CCTV for now." Swallowing hard, he continued, "There is no way my wife would've allowed herself to be drugged and leave the building with a stranger. Therefore, based on the camera's evidence, we are dealing with a kidnapping by an unknown assailant."

"The kidnapping of a United States Department of State agent," added Constable Thistlewhite. "Jesus wept." He shook his head at the unbelievable reality of their situation

Matt continued, beginning to regain his cop mojo. "I want to meet with whoever is the head honcho at Police Scotland. Can you make that happen right now? I need to make a phone call to my wife's parents, but I will have to explain to them what happens next."

"That would be Chief Constable Armstrong, Mark Armstrong," said Thistlewhite. "I was planning to alert his office next, as soon as I can restore our airport operations. Mrs. Horning has left our premises; do you agree?"

"Yes. She's gone."

"Let's go to my office. This way, please." While they walked, the constable called the forensic guy and gave him instructions.

Matt, seated at the conference table indicated to him, stared out Thistlewhite's window that overlooked the car park, while the constable attended to his immediate business of getting Edinburgh Airport back in operation. *Did you get in a car with that woman, Fern? Help me, darlin'. Give me a clue. A sign. I will come and get you if you just help me understand.*

"Alright," Thistlewhite said. "I have alerted our operations staff to return the airport to normalcy."

Matt thought, *But things aren't normal for us, are they, Fern?*

Thistlewhite joined Matt at the table and pressed a button on his phone. After a brief moment, he said into the speakerphone, "This is Constable Thistlewhite at the airport. We've got an emergency, and I need to speak with the Chief Constable." A pause. "Yes. Please hurry." Matt drummed his fingers on the conference table in front of him.

Another pause and then they heard, "Charles, this is Mark. What can I do for you? What's going on?"

"Thanks for answering," Thistlewhite said, emitting some air from his mouth. "I've got Matt Horning with me here in my office and you're on the speaker. Mr. Horning is a chief of police in the state of Oregon in the western United States. His wife has just been abducted, against her will, we all believe, from our airport. We have studied the CCTV recordings that show Mrs. Horning entering women's restroom #8—the one just before security—looking perfectly fine, and leaving it drugged and disabled, accompanied and being held by a strange woman. This is the first moment we've had to notify you. Mr. Horning would like to speak to you."

"You're telling me that an American tourist was forcibly removed from Edinburgh Airport?" the Chief Constable sputtered. "How in the hell could that happen under our very eyes?"

"Mr. Armstrong, this is Matt Horning. It's even worse than you think. My wife—her name is Fern Byrne Horning—is an employee of the U.S. State Department. We are not here on business, just vacationing. Looking at the CCTV footage just now and talking to a witness in the women's restroom, my wife was somehow drugged and rendered helpless by an unknown woman. It's likely a kidnapping, and Constable Thistlewhite and I are convinced they have left the airport grounds and are at large somewhere in the city. We have a description of both women, and we need your assistance in distributing it to all officers under your jurisdiction. I also want you to involve the public and make both descriptions widely available throughout Edinburgh. Can you do that for me?"

"Hold on a minute, Mr. Horning," Armstrong said. "This sort of thing is very alarming to the public, and we must keep a lid on it until we have further information."

"With all due respect, it's more alarming to me, her husband," Matt said. "Someone has taken my wife, Mr. Armstrong, and I intend to get her back as quickly as possible, with or without your help."

"If I may, sir," Constable Thistlewhite interjected, "there is reason to believe that Mrs. Horning's health might be in danger. In the last CCTV frame we have available to us, she appears to be the victim, not only of an obvious abduction situation, but perhaps, having had a nerve agent introduced into her body. We have observed two or more of the classic symptoms. I agree with Chief Horning that time may be of the essence."

"Oh, good Lord," Armstrong said, and paused. "Still, we can't run amuck. Please bring Mr. Horning to my office, and we will decide on a plan of action. I will access the CCTV airport coverage and see what we're dealing with."

With a clenched jaw, Matt said, "Again, with all due respect, we just told you what we're dealing with. We'll head your way as you request, but please have on hand your top detective or inspector, whatever you call them, in your crime division."

"I will invite whom I see fit to meet with you, Mr. Horning, once I've reviewed the CCTV in question. I'll see you soon, gentlemen."

The call ended.

"Is he always such a pompous ass?" Matt asked.

Constable Thistlewhite looked down at his hands on the table. "He has a difficult job."

. . .

Increasingly agitated on the painfully slow drive from the airport to the headquarters of Police Scotland at Tulliallan Castle in Fife, across the Firth of Forth—which shimmered in today's brilliant sunshine—from Edinburgh, and about twenty-five miles from the airport, Matt realized he left their luggage in the airport. *That poor old couple.*

"I forgot our luggage," he said to the constable.

"No worries, Mr. Horning. I grabbed them and threw them in the boot. You're all set."

"Thanks. It's probably time we started calling each other by our first name, don't you think? I'm Matt. You're Charles, OK?"

A hint of a smile graced Thistlewhite's face as he continued to focus on his driving. "I like that, Matt. We're going to help you, I promise. Police Scotland's Crime and Terrorism divisions are among the best in the world, and they will take your wife's disappearance as a personal affront. You are not alone."

Matt, afraid he was about to lose it emotionally, nodded silently, and looked out the passenger window. Once he'd collected himself, he said, "There's a chance this goes back to Port Stirling. We've had some tough cases lately in our neck of the woods, and it could be connected. But we have to keep an open mind in this early stage."

"Honestly, and not that I don't think we have heinous criminals in Scotland—we certainly do—but that does seem logical, considering both of your professions. Do you have competent detectives on your staff who can help you from afar while Police Scotland works it on our end?"

"Yes, the best. I'll talk to your Chief Constable and make him understand we need an urgent plan, and then make some calls to home. Fern's parents will be my first call, but then I'll get with my team."

They crossed the Kincardine Bridge into Fife, and Thistlewhite said, "Getting close now."

True to his word, the constable pulled into the impressive grounds of Tulliallan Castle, and the imposing gray fortified castle was just ahead. The three-story building looked like a cross between Gothic and Italian architecture, solemn and serious in its grayness and crenellated roofline, but with substantial arched Gothic windows that kept it from boredom.

"I'm relieved the Chief Constable won't be seeing my Port Stirling City Hall office," Matt said. "Although, I do have a knock-your-socks-off view of the mighty Pacific Ocean."

"I've wanted to visit your ocean. My understanding is that it's wilder than the Atlantic I saw on your eastern seaboard—more like the North Sea."

"Yep, that's true. Parts of Shetland looked like Port Stirling. We enjoyed our time there." Again, Matt's chin dropped momentarily to his chest, and he closed his eyes. Then he snapped back to attention, opened his car door as soon as Thistlewhite drew to a stop, and said, "Let's get this investigation moving, Charles."

• • •

"Chief Horning, we're all so sorry for the loss of your wife," started Chief Constable Mark Armstrong.

Matt interrupted him. "She's not dead, she's missing. And the sooner we cut to the chase, the better our chances of getting her back in one piece are. If I'm correct, this is a kidnapping, probably for some kind of ransom. Whoever took Fern wants money, or they want me, or they just want us to suffer from some perceived wrong she and I have done to them."

"If it is a kidnapping for financial ransom, what is your stance on that?" Armstrong asked, getting straight to the point now that he could see Matt wasn't interested in the pleasantries of Police Scotland.

"Normally, my stance as a law enforcement officer is that we don't pay ransoms. We pretend to, and stall for time, while we figure out who, why, and where, and set up a fake swap."

"Normally?" Armstrong quizzed.

"This is my wife, Chief Constable," Matt said heavily. "The love of my life. Fern. If it's money they want, I'll give it to them. Whatever it takes to get her back."

"Do you have any personal resources?"

"Yes, and they can have it all."

"Do the people in your local community know you have money?"

"I suppose they do. It's a small state, and there aren't many secrets. Plus, my wife and I have started a foundation with some of my family money, and the locals all know about that."

"Let's be prepared, then," the Chief Constable said. "Once you've had an opportunity to inform your families of this dreadful news, I am advising you to get a handle on your resources and have at the ready some serious cash."

Matt nodded. "Yes, I will do that. I will also talk to my detectives and have them start an investigation on our end. I want them to track down and talk to some of the bad actors we've interacted with lately. But I need help on this end, too."

"Police Scotland has a great deal on our plate currently, and while a missing American tourist is, of course, very important to us, we can't just drop everything else. Surely you can understand that."

Matt studied the Chief Constable and summed him up immediately. He was not only the pompous ass he'd heard on their initial phone call, but Mark Armstrong was also ignorant, and the worst kind of leader for a police force. He was a politician, not a cop.

"What I understand is that Fern is not just another missing American tourist, she is an agent for the United States government. She replaced the former agent for the west coast when he unfortunately got his head cut off. One of my first calls after notifying her family will be to her boss in Washington, D.C. So, yes, I do expect you to drop everything else and help me learn who is holding my wife, and where. Otherwise, you might be facing the ugliest of ugly international incidents. Surely you can understand that."

Matt stopped talking and stared into Armstrong's eyes. He could tell the Chief Constable was choosing between the lesser of two evils.

"I see." Armstrong turned and walked to his elaborate antique desk, picked up a landline phone, and said, "Please ask DCI Stuart MacLean from the Major Investigation Team in Leith to come here as soon as possible. Thank you."

CHAPTER 9

With huge relief, Matt could tell just from looking at DCI Stuart MacLean that he was a cop's cop. Forty years old, maybe forty-one, he stood six feet tall with an average build. What wasn't average about him—at least, not in Matt's usual law enforcement circle—was MacLean's shock of bright red hair, almost orange, brushed up on top and waved over to one side. It was neatly trimmed on the sides and back, but in front of his ears, the red hair continued in a well-groomed, narrow line, culminating in a bright red mustache and cropped, close-cut beard. The look was toned down somewhat by his black square eyeglasses that gave him an intelligent vibe. Behind the cool glasses were piercing blue eyes under also red, shaped eyebrows. He was dressed, not in uniform, but in street clothes; skinny black trousers, open-necked light blue shirt, and a sharp-fitted, black sport coat.

"DCI MacLean, thank you for coming," Matt said, approaching him with his hand extended.

Stuart MacLean took Matt's hand and shook it vigorously. "So sorry for the circumstances, but it's a pleasure to meet a states-side copper."

"I should probably know this, but what does DCI stand for?" Matt looked from MacLean to the Chief Constable.

"Detective Chief Inspector, but you should call me Stuart," MacLean answered before Armstrong stepped closer.

"DCI MacLean is the best DCI in all of Scotland," Armstrong puffed. "MacLean, I'm personally assigning you to assist Chief Horning in the investigation of the possible kidnapping of his wife. I will clear it with your Chief Superintendent Campbell. You may set up an office here in Tulliallan Castle or work out of your Major Investigations Team room in Leith, whichever you prefer."

"I think central Edinburgh works better than out here, and would be more comfortable for Chief Horning, sir," MacLean said. "He'll be needing accommodation, and we've got a nice hotel nearby. We can put him up there."

"Of course," the Chief Constable said to Matt. "You were on your way home, and probably checked out of your hotel, correct? I should have thought of that."

"Thank you, Stuart," Matt said. "Hopefully, I won't be needing it for long. We'll find my wife."

"We will," Stuart said. "Do you have a photo of her that we can distribute over the wire to all of Police Scotland? Something recent that we can also use to alert the media?"

Matt breathed a sigh of some relief. "Yes. Show me your station. Let's get to work."

• • •

Leith Police Station strung along, taking up much of Queen Charlotte Street in northeast Edinburgh near the Firth of Forth. They entered through a door in the middle of the block, and DCI MacLean said, "We're up two flights," and pointed to the ornate staircase. "The elevator is slow."

Matt waved at the stairs, and said, "After you."

They climbed the staircase with its white paneled walls, intricately carved dark wood stair rails, and frosted, stained glass windows, and followed it to a landing with two hallways taking off in opposite directions. About halfway down the hall on their right, MacLean opened a door with a brass door plate reading "Major Investigations Team".

There were only two people, one male, one female, in the high-ceilinged room that could have handled fifteen, if necessary. Desks were grouped in threes, and there were five groupings. The ceiling was a box beam coffered style, elegantly designed in two shades of muted green with cream interspersed. There was one good-sized window which Matt figured looked out on Queen Charlotte St., but a Venetian-style blind was pulled shut over it. An old-looking rectangular oil painting of Edinburgh Castle took up space on one wall, while a newer portrait of a judge in robes hung opposite. The room was lit by several modest antique chandeliers that dropped down from the tall ceiling. Two discreet doors at each end of the long room clearly connected to the next rooms.

Matt followed MacLean to a desk grouping at the far corner. They took seats, and MacLean woke up the computer on his desk. "OK," he said. "I've heard the basic story but there's no reporting to read yet, so I need you to tell me exactly what happened at the airport."

"We didn't take time to write a report," Matt said.

"Good, because, as you know, every minute counts. First, I need a personal photograph of your wife," Stuart said. Over his left shoulder, he called out loudly, "Scone! Did we get the CCTV films from the airport yet?"

"Yeah." She stood from her desk in front of the window and brought a manila folder over to Stuart. "Hi, I'm Meg Brown, DS Brown."

Matt rose to shake hands with her. "Detective Sergeant, right? Why did he call you Scone?"

She smiled. "Ah, the American. Yes, Sergeant. I'd be Chief Inspector if he would gracefully retire." She hooked her thumb at MacLean. "And Scone is my nickname. It's a Police Scotland tradition, giving everyone nicknames. I bake really smashing scones, so, therefore…"

"Now, Scone, you know I'm way too young to retire, but if I do, you'll be the first to know." They laughed together. *Clearly a regular joke*, thought Matt. It was obvious to him they were friendly colleagues.

Stuart studied the CCTV photos for a minute. "Is this your wife? Is this Fern?" he said, holding out the photo of her entering the women's restroom.

"Yes, that's her. Fern."

"I won't bother to tell you she's beautiful. I'm sure you've heard it before."

"Yep." Matt related the details of what he knew so far.

Stuart removed the photos of Fern and the other woman leaving the restroom, and the full image of Fern alone from the file, and along with the head shot of Fern that Matt had removed from his wallet and handed to him, said to Meg, "Please put these three photos on the Police Scotland wire, along with the physical description of the other woman from the witness in the restroom. Indicate that, at this point, we believe it to be an abduction, and officers should notify us first of any sightings. It's possible the assailant is carrying a nerve agent and should be considered dangerous. We believe they left the airport in a car, but we have no vehicle description at this time."

Meg's eyebrows raised at 'nerve agent', but she kept listening to Stuart MacLean until he finished his instruction.

"What about the media?" she asked when he paused.

"I was coming to that," he said with a smile. "We need the public's help, but you know what happens when we take this approach."

"The bloody phone rings off the bloody hook with every lunatic in the city," she said.

"Precisely. So, we need to be prepared. Before you share this with our favorite journalists, please set up this room to handle the influx of calls we no doubt will get. The fact that it's a beautiful American woman who is missing will likely double the number of callers who've just seen her. And it must follow, as the night the day."

"Huh?" Matt said.

"Hamlet," Scone said. She jerked her thumb at Stuart. "Quotes Shakespeare, does this one. It's his thing."

"Thanks for the warning," Matt said. "I would like the public to know that my wife is three-and-a-half months pregnant," he said somberly. "This is our first child. Fern is very healthy and in great shape, but it's extra urgent that we get her back immediately. If it's true about a nerve agent exposure of some sort, she will need medical care."

"Oh. Oh, my," Meg said.

"Do you have children?" Matt asked her.

"Yes. Two boys. I remember being pregnant for the first time. It was just over ten years ago. Fern does not need this about now."

The three cops were silent for a minute, and then Matt spoke. "Please arrange for a lot of coppers to answer the bloody phones."

Meg smiled, and patted Matt on the back. "Tons of bloody coppers coming this way. Don't you worry."

. . .

Matt went over today's movements with Stuart.

"Why were you and Fern separated at the airport?"

"Because I didn't think me going into the ladies' room with her would have been appropriate."

Stuart smiled. "Was that the only time today you'd been apart from each other?"

"Yes. We spent the morning together sightseeing the area around our hotel."

Stuart nodded. "Tell me about your trip to Shetland and the Highlands before you ended up in Edinburgh. Did anything unusual happen?"

"Not really unusual — we had a terrific vacation. Stayed in some amazing places, met interesting, friendly people, saw some great sights. What tourists do on vacation, I guess."

"Anything suspicious at all? Any of those hairs on the back of your neck that all coppers have when something's amiss stand up?"

"Yeah. I would have to say one thing. There was this guy." Matt related the story of the couple on the two planes, and then talking to him at Shetland Airport.

"The woman wasn't with him in Shetland?" Stuart asked, sitting up and taking notes.

"No, he said she had an emergency at home and had to return to the U.S."

"But he didn't accompany her? That seems suspicious right there."

"Then I saw him again outside our hotel in Inverness. Fern said it was just a coincidence."

The two policemen's eyes met for a silent moment, before Stuart said, "Could you identify him?"

"Yeah, of course." He described the man in detail for the DCI.

"Did the woman on the planes look anything at all like the CCTV mystery woman? Think hard, Matt."

"I already have. Tried to make her fit, but I couldn't. The two women are about the same height, but that was the only thing in common. CCTV woman is heavier with completely different hair color and style. The woman on the planes was wearing thick glasses and dressed like an American in casual sweats and sneakers. CCTV woman has no glasses, and was dressed like a Scot. I don't believe they were the same woman. And I didn't recognize either woman, or the guy."

"Which woman had the shorter hair?" Stuart asked.

"The one on the planes. It was very short and blondish gray. As you saw, CCTV woman has longer dark hair."

"Very likely a wig," Stuart said. "Maybe the other woman cut her hair in advance of the trip so a wig would slide on easily."

"Possible."

"Give me the exact date, airline, and flight numbers, if you have them, of the two flights the couple were on with you and Fern outbound from Newark to Shetland. We'll get the passenger lists and cross check them."

Matt pulled up their boarding passes on his phone, and Stuart jotted down the info as Matt read it aloud.

"Did you go through the TSA line at Newark? If so, did the couple? Do you know?"

"We were in the TSA line, yeah, but I couldn't tell you if they were. They were behind us at immigration our first time through Edinburgh Airport, and I only noticed them on the smaller plane to Shetland when they came down the small aisle—again, behind us—as Fern and I took our seats. The woman looked vaguely familiar, but I couldn't place her then or now."

"Did you see them anywhere in Shetland?"

"Just the man at the airport when we were all leaving."

"Did you see either of them in Edinburgh last night? Hotel? Restaurant? Pub?"

"No."

"Was the man in the concourse area with you today?"

"No. I never saw him again after we left our Inverness hotel yesterday. I'm pretty sure he wasn't on our train, and there was no sight of him last night around the city." Matt let out a sigh and ran his fingers through his hair.

"Do you remember where in the Shetland waiting room mystery man sat?"

"Yep. He took a seat in the far corner of the room. I can draw it if that would help. Are you thinking forensic team? After this many days? That seems like a waste of time to me."

"I am. A long shot, sure, but Shetland is a very small airport without heavy traffic. They have a forensics team in Lerwick, and it can't hurt. Draw the room and put an X on his chair. I'll take a photo and email it to them. We'll also have them check his ID and pull the info for us. How many people would you say were on that flight? Roughly?"

"Smallish plane. Probably about forty passengers. You don't think me seeing this guy three times in two weeks is a coincidence, do you, Stuart?"

"I do not."

CHAPTER 10

Early evening, they brought in food while they waited in the MIT room to see if their Police Scotland bulletin brought in anything useful. Meg reported that, so far, it was a quiet May night in greater Edinburgh, and most all of the patrols were out actively looking for the two women. Nothing had been reported yet, but the bulletin had only been live on the wire for about two hours. It would take a little longer for the media outlets to process the info and get it out to the public.

While they ate and waited—Matt had very little appetite but forced himself to eat—Stuart had gathered three more of his colleagues in Major Investigations, and they all listened and took notes as Matt detailed his and Fern's recent criminal cases in Port Stirling, starting with the most recent; Rohn Reid and Cold Rock Island. With the detectives asking many questions, Matt filled them in and worked his way backward to his first case on the new job, the murder of Emily Bushnell, which was also the case when he'd first met Fern in her then role as victim advocate for Chinook County.

"Guys, I need a break," Matt said. "I need to call Fern's parents and then talk to a couple of my detectives." He checked his watch. "Yeah, 10:00 a.m. on the west coast. I'm going to make my calls now. Is there a quiet room I could use?"

"Tom, please take Matt to the small conference room," Stuart instructed. "I'm going to go over these case notes and jot down any questions I have,

Matt, so take your time. One thing before you go: do you and Fern have any secrets or special signs that she might use to tip you off or warn you?"

"I think she did in the CCTV footage—her subtle patting of her stomach. But also, the color pink has had meaning in our relationship. It's a long story, but she might use an article of clothing, a flag, anything pink to send me a message."

"Pink. Got it." Stuart set down his pen. "Please relate to Fern's parents that Police Scotland will do everything in our power—and more—to find her and deliver her home safely."

Matt, dead tired and shattered, simply nodded.

• • •

The man and the woman, locked into their hidden space, checked the bulletin coming across his phone.

"Looks like we've been handed off to the Leith station," he said.

"Is that good or bad?" she asked.

"A little of both, I think. They are professional and will take us seriously. But they also have a better track record than some of the other stations. Step two in our plan will definitely get their attention in a hurry. Turn on the TV; let's see if they've alerted the public yet."

"They can alert all they want. Nobody will ever find us."

"True, but I want to know how much freedom we'll have to move around. You, my dear, have none, courtesy of CCTV." He turned his phone to her and showed her the photo still.

"Looks like it's time to ditch this wig." She pulled it off her head and flung it across the old stone room.

• • •

Matt took some deep breaths and tried to find some composure within himself. Alone in the conference room, and alone with his thoughts, he struggled with how to say what he knew he must say. He dialed.

"Hello?" answered Mary Byrne, Fern's mother.

"Mary, it's Matt."

"We were just talking about you kids. Are you home?"

"No, still in Scotland. Is Conor there?"

"Yes. Shall I get him?"

"Please. I have some news, and I want to tell you both."

"What's wrong, Matt? What's happened? Is my daughter alright?"

"Get Conor, please."

A few seconds went by, and then Mary said, "You're on speaker, Matt, and Conor is with me."

"What's wrong?" Conor said in a loud voice.

"I have some awful news," he began.

"Spit it out, son," demanded Conor.

"Fern has been taken, kidnapped, we think. I'm so, so sorry to tell you this." Tears sprung from Matt's eyes, and he wiped them off his chin.

"No!" wailed Mary.

"It happened at Edinburgh Airport as we were waiting for our flight home. She went in the restroom while I waited for her, but she never came out."

"How could you let this happen, Matt?" yelled Conor. "I trusted you with my daughter!"

Morose, Matt said, "I know. I know." He took a deep breath and attempted to pull himself together. "We have CCTV—security recording—of Fern leaving the restroom with another woman. I believe she was drugged. She was unable to walk normally—the other woman had a hold of her and moved Fern along."

Mary, through her sobs said, "How could she be drugged in a public restroom? I don't understand what you're telling me, Matt."

This was the part Matt was dreading. "We think the other woman exposed Fern to something. We have a witness in the bathroom who said Fern was smiling and herself when she came in, but different as they left when the woman was at her side."

"Exposed to what?"

"We don't know, Mary. But Fern was exhibiting some signs of nerve damage."

"Oh my God," Conor said. "Is she going to die? Give it to us straight, Matt."

"No. My wife is not going to die. I will not let that happen. We will find her. I'm working with Police Scotland, and they are competent and intelligent cops. And I think Fern gave me a sign that she's OK. She briefly looked up at the CCTV camera right outside the restroom and brushed her hand across her stomach. It felt like she was trying to tell me that she and the baby are alright."

"Oh, my grandchild," whimpered Mary. "This is so unfair."

"We believe it's a kidnapping, probably for ransom, and my next call is to line up some cash. I will pay a ransom if we have to, whatever they want."

"Just pay them, Matt," Conor said. "I'll get some money ready, too."

"Not necessary. I've got it covered. And the detectives here know what to do. We've got a bulletin out to all of Scotland's law enforcement, and the media will send it to the public. They've got Fern's photo and description, along with that of the other woman. Someone will have seen them, and we'll follow that lead. Edinburgh is not that big a city, and our chances of finding her are good."

"What if it's someone who hates her?" Mary said. "Or you? What if they just want her dead?"

"I don't believe that's the case," Matt said firmly. "It may very well be related to a previous case, but it's more likely they want me to suffer, and they want a bunch of my money. They'll let Fern go the minute they get paid. And if they're slow about it, we might find her first."

"We're coming," Conor said. "We'll get there as fast as we can, and we'll help you find her, Matt."

"I don't blame you for wanting to be close, and I can't stop you from coming. But I'd like to call you back once we see what kind of response we get from the public when the announcement airs. If someone out there saw her, we'll have a chance at a quick resolution. Will you give me that time?"

"It will take us several hours to arrange flights," Mary said, pulling herself together. "And we'll have to drive to Eugene or Portland first anyway. We'll book and then start driving. Call us when you can, OK?"

Before Matt could answer his beloved mother-in-law, Conor said, "Can your crew here help? Jay? Ed? All of them? There has to be a local connection, don't you think?"

"I do think so, yes. But we will cover all the bases here, too. We won't rule out anything yet. As soon as I get ransom money lined up, I will call Jay and get the ball rolling. I want them to immediately talk to anyone connected with our recent cases."

"Good," said Conor. "And you'll call Joe Phelps in D.C, too?"

"Yes. They've given me a small, private room here at the police station to make the calls I need to make. You were first, of course. I'll call Joe, and, based on when and what we hear from the kidnappers, Joe will handle things on his end, I'm sure."

"Having the U.S. government behind us can only help find my daughter, right?"

"Yes. We'll pull out all the stops. Joe will do his part to involve the full resources of our global intelligence operations, and my team in Port Stirling will stop at nothing to help us. Please have faith, you two. You know better than even me how tough Fern is. She will hang in there until I find her. There's not a doubt in my mind." *Except for the one where they've already killed her.* "Please be strong and stay positive. We'll bring her and the baby home together. We will."

"Mary and I will stay strong, for sure, and do what we can to find our daughter," Conor said. He paused. "How could you let this happen, Matt?"

. . .

Matt's next call went to Dallas, Texas.

"Dad, it's Matt. I'm in trouble and I don't have much time to talk. I need you to listen and do what I ask."

"What is it, son?"

"Fern's been kidnapped in Scotland, and I need a lot of cash as soon as you can help me arrange it. I haven't received a demand yet, but whatever it is, I don't think my Port Stirling bank will be able to handle it. I need you to get it together in Dallas and stand by to help me transfer it."

"Oh, no! Is she alive?"

"I think so, and I'm expecting a ransom demand in exchange for her life. I'm scared, dad. Can you get some money?"

"I can, certainly, and will do as you ask. How much do you think it will be?"

"I'm working with Police Scotland, and they predict it will be at least $1 million. If the kidnappers know that Fern works for the State Department, or they know about my personal resources, I'm afraid it might go higher."

"I have $1 million here at the ranch in a safe, and I'll have my bank ready another million, just in case. I'll take care of it, son. Do your thing and get my daughter-in-law back safely. I'll call you when I have it together."

Matt said, "Thanks, Dad," but his father had already hung up.

CHAPTER 11

"You aren't home yet, are you?" Jay asked. "I can tell because your voice is either bouncing off a satellite or travelling at warp speed under the Atlantic Ocean." Jay smiled at his grasp of the situation.

"Fern's been kidnapped." Matt knew that in order to get Jay's full attention, sometimes it was better to come right out with it.

"What do you mean?"

"She's been taken, Jay. Kidnapped out from under my nose. Edinburgh Airport. I'm still in Scotland."

"This is unbelievable," Jay sputtered. "What happened? How? Weren't you with her every minute?"

"Ladies room." Matt filled him in on all the gory details. "I need your help."

"You think it's connected to her work here, don't you?"

"Possibly. Hers or mine. Or both. Who knows? Someone who wanted to hurt one or both of us, for sure. Here's what I want you to do. The timing of this nightmare makes me think Rohn Reid has something to do with it. I want you and Tamryn to go out to Cold Rock Island and talk to him and his son, Randy. And anyone else out there who was connected to the Hiroshi Matsuda case. Talk to Captain Adams at the Coast Guard and get him to take you."

"OK," Jay said. "Have you talked to Joe Phelps yet? He'll have more pull with the CG than I have."

"Joe is my next call. I've talked to Conor and Mary Byrne, and then my dad to get the ransom money lined up so that we're ready if it comes to that. Tell Adams the story. He loves Fern and he'll help you out. I'll square it with Joe. Is Tamryn OK?"

"She's great. Everything is running smoothly here—you don't need to worry about anything. She and Rudy broke up a fight last night down by the harbor, and we have two guests in our jail today waiting for lawyers. No other action. Not that I wouldn't drop it for you and Fern even if we were slammed. This is terrible, Matt. Are you alright?"

"No, can't say that I am. Tired, scared, and pissed off."

"How are the Scottish cops treating you? Any help?"

"It started off badly with a pompous ass superintendent, but I got his attention, and he assigned Edinburgh's top detective to Fern's case. DCI Stuart MacLean. Good guy. Real smart. He took action immediately, and I can tell he really cares."

"Don't be scared, Matt. You're da man. You'll find her. Especially if you've got some good help on the ground over there. Rohn Reid seems too smart for something like this."

"Fern ruined his life. Tore his family apart. It's a strong motive to seek revenge."

"But this? He doesn't need the money."

"No, and that's the part that scares me the most. He might just kill her, knowing that it will kill me, too."

There was an ominous pause on the line while the two friends considered that, then Jay said, "I'm on it. I'll grab Tamryn, and call Captain Adams immediately. What else can we do?"

"Is Ed around?"

"We went fishing yesterday, but today the illustrious Lieutenant Edward Sonders of the Oregon State Police has been summoned to headquarters in Salem where he is receiving a highfalutin merit award for twenty-five years of service."

"Wow. I knew he'd been in the OSP for a long time, but I didn't know it had been that long. Must've joined when he was about twenty-five—isn't he turning fifty next month?"

"Yeah. He told me he worked for a small police force in southern Oregon right after college, and then joined OSP after three years. Anyway, said he will be back in Chinook County tomorrow."

"This is perfect. Please call him and ask him to stay where he is," Matt said urgently. "I want him to go to the Oregon State Penitentiary and have a conversation with Zhang Chen and the other guys we arrested the night of the trafficking raid. We also need a chat with David Dalrymple and his buddies Michael Winston and Ray Peng. Might not hurt to talk to Alex Bowen, too, although I can't see him being involved in something at this level."

"I can see Blake Bowen being involved, though," Jay said. "She's got no redeeming qualities whatsoever."

"Good point. Is she in the state pen, too, or is she incarcerated at another facility? I can't remember."

"No, Blake is at the women's prison, Coffee Creek in Wilsonville."

"Oh, of course. OK, call Patty Perkins and ask her to connect with Ed. I want them to go to the prisons together, and each of them to get a take on our old friends' current status."

There was a short silence while Jay scribbled some notes. "What else?"

"What about the Bushnells? Are they still in the Seattle area? Might be a good idea to see where their heads are these days."

"Sylvia will know. Jack is still in the state hospital; Fern and I checked when you got shot."

"I think that's everyone then. At least, everyone that Fern has been involved with and who has a reason to hurt her," Matt said and hesitated. "If we don't get a lead off any of these felons, we'll have to go back to my time in Dallas, but my gut is telling me it's about Fern as much as it is about me."

"Is there any chance it's random and related to Scotland?"

"A chance, yes, and we're exploring every avenue until we have more evidence, but personally, I don't think so. If I hadn't seen the guy I told you about in three different places with us, I might think that. But this guy started out with us in the U.S.—I'm 100 percent sure of that. It doesn't feel random, more like someone has been working on this for some time.

Not a spur-of-the-moment kind of deal. Everything points to it being tied to our work in Port Stirling. Do you disagree with me?"

"No. I think you're probably right. Some of our cases went down hard, and it's only natural for there to be lots of resentment—the kind that stews in people's minds over time."

"Call Earl, too," Matt said. "I have a lot of respect for the sheriff, and he needs to know what's happened. On second thought, wait a minute. When you talk to Patty, ask her if she can give him the news in person in Twisty River. He might take this real badly, and she'll know how to handle it."

"Yeah, that works better. What will you do next, Matt?" There was a hitch in Jay's voice.

"We're waiting at the station until the media gets the announcement on air to see if we get any sightings. They've booked a room for me at a hotel down the street, and when I reach my limit tonight, I'll go sleep for a couple of hours. But I'll leave my phone charged and on, and you are not to hesitate to call me with any news or questions. Got it? And, could you swing by my house and make sure everything is OK there? You know the door code, right?"

"Yes, I'll go right away. And the same goes for you to call me anytime, day or night. Two-way street, OK?"

• • •

DCI Stuart MacLean knocked on the conference room door and entered without waiting for Matt to respond.

"We've got a tip from the public," MacLean said. "Can you come back to the MTI room now?"

Matt said, "Gotta go, Jay," and hung up. He followed a silent, brisk-walking Stuart down the short hallway. They settled in the pod around Stuart's desk.

"BBC Scotland ran our announcement about fifteen minutes ago, including photos taken off the airport's CCTV," Stuart said. "Just now, a man called from Craigentinny, that's a neighborhood southeast of here, and he believes he recognized the woman on the BBC segment. He saw a woman matching the description meeting a man in the car park at the Palace of Holyroodhouse just a while ago."

Matt's eyes widened and his ears flushed red. "Did he see Fern? Was she with the other woman?"

MacLean shook his head. "No. He was leaving his shift as docent supervisor and says that there were two vehicles parked side-by-side, and they were located at the far end of one row, about six spaces away from where he was parked. The two stood talking between their cars. He did not see any other people. He noticed them because the palace was closed for the day, and there weren't any other cars remaining in the car park."

"Did he hear anything?" Matt asked.

"No. He said they were speaking low, almost whispering. He thought they might be secret lovers."

"Did he get a license number off either car?"

"He didnae, but he thinks he can describe both cars."

"Does that mean he did not in Scottish? Can we go see him now? Talk to him?"

In answer, Stuart turned to the coat rack behind him and pulled on a black fleece jacket. "Yeah, did not. Sorry, American friend. Let's go."

. . .

Still not used to the driver's wheel being on the right side of the car, Matt, hunched against the now steady rain, first walked to that door of the white Hyundai with its distinctive yellow and blue markings. "Other side, mate," Stuart said. And, with a smile. "How long have you been in Scotland?"

"One day too long," Matt said with deep sadness.

Settled in, Stuart plugged the man's address into the GPS, and they took off. Matt was silent with his thoughts most of the way and Stuart let him be. Finally, Matt said, "This car is quiet—is it electric?"

"Yes. Police Scotland spent millions on the fleet about four years ago. Lots of officers are still complaining and don't like the vehicles, but I believe it's great that we are doing our part to keep Scotland's pastures green, don't you think?"

Matt nodded. "I do. I need to do the same thing in Port Stirling, beginning with myself. Been thinking about it, just haven't had the time to get it going."

"You can tackle it when you and Fern get back home, yeah? America needs to do more about climate change or we're all toast."

"It's not just us, China and India have to do their part, too, but yep, we're behind you guys. If you help me get Fern back, I'll make sure every cop in my county drives electric."

"You don't need to make me any promises, Matt, I'm going to do everything I can to reunite you two. I don't need any extra incentives. What happened to your wife is disgraceful and unacceptable, and I'm embarrassed it happened in my city."

"Don't be. The world is a fucking crazy place these days. This could've happened anywhere, and the real truth is that it's likely because of our work in the U.S. There are too many unhinged folks out there, and our famous rule of law is meaningless to more and more people. I'm growing more pessimistic every day that we can right the ship."

"What's the answer?" asked Stuart.

"Well, if I had a genie and three wishes, I'd ask for heroin, fentanyl, and cocaine to be eradicated from our planet. Drugs are a major part of our problems, especially where homelessness and crime are involved. And, we need better leadership."

"In law enforcement, you mean?"

"Law enforcement, business leaders, political leaders—all levels. So many people get promoted a step or two above their capabilities, and we're not turning out real leaders anymore. There are some, but they're few and far between."

"Like our Chief Constable? At least two steps beyond where he belongs?" Stuart said.

"Precisely like your Chief Constable." They shared a muted laugh.

• • •

DCI MacLean pulled up to the curb in front of a modest stone semi-detached house. "Try to be calm, if you can," he said to Matt. "We have a respectful relationship with our people, and we need our interrogations to stay civilized. They're cooperative with Police Scotland, and it's vital we keep it that way."

"I'm not a cowboy," Matt said, indignant. "Well, actually, I was a cowboy, but I'm not anymore. I'll keep it under control. C'mon, man."

CHAPTER 12

A pleasant looking man, about fifty, in a dark blue cardigan sweater worn over a white collared shirt and a blue and grey patterned tie opened the door.

"You must be from Police Scotland," he said. "Please come through."

Stuart MacLean showed his badge. "I'm DCI MacLean and this is Chief of Police Matt Horning. He's from Oregon in the USA."

Matt extended his hand to their host. "Thank you for seeing us, Mr. Thomson."

"Please call me Graeme. Mr. Thomson is my father."

Stuart and Matt followed him into a cozy sitting room just off the front door. A fire was burning softly in the smallish grey stone fireplace, and the heavy wine-colored draperies were closed against the chilly darkness.

"May I offer you tea or a nightcap?" A gold-rimmed China cup and saucer sat on a small round table next to a recliner placed close to the fireplace.

"Normally, I would say 'yes, please'," indicated Stuart. "But time is of the essence on the case we're working on, and we need to just get to it, if you don't mind."

Graeme nodded, and the three men took seats.

"Matt's wife was abducted at the airport earlier today, and we believe it to be a kidnapping of sorts," Stuart started. "We understand that you saw our bulletin on the BBC, and you may have information related. Please tell us what you saw at Holyroodhouse car park."

"And when," Matt added quickly. "Don't leave out a single detail, sir."

"Certainly. I was leaving the palace shortly after 18:00, which is my normal stop time. Last admission this time of year is at 16:30, and the palace has a firm close of 18:00. I usually wait to say 'good evening' to the docents on my staff before I take my leave," Graeme said.

"Did anyone walk out to the car park with you?" Stuart asked.

"No, I left alone. Most of the staff had already left for the day. It was a slow day, and all of the visitors were well gone by 17:00, I would say. That's why I noticed these two vehicles in the car park—they were the only ones remaining."

"Where do the rest of the employees park? Night shift security? People like that?" asked Matt.

"There is a separate parking area for staff. It's around the back and has a different entrance than the visitors' park. I happened to be in the visitor park tonight because I had been off site at a management training at New College and was just popping in to pick up some papers and make sure everything was in order. I saw a man and a woman standing between the two cars, and they appeared to be deep in conversation."

"Did you approach them?" Stuart asked.

"No. It seemed as if they were having a very private conversation, voices lowered—that sort of thing. I didn't want to intrude."

"Did you see a second woman?" asked Matt, leaning forward. "She would have been taller than the other woman. Younger, with red hair, and slim."

"Your wife, I understand," Graeme said. "I'm very sorry, but, no, I did not see her. The only woman I saw was short with long dark hair and matched the 'other woman' description as the TV told it. I feel badly."

Dejected, Matt said, "And you only heard the two voices? The man and the one woman? No muffled cries or any noises coming from either of the two cars?"

"No. It was a still, early evening, and the car park is in a quiet area with parkland surrounding it. Only their voices, I'm sure."

"But you couldn't make out what they were saying?" Stuart asked.

"No, as I've said, they were whispering, and it was all quite muffled."

"What was the tone of the conversation?" Matt asked. "Were they animated? What was their body language telling you?"

"I wouldn't say animated. Perhaps the woman was a bit more excitable than the man. He was a cool customer. She waved her hand in the air in front of his face once while I was looking at them, but he didn't respond."

"Had you ever seen either of them previously?" asked Stuart.

"Not that I can recall."

"We understand you did not get a license number for either vehicle — is that correct?"

Graeme drummed his fingers on his armchair in an agitated manner. "Well, no. I had no reason to, did I?"

Soothingly, Stuart said, "No. No, of course not. You had no way of knowing they might be potentially of interest to us."

"Can you describe the cars to us?" Matt asked.

"I can tell you about the one closest to me, but not as much about the second one, and it wasn't a car so much as a people mover." Graeme answered.

"People mover?" Matt looked to Stuart for an explanation.

"What you call a van, I believe," Stuart said. "Continue please, Graeme."

"There was still some daylight, and the vehicle closest to me was a white Ford Transit. One of those cargo things with rear doors. The side nearest to me had a sliding door — no windows. Only the drivers' door had a window. I couldn't see the other side, but I would guess it had only a passenger window and likely another sliding, windowless door."

"New or old?" asked Matt, while Stuart was taking detailed notes.

"Somewhat in between," Graeme said. "Around 2019 model, perhaps."

"Were there any marks on it? Anything that could help us identify it?"

"None that I saw."

"What about the other vehicle?"

"It was definitely smaller than the white Ford, and I couldn't see it very clearly. It was black, and it could have been a Jaguar. It was closer to the ground than the other vehicle, sportier. It might have been an Audi. It looked brand new to me, but then I drive an older Vauxhall."

"Could you tell who was driving which vehicle?" Matt asked. "You're doing great." He tried a smile.

"Not definitively."

"Give us your best guess," Stuart urged.

"Well, I'd venture that the woman was driving the white one. She was standing closest to it, while the man stood next to the sport car. He was facing me, while her back was turned."

"How would you describe him?" Stuart asked.

"He had a Slavic look about him. Perhaps Russian, maybe Croatian. Wide, rounder face, pronounced cheekbones, kind of a big, bulging nose, light brown straight hair, pale skin. He also had a big mole or some kind of discoloration in the center of his chin. Brown thing. In his late forties, I'd guess."

"Excellent description, Graeme," Matt said. *Big mole, that was the man who was following us!* "Did you get all that, DCI?"

Stuart, scribbling madly, just nodded.

"Anything at all about the woman stand out to you?" Matt asked, desperate.

"Nothing about her looks. I didn't get a good look at her. Maybe I would say she wasn't skinny. I'm so sorry. She was dressed like they said on TV, plaid trousers and a solid jumper."

"Was she wearing a face mask?"

"I don't believe so, but I can't be certain."

"Could she have been wearing a wig?"

Graeme thought. "I don't really know. No women I know wear them—that I know of—and I doubt if I could tell the difference. You don't see many women in Edinburgh with glossy black hair, however, so I suppose it's possible. We tend to have brown hair, more chestnut colored, or ginger, of course." He waved his hand in Stuart's direction.

"Could you take a stab at any of the letters or numbers in the van's license plate?" Matt asked. "I know that's an unfair question, but occasionally something jumps out at witnesses."

Graeme shook his head, a sad look on his face. "I never saw either vehicle's plates because I was looking at them from the side. The only thing I could add is that the Ford may have had a rental logo sticker on the right-side windshield. Something caught my eye, but I can't say for sure. It may have just been the sunlight flickering."

"We have officers out at this moment showing the other woman's photo to car hire agencies," Stuart said. "We will add your description of the two vehicles."

"There's probably hundreds of white vans in the city," Matt said, disappointedly. "But adding that suspect car to the woman's photo might spur something." He looked at Stuart for hope.

"There may be hundreds of white vans, but we will stop every single one of them and turn them upside down if we must," Stuart said. "We will also go through our files and see if we have any male photos that resemble your description of our man. We will want you to come to the station in Leith and see if we can get lucky with an identification."

"That's no problem," Graeme said. "I will do whatever you ask of me. I just wish I would have taken a better look at the woman in question." He looked miserably at Matt. "I lost my own wife recently, and I know your pain is severe." He rubbed his hands on his thighs, and clearly couldn't think of what else to say.

Matt stood. "Fern is not lost. She's just temporarily missing, and I will get her back. You've aided my cause, Graeme, and I'm forever grateful to you." They shook hands, as Graeme, too, stood. "I'm sorry about your wife," Matt said. "How did she die?"

Graeme looked Matt in the eye. "She was hit by a bicyclist while walking in Hunter's Bog, fell and hit her head on a sharp rock. The polis believe the bicyclist didn't stop, and she bled to death alone. It can be a tough city, Chief Horning, but I hope it turns out better for you than it did for Lucy and me."

. . .

Back in the car with Stuart, and dead tired, Matt almost didn't notice his phone vibrating in his pocket. He looked at the screen — Patty Perkins.

"Patty," he croaked at his phone.

"Jay called me," said the Twisty River cop and the best detective in all of Chinook County. "I'm so sorry, Matt."

"Help me find her, Patty," he whispered. "Please help me."

"I'm on it. I'm driving now to Salem to meet Ed at the Oregon State Penitentiary. I wanted to tell you. He's cleared our visit with the law enforcement liaison inside, and we've requested a sit-down with Zhang Chen to start with. It will happen today, and we'll have some answers from that turd by the time you wake up in the morning."

"Will he talk to you?"

"Oh, yeah. Or I'll squeeze his balls until he passes out."

That almost got a smile out of Matt, but not quite. "I won't be surprised if Chen has something to do with this. Thanks, Patty, your instincts are good."

"Which is why when we've finished our work at the state pen, I'm coming to Edinburgh. Ted and I just talked, and he's been wanting to see Scotland, so we're coming together."

"You don't need to come. I've got good support here," Matt protested lightly. "The police are taking it seriously, and there's a hard-working, smart, detective chief inspector sitting right next to me." He cast a quick glance at Stuart, who stared straight ahead at the road.

"Don't care," Patty said. "Tell your guy I said 'hi', and I'll meet him in about twenty hours. If Fern is safe by the time Ted and I get there, great. We'll tour the Highlands. If not, we'll be by your side every step of the way. Gotta go."

"Wait," Matt urged. "Tell Zhang Chen that if he's behind this, I'll do worse to him than you will. Make him talk, Patty."

"That's a promise. Take care of yourself, honey." The line went dead.

Matt breathed a small sigh of relief.

"The cavalry's coming then, yeah?" Stuart said.

CHAPTER 13

While Oregon State Police Lieutenant Ed Sonders and Twisty River Detective Patricia Perkins waited in the lobby of the Oregon State Penitentiary for the public and legal information officer, Patty made a quick call to Jay.

The local cops had always worked together, but their bonds had been strengthened during the past couple of years as the southern Oregon coast had caught the attention of bad actors far and wide. Young cop, Jay Finley, and not-so-young cops, Patty Perkins and Ed Sonders, had worked together for three years before Port Stirling hired Matt Horning as its new Chief of Police. Within his first week on the job, all three tasked with keeping the area safe from crime knew he was a breath of fresh air after old George retired as the PSPD chief.

And, Matt's hiring had come in the nick of time because Oregon, traditionally on the fringes of neighboring California's problems, was now smack on the radar, and the law enforcement team had kept busy. But the arrival of Matt Horning, and his partnership and subsequent marriage with Fern Byrne, had not gone unnoticed by the crooks. As popular as Matt was in his community, he was twice as unpopular in the criminal underworld, a fact that local law enforcement lived with daily.

"You'd think even the bad guys would let them have a honeymoon in peace," said Jay now.

"Not allowed, apparently," said Patty. The nearing-retirement detective was wearing her police uniform today, which she rarely did. Her short blonde/gray hair wasn't as neatly coiffed as usual, but she'd done the best she could on such short notice. New Prada tortoiseshell glasses and a stripe of mauve lipstick brightened her up. "I talked to Matt, and he is distraught. How are you holding up, Jay?"

"I'm OK, I guess. I love Fern, too, you know. It's eating a hole in my stomach. How are you?"

"The same. I'm terrified for her," Patty said, her voice quivering. "But we're going to fight for her."

"Damn straight. I'm at their house now, checking it over for them."

"Everything look OK?"

"Yeah. Locked up tight, and nothing disturbed. I'll keep an eye on it until they are safely back home."

"What are you doing next?" asked Patty.

"Tamryn and I are headed to the Coast Guard station in Buck Bay, and we'll wait for Captain Adams to arrive. He's taking us out to Cold Rock Island. Matt wants us to grill Rohn Reid, and anybody else we can find."

"You were out there on the Matsuda case, weren't you?"

"Yeah. Can't believe I have to go back to that devil island. But there's a good chance that Reid might be involved."

"Agreed," Patty said. "The timing is suspect. Although his family destroyed themselves, he's had time to think about it by now and has probably assigned blame to Fern."

"That's what Matt said. I'm having a hard time believing Reid would risk everything to do something this stupid."

"Don't let that color your judgment, Jay," Patty advised. "Fern told me he's arrogant and thinks he's smarter than everyone else in the room. Sometimes, men like that won't be stopped by logic because they truly believe the rules don't apply to them."

"He is smarter than me," Jay said woefully.

"No, he's not. You are one sharp cookie, Detective Jay Finley. Just because he's made buckets of money doesn't necessarily mean he's the smartest. He may have cheated along the way. Ask the right questions and listen carefully to his answers; you'll know if he's clean or not."

"Thanks, Patty, good pep talk. Besides, Tamryn's with me, and her bullshit meter is off the charts. Between the two of us, we'll whittle him down to size."

In spite of her sorrow, Patty had to laugh. "If Reid thought Fern was strong-willed, wait until he comes up against the badass that is Tamryn."

"Fern *is* strong-willed, not *was*," Jay whispered into his phone.

• • •

When he and Patty hung up, Jay went outside through the double French doors of the Horning house to the large deck that overlooked the Pacific Ocean. He checked that the khaki canvas outdoor table and chairs covers were securely fastened against the wind, and that the gate at the top of the staircase leading down to the beach path was locked.

Once Jay was satisfied that everything on the deck was as it should be, he grabbed hold of the railing, breathed in the brisk sea air, held it, and let it out slowly, trying to calm his inner self. He was unsure if humans could feel their blood pressure spiking or not, but he thought his might be. He repeated his breathing exercise. His eye caught something out to sea. A harbor seal close to shore, bobbing and weaving in the vigorous surf.

"Might you be the famous Roger, Matt's talking seal?" Jay said out loud, and then quickly looked over his shoulder sheepishly to make sure there was no one around to hear him talking to a seal. The coast was clear.

The seal grinned at Jay. "Yep, that's me. I'm named after famous Dallas Cowboys quarterback Roger Staubach, you know."

"I knew that," Jay said. "Matt told me that on the day I threatened to have him committed for talking to a seal. He's still a Cowboys fan, if you can believe that shit."

"I suppose you're a Seahawks fan," Roger said.

"What's wrong with that?" Jay asked.

"Nothing, we do live in the Pacific Northwest."

"Exactly, and we should root for our teams."

"Although, sea hawks are actually ospreys, and they sometimes get in my way when I'm eating fish," Roger said. "So, not exactly my favorite. What brings you to Matt's home today?"

"Fern has been kidnapped in Scotland, and Matt has to stay until he gets her back."

"No!"

"That's what I said. It's awful and I'm afraid."

"Don't be scared. Matt is the best policeman I know, and he's very good at this sort of thing," Roger said reassuringly. "Could the evil man who shot at him on that very deck you're standing on be responsible?"

"He's in prison, so he couldn't have physically abducted Fern, but he could've arranged it, I guess. But that's true of all the criminals Matt and Fern put away. I don't know where to start, but I'll go to Cold Rock Island first as Matt instructed and take it from there."

"What's your gut telling you?"

"I don't go with my gut feelings like Matt does," Jay said. "Guess I don't have enough experience yet in this job to develop strong feelings until I've nosed around and talked to people. I like facts and evidence."

"I understand why you and Matt are a good team, then," said Roger, bobbing up and down in the affirmative. "So go forth and nose around. Keep me posted, young Jay."

"Thanks, Roger. You've been helpful. Time to go to work."

Roger grinned, ducked under the waves, and disappeared.

• • •

The state pen's law enforcement liaison, Amanda Wilson, came rushing into the lobby. "Sorry, I'm late," she said to Ed, whom she'd known since her first day on the job four years ago.

"You're never late, we're early," Ed replied. "Have you met Patricia Perkins?"

"No, I don't believe so," said Amanda, and the two women shook hands.

"It's been several years since I've had the pleasure of dropping in here,"

Patty said, with a smile. "But now that you're housing a few of our recent new friends, I thought it was a good time for a visit. Thanks for accommodating us on short notice."

"We take care of our law enforcement buddies. I've reserved one of the conference rooms for you to meet with Mr. Chen in private." Amanda hesitated. "He was — how shall I say — reluctant to talk with the two of you."

"Not surprising," Patty said. "How were you able to convince him to cooperate?"

"We have our ways. Follow me. Let's get you signed in." Nothing more was said by Amanda as Ed and Patty completed the sign-in process, stored their weapons in the lockers provided, went through the metal detector (Ed had to duck), and received their visitor badges. Patty relieved some of the tension by telling the young officer running the metal detector machine, "I wore underwear today just for you." She was disappointed when he didn't laugh, instead saying with a shake of his head, "You'd be surprised how many visitors don't bother."

After the second series of iron gates closed behind them, they turned left down a short hallway opposite the entrance to the visiting room. There were three small rooms, glassed in on three sides so the occupants were visible at all times. However, these meeting areas did have a door on each one for privacy, unlike the open visitors' room. The only furniture was a small round table and four chairs, and the room was brightly lit from overhead. A guard was stationed in the hallway and opened the door to the first room when he saw them coming through the gates. He didn't say anything but smiled and nodded in greeting.

Patty and Ed settled in the chairs, and Amanda said to the guard, "Please bring in Mr. Chen now." The guard walked to the end of the hallway, knocked on the door with a small window in it, and motioned to someone unseen on the other side.

Not knowing what to expect, Patty and Ed were nonetheless surprised when Zhang Chen came into the room — he looked exactly the same as he had the last day they saw him in the packed courtroom. Only the blue of the penitentiary standard apparel was different from the Chinook County orange prison garb.

He was still an imposing, slightly regal presence — tall, with his raven hair neatly clipped and styled. His posture was erect, and his sharp cheekbones more prominent than ever. Black eyes stared right through them, just as they always had.

He sat across from them without speaking and placed his hands on the table.

Patty looked down. "You have a manicure?" she said incredulously. "A fucking manicure?"

That brought a tight smile to Chen's face. "One has standards, Detective Perkins."

"You're in prison, Chen," Ed said, stating the obvious. "I guess it hasn't crimped your style."

"I have resources, and this is a building that appreciates some extras from time to time. It's all very civilized, as long as you don't flaunt it or become obnoxious. I'm a model adult in custody. There is simply no reason to be otherwise."

"How do you get the money inside?" Patty asked, pretty sure she knew the answer. "We had to leave all of ours in the lockers at reception."

"My friends and family have not deserted me, in spite of my unpleasant circumstances." He sat back and stared at her with a look that still gave her chills. It said to her, 'I'd just as soon slit your throat as answer that question.'

"Moving on," Ed started, "we're here because we want to know if you know anything about the kidnapping of Fern Byrne in Edinburgh, Scotland, earlier today, UK time. Do you?"

A brief silence while the three stared at each other, nobody blinking. Cool as always, Chen finally said, "I do not."

"Would you tell us if you did?" Ed asked.

"I would not."

"What if there was something in it for you?" Patty said.

"What could you possibly do for me?" Chen said to her, ice in his voice. "We hate each other, remember?"

"Oh, yes, I remember," Patty said forcefully. "You did terrible things, Chen, horrid, disgusting things to innocent human beings, so, yes, it's fair to say that I do hate you. But it's also possible that I love Fern Byrne more than I hate you, and Lieutenant Sonders and I will leave no stone unturned to bring her home safely."

Chen held her gaze and was silent.

"How many years did you get?" Ed asked, knowing full well the answer.

"Minimum twenty-five. Your lot would like me to die in here," Chen answered.

"The best years of your life in prison? Awful, just awful," Ed said, shaking his head, and leaving it hanging in the air.

"It is a shame," Patty added. "I remember when we arrested you at your Port Stirling home how you were wearing a luxurious red cashmere sweater, perfectly fitting black jeans, and to-die-for black Italian loafers. It was so you. So pulled together. A man in his fabulous beachfront home with everything to live for. And yet, here you are." She spread her arms and waved at the room.

Again, Chen didn't react. Serene and imperturbable.

"How are your sweet parents coping with your imprisonment?" Patty asked, trying to goad him.

"My parents are none of your business."

Patty grinned at him, knowing she'd hit a nerve. "Do they come to visit you? It must be very unpleasant for them to see their son behind bars. Wasting his life." She made a tsk-tsk sound.

Chen suddenly stood and motioned to the guard. He turned to Patty and leaned over the table; his face close to hers. "Put an offer in writing and leave it with Amanda. If it appeals to me, I'll ask around. If not, I hope you will invite me to Mrs. Horning's funeral. On some level, I did admire her."

Ed and Patty watched Zhang Chen disappear through the door at the end of the hall. They stood motionless until the door clanged shut.

"That went well," Ed said.

Patty fumed. "That flaming asshole. I can't stand that man. He's in prison for the rest of his life — how can he still be so flippin' arrogant?"

"Was that a rhetorical question or do you want me to answer?" Ed sat back down and motioned to her to do the same.

"And he calls a prison official by her first name?", she continued to rant. "Doesn't that seem awfully informal and completely inappropriate to you?"

"Agreed. Take a deep breath, Patricia, we have some thinking to do."

After Amanda watched the guard escort Chen back through the set of gates into the prison proper, she came to the door and waved through the glass. Ed shook his head 'no' vigorously, pointed to his watch, and then held up ten fingers. She mouthed 'got it', and turned her back to the door, standing guard.

"He wants a deal. We can't let him out of here," Patty said. "We just can't."

"We also can't let Fern die in Scotland," Ed said calmly, and they locked eyes.

"No, we can't do that either," Patty conceded. "Not if there is a chance that asshole might be able to learn something in this hellhole." She rubbed her face with both hands and followed it with light slaps on her cheeks. "What do you think it will take to get him to help us?"

"Well, he knows we can't set him free. He's definitely an asshole, but he's not stupid. He's never been stupid; it was his greed and arrogance that landed him here. Plus, he's a young man—forty-three, right?"

Patty nodded.

"If we could get the powers that be to take five years off his life sentence, he could hypothetically be out in his early sixties. It's not an ice cream sundae, but it is a carrot."

"Do you think Judge Hedges would even consider it? She delighted in giving Chen a long sentence."

"This is Fern's life we're talking about, Patty. Cynthia Hedges is fond of her, too."

"I know that, but it's still asking a lot of someone whose entire life has centered on the law. Not to mention right vs. wrong. Cynthia has always acted by the book."

Ed lifted his head slightly and scratched under his chin. "I hear you, but we have to try, don't we? Also, we could go to the Governor if Cynthia balks."

"Or Joe Phelps. Wonder if Matt has contacted him yet. Joe will be beside himself if a second agent of his gets murdered, especially since her predecessor was beheaded."

"Please don't say that word again, Patty. I'm a tough cop, but I can't go there this time."

"How do you think I feel?" she said, her face flushing. "Fern is like the daughter I never had. This cannot be happening!" She slapped the table viciously, and Amanda turned quickly around. Ed waved her off for a second time.

"Then let's act," he said. "Our choices are to get Zhang Chen some relief from his sentence, or to talk to some of his pals in here ourselves. Like David Dalrymple and Ray Peng. And we need to call Multnomah County and find out where Michael Winston is incarcerated — I think it's in Washington's Stafford Creek Correction Center in Aberdeen, but I'm not positive."

"I think we need to do all those things, Ed. You're right. My hatred for Zhang Chen is not as important as doing everything we can for Fern and Matt. Let's make a plan. Besides, if he does get out of here, it would give me a purpose in retirement to dog him to death."

"That's the spirit. Here's another thought; let's talk to the guard who just escorted Chen back to his cell. Maybe he's heard something."

"I was just about to suggest that," Patty said. "We should talk to some of the guards who are around our friends. Most of them look bored to me, and maybe they listen in on inmates for their fun."

Ed stood, knocked on the door, and when Amanda opened it, Ed said, "We need to talk with you for a moment."

"Sure," Amanda said. "What can I do next for you?"

"Are we allowed to have brief chats with the guards? If so, we'd like to talk with the guard who escorted Chen just now."

"That's no problem. I'll contact him. Wait here."

Five minutes later, the guard appeared at their door, looking uneasy. He was Hispanic and young, in his late twenties, Patty thought as she opened the door and asked him to come in.

Patty and Ed introduced themselves, told him why they were there, and asked him to sit down. "Please tell us your name and about yourself."

"Luis Garcia. I've worked here for two years, and I moved to Salem from Medford, where I was born."

While Ed made a note, Patty looked him over. He was a nice-looking kid, slender but substantial shoulders with good facial features and close-cropped black hair. She thought he looked like a soccer star.

"We appreciate you talking with us," she said. "Please don't be nervous, we just have a few questions about some of the adults in custody."

Luis nodded.

"We are investigating a crime that took place earlier today in Scotland, but it may have a local connection," she continued. "Have you heard any of the inmates talking about Scotland, or have you heard the names Matt or Fern mentioned?"

Garcia was a cool customer, and if he did recognize the names or the topic of the conversation, he didn't let on.

"Scotland?" he said. "No, I haven't heard anything about Scotland. Always wanted to go there, though. And those names don't ring a bell. Who are they?"

"They work in law enforcement in Chinook County and are friends of ours," Ed told him. "Fern is missing — she's been kidnapped."

"No, I haven't heard anything about her. Sorry I can't help you."

"Do you spend much time around Zhang Chen, the prisoner you just took back inside?" Patty asked.

"Not that much. I'm assigned to his wing on this shift, but they move us around."

"What about David Dalrymple?" Ed inquired.

"I know who he is, yes, but again, we're rotated regularly."

"Ray Peng? Alex Bowen?" Ed again.

"Yeah. Same thing. We all know them. The 'beach boys' we call them. From down south on the coast. Rick Reid is a relatively new arrival, and we group him in that crowd, too, although, so far, he doesn't have anything to do with the other four. Keeps to himself as much as possible."

"Do the other four beach boys hang out together?" asked Patty.

"Kind of. They all know each other for sure. I couldn't tell you any specifics about their relationships though."

"And you're quite sure you've not heard any chatter about Scotland in the past few weeks?"

"Nope. Not a whisper."

Patty and Ed looked at each other, and she shrugged. "I guess that's it for now then," she said to Garcia. "Thanks for your time. Please let Amanda know if you do hear anything, won't you?"

"Sure thing, ma'am."

CHAPTER 14

Three hours southwest of Salem and the Oregon State Penitentiary, Detectives Jay Finley and Tamryn Gesicki had just boarded the Coast Guard cutter Resolve with Captain Bob Adams. Adams and his crew were instrumental in helping Fern solve the murder of Hiroshi Matsuda and bring the perpetrators to justice. He, too, was horrified at this new development.

"Let me make sure I have the facts straight," the fit, dapper, fifty-something captain said after Jay had introduced him to Tamryn, and they had been welcomed aboard. "Matt and Fern are in Scotland, she's been abducted by persons unknown, and you think Rohn Reid may have something to do with this?"

"In a nutshell," Jay answered.

"So, we're going back to that island to confront him?"

"Yes. Matt wants us to question him face-to-face, and his son, Randy, too. We all agree that the timing of Fern's kidnapping is highly suspicious, coming so closely on the heels of her last case."

"Do you know for a fact that they are on the island?" the captain asked. "Not at one of his other homes?" Billionaire Reid owned at least three other homes that they knew of in addition to owning all of Cold Rock Island—Seattle (his original hometown), Palm Desert, California, and an apartment in Paris.

"He is on the island," Jay nodded. "I checked with one of his permanent employees there, Aaron Rogers, and he confirmed it. You might remember Aaron, Bob, he is one of the caretakers…a nice kid caught up in a whole lot of ugliness."

"I remember everyone on that island," the captain said, grim-faced. "Fern liked Aaron—thought he was sweet. I remember when I met him thinking that he didn't look anything at all like the NFL QB with the same name. Small guy, kind of timid."

Jay smiled at the thought. "Our Aaron will tell you that his name is spelled Rogers, not Rodgers. He told me that Reid's airplane is in the island's hangar, and he saw him walking around outside this morning. Aaron's agreed to keep our arrival a surprise, and said he'd meet us at the dock."

"That won't make Mr. Reid very happy."

"No, I don't suppose it will. But Aaron learned from the Matsuda case—all of them did, I believe—that it's a good idea to cooperate with the police."

"Have you met him, Tamryn?" asked Adams.

Trying to tame her untamable curly black hair in the stiff ocean breeze—she loved the Pacific Ocean, but she would never love the wind—the diminutive detective said, "No, I haven't had the pleasure. I was, umm, detained during the Matsuda case and unable to help my colleagues." Her Boston accent and spunky, straightforward demeanor took the captain somewhat by surprise. She seemed out of place in Oregon. But he also liked her instantly.

"He's an interesting man," Adams continued. "As a father myself, I almost feel sorry for him, even with all his billions."

"You would've been paying closer attention to your family, Bob," Jay said.

"I certainly would like to think I would have. Are you ready to go?"

"Ready if you are, Captain," Tamryn said. "Let's get this show on the road. Or, on the water, I guess I should say."

"We have about a thirty-minute ride. Most visitors to my ship enjoy the forward deck, especially as we get close to the island, but there's less wind on the aft deck," he pointed behind him.

"I'll take the aft," Tamryn said, "for now, anyway. When we get closer, I'll want a look at the island. OK with you, Jay?"

"I do not need to watch our approach to this place. Thought I was done with it for good."

Tamryn and Jay zipped up their jackets against the freshening breeze and headed to the stern deck. The day was typical for an Oregon beach day in mid-May: it was fifty-nine degrees but dry when they left Buck Bay. However, despite the mostly sunny sky, there was more of a chill on the water, and they huddled close to each other on the deck.

"Have you heard anything new from Matt?" Tamryn asked him.

"No, not since the one call. If I know him, he's pushing the Edinburgh police hard, even though it's getting late over there."

"He's probably exhausted, poor guy," she added. "We're going to do our part, Jay. Have you told the rest of our team? Cancelled any time off?"

"Yeah, I told Sylvia, and asked her to fill in the others, including the city manager. Matt's put me in charge of the local investigation — are you OK with that?"

"Silly goose," she said, elbowing him hard in his skinny ribs. They were a funny cop team; Jay tall, gangly, always with a cowlick in his brown hair, having just turned the dreaded thirty years old, and Tamryn, about ten years older, and east coast all the way. Beautiful blue eyes to contrast with her black hair, but she'd be the first person to tell you that she wished her legs were longer and her generous hips smaller.

"Of course, you're in charge with Matt away," she continued. "You proved your leadership skills when he got shot. The locals say you were nothing short of brilliant during that scary period. I'm proud you're my partner, in case I haven't said that lately."

"Thanks, Tam. I probably should be more ambitious, but I like having Matt as the boss. I've learned so much from him, and I trust him to always know the right thing to do. I'm uncomfortable when he's not around."

"It's alright to not aspire to higher leadership. It often comes with a bunch of gunk that cops like you and me don't want or need."

"My girlfriend, Amy, doesn't agree with you," he lamented. "She thinks I should capitalize on my role in the department last year when Matt was in the hospital. Says I should be applying at other PD's, even if it means moving out of Oregon."

Tamryn gave him a sideways glance before carefully speaking. "I'm sure she has your best interests at heart."

"Don't think so. Increasingly, I don't think she does. Amy's a good person, but I think she wants me to be a big shot more for her than for me. I'm not sure how to handle our relationship these days."

"This is why we date people, Jay, and why we don't get married after one week together. It's about learning who the other person really is; their values, what they want out of life. You're in that phase now. Where does Amy want to live, where does she want to go on vacation, do your energy levels match? Your intelligence match? Do you have the same outlook on money? I should have done more research, rather than assuming Barry Gesicki should be my husband just because he lived in the neighborhood and my parents liked him. Take your time and be sure."

"Do you think you'll ever marry again? You know, based on what just happened to you?"

"My instant response to your question is, 'What, are you nuts?'."

Jay laughed.

She continued. "But I had a long talk with Matt the night I spent at his and Fern's house. He convinced me that there are good men in the world, and that I would get it right the next time. And, I have to say, working with guys like you, Rudy, Walt, Ed, and the sheriff—not a bad apple among you—makes me think Matt is probably correct."

"You sure as hell know what to look out for now, huh?"

"Yes, and you have the benefit of my dreadful experience," Tamryn said, now serious. "Use it, Jay. I'm certainly not implying that Amy is a psychopath like you-know-who, but pay attention to her signals. If she believes in you and wants you to be the best you can be, that's one thing. But if her motives are selfish, that's entirely another thing."

"How will I know?"

"You'll know. Something deep inside will poke at you. It could be this thing about ambition. If you know yourself well enough to know that you love your current job, your current life, and this ocean, and she doesn't…" Her voice drifted off and she let that sentiment stand.

"Yeah. I'm tired of being alone, though."

She elbowed him in the ribs again. "You're not alone, dude, you have me, the greatest partner a cop could ever want."

"There is that."

. . .

The ship approached the man-made harbor at Cold Rock Island, and Jay shivered.

"This is déja vu all over again," he said. "Along with bad juju, and whatever other vu and ju you want to add. I hate this place, and I didn't even have to see the body swinging from the rafters like Fern and Bernice did."

"Bernice told me about it when she was taking care of me," Tamryn said. "Said it was one of the worst things she's seen, and she's witnessed a lot of bad things. Surely, Rohn Reid can't blame Fern for doing her job."

"You wouldn't think so, but there's a lot of psychology involved. He should take some of the blame himself, but men have a hard time with that."

"*People* have a hard time with that," she corrected. "It's not just men who can't look in the mirror sometimes and see the real truth."

"That's true. Mrs. Bushnell comes to mind. That was Matt's first case in Port Stirling, and last time I looked, she still hates Matt for the outcome, even though it probably saved one of her kids' life. If she'd acted instead of sweeping the evidence under the rug, everyone would have been better off."

"Matt told me about this case during our interview process," Tamryn said. "Where is she now?"

"Fern and I checked on her last year, and she's moved to Texas. Her husband divorced her."

"We'll track her down again and have a new chat. OK with you, partner?"

"We're going to talk to everyone who has a reason to make Matt and Fern suffer," Jay said with a steely tone. "And I mean everyone. Buckle up, Tam, you're about ready to get a crash course in "Matt and Fern do Port Stirling.""

Aaron, as promised, met them on the dock. Captain Adams insisted that two of his crewmen accompany Jay and Tamryn up to the house. Most of the crew who'd been on the island recently with Fern volunteered; they recognized what could happen here. The Coast Guard guys took off walking up the narrow, paved road that led to the top of the island. They knew where to go.

"Thanks for coming down," Jay said to Aaron, extending his hand. "It's nice to see you again. How are you doing?"

"I'm OK," the young man said. In his jeans, Seattle Seahawks sweatshirt, and Mariners cap, he looked about twelve, even though he was in his twenties. "It's back to being pretty quiet around here, which I like better."

"Better than all sorts of law enforcement swarming around, and a body hanging in your airplane hangar, you mean?" Tamryn said, coming forward to shake hands as well. "I'm Tamryn Gesicki, a detective with the Port Stirling police. You must be Aaron Rogers."

Aaron nodded and shook hands, his face pale. "Yeah, better than all that fuss, and poor Mr. Matsuda. It's nice to meet you, ma'am. Am I allowed to ask why you guys are here?"

Tamryn and Jay exchanged a quick glance before Jay said, "You liked Fern Byrne—Mrs. Horning—didn't you, Aaron?"

"Affirmative," Aaron answered. "She was nice to me when she didn't have to be. I think she could tell how upset and scared I was. Fern told me that anybody would be upset seeing Mr. Matsuda up there like I did."

"She was right, and she liked you, too," Jay said. "Fern knew early on that you couldn't have done such an awful thing."

"Why didn't she come with you today?"

"Well, that's why we're here. She and Matt are in Scotland, and Fern went missing earlier today. We believe she's been kidnapped."

Aaron's eyes got so big, Jay was afraid they'd pop out of his head. "No!" And then, "You don't think Mr. Reid has anything to do with it, do you? He wouldn't. Why are you here? I don't understand."

"We don't know, Aaron," Jay said. "We do think the timing of this is suspicious, seeing as how your employer's case just ended. But we will talk to everyone who might have a reason to want to hurt Fern. And your boss might blame her for what's happened to upend his life."

"He doesn't hate Fern," Aaron argued. "Randy does more than Mr. Reid does. He—Mr. Reid—is still grieving, but that's natural, don't you think? Randy is the bitter one. Talk to him—you'll see."

"It's not surprising that Randy hates Fern," Tamryn said. "The way I understand this case, he's to blame, so he has to transfer that guilt somewhere."

"I guess," Aaron conceded.

"Can we ride with you up to the house?" Jay asked, pointing at the golf cart.

"Hop in. I think Mr. Reid is in the house."

They wound up the rocky island from sea level to an assortment of buildings spread horizontally along the highest point.

Aaron dropped them off at the front door, and skedaddled away, as Jay advised him to do. A cold blast of air hit the two detectives while they stood silently waiting for someone to answer the doorbell.

CHAPTER 15

A man who Jay recognized as Leonard, the caretaker slash butler for Mr. Reid, opened the door, an astonished look on his face.

"It's Detective Finley, isn't it?" Leonard inquired.

Jay and Tamryn both produced their badges, so there was no mistaking why they were there.

"Yes. Hello, Leonard," Jay said. "This is my partner, Detective Tamryn Gesicki. We're sorry to bother you folks, but we need to speak to Rohn Reid. We understand he is currently on the island."

"That's right, he is here. We are spending about three weeks before we head to Seattle for the summer. Does he know you are visiting us?"

Jay shook his head. "No, this is a spur-of-the-moment deal."

Leonard frowned, but said, "Please, come in." He stood aside to allow them entrance.

"I'll tell him you're here. May I tell him what it's about?" Leonard asked.

"We'll explain to him," Jay said. "It won't take long."

Leonard looked out the front door toward the dock down the hill. He saw the ship, and the two crewmen who were hanging out in the front garden. "The Coast Guard? Again? Please tell me if something is wrong, Jay," he pleaded.

"Something is very wrong, but we don't think Mr. Reid has anything to do with it. We're just covering all the bases. It's what we cops do," Jay said, and tried out a smile that didn't quite get there.

"I hope so. Mr. Reid can't take much more tragic news this year. I'm quite worried about him. You'll see." And with that he took off down the hallway toward Rohn's suite of rooms at the east end of the sprawling, luxurious house.

Tamryn took advantage of Leonard's departure to look around the home's entry. To their right was the huge living room with three separate, plush seating areas, floor-to-high-ceiling windows looking out to the sea, and a giant stone fireplace. Off to the left, was a library with wall-to-wall book shelving climbing high up the wall—a room just as she had imagined someday owning in her fantasy house.

"It's good to be the big cheese, I guess," she whispered to Jay.

"Yeah, it's a nice place." His jaw was clenched, and she saw him ball up his fists and then release them, only to repeat the move.

"What's up, partner?"

"I'm not wild about this place or its occupants," Jay said. "Except Leonard. I like him."

"You're not afraid of Rohn Reid, are you?" Tamryn asked. "Just because his paycheck is a little bigger than ours?"

Jay snorted.

"Because if you are, you shouldn't be. The laws apply to him just like everybody else. And you've already proved that to him. He can't touch you."

"Maybe. But maybe he's touched Fern. And got some measure of his perverted justice with Matt. I swear I'll kill him if he has."

"Slow down, Jay, you're not going to kill anyone," she said, taking a hold of his arm. "This is a fact-finding mission. If we don't like what we learn, we'll retreat to the ship and decide what to do about it. With me?"

He looked down at his partner who was about a foot shorter than him. "I'm in. But I don't have to like it."

"Don't go there. Let's get his reaction first and try to remain objective. Our instincts are good, Jay, and if we stay professional and do our jobs, we'll know what to do. And if he had Fern kidnapped, we'll blow his head off."

Jay wheeled, eyes big, and looked at Tamryn.

She grinned. "Kidding, I'm kidding. But I am good at that, you'll recall."

Rohn Reid came into the foyer where Jay and Tamryn waited. Jay saw immediately what Leonard meant; Rohn did not look good. He'd lost about thirty pounds, which he needed to do, so that was OK. However, he seemed very frail, stepping carefully and slowly—more of a shuffle, really—and his skin looked slack. Never the tidiest of men, he was even more disheveled than usual. Everything about him looked gray—hair, face, and attire.

"Jay," Rohn said, as he approached to shake his hand. "And who is this lovely creature?" He stared at Tamryn.

"It's a pleasure to meet you, Mr. Reid," she said, moving to shake his offered hand. "I'm Jay's partner in Port Stirling—Tamryn Gesicki."

He completely ignored Jay and seemed to be fascinated by Tamryn. "You're not from the west coast, are you?" he asked.

Tamryn smiled. "Good ear. I'm from Boston originally. Only been here for a few months."

"And you're a police officer?"

"Yes. Detective, actually. I love my job."

Rohn turned back to Jay. "I'd say you lucked out with Ms. Gesicki for a partner."

"I did, sir. She's a great addition to our police department. Can we talk to you for a few minutes?"

"Of course. I assumed you didn't sail out here with Captain Adams just to check on me. It's nice to have some company, even if it's the police." He moved into the living room, taking a seat in his favorite leather chair close to the fireplace where a warm fire crackled. He motioned to the chairs opposite him.

"How about some coffee or tea for everyone?" Leonard asked once he saw the boss was settled.

"Terrific idea, Leonard," Rohn boomed. "I'll have coffee. Tamryn? Jay?"

"Coffee would be great," Jay said, looking at Tamryn who nodded in agreement. "It was chilly on the ship, and coffee will help."

"Do we have some of that dark roast from Seattle?" Rohn asked Leonard. "If so, brew up a pot. It'll warm all of us on this chilly day."

"Coming right up," Leonard smiled.

"Now, what is it you two need from me?" Rohn said to Jay.

Jay started, while Tamryn eyed Rohn rigorously. "Earlier today, Fern Byrne was abducted at the airport in Edinburgh, Scotland, kidnapped, we believe, and we're investigating. Talking to people who may have a reason to wish her or Matt Horning harm."

Rohn calmly said, "I don't wish either Fern or Matt harm. My family caused its own demise, and I have to live with that. If it hadn't been Fern and Matt doing their job, it would have been other law enforcement, probably with even more tragic results. At least, my family is alive."

"So, you don't know anything about a plot to take Fern?" Jay persisted.

"No, I don't."

"Have you been to visit your family at the Oregon State Penitentiary and Coffee Creek recently?"

Rohn shifted in his chair, putting one foot up on the edge of the coffee table in front of him. "Not only 'recently', but I'm ashamed to admit that I have never been to visit. I'm not ready yet to see Rick and Moira behind bars."

"You do understand that we can check visitor logs?" Tamryn said politely, with just the slightest edge in her tone.

"I'm telling you the truth," Rohn said to her. "I haven't been to visit. Randy has been to see both his brother and his mother, and, in fact, he's at the state penitentiary now."

"Your son?" Tamryn asked.

"Yes. He goes to visit fairly often and reports back to me. Says they're being treated well and are both OK. That's all I need to know for now."

"Do you miss them?" Jay asked.

"Look at me," Rohn said with sadness. "Of course I miss them. We were a family. A unit. And that's been torn apart. I'm not as good on my own. I need the people I love around me."

"But you don't resent Fern and Matt's role in what happened?" Tamryn asked. "It would only be natural, you know."

"Do I wish they'd never come to Cold Rock Island? Yes. But the Secretary of State would've come, and he would never have settled for no answers." Rohn shrugged. "I'm a pragmatic man. It doesn't matter who was ultimately responsible for their arrests; it would've been someone."

"Why is Randy there now?" Jay asked.

"He goes twice a month. Just happens that today is his day."

"So, he was there around the first of May, and probably twice in March and April? Does that sound right?"

"Yes, I would say so. I have it on my calendar if you need the exact dates," Rohn said resignedly.

"I would like the exact dates," Jay said. "We'll get them when we're through talking, and I will compare with the prisons' records. What does he do while he's there? Does he take them anything?"

"They're in maximum security; visitors aren't allowed to take them much of anything. Photos and some food, I think. He gets one hug with each of them. That's about it."

"What do they talk about?" Tamryn asked.

"Oh, you know, just life. Business. Filling them in on what we're doing. He mainly checks to make sure they're healthy and getting what they need. We may appeal their verdicts."

Jay and Tamryn looked at each other, surprised.

"On what grounds?" Jay choked it out.

Rohn rubbed his thigh. "I won't give you the details, except to say that our attorneys believe there may have been some irregularities in their trials."

"That's ridiculous!" Jay spat. "Everything was done meticulously, by the book. You're grasping at straws."

Rohn stared at him. "Yes. Yes, I am grasping at any straw within my reach. You would do the same, Jay, if it were your loved ones."

"I suppose I would," Jay conceded. "Moving on, do you have any reason to believe that Randy might be involved in this plot? To kidnap Fern?"

"And does he have any connections in the criminal world that we should know about?" Tamryn added.

"No. And I resent that question." He frowned at Tamryn.

"It's a fair question, considering his past dealings," she shot back at him.

"He was an innocent bystander," Rohn said. "You need to read the trial transcripts."

"I have. I just don't believe some of the testimony on record," she said. "My colleagues like to say that I have a high bullshit detector, and I believe your son is full of it."

To their surprise, Rohn laughed. "He can be, Tamryn, yes, I'll give you that. But he wasn't in this case."

"Does he resent Fern?" Jay asked.

Rohn thought for a moment. "Yes, I would have to say that he does. Certainly, more than I do. He's young, Jay, and like you, wears his heart on his sleeve. But he's not impulsive and he's absolutely not stupid enough to get involved in kidnapping a cop."

"He was stupid enough to get involved in a fraudulent crypto Ponzi scheme that hurt a lot of people," Jay reminded him, his face reddening. "Why wouldn't he hurt Fern and Matt if he blames them for your troubles? Why do you think that?" Jay's right leg was moving up and down rapidly, and he was becoming enraged.

"We will talk to Randy," Tamryn said quickly. Her tone was quieter in an attempt to defuse the escalating situation. "Please understand that at this early point in our investigation—we just learned of this a few hours ago—everyone in the Hornings' past is a suspect until we rule them out."

"And you came rushing out here first." Reid shook his head. "I think you'll find that Randy is not involved," Rohn said coolly. "You should look elsewhere."

"We'll look wherever we damn well please!" Jay roared. "It's not up to you to tell us how to do our job. In fact, Randy is number one on my list, and you are probably number two."

Tamryn stood. "We're going now."

Neither man was sure to whom she was talking, so both also stood. "Detective Finley and I will talk to Randy as soon as possible. We'd prefer that you do not warn him in advance. Notify us if you go anywhere, will you, please?" she asked Rohn.

"I'm staying put. I'll be here if you want to talk again," he said to Tamryn, turning a shoulder on Jay. "I'm sorry about Fern. Truly, I am."

• • •

"He's a lying sack of shit," Jay fumed, once outside the house.

"I think he was sincere," Tamryn said. "I'm sorry, but I think he meant it when he said he doesn't hold a grudge against Fern. It almost felt like he's too broken to be anything but sad…at least, right now."

"It's an act, Tam, he's acting. He's smart—I told you. He wants us to think he's an old, sad man. I don't buy it. You shouldn't either."

"OK, you know him better than I do, so I'll roll with you. But I'm way more interested in talking to Randy. Unless Rohn or his attorneys have underworld connections, it would be difficult for him to organize a global kidnapping. Plus, I'm convinced he hasn't talked to anyone in the penitentiary. He's smart like you say and would know that we will check the visitor logs, for sure. And, honestly, the attorneys that represented Randy in court didn't come across to me as sleazy. I don't see where Rohn has the opportunity to hire the kind of people who did this thing."

Jay thought that over. "I suppose you're probably right. Randy has more experience in the criminal world, and he's sure spending time at the prison. But I'm not ruling out Rohn just yet," he said stubbornly.

The door opened behind them, and Leonard came out, pulling it shut behind him.

"Was Mr. Reid able to satisfactorily answer your questions?" he asked Jay.

"He answered them, but we're not sure how satisfied we are with his answers," Jay said. "He said he knows nothing about why we're here."

"My guess is that he genuinely doesn't know anything," Leonard said. "He's not paying attention to the world right now and is not as engaged as he usually is. Since we've been here, he mostly spends his days reading in his room, and his nights watching television. I suppose he works some, but it's without his normal enthusiasm."

"Classic depression," Tamryn noted. "Do you think he might sell this island? You know, bad memories and all that?"

"I suggested it to him several weeks ago," Leonard answered, shaking his head. "But he said no. He told me that his family will want to return to Cold Rock Island when they are free again."

"Not gonna happen," Jay said. "They murdered a man in cold blood. The state pen is their forever home."

"People get paroled, do they not? Or the verdict gets overturned on appeal?" Leonard argued. "It happens."

"It does, but Mr. Reid will be dead by the time his family might become eligible for parole," Tamryn said. "And winning an appeal is about as likely as me winning the Boston Marathon. Honestly, I agree with Jay, and if you care about him, it would be better for his mental health if he moved on from this island."

Leonard shrugged. "It's his life. His money to do with as he pleases. I can continue to talk to him about it, but I'm more hopeful that he's just still in the grief phase and will gradually improve over time."

"That may happen," Tamryn agreed. "But I think the more time you all spend here—the scene of a horrific crime—the longer it will take."

"Are you leaving now?"

"We want to talk to the other employees," Jay informed him. "We saw Aaron, but are Noah, Lynette, and Tyson here?"

"Yes. Everyone you met before except Simon, the gardener," Leonard said. "He has chosen to not work for Mr. Reid anymore. I believe he's decided to only work near his home in the U.K."

"Why?" Jay asked.

"He told me he doesn't like to see dead bodies hanging from rafters. Can't say as I blame him."

Leonard went back inside the house.

Tamryn said, "Before we go looking for the employees, let's call Patty and Ed and ask them to see if Randy is still in Salem."

"Good idea." Jay pressed the button for Ed on his phone. "Can you talk?" he asked his buddy.

"Yes. Patty and I are sitting in the car outside the state penitentiary," Ed told him. "We just finished with Zhang Chen, and I'm trying to calm down my girlfriend here."

"I'm not his girlfriend!" Jay heard Patty yell in the background, and he laughed for the first time today.

"Putting you on speaker," Ed said.

"It went well with Chen, then," Jay said.

"He will snoop around this god-awful place on our behalf," Ed answered.

"If?" Jay asked, knowing there was more to this story.

"If we give him something in return."

"Like what?"

"That's why we're sitting here. Talking it through. I think we've decided to ask the prosecuting D.A.'s office and Judge Hedges if they're willing to take five years off Chen's sentence and parole him when he's sixty-ish. It was my distinct impression that he might be able to learn something about Fern's situation. Amanda Wilson, the public liaison here, says that other prisoners are afraid of Chen, and the guards suspect he's still running things somehow."

"Do it," Jay said. "We need to use what we've got. Cynthia will go along with whatever you and Patty recommend if it might save Fern."

"OK, that's three-for-three then. Why did you call? Have you heard anything more from Matt?"

"No. Tam and I are on Cold Rock Island. Just talked to Rohn Reid. He told us that Randy, his son, is in Salem today at the prison. We're wondering if you can go back in and ask at reception if he's still there."

"Sure. If he is, we'll talk to him. Patty still has some pent-up rage to unleash," Ed said.

"There he is now!" Patty exclaimed. "Coming down the front steps." She was out of the car in a heartbeat.

"Later," said Ed, ending the call.

CHAPTER 16

It was now 1:00 a.m. in Edinburgh, officially the day after Fern's abduction. Matt, refusing offers to take him to the nearby hotel, was still at the police station. His eyes were red, his skin was pale, and his hands had a slight tremor.

"You look a wee bit bushed," Stuart said to him, trying again to get him to a bed for some rest. He knew Matt wouldn't sleep, but even resting his body for a couple of hours would help him regain some of his strength.

"You don't look so hot yourself," Matt answered. "You should go home, DCI. I want to hang out here until the tip line stops ringing for the night. And, in case any of your patrols turn up either of our witness's vehicles. What time do they circle back into a station and change shifts?"

Stuart looked at his watch. "About now. I'll stay until our guys get back here. I want to ask them what the city looks like. Then I'll go kip for a few hours."

The tip line rang again. It had been about thirty minutes since the station had received any further calls, after the deluge that occurred immediately following the BBC bulletin. As a group, they had decided that Meg should answer the phone because callers might find her less intimidating than a male voice.

Meg picked up, saying, "Police Scotland", and immediately stood up and started gesticulating wildly at Stuart and Matt. They ran to her desk.

"Yes, DCI Stuart MacLean has been assigned to the missing American woman's case. He is beside me, along with the woman's husband."

Meg paused and listened intently, staring at Stuart with wide eyes and her mouth slightly agape.

"I understand. May I put you on speakerphone?" Pause. "Thank you." She pressed a button on her phone. "You may now talk to Mr. Horning."

The voice on the phone was clearly using a voice modifier, and they were unsure if it was a male or female. But the substance was loud and clear: "Mr. Horning, we have your wife, and we want to arrange to return her to you."

Matt lunged at Meg's telephone, but Stuart grabbed him and pulled him back sharply. That move seemed to settle Matt somewhat, and he said, calmer than he felt, "Is she alright? What do you want?"

The voice said, "Mrs. Horning is fine, and she will continue to be fine until you manage to pull together two million dollars of your greed money. You must have the cash in hand within 24 hours, and then we will instruct you where to deliver it. Once we have the cash, and it must be in U.S. dollars, Mrs. Horning will be set free with instructions on where to find her. Do you understand?"

"Did you give her some kind of nerve agent? Is she conscious?"

"Your wife is fine, as I just told you. Do you understand our instructions regarding the money?"

"I understand, and I will do as you say," Matt said. "I need to speak to her, please. To know she's alive and alright."

"We can't do that, Chief. We know you cops have tricks between you, and we won't allow that." An icy cold voice came through, even with the transformer application, and Matt felt a stab in his heart. "You must take our word that she is safe...for the moment...and trust us. Otherwise, you will never see your beautiful young wife again."

"Trust you?!? How can I trust you? You stole Fern," Matt said, spittle coming out of his mouth. "You are despicable. I need to hear her voice. Please, give me that. I will get your money, I promise, if you let me know she's alive."

"You don't get to set the terms this time. We will call back on this number tomorrow at midnight. Get the cash or it gets ugly fast."

The line went dead.

Matt, Stuart, and Meg stood mutely staring at the phone, as if it was a live creature.

Matt broke the silence. "She's dead. They've killed her." His voice was choked with emotion and the gravity of the moment.

Surprisingly, Meg, her shoulder-length red hair flying, took Matt by the shoulders and shook him. "You don't know that. And I don't believe it. They are afraid that you and your wife have a secret code of some sort for just this situation. I've seen it happen before with married cops, even partners. They are just being super cautious, and you must believe that she is alright."

Stuart added, "She's right, Matt. Fern could've quickly said something meaningful to only you that would indicate who has her, where she is, or some other tipoff. They couldn't risk it. I know you're scared and frustrated, but we have to play by their rules until we find Fern. Let's concentrate on getting the money together. We can contact anyone you want us to — just tell us what you want to do."

"My father is working on the money already. He will get it done, and we don't have to worry about that." Matt sat down. "Play back the recording, Meg. There has to be a clue or two in there. I think I heard one."

Meg responded, and the three of them huddled around the machine and listened intently to the call from beginning to end.

"There! Pause it there," Matt said. "The voice called me 'Chief'. It's someone who knows us and knows that's my title."

"Aye," Stuart said. "I caught that, too. A Scot would not say 'Chief'. Keep playing, Meg."

Three sentences later, Matt stopped it again. "*'Young*', the caller said. That probably means they are older than Fern. If they were, say, Randy Reid's age — late twenties — they wouldn't think Fern is young."

"Who is Randy Reid?" Stuart asked.

"A suspect in our last case. The Hiroshi Matsuda murder that was Fern's operation. I told you about it."

Stuart nodded. "Right, the crypto kid. I agree with you. Fern would just be 'your beautiful wife' to him, not your young wife. I would venture a guess we're dealing with people in their forties, at least."

"Someone at least forty who knows me," said Matt. "Pretty wide open. Hit play again."

Again, Matt stopped it. "'*This time*'—What is that about? They've dealt with me before when I did get to set the terms? Do you think that's what they meant here?"

"I do think that, yes," answered Stuart. "It's someone with a grudge against you from a time when you were in charge. They didn't like the terms. Someone you hurt, put in jail, or even killed? This is about revenge. Told by an idiot, full of sound and fury, signifying nothing."

Matt stared at him.

"MacBeth. Sorry."

"Or, they are desperate for money," Meg said. "Maybe you took away their breadwinner—something like that. And, there's at least two of them; the voice said, '*our* word' and 'trust *us*', and 'we'."

"Probably the man and woman Graeme Thomson saw in the car park," Stuart said. "Although it could still be just the woman, and she's trying to make it sound like there's more than one person."

"Or it could be a gang of some sort," Matt added. "Like the thievery gangs that work together. Have you had any experience recently with other kidnappings that remain unsolved? Where the perpetrators got away with the ransom money?"

"We have had two recently that come to mind, and might be relevant," Stuart answered. "Both were government ministers, however, and the separate incidents were politically motivated. The ransoms were paid, but no one was apprehended—they got away clean. Real pros. But again, these were likely UK based and wouldn't know you."

"How recent were the episodes?" Matt asked.

Meg answered. "The last one was a couple of days before Christmas, and he was let go and found on Christmas Eve day." She looked at Stuart. "And the other one was last fall sometime, wasn't it? October or November?"

"I think that's right," Stuart agreed. "Wasn't it Guy Fawkes Day? Five November?"

"Of course," Meg said. "That's it."

"Where were the two victims found?" Matt asked.

"The first one was found at Waverly Station," said Stuart. "She was disoriented and wandering around. The second one was weirder. He was tied to some stakes off a path to Arthur's Seat. Heavily drugged and badly beaten. If a hiker hadn't found him, he probably would've died."

Matt winced at that, and looked at the ceiling, taking a deep breath before saying, "So, both near the city center." He was trying so hard to keep it together and willing his brain to connect the dots.

"Correct. We have two working theories," Stuart said. "One is that they were politically motivated. Because both victims were in the same party—the Scottish National Party. And, while they demanded ransom money, there was a lot of political rhetoric from the kidnappers all along the process. Our second theory is that it could've been the work of a cartel."

"What cartel?" Matt asked.

"Essentially, there are two operating in Scotland and the U.K," Stuart explained. "One is home-grown and is composed of two Glasgow crime families who have joined up. They operate mostly in conjunction with bad actors in Spain and Portugal and specialize in drug and human trafficking, and money laundering. We got some of them in a big operation two years ago, but they're still operating at a high level, and there is some evidence that they are slopping over into Edinburgh.

The big cartel is out of the Balkans. This organization is responsible for up to eighty percent of the hard drugs entering the U.K, along with a nasty pipeline of youngsters used in child porn. They are violent, resourceful, and efficient. We don't know where precisely they are located, but we know there are some ties to Budapest."

"Nothing from China or southeast Asia?" asked Matt.

"Not that we know of, and our informants are deeply embedded in both of these organizations. It's been a 'two steps forward, one step back' kind of a deal. Why do you ask about Asia?"

"We've had some recent action from a Chinese connection through California. The ringleader, a very wealthy global businessman, is currently in a maximum-security prison in Oregon, but we're convinced he's still active somehow. Fern and I are not his favorite people on the planet. I've asked two of my local associates in law enforcement to go there and have a chat with him. We'll see what that shakes loose."

"Sounds like he would fit our phone clues, but, again, we've seen virtually no Asia connections in Scotland's organized crime," said Stuart.

"Don't you think the timing of Fern's abduction—on the recent heels of your other two unsolved kidnappings—is suspicious?" Matt asked. "Maybe it's a combo; someone with a grudge from Oregon who's hired a local gang to get it done."

"Possible," nodded Stuart.

Matt reached for his jacket on the coat rack behind him. "Let's go out."

"Now?" Stuart asked.

"Now. I want to look around your city a little. Meg, will you survey your patrol officers as they come in? See if anyone noticed anything?"

"Of course."

"And call me if you get any leads, OK?"

"I will, Matt," she promised. "Be careful, gentlemen, it's an evil night."

Matt, looking grim, inclined his head toward Meg, acquiescing.

CHAPTER 17

The night even looked evil. Shrouded in a thick, damp fog, the bricks on the police station's Edinburgh street were deceptively wet and slippery underfoot. The yellow light from the street lamps was a halo of diffused light that reflected off the cobblestones. There was no one about. No cars, no shop lights, no nothing, only the two detectives walking through the eerie quiet. The dense mist sat heavily on Matt's head, but he barely noticed.

Stuart reached over and pulled the hood on Matt's jacket up over his head. "Don't be daft. Where do you want to walk?"

"Just want to walk. How far is it to Holyrood? To the car park?" he added on second thought.

"Far. About forty minutes, walking. And, it won't do us any good to go there now. Not in this pea souper. We'll go in the daylight. Let's go this way." Stuart took off walking straight ahead, the street eventually curving around a shadowy corner in the next block. Off to Matt's left, a medieval building with a severe dark stone arch led to a narrow, chilling passageway with irregular stone steps.

"Why are we doing this?" Stuart asked. "It feels a wee bit crazy."

"I like to walk when I have things to think about," Matt answered.

"In the feckin' dark?"

"Not usually at night, unless I can't sleep. Then, I'll go down to the beach at home and follow the shoreline for a while. The solitude and the waves crashing ashore always clear the voices in my head. And the air… it's so clean and fresh. Briney, you know? Smells like the sea should smell."

"You miss home, don't you?"

Choked up and silent, Matt nodded in the darkness.

"We like to think we have good air in Scotland, too. Do you not find it so?"

Composing himself, Matt said, "The Shetland Islands felt the closest to home. It was brisk and refreshing, but that relentless wind…"

"Aye, the wind. It's a rare day in Shetland when the wind doesn't blow like it means business. Not that we don't get the occasional gale in Edinburgh, too, but it's not constant."

After another two blocks, Stuart pointed to a tall building with lights sparkling through big street windows—the only sign of life in this part of the city. A discreet sign indicated it was a hotel.

"This is your bunk, if you're interested," Stuart said, slowing on the sidewalk. "I highly recommend you go in, make some calls to ensure your parents have the ransom lined up, and talk to anyone else you need to. Nothing else is likely to happen tonight, but if it does, we'll fetch you."

"I can't sleep, Stuart. There's no way. My pulse is pounding, and my brain is keeping time with it."

"You won't sleep," he agreed with Matt. "I couldn't either, under these circumstances. But you can get comfortable in the hotel, rest on the bed while you talk to your colleagues and friends. I will not desert you. I live nearby, and my phone is charged and always on. Tomorrow is going to be long, and we'll need to be sharp to achieve the outcome we all want. What's it to be?" He came to a halt in front of the hotel steps.

"I do need to make some phone calls. Fern's boss in Washington, for sure. He doesn't know yet, and he needs to be informed sooner rather than later. It's probably a good time in D.C. to reach him. I wanted to wait until we knew something, but I guess we now know what we're dealing with. He's a powerful man with more resources at his disposal than you or I could imagine."

"Call him. What's his name?"

"Joe Phelps."

Stuart scribbled a note in his police notebook pulled from his pocket. "OK, and please call your parents. Police Scotland will kick in some ransom money if necessary, but it's more red tape than I appreciate."

"I can imagine," Matt said with a tight smile. "I'll handle it with dad and Fern's father. That's another clue from the call, by the way — U.S. dollars, not British pounds. There's an Oregon connection sure as hell. I hope my team can unearth it."

"Let's go inside and get you registered." Without waiting for Matt to respond, Stuart went up the stairs and pulled open the front door.

・・・

Matt pulled off his shoes but laid fully dressed on top of his hotel room's small bed. For a boy originally from Texas and then wide-open Oregon, everything in Scotland felt small to him. He yearned to have Fern snuggled up to him in their giant King bed in Port Stirling, listening to the surf below them. *It will happen again. I will make it happen.*

Hotel reception had given him some bottled water, and he drank from it now, and then pushed Joe Phelps' number on his phone.

"Howdy, Chief," Joe answered. "Are you and my girl home?"

Tears finally rolled down Matt's cheeks. "No," he managed to say through the waterworks.

"What is it? What's wrong?"

Between sobs, Matt spilled out the events of the day to a silent Joe Phelps, who let Matt go at his own pace. When he stopped talking, Joe said, "I'm so sorry. We'll find her. We will. That's what we do, you and I, we solve problems." His voice was strong, but his insides were mush.

"I think she's dead, Joe. They wouldn't let me talk to her."

"I wouldn't have let you talk to her either. Doesn't mean shit. Do you want me to come?"

"No. But I do want you to check in with Jay. It's connected to Port Stirling, I'm sure. Our parents are coming; I couldn't stop them. They're taking care of the ransom and are beside themselves. Conor Byrne will probably never speak to me again."

"I'm sure that's not true. I don't know the man, but if he and his wife gave birth to Fern, they are good people. We'll get her back, and he will come around. You'll see. That's the least of your worries, Matt. What's the status of the investigation on the home front?"

Matt told him his instructions to Jay, Patty, and Ed. "I haven't talked to them for several hours, but I will make those calls next. Patty and her husband, Ted, are going to come tomorrow — your time — after she chats with Zhang Chen and any other asswipes at the state prison who hate my guts. I couldn't talk her out of it, and if I'm honest, I'll be glad to see her and Ted."

"Patricia is a crackerjack detective, and I like her call on this one. You need some hometown support. But it sounds like Police Scotland know their job. From what you told me, DCI MacLean seems like the real deal. I'll call the brass and reinforce Fern's importance to the U.S."

"Appreciate that, Joe. The guy you want to call is Chief Constable Mark Armstrong. He's the head honcho of Police Scotland. Has an office in a place called Tulliallan Castle in Fife. That's across the water from Edinburgh city center."

"Sounds like you're getting to know the place."

"Trying. I'm in a hotel now, and we'll be up at dawn to survey a site where a witness may have seen Fern's kidnappers. Until then, there's nothing else we can do. It's a needle in a haystack, Joe. Except it's Fern."

"I will get you help. You are not alone."

"That's what everyone says, but I am alone. Inside." He gulped loudly, and a puff of air came over the line, and then he said, "Don't expect much from the Chief Constable — he's a suit."

"I have the power of the United States government behind me; that usually gets me the proper attention for my needs."

"This is the time to put it to use. I don't much like to ask for help, but I need it now, Joe. I'm sinking. Feel like I'm in quicksand."

"You're fine. You're just tired. Get through the night and bounce back to the Matt I know at dawn. You know what to do, and you're not on an island. Well, technically, you are on an island, I suppose. But we will all do our parts and help you. I always get my man, and this kidnapping will have the same result."

"What if it's a woman that's taken her? Not a man? Will you get her?"

"I not only will get her, I will personally put a bullet through her forehead if that's what it takes."

"Not your style, Joe."

"It's Fern. My style and the rules don't apply. Get some rest, and we'll talk again in a few hours."

. . .

OSP Lieutenant Ed Sonders and Detective Patty Perkins approached Randy Reid as he started down the path to the penitentiary's parking lot. Randy looked up and saw Ed and stopped dead in his tracks.

"You?" was all Randy could get out of his mouth.

"Yep, me," Ed said, and flashed his badge.

Randy took it in, turned to Patty and said, "Who are you?"

"Mary Poppins," Patty snapped. "What's it to you?" Criminals who got off scot-free were not Patty's favorite animals. "We need a few minutes of your precious time."

"I'm in a hurry," Randy said.

"Let's go sit over here," Patty said, pointing to a picnic bench under a huge oak tree, and ignoring his comment.

Ed took Randy by the elbow, possibly a bit more forcefully than he needed to, and guided him to the bench.

"Why are you here?" Patty started.

"Visiting my family. It's allowed, you know," he snarled at Patty.

"My partner's not in a very good mood today," Ed advised him. "I wouldn't poke her too much if I were you. Why don't you politely tell us what you talked about during your visit with your family." Ed drew himself up to his full stature on the bench, which made him about two feet taller than everyone else.

"I try to bring them some sense of the normal world," Randy said. "Ask them if they need anything. That sort of thing. It's not a normal environment, and I want to do what I can to make it the best it can be for them."

"Did the name Fern Byrne—Mrs. Matt Horning—come up?" Patty asked. She gave him a hard, unblinking stare.

"Fern? You mean the woman who put my family here?" he said coldly.

"Fern didn't lock them up," Ed said. "You are responsible for that. All by your lonesome."

"A jury thought otherwise," Randy said.

"Every once in a while, juries get it wrong," Patty said. "Yours is one of those cases. Sometimes we cops get a second chance to right a wrong. Wonder if this will be one of those times, Randy?"

"I don't have a clue what you're talking about, Mary Poppins. But, no, we didn't talk about Fern. We talked about business and baseball. We try to not think about what your lot has done to our family."

"So, no mention of Matt Horning either?" Ed questioned.

Randy shook his head. "No. What's this about anyway?"

"We ask questions, we don't answer them," Patty said. "Have you heard the word 'Scotland' today or anytime in the recent past when you've visited this lovely hotel?"

Randy thought for a minute. "Scotland? Don't think so."

"What about any talk of kidnapping? Does that topic come up at breakfast?" Ed asked.

"No matter what you think, Lieutenant, my family are not common criminals. We don't talk about crime; we discuss how we can hold our family together and keep dad and our businesses thriving. This mess has destroyed him, and he's unwell. We're all worried about him."

"Guess you should have thought of that before you defrauded thousands of people, and caused the homicide of a fine human being, huh?" Patty said. "But no matter about that now." She waved her hand. "So, you don't like Fern. Is that fair to say?"

"I did like her," Randy replied. He stuck his chin out, a slight move that Patty caught. "Until she did this to us."

"Fern was doing her job," Ed said. "See, in the U.S., when you take the life of another human being, society demands that you pay for it. All Fern did was unravel the truth. If you've heard anything about her or Matt today, it would serve you — and perhaps your family — well if you would tell us what you know."

"Fern's been kidnapped?" Randy said, clearly stunned. "Is that what this is about?"

Ed nodded.

"Oh my God. And do you think my family did this? No way!" He started to stand but stopped when Patty said in an unlike-Mary-Poppins vicious tone, "Sit down, Randy."

He sat back down on the bench.

"My real name is Detective Patty Perkins of the Twisty River police department. Fern Byrne and Matt Horning are two of my very best friends," she said, calm now. She produced the grainy CCTV photo of Fern and the woman. "Please look carefully at this photo and tell me if you recognize the people in it."

Randy stared at the photo and then pointed to Fern. "That's Fern. I don't know who the other woman is."

"You're sure?" Patty asked. "You've never seen her before? It's not your girlfriend?"

Randy looked up at her. "What? Of course it's not my girlfriend. She's young; this woman looks old."

Patty picked up the photo. "Just checking. I believe there might be people in that building"—she nodded toward the prison without taking her eyes off him—"that are more involved in this case than you. However, if you have heard anything about Fern's kidnapping, it would behoove you to tell me now. Do you know what 'behoove' means? Otherwise, if I learn later on that you are protecting anyone, or involved in this horrendous crime, I will hound you to the ends of the earth until you are safely behind those same bars." She nodded at the state pen again.

"I swear," Randy said hurriedly. "I know Fern was just doing her job. I don't hate her. I'm just sorry this all came down the way it did. I don't know anything about it. And I don't think my family does either—they would have mentioned it to me."

"I was best man at their wedding," Ed said quietly. "I feel the same as Patty. We will find out who did this, and if there is an Oregon connection, we think it may have started in this building. If you hear anything that can help lead us to Fern's kidnappers, we are prepared to hand out favors. Do you catch my drift?"

"Are you saying you might help my family if they can give you any information?" Randy asked. "Just to be clear."

"Yes, that's what the lieutenant is saying," Patty said. "Help us, and we'll hold our noses and help you."

CHAPTER 18

Jay gave Tamryn, who was curious about the various buildings on the island, a tour of the recent crime scene, and they found Lynette, the housekeeper and now the cook, in the hangar where Reid's plane was housed.

"Jay," Lynette smiled and bounded down the plane's steps when he and Tamryn approached. In her mid-twenties, with shoulder-length, glossy brown hair, and a peaches-and-cream complexion, Tamryn was slightly envious of both the younger woman's energy and fresh innocence. Tamryn had left that innocence behind in Boston when she relocated to Port Stirling, wiser to the frequent difficulties of the real world.

"It's nice to see you again, Lynette," Jay said. "Do you have a minute to talk? This is my partner, Tamryn Gesicki. We're here on official business."

"Oh, God, what have the Reids done now?"

"We don't know that they've done anything," Jay said hurriedly. "We do have a serious problem, however, and we're investigating all avenues."

"I'd like to see the inside of a personal jet," Tamryn said to Lynette, smiling. "Can we go in there to talk?"

"Don't see why not. But I just cleaned it, so you'll have to take off your shoes." She bounded back up the stairs, and Jay and Tamryn followed her.

The two cops looked around the plane and then all three took seats in a seating area with four swivel chairs facing each other. Tamryn ran her sock-clad feet over the plush, fluffy carpet underneath.

"OK, I need my own plane," Tamryn grinned. "This is totally sweet." She swiveled in her chair to make the point.

"It's nice, for sure," Lynette agreed. "I don't get to ride in it much, but when I do, it's a lot of fun." She paused and looked worriedly at Jay. "Why are you here again?"

"I think you and Fern got along well, didn't you?" Jay asked.

"Yes, I really like her. She's inspirational to me — a smart, tough woman doing an important job. She told me I could, too, if I wanted to and worked hard. But she's way more courageous than I could ever be." She shivered.

"Well, Fern has been kidnapped while she and her husband are in Scotland," Jay informed her. "We are investigating any ties to Oregon. You know, people who might have a reason to want to hurt Fern. Have you heard anything here that might be relevant?"

"Is she OK?" Lynette's concern was real.

"Truth is, we don't know for sure."

"Fern might be dead? Is that what you're saying?" Lynette paled.

"We are operating under the assumption that they just want the ransom money, and that she will be released when that happens. But, no, we don't know if she is dead or alive. We're determined to do everything we can to find out who is behind this. If she's alive, maybe we can find her. Can you help us? Have you heard anyone talking about Fern or Matt? Mr. Reid? Randy? Tyson or Noah?"

Lynette's brow puckered, and it was obvious she was thinking hard. "Maybe about two months ago, when I was serving Mr. Reid and Randy dinner one night the last time they were here, they might have been arguing about Fern."

Tamryn and Jay exchanged glances.

"Please tell us precisely what they said," Tamryn instructed her, "as much as you can remember and as close as you can come. It's very important." She nodded to encourage the young woman.

"Well, when I first came into the dining room, Randy said something like 'This is all Fern's fault', and he kinda slapped the table. Then Mr. Reid said, 'No, Hiroshi's death would have been investigated no matter what. We couldn't have hidden it forever.'"

"Mr. Reid definitely said, '*We* couldn't, not *you* couldn't'?" Jay asked.

"I think so," Lynette said. "That's the way I remember it. Then, Randy said 'But she was so mean to mother. How can you defend her?', and Mr. Reid said something like, 'Your mother made a stupid mistake. Fern did what she was trained to do'."

"What did Randy say then?"

"I don't really know. I left the room and went back to the kitchen, happy that Mr. Reid defended Fern. But when I brought out dessert, Randy said 'Maybe you're going to accept this and do nothing, but I'm going to do something.' Mr. Reid told him that there was nothing he could do, and Randy said something like, 'We'll see about that'."

"What do you think Randy meant by that remark?" Tamryn asked.

"Who knows?" Lynette answered. "I guess at the time I thought he meant he would talk to the lawyers or something. But maybe he had something else in mind?"

...

With Aaron's help, Jay and Tamryn hunted down Tyson, in charge of security for the island, and Noah, the handyman. Although all three men had been cleared of any advance knowledge of Matsuda's murder, Jay couldn't forget the fact that they had initially lied to Fern and Joe Phelps at Rohn Reid's direction. Aaron and Noah had been sincerely remorseful, but Jay still didn't trust Tyson and wasn't one hundred percent convinced he had nothing to do with it. He shared that feeling with Tamryn now.

"Why do you feel that way?" she asked him.

"I don't exactly know. He lied, but so did all of them. He just seems tighter with the Reid twins, and he's a big guy, you know."

"So, like, he could have helped after Matsuda was murdered; is that what you mean?"

"Yeah," said Jay. "I still have trouble visualizing the two of them stringing him up there. And, he's got this attitude like he knows more than we do."

"But he came around after the fact, didn't he?"

"Reluctantly, I would say. I don't know, it's just kind of a gut thing. I'm not a cop that relies on my gut feelings much—not like Matt, for sure. But then, his gut feelings are always right, so there's that," Jay said.

"From what I've heard, yours are usually spot on, too, partner," Tamryn said. "I wouldn't discount them completely, and I will pay close attention to Tyson. Let's do this."

They went to the far end of the hangar where Lynette waited with the three male employees.

Tyson approached them, stepping out in front of his two co-workers. "Aaron tells me that you want to talk to us about Fern," he said, taking charge of the conversation. "Has she really been kidnapped?" There was fear all over his face. Lynette stood by silently and looked down at the floor.

"Yes," Jay said briskly. "This is Detective Tamryn Gesicki, my partner, and we have just a few questions for you guys." Tamryn showed her badge, Jay saw it out of the corner of his eye, and quickly produced his, too. "It does appear that Fern has been kidnapped," he said, and shared what they knew with them.

"Scotland?" Tyson said, his face screwed up. "That's bad news. We all like Fern. She was straight with us."

"Yet I understand you lied to her," Tamryn said.

Tyson locked eyes with her and said, "We did what we had to so we could keep our jobs. The three of us, we like working here. Wasn't nothin' to do with Fern."

"Did you apologize to her?" Tamryn asked.

Aaron jumped in. "Yes. We all told Fern we were sorry, and we meant it. She knows."

Tamryn nodded and looked at Jay, who said, "Have any of you heard Randy or Mr. Reid mention Scotland in the past couple of months?"

Three heads shook 'no'. Tamryn made notes in her police notebook.

"Have they talked to you about Fern or Chief Horning? Mentioned them in passing? Did you overhear anything that might help us?" Jay asked.

Noah cleared his throat and shuffled his feet slightly.

"What is it, Noah?" asked Tamryn, immediately picking up on his body language. "Tell us."

"Well, you know, Mr. Reid did talk to me about Fern after you all cleared out."

"Why?" she asked.

"Because Fern caught me checking up on her and Joe the first night they stayed here. Mr. Reid wanted me to know that he appreciated my loyalty, but in the future, I'm not to bother guests. Especially in the middle of the night like I did Fern."

"Did he say anything else about her or Matt?"

"No. Just that it was all over, and we're to go back to normal. I appreciated him telling me that," Noah added.

"Did Randy say anything that we should know?" Jay asked, not looking at Aaron. He didn't want the other two to know that Aaron had already talked.

Nobody said anything.

"Noah," Jay said, "has Randy indicated his feelings for Fern or Matt to you? That's a direct question."

Noah looked ill. "Randy said he hopes Fern comes to the same ending as Mr. Matsuda." He gulped. "But he didn't mean it, he was just spouting off. He misses his family and the way things were."

In the background, Lynette let out a gasp.

"When did he say this?" Jay followed up.

"It was not long after they came back here after the trials. Maybe the end of March. He didn't really mean it — honest."

"Did either of you two hear Randy say that, too?" Tamryn asked.

"Yes," Aaron said. "I was with Noah when he said it."

"Tyson?" Tamryn said.

"I wasn't with these guys when that happened, but he's said a couple of things to me. He blames Fern for everything that happened on Cold Rock Island."

"He hasn't taken any personal responsibility for the tragedy here?" Tamryn asked Tyson.

"He has not. But that's Randy — it's always someone else's fault."

"Is he capable of doing something like this, in your view?" she asked.

"Oh, yeah," Tyson said forcefully. "He's got the resources and the smarts to get whatever he wants. If he was determined for some sort of sick revenge, he could pull it off."

"Do any of you know much about what kind of connections Randy might have out there to pull off a kidnapping in another country?" Jay asked.

"That's the only part that makes me think he couldn't be involved," said Tyson. "Randy's led a pretty sheltered life — Mr. Reid's money saw to that. Seems like you'd need some help on a deal like this."

"What about girlfriends?" asked Tamryn. She showed the grainy CCTV photo of Fern and the woman leaving Edinburgh Airport to all three men. "Any women who might resemble the woman with Fern here? Don't pay attention to her clothes or hair."

They scrutinized the photo, and Aaron moaned quietly. "Poor Fern," he said.

"Randy's got a new girlfriend, but this woman" — Noah pointed at the image — "is too old and too fat. I've never seen her before."

"Nope, me neither," agreed Tyson and Aaron, who said, "I can't even think where Randy would have met a woman like that. She looks mean. Maybe he met her when he visited the prison."

"Maybe he did," Jay said.

• • •

On the Resolve sailing back to the mainland, Jay got a text from Matt.

> Matt: Ransom demand — $2 million. Things moving now that it's official.
>
> Jay: Wow. At least, we know what we're up against.
>
> Matt: Yeah.

CHAPTER 19

Patty and Ed wrapped up with Randy Reid in the parking lot of the Oregon State Penitentiary and watched him race off in a fancy white sports car, top down on this fine Oregon spring day.

"That pisses me off," said Ed, watching the car exit at the far end of the parking lot. "We all know Randy's role in Fern's case, but he skates away free as a bird and gets to drive that car."

"What kind of car is it?" Patty inquired, feeling that Ed wanted to further rant.

"A Lamborghini Gallardo, if I'm not mistaken. And if you happen to have about $150,000 you don't need, you could have one, too."

"I can think of so many other things I would do with $150K. Must be a guy thing."

"You are judged by your beauty and intelligence. We guys are judged by the car we drive, and the shoes we wear. You are winning, Patricia. I am not."

"I like your shoes," she grinned at him. "Not wild about your old Jeep, though." She sighed, discouraged with their two interviews, and, back to the business at hand, said, "Nobody knows nothin'."

Ed agreed that they were no closer to any solutions except that Zhang Chen might help if they could strike a deal reducing his sentence, and that Randy promised to see if he could learn anything about Fern's kidnapping from his incarcerated family members. Neither one of those options was even close to a sure thing.

"It occurs to me that Randy, and Rohn Reid, for that matter, do not need the ransom money," Patty said. "If they are involved, it's likely purely about revenge."

"So, why demand ransom?" Ed asked.

"To throw us off?"

"Maybe. But maybe we're really looking for someone who needs money."

"Zhang Chen doesn't need money either," she noted.

"True," Ed agreed. "But he needs to show he's still the boss, the Godfather, if you will. And, even if revenge is his motive — or whoever may have asked him for help — Chen is shrewd about money, and he wouldn't leave $2 million on the table if he thought he could get it."

Patty's phone buzzed. Amanda Wilson.

"Hi, Amanda. Whatcha got?"

"I'm bringing David Dalrymple into the room I've reserved for you, as you requested. He's willing to speak to you."

"That's terrific," Patty said, and mouthed to Ed, 'Dalrymple'. "We're sitting in the parking lot on a short break, and will be right in. Thanks, Amanda — you're good at your job. It's very refreshing in this day and age."

"Back at you, Detective Perkins," Amanda replied. "You cats down in Chinook County are doing your jobs, too. Gives me job security," she laughed and hung up.

"This is good," Ed said. "All we can do is talk to everyone in Matt and Fern's past in this building today and get a hit from them if they know anything or can help us. Unfortunately, our list of potential suspects is long, and we've only talked to two of them so far — too soon to be discouraged. We'll see if Amanda can round up the Bowens and Ray Peng today, and if she's had a chance yet to find Michael Winston."

"I know she's on it and doing the best she can under these immediate circumstances. I didn't expect any of these dregs of humanity to say, 'Yeah, I arranged Fern's kidnapping'; I knew we'd have to dig for it." She checked her watch. "My issue is that I need to meet Ted at the airport in four hours for our flight to Seattle, and then on to Edinburgh."

"That's not a problem. Jay and Tamryn will join me here as soon as they finish on Cold Rock Island. I expect them to be in Salem by seven o'clock-ish. I will run you up to Portland, join them back here, and we'll keep going until our list is exhausted. Jay said he and Tamryn each quickly packed an overnight bag and left it in their car at the Coast Guard station in Buck Bay—they're ready to hit the highway fast to help me. I got the feeling Jay is looking forward to seeing Ray Peng again…and, locked up."

"Too bad he'll miss our chat with Dalrymple; Jay owes him some bad juju, too."

"So do I," Ed said with a steely tone. "So do I."

. . .

Former Chinook County District Attorney David Dalrymple was seated in the small meeting room in the seat his pal Zhang Chen had occupied not an hour ago.

He looked up as Patty and Ed entered the room. "You're looking well, Ed," he said. "You, too, Detective, although I heard you were going to retire."

"I considered it when I had the pleasure of seeing you locked up," Patty told him. "But as long as there are still more of your ilk causing grief in my world, I appear to be needed."

Dalrymple addressed Ed. "I was told there were two law enforcement officers who wanted to talk to me about a Port Stirling PD issue. I was rather hoping it would be someone more reasonable like Matt Horning or Jay Finley instead of her."

"You mean the same Matt Horning you hired an assassin to kill?" Ed said, an angry expression on his face, "causing the worst day of my life in my fifty years. I'm afraid you're stuck with your old friends Patty and me. And when you are a guest of the State of Oregon, your choices are limited."

Dalrymple, already gray-ish, paled further. "You know I was only doing what Zhang Chen demanded, Ed. I had no choice. It was kill or be killed. What would you have done?"

"Let me answer that stupid question," Patty said. "Ed would've done the right thing. Turned in Chen and his band of merry men to face justice. You were weak. And greedy. You know, David, I always thought your bullying and bluster hid a weak man, but since the voters kept you in your job, I respected them and went along as best I could. I suppose this," she waved her arms around the small room, "was inevitable in your life."

Dalrymple leaned forward toward her, clasping his hands on the table, his face flushed. "I would show you 'weak', Patty, if I weren't determined to be a model prisoner."

"Back it up, buddy," Ed said, pushing Dalrymple's shoulder back in the chair. "Let's all acknowledge that we don't like each other, and get down to business, OK? Maybe we can add to your model prisoner resumé if you hear us out."

"How's that?" Dalrymple asked.

"Fern has been kidnapped, and Patricia and I are here today to talk to those of you in the building who aren't fond of her."

"I always liked Fern," David said. "I have no reason to want her to come to harm."

"Fern tracked down your hired killer," Ed reminded him. "Without her courage and skills, you might still be on the outside instead of, well, in here."

"You don't seem that surprised at our news," Patty said. "Don't you want to know the circumstances?" Her eyes never left Dalrymple's face.

"I am surprised. I can't imagine who would want to hurt Fern." His color had returned to normal, and Patty detected a slight hint of smugness about him.

"Did Chen tell you the details?" she persisted.

"I don't talk to him much; he's in the max security wing. I'm not as big a threat to humanity as he is, apparently." He leaned back, crossing his arms in front of his chest, tight-lipped.

Nothing else to say, I guess, Patty thought. "Still, you don't ask us what's happened," she said. "Why is that?"

"You're going to tell me. And, clearly, I'm at your mercy and not going anywhere soon."

"Fern and Matt were on vacation in Scotland, and she was abducted at Edinburgh Airport," she told him. "Matt is there now, working with Police Scotland. He has received a ransom demand."

"Which he intends to fulfill," Ed added.

"Wow," Dalrymple said. "Now I am surprised. An international crime involving our little local friends. How on earth could I possibly have anything to do with this? Last time I checked, I'm not allowed to fly to Scotland."

"We didn't say you did it, David," Patty said, trying to be calm and not slap his smug face as hard as she possibly could like she really, really wanted to do. *I would use my open palm and get my whole arm into it. It would be such fun. Maybe the most fun ever.* "We want to know if you've heard anything about this inside this building. Has anyone mentioned Fern or Matt to you? Have you heard anything about Scotland?"

"What's in it for me if I talk to you?"

"Assuming you mean other than doing the right thing for the first time in your squalid, pathetic life?" Ed said. Not really a question.

Dalrymple stood and waved at the guard, and then he leaned over the table, his hands supporting his weight. "As an adult-in-custody, I'm not required to sit here and be abused by law enforcement. I know nothing about your case, Batman and Robin," he said, looking at one and then the other cop. "I've not heard Fern or Matt mentioned since I arrived here, nor have I heard the word 'Scotland' come out of any of my colleagues' mouths. If you can learn how to speak to me in a civil fashion, I may ask around on your behalf. Good day." He turned to watch the guard unlock the room's glass door.

"Please wait," said Ed. "I apologize for the insult. It was uncalled for, and it won't happen again."

"We need your help, David," added Patty. *But I'm not promising to be nice to you—ever,* she told herself. "Fern might already be dead, but we have to do everything we can to try to find her, and help Matt. Please stay and hear us out."

"That's more like it," Dalrymple said, taking his seat, and waving off the guard. "I honestly haven't heard a word of this incident, but I will try to help you. You need to know that Matt, in particular, is not very popular in here. He's ruined several lives, and inmates are resentful types. Taking something he loves would be a nice revenge."

"There is nothing he loves more than Fern," Ed said, subdued.

"My point. But it would be difficult to pull off from here. Kidnapping someone in a public place would be hard enough, but grabbing a cop like Fern…that's a whole other game, I would guess."

"And the details are even more complicated," Patty said. "They've got CCTV footage showing a woman taking Fern from the women's restroom, and it looks like Fern's been drugged somehow. Maybe injected with something to disable her."

Dalrymple paled. He hesitated for a moment and then, "Good God. That's awful. Matt must be devastated. I wouldn't wish that on my worst enemy. And you don't know if she is dead or alive?"

"We don't know. When the kidnapper called, they wouldn't let Matt talk to her."

"That's smart from the kidnapper's perspective. She could have tipped him off somehow, I suppose," David said.

"Yeah, that's the general consensus," Patty said.

"You mentioned Matt will pay the ransom. Do you know that for sure?"

Ed nodded. "Yes, he's working on it now."

"How much?"

Patty hurriedly said, "We aren't at liberty to disclose that."

Dalrymple shrugged. "Idle curiosity. If I were in his shoes, I'd just pay it and hope the kidnapper is honorable."

"If we can't turn up a link in Oregon soon, that's all Matt can do," she noted.

. . .

Tamryn and Jay returned to the Coast Guard ship empty-handed. No one on Cold Rock Island knew anything, or they were shiftier than the cops gave them credit for.

"I'll write up this visit," Jay said, "but I don't think there's much here to go on other than Randy's apparent bitterness of Fern."

"Saying he hopes she comes to the same end as Hiroshi Matsuda is more than just bitterness," said Tamryn. "It's down to Randy, in my view. Those three stooges couldn't plan a BBQ, much less a kidnapping in Scotland. And Lynette is a sweet thing with absolutely no worldly experience."

"Barely any mainland experience," Jay added. "She's from Seattle originally, but she's spent most of her adult life on this island. I can't see it, personally."

"Sweet Jesus, me neither. It feels like the three guys and Lynette are hiding from the world. Wonder what it did to them to make them choose this lifestyle."

"I suspect the money is very good. They all probably decided to do this work now and save up a pot of dough, and then get on with their lives."

"Possibly," Tamryn said. "That certainly makes sense for the men, but I can't see a young woman — and she's very cute, did you notice? — making this choice at her age."

Jay smiled. "I did notice. And she's smart. She helped us solve the Matsuda case. She's wasted out here, don't you think?"

"So you like her?" Tamryn teased.

"I like her. Period. And we've probably discussed my personal life enough for today. Are you ready to head to Salem as soon as we dock?"

"I am. I'm actually looking forward to meeting some of these deadbeats you put away before I got here to help you. You should drive...I have no idea where Salem is. Ed tried to tell me, but it seems like it's a long way."

"It's a good four-hour drive. Oregon's big, new partner."

"Even our little southwest corner feels big at times. No people, but lots of miles to cover. I didn't even own a car in Boston."

"If we can solve this case at the state pen and save Fern, maybe we'll run up to Portland afterwards and I'll show you our big city for a few hours."

"That would be terrific," she said. "I saw it from the plane, of course, and it's a gorgeous setting — mountains and rivers. It looked cool. Let's figure out who snatched Fern, and get her safely reunited with Matt, OK?"

"OK, we can do this!" Jay said.

. . .

Jay and Tamryn's confidence hit the skids after a couple of hours at the Oregon State Penitentiary. Ed and Patty had headed to the Portland airport just before Jay and Tamryn arrived, but Amanda Wilson had been instructed to expect them.

Jay wanted to talk with Alex and Blake Bowen, but he was met with some shocking news. Blake Bowen had been paroled last week — she'd been incarcerated at the Coffee Creek Correctional Facility up the road in Wilsonville — and had returned to her Buck Bay home.

"What do you mean Blake was paroled?" Jay asked Amanda when she delivered the news. "How can that be? Why weren't we informed?"

"I can't tell you why the Port Stirling PD was not told," Amanda said. "I'm sorry. It should have come from the Board of Parole. All I know is that she and her lawyer convinced the Board that she was not a threat to the community, as she only aided her husband after the crime. She gave her home address in Buck Bay for parole supervision, and the Buck Bay PD is handling post-prison supervision. I'm surprised their chief didn't call yours."

Jay scowled. "Yeah, so am I, although he probably knows that Chief Horning is on vacation in Scotland. But it still sucks that they didn't call us." He looked at Tamryn and shrugged.

"We'll talk to Alex Bowen, if that's possible now," Tamryn said to Amanda. "Once we've worked through our list of suspects who are in custody here, we'll head for home and hunt down Blake. Does that sound like our plan, Jay? Or do you think Blake is more important than the other names on our list here?" She scratched her nose.

"I think we should wait to decide what's next until Ed gets back. We need to hear his view on the vibe here — our phone call was short, and I need more details."

"OK, here's another idea," Tamryn said, turning to Amanda. "Can we get your visitor logs and outgoing phone calls for the prisoners we want to talk with? Find out who's been to visit and who they might have called, say, in the last couple of months?"

"Yes, I can make that happen," Amanda said.

Jay said to her, "While you work on that, Tam and I will talk to Alex Bowen and see what he knows about his wife's release."

Tamryn nodded. "Agreed. Can you bring out Alex Bowen now?" she asked Amanda.

"Be right back," Amanda answered and motioned to the guard.

Tamryn, who'd never met Alex Bowen, thought he looked like a respectable businessman as he took his seat in the conference room. Handsome, on the tall side, probably in his early fifties, with a full head of brown hair with gray beginning its assault around his face. Jay would tell her later that Alex had considerably more gray hair and looked even leaner than the day they arrested him for the murder of Hannah Oakley at Mourning Bay.

"Hello, Jay," he said politely across the table.

"Alex, thanks for talking with us," Jay responded, and introduced Tamryn. Jay had actually felt somewhat sorry for Alex Bowen in the way his case came down. He was convinced that Alex's wife, Blake, had been the real reason why Alex snapped, that she had goaded him into his crime. But here he sat while his wife was comfy at home. At the ripe old age of thirty, Jay was only now beginning to realize that life was often unfair. He was still an optimistic sort and believed in the goodness of most people, but a sliver of anger at injustice occasionally wormed its way into his heart. It had found its path there now.

"I have to tell you that we just learned that Blake has been paroled, and I'm angry," Jay started.

"Why? She didn't kill Hannah, I did," Alex said. "I belong here, my wife does not."

"Can you honestly sit there and tell me that she didn't coax you into doing it? That you didn't kill Hannah to make Blake happy?"

"I lost my cool, Jay. That's the honest truth. I will regret it until my dying day, but I can't change the horrible thing I did, and I will not allow you or anyone else to blame Blake. It's my burden and mine alone."

"That's quite admirable of you," Tamryn said in a friendly manner. "My former husband would never put me before him if it came to that."

"Are you divorced?" Alex asked her.

"No. I blew his head off when he tried to kill me," she answered sweetly. "How's your wife handling her newfound freedom?"

Jay noted that Alex sat back in his chair, seemingly unwilling to get too close to Detective Gesicki. "It was self-defense," Jay told Alex. "She's really a nice person."

"If you say so," Alex said, daring a look in Tamryn's direction. "My wife is, as you can imagine, happy to be home. She will rebuild her life in an admirable way, just as she has managed her career. I will assist her in that effort any way I can. I don't want Blake to suffer because of my deeds."

"Again, admirable," said Tamryn. "Is there any chance your wife would try to get revenge on Matt and Fern by arranging a kidnapping in Scotland?"

Alex actually laughed. "Of course not. She's thrilled to be out of here; why would she risk being sent back? It's a ridiculous idea."

"I've read up on your case, and I understand Blake was a global star earlier in her life," Tamryn said. "Would she have any connections in Scotland, do you think? Possible?"

Alex shook his head. "No. I see where you're going, Detective, but it's a road to nowhere. My wife does have friends all over the world, that's true, but not of the type you're looking for."

"How do you know what we're looking for, Mr. Bowen?" she asked. "We haven't told you."

Alex shifted in his chair, suddenly not so comfortable. "Well, you said 'kidnapping'. That implies a scurrilous character. My wife doesn't know anyone like that."

"I've always liked that word," Tamryn said. "Scurrilous. It sounds exactly like what it is. Someone up to no good. Vulgar. Abusive. Bet there's plenty of guys in here that fit that description. Might you have asked around at Blake's request if there was anyone who could help her carry out revenge on the Hornings?"

"Is that what you think?" Alex asked, incredulous. "That I got help from my cell mate so Blake could arrange Fern's kidnapping? Are you completely deranged?"

Jay and Tamryn exchanged a swift glance.

Jay said, "We didn't tell you it was Fern who got kidnapped." He stared at Alex.

Alex shrugged. "People in here talk. I heard about it."

"Maybe you heard it from your wife," Tamryn leaned in. "Did your cell mate—God forbid, poor soul—know someone in Scotland who could help out Blake with the job? Or someone you meet for breakfast every morning in here? Did that guy know someone? An expert at carrying off a kidnapping?"

"No," Alex said simply. "No, you're on the wrong trail."

"Would that be the trail you buried Hannah on at Hedgehog Mountain?"

Jay asked sarcastically. "Did you give Blake a lead, Alex? Tell me the truth and it might help you. We are desperate to get Fern back safely. If you know anything, anything at all, you have to help us. It's the right thing to do and would make up for a lot of the wrong you've done."

"I can't help you, Jay. At least, not at this moment. I can only promise that I will pay attention and let you know if I hear anything. Just so you both know: I am fond of Fern. I got to know her when she was forming her non-profit foundation, and she's a wonderful human being. I hope she survives this ordeal."

"Does Blake feel that way, too?" Tamryn asked. "Or does she give a shit about anything other than revenge with a little ransom money thrown in to ease her transition back to a normal life?"

CHAPTER 20

Matt awoke with a start. Daylight was just beginning to creep in around the edges of his hotel room windows where the tartan plaid drapes didn't quite cover. He looked at his watch; 6:00 a.m. The last time he looked at his watch, it had been 4:30 a.m. *Ninety minutes sleep, I'll take it*, he thought, surprised that he had dozed off at all.

He reached his left arm across the bed, reaching out to his beloved wife, as he did every morning since their marriage began. He knew Fern wasn't there, but he had a sliver of hope that maybe he'd dreamed yesterday—a very bad nightmare of a dream. Her side of the bed was cold, icy cold to him. In one hand, he clutched a scarf he'd retrieved from her suitcase. She'd brought two with her to Scotland and wore them every other day on their trip. It was a cliché, but he held it up to his face, and, yes, it held her fragrance.

Where are you, honey? I know you're here somewhere in this city, but I can't feel it or visualize it yet. I'm a tough cop, and you know I don't buy into your woo-woo shit, but I'll try anything to get you back. So, here's what we're going to do, my love; I'm going to lie here, very still, with my eyes closed, and place my right hand over my heart while I hold your scarf. I want—need—you to do the same wherever you are. I need a picture in my mind of the space you're in. Are you alone? If not, who's there with you? Male? Female? Both? Are you tied up? Is it dark or are there lights on? You know in your heart that I'm here with you, searching. I have some help. We just need a start. So, here we go, Fern.

Matt held his body rigid, his eyes closed tightly, and he slowly brought the hand holding her scarf up to his naked heart. Nothing happened.

• • •

Ed dropped off Patty at the Departures area of Portland International Airport. Ted, her husband, was out front at the United Airlines entrance to meet them as planned. His flight from Buck Bay had landed forty-five minutes ago, and Patty gave him a tight hug, so happy to see this man she so loved, even at his late arrival in her life.

"Thanks for bringing my girl, Ed," Ted said. "Off to Scotland we go."

"I'm glad you two are up for this," Ed said. "I can't guarantee that your wife is in a good mood, however. Some of her old pals pissed her off in Salem."

"They did you, too," Patty noted. "A miserable bunch of human beings."

"That they are. Anyway, Jay and Tamryn will pick up where you left off, and we'll get the job done. You go support our Chief, OK?"

"Will you keep me posted?" she asked, and then, without waiting for Ed's answer, "and make sure someone tracks down Blake Bowen. My gut's not liking her being a free woman."

"We'll have a chat with her, for sure. I'll text you with updates. That way, I won't bother you if you're sleeping or in the middle of something. That work for you?"

"Yes. But call either Matt or me if you get anything crucial."

"You know I will," Ed told her. "Get going, and safe travels."

Patty turned to Ted and asked, "Did you bring my passport?"

"No, I left it on the kitchen counter."

She poked him in the ribs, laughed, and said, "Let's go, honey."

• • •

Ed quickly drove back to Salem, and, thankfully, I-5 was moving right along in the early evening. For the third time that day, he entered the penitentiary and waited for Amanda to escort him to where Jay and Tamryn were still with Alex Bowen.

"Lieutenant," Bowen greeted him. "It's nice to see you again." Somehow, he said that with a straight face, even though Ed had been the one to place handcuffs on Alex and Blake the night they were arrested.

"You look well, Alex," Ed said politely. "Considering."

"We're trying to make him understand how we could help him have a better future," Jay explained to Ed. "We agree with you and Detective Perkins that someone in this building knows something about Fern's kidnapping."

"And whoever gives us info that leads to Fern's release will be rewarded," added Ed.

"Did you know that Blake Bowen has been paroled?" Jay asked Ed. "She's home in Buck Bay." Jay's face looked like he'd just eaten a plate of bad oysters.

Ed nodded. "I just heard. When did it happen?" he directed at Alex.

"Last month," Alex said defiantly. "She's innocent, and the parole board agreed. You all need to leave her alone. Let her begin a new life."

"No can do," Ed said, shaking his head. "From where I sit, what with the timing and all, that makes your wife a prime suspect in our case." He turned to Jay and Tamryn. "Let's get Alex back to his cell, and think over what you've shared with him, and the three of us can discuss how we'll drag Blake into police headquarters and grill her until she breaks, OK?" Then, uncharacteristically, he suddenly got up in Alex's face, slammed his huge hand down hard on the table, and said forcefully, "Give us information, Bowen, and make it quick! Do you understand me?"

"I don't have information," Alex cried, with Ed's face inches from his.

"Then get out of here and go get some before I snap like you did when you killed Hannah!"

Jay reached out and tugged on Ed's sleeve to get him to sit down.

Tamryn snapped a rubber band which was inexplicably wrapped around her wrist, exhaled loudly, and said, "What Lieutenant Sonders meant to say is that it's in both yours and Blake's best interests for you to put your ear to the ground inside these walls, and see if you can learn anything about Fern's kidnapping that would be helpful to us. And time is of the essence."

Alex sat up straight in his chair. "I will ask around. Blake doesn't know anything about this, I swear. May I go now?"

Ed went to the door, beckoning to Amanda, who opened the door. "Mr. Bowen would like to return to his cell now," he told her, but held his position, partially blocking the doorway with his intimidating frame. Alex squeezed past him. "I'll do what I can," he rasped.

"See that you do," Ed replied quietly.

• • •

The three cops sat silently for a few moments until Alex, with Amanda escorting him to the care of the visiting room guard, was out of earshot.

"I did that on purpose," Ed said. "I don't often resort to my intimidation factor…"

"Thank Jesus for that," Tamryn interrupted, grinning.

"but, on occasion, it can be very successful," he continued. "Alex Bowen will be my puppy. And, if Blake is up to no good, he'll have to decide who he's more afraid of—me or his wife. Probably a close call."

"I'm more afraid of her," Jay said. "She's a nutcase. You're just a very large human being. I'll bet that by the time she'd arrived back at her home, and had a nice hot bath in her own bathtub to wash off the prison stink, she figured out how to get revenge on Matt and Fern."

"Tell me more about her," Tamryn said.

Jay responded, "She's cagey and has no moral compass. She's one of those people that has zero empathy for others. It's all about her. No matter what Alex says or how hard he tries to protect her reputation, I'm convinced she was responsible for Hannah's death. And, I don't think she would bat an eye at planning Fern's kidnapping or carrying it out herself. We need to know—right now—if she's home or not."

"But Matt has seen photos of the woman involved," Ed said. "He'd recognize Blake Bowen, for sure, even if she was disguised pretty good."

"You'd think so, but he was upset real bad when I talked to him."

"So, you're not sure if Matt has on his cop hat?" Tamryn said, a worried look on her face. "Is that what you're saying?"

"He said the right things," Jay said, "but it's Fern we're talking about. So, no, I'm not sure he's thinking as clearly as our Matt."

Ed pulled out his phone. "I'm calling Dan McCoy. Why didn't that jerk of a police chief tell us that Blake Bowen was out?"

Jay and Tamryn didn't answer Ed's question. They had no answer.

"McCoy? It's Ed Sonders. I need to talk to you." A pause. "Don't really care if you're headed home for dinner." He rolled his eyes at his two colleagues. "I'm at the state pen with detectives Jay Finley and Tamryn Gesicki from Port Stirling, and we just learned that Blake Bowen was paroled and that your PD is in charge of her probationary care and feeding. Didn't you think the arresting officers might have been interested in knowing this shocking tidbit? Putting you on speaker." He clicked the button and set his phone in the middle of the table.

"I was about to call Matt, but I heard he was on vacation," McCoy said through the speaker.

"Dan, this is Jay. I'm not on vacation," he said vigorously. "Remember me? I'm the one who found Hannah in the ground, and I'm in charge while Matt is away."

"Sorry, Jay. I thought it could wait."

"Well, it can't. We have a situation here, and I want to know if Blake Bowen is home in your town."

"I believe she is. We delivered her there, and she seemed happy to be home. Who wouldn't be, I guess?"

"That's not good enough, McCoy," Ed interjected, growing irritated. "We need to know if she is home currently. Like right now."

"What's going on?" McCoy asked.

"How about you personally drive out there and see if she's home," Ed said, "and then we'll fill you in."

"Now?"

"Correct. Now. It might be a case of life and death, and you don't want to be on the wrong side of this one, Dan. Please call me back on this phone when you've established her whereabouts."

"OK, I'm turning around. I'll be in touch soon." McCoy hung up.

. . .

Dan McCoy had just celebrated his 20th anniversary as chief of police in Buck Bay, Oregon. For the most part, he'd done a decent job holding down the crime rate and keeping his town of 18,000 safe. He had friendly relations with the other local law enforcement jurisdictions in Chinook County for all of those twenty years, except for the past couple of years, when Matt Horning arrived from Texas.

As police chief of Port Stirling, Horning had burst onto the scene his first week on the new job when he and his officers had solved the horrific homicide of the mayor's daughter. Overnight, Chief Horning had become a legend throughout the county and beyond. It didn't hurt that Horning was a young stud, the kind of chief that women loved, and men wanted to be.

McCoy had once been the young stud police chief, but he'd turned slightly paunchy and had begun to lose his hair. He supposed he was a little jealous of Horning and the adoration he inspired, although he tried to hide it and be professional around him.

But the honest truth was that Matt Horning was a better police chief, and a better cop than McCoy ever was, and they both knew that truth. Their rift had grown during the Hannah Oakley case when McCoy had blown the initial investigation of her disappearance, and it took Matt and his detectives to clean up the mess and bring the right perpetrators to justice.

He knew Horning no longer trusted him. *Maybe he could right the ship by helping out Jay with whatever's going on that has his knickers in a twist.*

McCoy pulled into Blake Bowen's gravel driveway, killed his lights, and sat studying the house further up the hill that overlooked the Pacific Ocean. He rolled down his window and listened to the waves crashing at the bottom of the cliff behind him. It was dark, and the fog had rolled in obscuring the starry sky with its sliver of moonlight.

Blake's house was lit up; both floors of the huge place were ablaze. *Maybe she's scared living alone*, he thought. There were no curtains on the big picture windows that faced the ocean, didn't really need them. No one could see in unless they were in Blake's driveway, as he was now. He didn't see her, but she must be home. It looked like her antique Thunderbird parked at the top of the hill.

He approached the driveway's gate and stopped in front of the speaker box, punching the button. A woman's voice said, "Yes? Who is it?"

"Dan McCoy, Buck Bay PD Chief. Is this Blake Bowen?"

"Yes."

"I'd like to talk to you for a few minutes. Please open your gate."

"This is not a good time."

"Open your gate, ma'am."

Wordlessly, the gate slowly opened, and McCoy drove through it and up the hill. He climbed out of his car and approached the steps leading to the front door. Blake Bowen stood on her porch, dressed in some kind of dramatic wine-red kimono thing, hands on her hips.

"You can't pester and harass me," she said loudly. "I'm a free woman."

McCoy nailed her with a cold stare and flashed his badge in her face. "I would think by now you would have a better understanding of what the police can do. Let's go inside, it's chilly out here."

Blake did as she was told, leaving her front door open behind her. She moved into the great room, its wall of windows looking out to the foggy night, and plopped down on the brown leather sofa, tucking her feet under her. McCoy sat in a cream-colored fabric chair opposite her.

"I'm here because the Port Stirling police wanted me to check on you. Make sure you were in Buck Bay."

"I'm here, so now you can leave."

"Have you been home since we brought you here?"

"If by home you mean Buck Bay, yes," she said snottily. "I've been out of my house which I'm allowed to do, as you well know." She placed a strand of tired blonde hair behind her ear. Pale skin with dark circles under her eyes, indicated lack of sleep.

"Where have you been?"

"I don't have to tell you that."

"It would make both of our lives easier, Blake, if you just answer my questions. I'd like to go home and have dinner with my family instead of taking you down to the station for questioning."

"Has something happened to Alex?" she asked. "Why do they want to know where I am?"

"No, Alex is OK. I don't know why they are suddenly curious about you. They didn't tell me. Just said it was important to know where you were. Obviously, something serious has happened because it was urgent to verify your whereabouts. So, let's try this again. Where have you been in the last week?"

She stared him down, and then said, "Safeway and the liquor store."

"Which liquor store?"

"Buck Bay. The one down by the bay. I went there the afternoon you dropped me off. Couldn't wait to take a spin in my car, and it seemed like a good destination. I also got a burger and fries at McDonalds—much tastier than the prison version."

"Have you talked to your husband?"

"Not since the morning I left the penitentiary." She twirled the ring on her left hand. "He told me to go home and get my life back together. That's what I'm trying to do, Chief. You really need to leave me alone."

Ignoring that remark, McCoy said, "Have you had any visitors here?"

"Nope. People are afraid of ex-cons, don't you know?" She smiled, a sickly smile.

McCoy looked around the house. "You're pretty isolated here, Blake. Without your husband. Have you considered selling this house and moving someplace without all the bad memories? Maybe closer to friends or family?"

"I'm good on my own, and I prefer my company to most people because I'm smarter than most people, especially in this shithole county. Besides, I can't afford to sell this house right now. I need to reinvigorate my music career and make some dough first. Not that it's any business of yours."

McCoy nodded in an attempt to show unity with her. "Sounds like a good plan. What have you been doing with your time?"

"Sleeping, mostly," she answered. "It's so quiet and peaceful here. Walking on the beach. Watching movies. Cooking and eating. Drinking vodka tonics—you know, the usual. Giving myself some time to decompress before I get serious about work again."

McCoy stood. "OK, thanks for your time, Blake. I'll let myself out, and I will let you know when I find out why Port Stirling wants to know about you."

She waved her hand. "Doesn't matter. They can't hurt me anymore."

CHAPTER 21

It was close to lights out time at the prison. Jay told Matt he'd call him before they went to bed — early morning for him — and he really wanted to be able to report some progress. He was holding out for the possibility that David Dalrymple, Zhang Chen, or Alex Bowen might do some reconnaissance on their behalf during their dinner time, but that was three hours ago, and no one had approached them yet.

Ed wanted to talk to Ray Peng, or as he referred to him "Mr. Ghost Gun", but it would have to wait until morning, as they were too close to lock down for the night.

They went over the visitor logs and phone calls list that Amanda had provided for them earlier. And then, went over them again.

"There's nothing unusual here," Tamryn groaned. "It's all family members. Not even any calls or visits from their attorneys or friends. Just family."

"Then that's who we need to focus on," Jay said. "We'll call each of these numbers and talk to them. I'll divide them into three." Jay studied the logs and then said, "Ed, you take Rick Reid and Alex Bowen. Tam, you've got Zhang Chen — his list is the longest. I'll do David Dalrymple and Ray Peng. Let's get to work."

After an hour with limited results — only Tam got through to a live person — they knew this project was to be continued. She and Zhang Chen's mother had a nice talk, but one which provided zero clues or evidence.

Jay said, "Clearly, this will take some persistence on our part." He looked at his watch. "Damn, it's getting late."

Amanda appeared at the door of their conference room, and peeked her head in. "I'm afraid you need to leave soon. The warden is bugging me. And I'd like to get home to make my teenager go to bed."

The three cops looked at each other. Tamryn spoke. "We've done what we can until morning, guys. It's a wrap." She stood and gathered her notes, which had to be presented to the final gatekeeper for inspection.

"I don't give a hoot about the warden," Ed said, "but I want your teenager to get to bed." Ed stood, too.

"Can we give it another fifteen minutes?" Jay pleaded with Amanda. "There's still a chance that one of your guests might have something for us before he goes to beddy-bye for the night?"

Amanda looked at her watch. "OK, fifteen minutes, but that's it. Then it's adios until 8:00 a.m."

Jay smiled at her. "Deal. Thanks."

Tamryn and Ed sat back down.

"Dalrymple is the most likely to try hard on our behalf," Jay said. "He stands the best chance of getting out of here early and he knows it."

"I'm not so sure," Ed said. "Bowen is the most upset about Fern, and I felt he genuinely wanted to help if he could."

"Alex Bowen strangled a woman with his bare hands," Tamryn pointed out. "He has the same chance as a snowflake in a blizzard of getting out of this place. My money's on Zhang Chen because he's the smartest of the three men. His sweet mother still thinks he's perfect, by the way." She rolled her eyes. "We also know he didn't personally pull any triggers, and he knows a desperate judge might use that as an excuse to offer him a deal."

"Dalrymple didn't pull any triggers either," Jay reminded her. "It doesn't mean either one of them aren't as guilty as Alex Bowen of causing a ton of grief to their victims."

"I didn't say Chen isn't guilty of crimes against humanity—he's major scum. But I think he will turn this prison upside down if it might help him, and we already know that he's got a certain cachet in here with the other prisoners and some of the staff. He'll take advantage of that, mark my words."

"I hope you're right, Tam," Jay said. "I really, really hope you're right. Someone has to tell us something. Something to help Matt find our Fern."

Tamryn stood and hugged Jay. She knew her partner well enough by now to understand that he was traumatized. "Let's go, and let Amanda go home," she said quietly. "Tomorrow is a new day."

. . .

They had a quick beer at a restaurant Ed knew while they waited for halibut fish and chips to take out to the Best Western Inn, their home for the night. The three colleagues went their separate ways; Jay went off to make the call to Matt after promising Ed and Tamryn he would call them if Matt had any news to report. Otherwise, they agreed to meet at 7:00 a.m. in the lobby.

Jay quickly ate his dinner, accompanied by a Coke from the mini-bar, and then called Matt's cell.

"Hi, pardner," Jay said when Matt answered. "Where are you? Can you talk?"

"Yeah. Your timing is perfect. I just woke up, and I'm going to take a quick shower and get some breakfast. Going to need my strength today and tonight. Anything on your end?"

Yes, Zhang Chen confessed to planning the whole thing, and we know where Fern is, Jay wanted to say. Instead, he said, "Nothing. But we've got the visitor logs and phone calls list for all our suspects, and we've started making calls to mostly family members, which are the only people who've been in and out. We've also dangled carrots in front of Dalrymple, Chen, and Alex Bowen, and they will ask around. We think they're all highly motivated to help us. I believe we'll have something tomorrow morning."

Neither man said what they were both thinking: *That's too late.*

. . .

Stuart MacLean was waiting in the tiny lobby when Matt went downstairs to get a bite of breakfast. MacLean sat in an old chintz armchair reading a newspaper with a cup of tea on the spindly wood table next to him. An equally spindly floor lamp produced a weak shaft of light over his right shoulder.

"Why didn't you call me?" Matt asked, surprised to see him. "Tell me you were here?"

"I wanted you to sleep if you could. I knew you'd show up for food at some point." He stood. "How are you doing? Holding up?"

"I'm peachy," Matt said sarcastically. "The love of my life is likely dead somewhere in this God forsaken city. How do you think I am?"

"Fern is not dead," Stuart said firmly.

"I'm so desperate to find her, I even tried some of her weird woo-woo stuff. It didn't work. I didn't get any hits about her."

"That's because you don't really believe in it."

"And you do?" Matt asked, raising an eyebrow.

"Not really," Stuart admitted. "But every once in a while, Meg on our team will have a moment, and see something the rest of us don't see."

"Same with Fern. I make fun of her, but there have been a couple of times when her premonitions were correct."

"Maybe it's a woman thing. Best to not pooh-pooh it. I'll take all the help we can get." He pointed at Matt's phone, sticking out of his jeans pocket. "Have you heard from your family yet? Are they here with the ransom money?"

"Not yet. Dad said their flight from Dallas was due to arrive at 8:20 a.m. and he would call me the minute they landed."

Stuart looked at his watch. "About an hour-and-a-half then. Let's get a good Scottish breakfast in you, and head to the airport. We'll pick them up, get them and the cash settled, and then you and I will go to Holyrood car park and see if we can ferret out any evidence. That meet with your approval? And, did you get any rest?"

"A little. You?"

"Catriona, my wife, made me drink some hot milk at midnight, and, lo and behold, it did put me to sleep. She wants me to tell you that she's looking forward to meeting Fern, and that the four of us will celebrate mightily when she's safe."

Matt smiled a sad smile. "That would be nice."

Matt wolfed down a platter of food: porridge, sausage, egg, baked tomato and baked beans. He asked for coffee instead of tea and was pleasantly surprised when a small pot appeared at his table. He was on his third cup — hey, the cups are small — when his phone rang.

"Dad! You're early."

"We had a tailwind across the Atlantic, according to our pilot. We're just taxiing now, and have to clear customs, etc. etc. etc. How are you, son?"

"Awful," Matt answered, as a rogue tear spilled out of his eye and ran down to his chin. "I'm so glad you're here. DCI MacLean and I will leave right now, and we should be in the Arrivals hall by the time you come out. Do you have the cash?"

"Most of it. We have to go to the Royal Bank of Scotland this morning and get the rest. Our Dallas bank set it all up. Don't worry."

"Thanks for doing this, dad. I'll make it good for you."

"Matty," Ross Horning said, "the money is the least of our worries. We need to get my daughter-in-law home safely — it's the only thing that matters. We all love her, too, you know."

"I know."

"Conor and Mary are with us on the plane, and I have to warn you that they are both basket cases. Not that I blame them, of course."

"They hate me, right?"

"No, they don't hate you. But they are scared to death, and that can manifest itself into anger. We can't let that happen, because we all want to go on with our lives once Fern is safe. Your mother and I will do our best to make sure that all of our relationships stay intact. You don't worry about the Byrnes; Beverly and I will take care of it."

"I appreciate that, dad. I need to focus on finding her and making sure Police Scotland makes us a priority." Matt looked sideways at Stuart, who nodded in agreement. "As soon as we get you settled, we're going to check out a location where a witness reported seeing a woman who may match the description of the woman who we believe took Fern."

"So, there were no other leads overnight?" Ross asked.

"No, but we are hopeful that could change today. The BBC didn't run the announcement until last evening, and Stuart thinks many more locals will see it this morning. So, we'll cover the one lead we have, and hope we find something. Police Scotland is out looking for the two cars our witness remembers seeing, but nothing has turned up yet. Stuart has also put the word out to local informants who he trusts. Otherwise, we wait for the leads phones to ring again, and, worst case, we wait for midnight instructions."

"I'm sorry you are going through this, son. It's a big ol' fat nightmare. Oops, we're up at the gate now. See you soon. Keep your chin up."

"Right. We'll leave now," Matt said, ending the call. To Stuart, he said, "We're going to get the parents," and there was dread in his voice.

• • •

In Edinburgh Airport's arrivals hall, Matt got the reception from Fern's parents he expected, both of whom looked ten years older than when he last saw them before they left home for Scotland. Conor hugged him, but it was stilted, and he didn't say anything. Mary was pale, and a sobbing mess, but clung tight to Matt. "You have to get her back. You have to," she choked out between tearful wails.

Stuart stepped forward. "Mr. and Mrs. Byrne, I'm DCI Stuart MacLean and I'm heading up the investigation into your daughter's kidnapping. As you Americans like to say, we're pulling out all the stops on Fern's case. Every member of Police Scotland is working on this with the public, with our informants, and with the information a potential witness gave us. You are not alone, and Matt is not alone. If there is anything you need, please do not hesitate to ask us."

"That's very kind of you," Conor said. "Our daughter has some Scottish blood in her on my side of the family. My grandmother was one-half Scot and one-half Irish, thus the hair," he smiled a tight smile and pointed to his head of red hair. It wasn't as lush as Stuart's, but it was a welcome gesture.

"All the more reason why Fern's kidnapping must not stand," Stuart said.

"Let's drop the mothers off at a hotel and let them rest while Conor and I go to the bank to retrieve the rest of the ransom," said Matt's father. "Does that work for you, son?"

"Yes. Stuart and I will take you, and then he and I have some work to do. Mary and mom, will you be OK at the hotel?"

Beverly put her arm through Mary's and said, "Don't you fellas worry about us. We're tougher than all of you put together. Right, Mary?"

Fern's mother said, "Usually. Perhaps not at this moment." Then she started crying again. Beverly put her arms around her friend and held her close.

"Understood, then," said Ross. "Can I leave this cash with you, Stuart? I'm getting tired of carrying it."

Stuart reached for the hefty suitcase, and said, "Our car is parked at the curb. It will be a tight squeeze, but let's go back to HQ and get these cases properly stored."

On the drive back to Queen Charlotte Street, the parents asked a lot of questions, and both Matt and Stuart answered them truthfully, not holding back.

Once they arrived at the Major Investigations Team room, Stuart went in first and yelled across the room, "Scone!"

Meg sprinted across the room, dodging cubicles to reach Stuart's side as he set the bag down on the floor. Introductions were made, and Meg took control of the suitcase. "So that's what two million feels like," she whispered to Matt's father.

"$1.4 million to be exact," Ross said. "I know you will put it somewhere for safekeeping until midnight. We're off now to secure the remainder of the ransom."

Scone, choked up at the ashen faces of all four parents and the trust the Americans put in her, just nodded.

• • •

The mothers were settled at Matt's hotel, and the fathers were united with a driver who would transport them to the bank.

Stuart and Matt got to work. The Leith station forensics team met them in the Holyrood Palace car park. Forensics had arrived earlier, before the palace opened to the public, and cordoned off the area in question, where they were now at work. Stuart and Matt donned the white suits and booties.

"Anything?" Matt asked, urgently approaching one of the investigators who had the look of a distinguished science professor.

"Not much, but perhaps two findings that might be of help," the older man, with silver hair and beard but bright blue, lively eyes, answered. "We do have one tyre tread imprint from the grass right here." He walked over to the edge of the asphalt and pointed out a distinct tread mark in the wet, somewhat muddy lawn that surrounded the park. Matt leaned over until his face was about one foot from the grass, carefully inspecting the imprint.

"This is a high-performance, relatively new tire," he said to Stuart. "It could be off a Jaguar, but probably not an Audi, like Graeme Thomson said. Let's take his description of the man to all the Jaguar dealerships and see if we can jog anyone's memory about a recent sale of a black Jag." He turned to the forensic investigator. "I'd shake your hand if we weren't wearing these suits. Nice work. This might be a lead. Thank you so much."

"Aye, it's pattern evidence, but if you have a witness who may have seen the vehicle, it's a point of interest," silver beard said.

"What's the second item?" Matt asked.

"Follow me," the man said and moved carefully along a path of butcher paper they'd laid in an already-searched area just beyond the tire imprint. "We have searched this entire grassy area, and once we found the imprint I showed you, we moved beyond a meter or so and found this shoe print. The striations and wear pattern are fairly pronounced, and we believe we can match it against our footwear database." He pointed to a distinct footprint in the wet, muddy grass, and Matt and Stuart grinned at each other, overjoyed at the prospect of potential evidence.

"Once we make a cast of it, I will be able to give you more information, but based on my experience, I would say this is from a man's shoe, probably a trainer—athletic shoe, to you—and approximately a size ten, or eleven in a U.S. size."

"I'm sure I don't have to tell you how important a clue this might be, sir," Matt said. "Will you be able to process right away, and give us the evidence? And, what's your name? We haven't been formally introduced."

"Name's Neil Aitken," said silver beard. "Of course, we'll work on this forensic evidence immediately. Your wife's kidnapping is our most pressing matter. Our team wishes you good luck, Chief, and we'll keep looking, but beyond these two imprints, there's not much joy in this space. No clothing, no liquids, no hair even. We will come back tonight and do an illuminated search for body fluids if your case is not resolved by then."

"Thanks," Matt said. "I am grateful to you and your team, Neil, and I understand that you can only find what's here."

• • •

Ross and Conor were escorted to the Royal Bank of Scotland on St. Andrew Square by two armed members of the Major Investigations Team. Both the Texan and the Oregonian were sophisticated, and worldly travelers, but still, they were impressed by the bank's edifice.

The bank was located on a tidy, small, gated square. The four men on their grim mission were met at the ornate door by a uniformed, but unarmed guard. One of the MIT detectives said, "This is Mr. Horning and Mr. Byrne from America. They're expected."

"Ah, yes, right this way, please, gentlemen."

They followed him through the high-ceilinged, elaborate 1800s grand hall with its marble countertops and gilded cashier stations to an enclosed office at the far end of the huge room. This room, too, was painted cream with gold touches, and featured matching, but smaller, chandeliers as found in the grand lobby. A man in a tailored gray wool suit with vest, white shirt, and red patterned tie rose from a mammoth desk to greet them.

"I've been informed of your situation," he said, shaking hands with both men, "and please accept my condolences. We're terribly sorry this has happened to your family in our country. Please sit." He indicated a small seating area opposite his desk; sofa and two chairs with a low table between them.

"Is my money ready?" Ross asked the gentleman. "We've left our wives at the hotel, and we're eager to get back to them."

The bank manager cleared his throat. "I'm afraid there is a slight problem." He paused, rubbing his hands on his thighs, buying time to let the two visitors prepare themselves for what he had to tell them next.

"There can't be any problems," Conor said loudly.

"I understand how you feel, but we have strict banking rules in this country."

"Such as?" Ross asked.

"The Bank of Scotland belongs to an international consortium of financial institutions that does not condone paying ransom to kidnappers or cyberattacks, or anything of an illegal nature. It has come to our attention that you are seeking this large withdrawal of U.S.A. dollars to pay a ransom demand. Is that correct?"

"My daughter has been kidnapped, and we need this money to secure her release," Conor said, his face turning beet red. "My daughter who is pregnant with our first grandchild."

The bank manager looked ill. "I'm so very sorry, but my hands are tied. There is nothing I can do. You can, of course, withdraw amounts up to your local bank's daily limits."

"We need $600,000, sir," Ross said frostily. "I believe my daily withdrawal limit is $10,000, so you can plainly see that won't work. Not in time to save my daughter-in-law's life. It is my money, and I demand you produce it immediately." The tall Texan with broad shoulders leaned forward in his chair toward the slight bank manager.

"I do understand your distress, and I'm terribly sorry, but it's no good, Mr. Horning. I would be fired if I concede to your demands."

Ross looked at Conor who had started to cry again, and then said, "When I get finished with your bank's board of directors and the United States Department of State, you will also be fired. But if you do as I say and produce my money, I will see that you are offered a job at my bank in Dallas, Texas, at double your current salary. That is our final offer—take it or leave it."

The bank manager stood, pale and trembling. "Please leave my bank immediately. I'm very sorry."

Conor Byrne fainted and crumpled from his chair to the floor.

CHAPTER 22

Matt thanked the forensic crew at the Holyrood car park for their meticulous work, and they promised to process the results as fast as possible. DCI MacLean looked at him as they walked back toward their car.

"What now?" Stuart asked.

Matt turned away from the car and started walking away from Queen's Drive, and toward the narrow road that ran on the east side and behind the palace. "Let's walk around a bit, OK with you?"

"I could fancy a stroll—let off some steam, shall we?" Stuart said, and they took off down the road.

Under different circumstances, Matt would've thought it was a pretty road, with its overhanging old trees and ancient stone walls separating it from the palace grounds. On this braw morning, the sun was trying to peek out among the colorful clouds, and an occasional ray made it through the tree canopy. It was quiet, and they continued their walk down the middle of the narrow cobblestone way in a comfortable silence.

Matt spoke first. "You don't know my wife, of course, but she is a highly skilled detective…and more, that I can't really talk about."

"Fern is a spy," Stuart said matter-of-factly. "We play close attention to the U.S. and work regularly with the State Department on international espionage issues. It's been clear to me since last night when my superior got a call from Joe Phelps."

"I see. It's beginning to feel that too many people know of Fern's real job," Matt said with a scowl. "I wonder if that's what is behind this. Maybe it's not connected to Port Stirling after all, but the broader crime universe."

"No one else knows the truth about Fern. My Chief Constable, with all his flaws, is a sharp observer of his counterparts, and I've learned to read the signs. And I wasn't sure I was right until you just confirmed it. I believe that your first thought about her kidnapping being related to her Oregon cases is likely accurate. We need to keep the focus there."

"It is the most logical answer. What I started to tell you is that Fern — if she's able to — will help herself in this nightmare. She'll know that I am doing all I can to find her, and she will give me a sign of some sort. I need to look around in this area because this is our only lead so far."

"Do you mean like the sign she gave you outside the airport restroom? Patting her belly?"

"Exactly. Even in her drugged state, she understood that I would be looking at CCTV. She wanted me to know that she was conscious, and our baby was alright. That's why it's important that I keep my wits about me and look around as much as I can."

"I understand, and I'll walk this entire city with you if that's what it takes." Stuart hesitated for a moment, and then asked, "Do you know the sex of your baby yet?"

"No, it's too early, but we decided we'd rather be surprised anyway."

"Do you have a preference?"

Matt stared straight ahead and clammed up for a minute, and they kept walking. Finally, he said, "I suppose like most men, I'd love a son. But today, the idea of a little girl with Fern's red hair is pretty appealing to me."

Stuart reached out and put one arm around Matt's shoulders. "You just want your wife back and a healthy baby, whatever it is."

Matt wiped away tears, and the two continued down the road. After a bit, they came to an elaborate black iron gate that connected two rough stone walls. Above the iron bars was a stone that ran the width of the gate with the words 'Croft An Righ Cottage' carved into it. An ancient-looking stone sculpture that topped the gate, all curly-cues and open carvings that let the sky show through, was both stately and fanciful.

Matt stopped in front of the gate, grabbed the iron bars, and looked through to the slightly wild untended garden beyond. "What is this place?" he asked.

"It's a mansion that we think dates from the 16th century, although it was remodeled in the 17th. Historic Scotland uses it today for its offices, and the building is much-loved. You'll see their plaque when we get further along."

"It looks like it's L-shaped."

"It is. There's a round turret on the far end that's quite nice."

"Americans love turrets, you know," Matt said, trying to smile.

"We know. We always put you in the turreted rooms whenever possible." Stuart grinned.

Matt tried the latch on the gate, and to his surprise, it opened. "Will you get in trouble if we go in?"

"Of course not. We Scots love to share our heritage." He motioned with his hand for Matt to go in.

Inside was a sort of garden, but it was too wild for Matt's taste, with vines and weeds attaching to the side of the building. He would break out his weed-whacker if it was his property. He walked over to one area where five ancient, uneven stone steps with a more modern black railing went down to a seriously old door. He tried it, but it was locked and didn't budge. As he turned and climbed the steps, a whiff of some flower—gardenia, maybe?—wafted over him, but it didn't resemble Fern's fragrance. She wore a modern blend body lotion that smelled nothing like gardenias.

"Let's go. Zilch here."

They headed back toward the car park. "What's on the other side of that busy street that borders the parking lot?" Matt asked.

"Only my favourite place in the city," Stuart said with a smile. "Hunter's Bog. Come along and I'll show you."

As they walked, Matt asked, "Where would be a good place in this area to hide someone?" He looked around at the wild, natural surroundings they were headed into. "Would this Hunter's Bog be a good place?"

"Well, I've never thought of it in that regard, but I suppose so. Yes, actually. It's in the heart of the city, but it feels remote and lonely when there's no one there. You'll see."

While they walked, Stuart told Matt the colorful story of how Hunter's Bog got its name, and the various iterations of the park over time. After they crossed Queen's Drive and stopped for a moment at historical landmark St. Margaret's Well, they began the hike that led into the Bog.

Coming up over a rise, Matt was stunned at the view of the lush green valley below him with its watery bog, and its hills on either side covered with the brilliant yellow flowers of the springtime gorse.

"It looks just like home!" he exclaimed. "The gorse! It was all over Port Stirling before we left."

"You have this same plant?" Stuart asked.

"We not only have it, it's invasive and a real pest. Fern hates it. But I always think it's pretty when it blooms in the spring. Like it is here today."

They sat for a minute on an ancient rock, carved by centuries of rough weather. A few trees scattered throughout the Bog, trying to be a presence, but the valley was mostly a carpet of luxurious green grass, carved into areas by various hiking paths. Above them rose the Salisbury Crags, and Matt chose the path that led to the top after Stuart explained it would give them a good view of the area.

From the top, Matt looked out to the incredible view and seemed to land his gaze particularly on the Old Town section of Edinburgh below them. "My wife is down there somewhere, Stuart. I think we're close to her. I believe the man and woman that Graeme Thomson saw in the car park are who we're looking for, and I believe they chose that location for a reason—they are holding Fern nearby, and it was a convenient meeting place."

"That's one theory," Stuart agreed. "Or, they knew that the car park at Holyrood would be deserted after closing hours and chose it for that reason. But let's do a concentrated sweep of Hunter's Bog, and a door-to-door campaign in the area down below. I agree with you that it's close to where our lone witness might have seen the woman who took Fern out of the airport." He swept his arm to show Matt where he was talking about.

Matt continued to stare at the old-looking area with its steep inclines and multiple staircases. "Is that an area where many tourists go?" he pointed, "or do locals live and work there?"

"Both. It's got a lot of pubs and shops, and a different view of the castle, so many tourists find it. But as you can tell from the topography, it's not as accessible as in some parts of the city. I would recommend we begin our search at Hunter's Bog and surrounds, and then do Old Town. And I say that only because of where last year's kidnapping victims were eventually found, on the off chance they are related to Fern's." He pointed to a place high up the slopes from where they were standing. "That's Arthur's Seat, where I told you one of last year's kidnapping victims was found."

Matt nodded his agreement. "Make the call, Stuart. We can't just wait until tonight for the kidnapper to contact me."

While Stuart was occupied handing out instructions and assignments to Police Scotland, Matt walked around the top of the Crags' viewpoint and memorized the lay of the land below. His phone buzzed—his father.

"Dad."

"Hi, son. Can you talk for a minute?"

"Yes. Where are you?"

"Conor and I, along with our police escort, are still at the Royal Bank. There's a hitch, Matt."

"What do you mean?"

Ross explained the bank's position on kidnappings.

"Are you telling me that they won't give you your own money?"

"I'm afraid so. I got what I could within my daily limits, but we're short of the $2 million ransom demand. Unless someone can successfully intervene—and I tried every desperate maneuver and threat I could think of—we will miss the midnight deadline for the full amount."

"But that's outrageous!" Matt shouted. "It's our money. We need it! They will kill Fern if we don't give them what they want."

"I know, but they're stubborn. You need to talk to the big shots at the police and get them to talk some sense into that contemptible bank manager. I'll stay here, but they're done listening to me and my threats."

"How is Conor?"

"He passed out in the bank manager's office when they told us the news. He's fatigued from the flight and not eating or sleeping, but he's OK now. We're taking care of him on the sofa in the office, and they brought in some tea and sandwiches. He'll come around, but he's so frightened. I'm sorry."

"Don't apologize and don't worry. I will take it from here. Last night, Stuart mentioned they could kick in some of the ransom if necessary. Apparently, it's not easy — or fast — but he will help us. How much are we short?"

"$550,000. If we had a week, Conor and I could pull it together even under their arcane and stupid rules, but we can't do it today."

"We don't have a week, dad. Fern might already be dead, but if not, she will be for sure at midnight if we don't meet their demands."

• • •

Matt explained the problem to Stuart, who slapped himself in the forehead, knocking his black frame glasses askew. "Dammit! Our banks can be obstinate about this, but I figured they would acquiesce to Americans. Clearly, I have to get Chief Constable Armstrong involved, but we'll have to hurry."

"Then let's hurry. I can't believe this is happening. The one thing in life I thought I'd never have to worry about is money. And now, my life will be over in thirteen hours if I can't come up with half-a-million dollars, and these bastards take the time to count it. I'll talk to your chief with you. He needs to hear it from me that I can personally pay Scotland back if these guys get away with the ransom."

"You have that much?"

"About twenty times that amount. Texas oil. Don't ask," Matt answered.

"I'm sure it's an interesting story, but we don't have time. The searches are starting, and I'd like to join in with the troops."

"That's great news, Stuart — thank you. Do they know who and what we're looking for?"

"Tall, 30-something red-haired American woman in the company of at least one older woman, and possibly one or more men. Descriptions have been sent, as have those of the two vehicles Graeme Thomson described."

"CCTV photos of Fern and the woman?"

"Yes, every searcher will have the airport CCTV photo."

"Nice work, my friend. Let's go find my love."

CHAPTER 23

The day wore on for Matt, Stuart, and the families; sometimes it felt endless, and sometimes panic set in at the speed it was moving with no further results on getting the remaining ransom cash in hand.

Chief Constable Armstrong agreed with Matt that it was crucial to show up with the ransom once they received instructions from the kidnapper. Without the remaining money, Matt would have to throw himself on their mercy and explain the bank's balking at the last minute. After all, he could give them $1.4 million plus change; surely that would prove their intentions. Nobody could argue how short and condensed the timeframe was to come up with that large sum. They would be reasonable, wouldn't they? *No, they won't*, Matt thought. He was terrified.

But the search of the area around Holyrood where the woman matching the description of Fern's abductor had been seen was going well. The Scottish people were going out of their way to be helpful, as was their very nature; some even grabbed their coats and joined the police searchers. To Matt, it felt somewhat like the 'we are all in this together' spirit he felt in Port Stirling, and it was deeply touching.

And, not to be outdone by the goodwill of the Scots, Joe Phelps and the State Department had stepped up big time. On a highly clandestine note, Joe Phelps had agreed to have his counterpart in the U.K. arrange for the $550,000 to be hand-delivered to Matt.

"There are two problems with this arrangement," Joe said on the burner phone he was using to update Matt. "One is that the only person who can get this done by midnight is in London, and she will have to personally deliver it to you in Edinburgh. The second issue is that if word ever got out that the U.S. government was paying ransom money to save one of its own employees when we don't generally do it by policy, you can imagine what would happen to my job, among others."

"I get it, Joe," Matt said.

"So, what I'm saying is that you can't share this information with a single living soul, especially not your new best friend, DCI MacLean, or anyone in Police Scotland. Do you understand?"

"Yes. I won't even tell my father, who is completely distraught that he failed in his mission."

"He didn't fail. The Scottish bureaucracy let you down."

"Would it help if I met your courier halfway? Between London and Edinburgh someplace?"

"I asked her that—and it is a 'her'—and she laughed at me. Said it would only slow her down, implying that we Americans aren't up to the task in the good old motherland."

"She's probably right. I would have no idea where to go. Fern did most of the driving." Matt choked on her name, and Joe took over the conversation.

"Here's what you're going to do. You will make an excuse and go to Waverly train station when I call you back on this phone. It might not be until about 8:00 p.m., so don't worry. You will meet a woman getting off a train from London—I don't know which one yet, but she will let me know—and she will hand over a somewhat beat-up, older suitcase for you to carry. The two of you will act like a couple, get in a taxi and ride somewhere near the police station, but not directly to it."

"I can do that. How will I know her?"

"Her name is Lisa Perry, and I've known her for years. We last met in London about eight months ago. She is fifty-eight years old, 5'6" tall, about 150 pounds. Hair is dark, kind of a shiny brown, and she wears it in a pageboy, chin-length, parted in the middle, no bangs. Kind of severe looking. She will be wearing black slacks, a white sweater, and a purple jacket, with a purple and white scarf.

Matt jotted down notes as Joe kept talking. "Lisa is bringing big notes so her case is lighter to carry. The kidnapper didn't mention what size notes he wanted, did he?"

"No, nothing specific, just $2 million." He hesitated. "Time out, Joe. I have to say thank you for this. It's above and beyond the call. If we lose the cash in the exchange, I promise I will pay you back every penny."

"I don't care. I just want my employee returned home safely." Joe sounded cool, but Matt knew he was only trying to calm him down by being unemotional and businesslike. He also knew that Joe's stomach likely felt like his own did—a churning mess.

"Lisa will stay in Edinburgh until the situation is resolved. She is an exceptional resource, Matt, and you can rely on her, no matter which direction this thing goes. She was the first person I thought to call for a reason. And, it doesn't hurt that I did her a big favor a few months ago."

"What was that?" Matt asked.

"I would tell you, but I'd have to kill you."

"Ahh, a spy joke."

"More seriously," Joe said, "Lisa is also well-versed in the use of nerve agents. I'm not saying that's the deal with Fern, but if it is, Lisa will be an asset to you when you get your wife back."

Matt was silent, unable to respond to that painful possibility.

"I said, I'm not saying that I believe Fern has been exposed—do you hear me?"

"Yeah."

"I'm only trying to prepare for all the eventualities. The truth is we don't know the who or the why yet, so everything is on the table. I refuse to be surprised by any outcome tonight because you might have to act fast and not think through all of your options."

"I am trying my hardest to stay focused, and to get my composure back."

"Of course you are, and you know what this state of affairs takes. But it's Fern, Matt, and everybody, most of all me, would understand if you aren't quite as unflappable as usual. Superman may have left the building."

Matt gripped the phone tightly. "No, he's still here. And he's pissed off."

• • •

"She's home, but she's fucking weird," Dan McCoy said into his phone to Jay. "Says she's going back to work, to resurrect her career. Doesn't know anything about Fern or Matt and hasn't talked to her hubby since she was released. I got the distinct impression that she might not ever talk to him again."

"She used him, didn't she?" Jay responded. "Poor Alex. What a schmuck. The tragic part is that she might be trending again in a few weeks because of her notoriety. Wouldn't that be perfect?"

"Wouldn't surprise me one bit, since our whole country seems to be celebrity obsessed. How did our standards sink so low?"

"Did you get the feeling that Blake really didn't know anything about Fern? Did she mention Scotland?"

"Scotland? What the hell is going on, Jay?"

"Fern's been kidnapped. It happened at Edinburgh Airport, and there's a ransom demand for her. Matt believes it's connected to one of her cases here. Or, one of his, and it's persons unknown trying to get revenge on him."

"Holy crap."

"Yeah. Ed Sonders and my partner, Tamryn Gesicki, are with me now at the Oregon State Penitentiary trying to get a handle on what some of our favorite adults-in-custody might know about this case."

"So, the timing of Alex and Blake's arrests is suspect?"

"Bingo. But there are other cases we're taking a hard look at, too," Jay said. "I'd really like to give Matt a lead soon."

"How's he taking it?"

"Not good."

"Matt and I don't always agree," McCoy said, "but this sucks to high heaven. Please tell him I'll join in the effort on the home front, and that my thoughts and prayers are with him."

"This one is going to take more than thoughts and prayers, Dan, it's going to take our best detective skills and a shitload of action. Keep an eye on Blake until we get back home, OK?"

CHAPTER 24

At 4:00 p.m. in Edinburgh, things began to happen. First, Neil Aitken called from forensics with early results from their findings at the Holyrood car park scene. Scone sent the call to Stuart's desk, and he put it on speakerphone.

"You know your automobiles, Chief Horning," Aitken said. "You were correct about the tyre imprint; it is that of a 2024 Jaguar coupe F-Type. I checked, and that automobile sells at upwards of 75,000 Euros, so I wouldn't think that every bloke on the corner could own one."

"Woot! Woot!" Matt cheered. He wasn't sure if the Scots high-fived or not, but he held up his hand, and Stuart slapped it. "You're absolutely certain?"

"One hundred percent. I personally went to a local dealership an hour ago to compare. Find that particular Jaguar in Edinburgh, and you might be closer to finding your wife."

"Oh, we'll find it," Stuart said. "Well done, my man. What's next for your gang?"

"We're working on the footprint now, but so far, we haven't been able to narrow it down enough to a brand so it would be useful to you."

"Keep trying," Matt said. "What's your favorite whisky, Mr. Aitken? When my Fern is safe, I'll have a bottle coming your way."

"Not necessary. But I would never say no to an Aberlour Speyside single malt. Keep the faith, Chief."

Shortly after Matt and Stuart talked with Aitken, Scone came to their cubicle and reported that the Police Scotland canvassing of Jaguar and Audi car dealerships turned up no new black car sales in the past few months to anyone matching the description of the male in the parking lot. This news was particularly upsetting to Matt because of Aitken's evidence that the tire tread mark was that of a new Jaguar.

"Can we get an artist's rendering of the man in the car park based on Graeme Thomson's description, and go back to the Jaguar dealers?" Matt asked, his hope fading. "We have to try again based on the forensic evidence."

"Ahead of you on that front, Chief," Scone said. "I've sent the description to our staff person, and she's working on it now. I've got four of our officers standing by, and they understand that we were waiting for the forensic results on the tyre tread to narrow it down."

"There are approximately 200 car dealerships throughout Scotland," Stuart said. "But if I recall correctly, only about twenty offer Jaguar and Land Rovers."

"I know our guy could have bought the car anywhere, but let's start here," Matt said. "How many of those dealerships are in the Edinburgh area?"

"Not many. Somewhere in the four-to-six range, depending on what you consider 'the area'."

"So, if you and I go to one or two, you've got officers ready to cover the rest, right, Meg?"

"Correct. I'd go myself, but someone needs to man the phone," she said.

"I'd like to see the artist's sketch when she's got it," Matt said. Stuart raised his hand. "Me, too," he said.

"Of course," she said.

"And, we're still staffing the tip line, correct?" Matt asked.

"Yes, DS Barclay is on shift now, and he's reporting no new calls during the past two hours. But it may pick up as people get home from work, and so on," she said. "My desk phone is on it as well."

"Good," Matt said. "How long do you think it will take your artist to finish the sketch?" he asked, trying to sound patient and reasonable.

"Not long," Scone said and patted him on the arm. "I will see to it, and keep you posted. Hold good thoughts."

"Thanks, Meg," Matt said. He couldn't call her Scone, didn't feel right.

At 4:30 p.m., Detective Patty Perkins and her husband Ted arrived. Patty burst through the Major Investigations Team door, brushed hurriedly past the Scottish detectives, and made for Matt, enveloping him in a tight hug. She whispered something in his ear, and he slowly pulled away from her.

"Don't be nice to me," Matt choked out. "I'm trying to keep unemotional and stay focused." Then he grabbed her again in a bear hug. "But it's dang nice to see you two!"

Ted moved in for the group hug. "Please put my wife to work, she's driving me crazy."

Matt could hear the smile behind Ted's remark. "Why wouldn't I use the services of the world's greatest detective to help me?" Matt said.

"How are Conor and Mary holding up?" Ted asked. He'd known them for thirty years, and Matt knew he understood how much they loved their daughter.

"It's not easy. Won't be until we get her back."

"What can I do right now?" Patty demanded.

Matt filled her in on the snafu with the ransom cash (but not about Joe Phelps' role in obtaining the remainder), the possible witness, and the forensics news, while Ted went in search of coffee for all of them.

"What's your take from your visit to the Oregon penitentiary?" he asked her.

"Nothing concrete, I'm afraid," Patty said. "But I have my suspicions that this plot may very well indeed have originated there. Zhang Chen and David Dalrymple were the two that Ed and I interrogated together. Both told us nothing new, but we dangled carrots in front of them. My brain says Chen might be behind this, Matt. He's got the international connections and the clout still — unbelievable, I know — but he's still in charge."

"What does your gut say?" Matt asked.

"My gut didn't love David Dalrymple's response. I got a feeling that he already knew something before we got to him. He was awfully cool and relaxed talking to Ed and me, almost felt like he was trying too hard."

"Do we know if David's buddy Michael Winston is still in prison? Oregon or Washington?"

"Not for certain."

"I'll ask Sylvia to track him down," Matt said. "We need to talk to that asswipe as well."

"I think Jay already asked Sylvia to find him and set something up. Are you in regular communication with Jay on the home front now?"

"Yeah, we talked this morning, my time. He, Tamryn, and Ed were still in Salem and were planning to overnight there and go back to the prison in the morning as early as they're allowed. They want to talk to Ray Peng, but they got kicked out of the pen last night when it got late."

"I doubt if a second-rate player like Peng could pull this off, but he would likely know if his pal Zhang Chen was involved. Peng might be a good candidate for a deal."

"Agreed," Matt nodded. "Anything else come up yesterday?"

"Yes, I met Randy Reid, and I don't like him."

"Big shock there. Me neither," Matt said. "Could he be involved?"

"Possible. He holds the two of you responsible for breaking up his family."

"No surprise. Entitled guys like him wouldn't ever think of looking in the mirror for the problem. My gut is telling me that we have to press hard on our bad guys with the money and connections, and that's Zhang Chen and Rohn Reid. With their minions to carry out the deed."

"Is there any chance it could simply be Scotland related?" Patty asked. "A crime ring here?"

"A chance, yes. Probable on its own? No, not in my opinion." He shared the info on the recent kidnappings in Edinburgh that Stuart told him about.

Suddenly, Meg started shouting and waving at Matt from across the room. "It's him! On the phone! Come quickly!"

Matt outran Stuart and Patty to Meg's desk.

"Do you have the money?", came the disembodied voice over the speakerphone.

Matt held up his hand in the 'stop' gesture to his three colleagues gathered round Meg's desk. "Yes," he said. "We have the cash. $1.5 million in hand." Meg scrambled to start a tracer on the call.

"The ransom is $2 million. You know the number. Hanging up now."

"No, wait!" Matt yelled into the phone. "The other half million is on its way here now. It will be here any minute, I promise."

Stuart gave Matt a raised eyebrow, accompanied by an odd look. Matt gestured with his hand that indicated 'don't worry.'

"Will you be ready by midnight?"

"Yes. Yes, we're ready. Please let me speak to my wife. To Fern. I just need to hear her voice. Please."

"No. I will call back. Your wife is fine…for now."

"What about our baby? Is the baby alright?"

"Good-bye, Chief Horning. And good luck."

The phone call lasted forty seconds. Matt put both hands over his face, and bent over, his shoulders shaking. In a rush of rage, he cried, "Noooo!" Patty stood frozen with one hand over her mouth for a second or two, and then grabbed Matt and held on tight. "It's alright, Matt, it's going to be alright. Fern is still alive, and we will get her."

Slowly, Matt straightened up, wiped the tears from his face, and said to Meg, "Did you get a trace?"

"Partial," Meg answered with a tight-lipped half-smile. "An area, not any more specific—the call was too short. It came from south of where we are here, and not far. Maybe a little southeast."

"How big is the area?" Matt asked.

"Hard to tell, but most likely over half a kilometer in each direction. I'm sorry, but I can't be more specific."

"Possibly near Holyrood, then?" Stuart suggested.

"Maybe," Meg said. "If not, it's not too far."

"This is progress, then," said Stuart. "We can narrow the area of the city that will allow us to concentrate our door-to-door search. Get a printout from the tracer—best guess is all we're looking for, Scone. You and I will draw an outline of the search area. Call all the troops here and have them on stand-by." He turned to Matt. "What was that bit about the rest of the ransom cash?"

Matt looked him directly in the eye and said, "I have a Plan B, and we will have the rest of the cash soon."

His look told Stuart not to ask a lot of questions. Instead, he joked, "You're not about to rob one of my banks, are you?"

Patty, with red eyes but regaining her composure somewhat, said, "He should. What would you do if it were your pregnant wife, DCI MacLean?"

Stuart's color rose up his neck, making his cheeks red. "Exactly what Matt is doing. Raise the money however I had to and negotiate with her kidnappers. We're doing everything we can, Detective Perkins."

"What's our illustrious State Department doing on Fern's behalf?" Patty asked Matt.

"Joe is working it behind the scenes. We have every resource helping us, but now we need to focus on the exchange as well as the search," Matt said, changing the subject from the cash. He looked at his watch; 5:00 p.m. "I'm not giving up yet on the search, especially now that we can narrow it, but we only have about four more hours before we have to concentrate on the exchange. Stuart, talk to us about how you've handled your most recent kidnap situations."

Stuart ran his hand through his red wavy hair and made it stand up on top like it was afraid and running away from his head. "The bloody awful truth is that we haven't done a good job. But we've learned from our mistakes. Knowledge that will help us tonight, I believe."

Patty rolled her eyes. "Well, now I feel better."

CHAPTER 25

Jay's watch alarm woke him at 6:00 a.m. Momentarily, he forgot where he was. *Oh, yeah, a motel in Salem close to the state pen. Fun.* Born and raised in Chinook County, Jay wasn't comfortable when he was away from the south coast of Oregon. He was adventurous and enjoyed seeing new places, but he was always super eager to get home again.

Recently, he'd bought a small bungalow—which Fern had found for him—within walking distance to the Port Stirling beach. It was set back in a friendly neighborhood on the other side of Ocean Bend Rd and was just the right size for him. For the first time in his thirty years, he had a garage all to himself. It was small, but it was his favorite thing about being a homeowner, and upon moving in, he had outfitted it first with new tools. Actually, a big screen TV had been his first purchase, but the garage stuff had come before living room furniture. He would order that online because going shopping for furniture was his idea of some kind of hell.

He laid there in the lumpy motel bed, thinking about the day's priorities and realized he already missed his new home. And the PSPD, along with his colleagues and his desk overlooking the Pacific Ocean. But there was no point in longing for home and routine; he had serious work to do today.

Jay showered, slicked down his ever-present cowlick as best he could, and dressed quickly and was downstairs in the motel's breakfast room getting coffee when first Tamryn then Ed joined him. "Coffee?" Jay asked, holding up two mugs. Both cops nodded, and took a seat at a table separate from the others.

"How do you want to handle the questioning of Ray Peng?" Jay asked.

Ed waved his hand. "Don't talk to me until I've had some coffee. You two discuss and I'll listen."

"I talked to Matt last night before I went to bed, and we both feel that Ray Peng might be our best chance at a play-for-pay deal," Jay started. "If he knows anything about Fern's kidnapping or will snoop around the prison and help us, he's a prime candidate for early release."

"Why?" asked Tamryn.

"Because he was only convicted of conspiracy, and manufacturing ghost guns illegally. He never pulled a trigger, and he doesn't have the brains to be the mastermind, like Chen."

"How long is he in for?" she asked.

"I don't remember his exact sentence, but it's not as long as Chen's twenty-five or the Reids' life, and not as long as Dalrymple's either, if I recall. I think Peng is our best chance, next to Randy and Rohn Reid trying to help their family."

Ed sat drinking his coffee and looking pensive.

"What?" Jay asked him.

"Ray Peng is a complete wuss. Even if he knows Zhang Chen masterminded the Fern operation, he doesn't have the balls to rat him out. And he would probably be right; Chen would kill him, one way or another. I'm all for talking to him this morning, but I have zero-to-low expectations."

"Couldn't we offer him witness protection?" Tamryn asked. "Put he and his young family somewhere safe?"

"Possibly," Ed said. "It's worth a try, but I still think he will clam up. Do we have the Reids lined up after Peng?"

"Yes," Jay answered. "Amanda said they aren't eager to see us, however."

"I wouldn't be either, if I were them," Ed said. "Too bad."

"I take it there was no positive news from Matt last night?" Tamryn asked.

"Nothing definitive, but he was looking forward to inspecting a location where a witness provided a possible ID of the other woman. I hate this time zone difference. It makes everything hard," Jay lamented.

"It was a little easier in Boston," agreed Tamryn. "This eight-hour difference sucks." She checked her watch. "It's mid-afternoon there now. I'd like to know if anything has happened today so far."

"As soon as we're finished at the prison, we'll call Matt," Jay said. "There's no point in talking now, we've got nothing to tell him."

"I'd like to give him a thread to hang onto," Ed said, dipping his head down dejectedly to his chest. "You know he's suffering mightily. As soon as we get through these prison chats, we'll circle back to Chen, Dalrymple, Alex Bowen, and Randy Reid. See if they've thought things through during the night. OK with you two?"

"It's a plan," Jay said. "At least, we have something to do so we can feel useful." He, too, was dejected.

"Guys, snap out of it," Tamryn said. "We likely have the culprit right here. Be at your best today, and they won't be a match for the three of us. Am I right?"

Ed looked at Jay, and Jay looked at Ed. "You are right," they said in unison.

"Then let's get some breakfast and power up," she said, standing and heading to the sad buffet.

• • •

The last time Ed and Jay had seen Ray Peng he was throwing up in the Chinook County courtroom immediately after the jury had found him guilty of the charges entered against him. He didn't look much better today. His skin was sallow and pitted, and he had lost weight on his already thin frame. Peng's best feature — his glossy black hair, always styled in a trendy fashion — had been cut close to his scalp.

Ed gestured to the chair across from him at the small table in the penitentiary's conference area, and Peng took a seat, his eyes staring straight ahead.

"Hello, Ray. It's nice to see you again," Ed began. "But you're not looking so good — have they been treating you well in here?"

"I'm alright," Ray said sullenly. "Why are you here?"

"We are talking to all of your Chinook County incarcerated friends—Chen, Dalrymple, and so on. You know, the upstanding citizens who got you arrested and sent here."

"Those guys aren't my friends."

"No, they truly aren't your friends and never were," Ed said, leaning toward him with his big hands clasped on the table between them. "But we want you to pretend that they are your friends and help us get some information."

"What kind of information?"

Jay stepped into the conversation. "You remember Fern Byrne, Chief Horning's wife, don't you?"

"Yeah. Why?"

"She's been kidnapped while she and the Chief were on vacation in Scotland, and we think the plot may have sprung from this place. You ever been to Scotland, Ray?"

He shook his head.

"You hear anything about Scotland or Fern in here?"

"Nope."

The three cops sat back and waited for Peng to put the pieces together. The silence lasted almost thirty seconds.

"You want me to be an informant on Zhang Chen?" he asked, his eyes widening. "Are you crazy?"

"Probably," Ed said. "He'd kill you, correct?"

"In a heartbeat," Peng answered, his hands now shaking.

"We can protect you, Ray," Tamryn said, speaking for the first time. "I'm Tamryn Gesicki, a new police detective in Port Stirling. I've had a lot of experience on the east coast with witness protection programs."

Peng stared at her for a moment, and then waved both of his hands back and forth. "No. No. No. Not gonna happen. No."

"Hear me out," Tamryn said. "We can get you out of here. Get your freedom back. And move your wife and two children someplace safe. We'll even let you choose your destination, within our reasonable boundaries. We'll help you find work."

"It's suicide! No, I can't do it," Ray said.

"Zhang Chen will spend his life down the hall," Ed said. "Once we have you out of here, he can't ever hurt you again."

Ray laughed. A nervous laugh with no mirth whatsoever. "You're wrong, Lieutenant. Zhang Chen has tentacles all over the world. He still has hundreds of people loyal to him. You think these walls could ever stop someone like him? They can't. I'm probably already dead just because I'm sitting here with you."

"Give us a chance to help you lead a better life, Ray," Tamryn tried again. "We can do it. I can do it, because I've done it successfully for others in your situation."

"All we're asking is for you to listen to the chatter in here," Ed said, "and tell us if you hear anything, anything at all about Fern, Chief Horning, or Scotland."

"You don't even have to ask any questions," Jay added. "Just listen and let us know if anyone is talking about Fern's kidnapping."

Ray sat, and it was clear he was thinking. "If I do hear anything, how would it work?"

"Tell your guard you want to talk in private with Amanda Wilson. She'll know what to do," Jay said. "You know her, right?"

Ray nodded. "If I help you, you'll get me out?"

"You have our word," Ed said. "Will you help us save Fern?"

"Maybe." Ray stood and motioned to the guard.

. . .

Next up was Rick Reid.

"Randy told me you'd be here to talk to me," Rick said, as the guard brought him to the room. "How can I help you fine officers of the law?" He smiled at Tamryn, and she introduced herself to him.

"Did your brother also tell you that we're about to arrest him for the kidnapping of Fern Byrne, and send him here to join you?" Ed said.

That wiped the smug smile off Reid's hollowed-out face. For a moment, Tamryn thought Reid wanted to say something, but he held back.

"Everyone in here seems to be losing weight," Ed noted.

"Randy doesn't know anything about your kidnapping ordeal, and neither do I. I made one big mistake in my life trying to protect my brother, but I'm not like the other people in this dreadful place."

"What about your mother, Rick, is she like the other people in here?" Jay asked. "Evil to the core?"

Rick glared at Jay. "We did what we did to try to save our family. We are not 'evil'. We regret our actions, obviously, and we'll pay for them with our lives, but we are not hardened criminals. You're barking up the wrong tree."

"We want to believe you," Jay said.

"But I don't," Ed said. "I believe that you Reids think the laws don't apply to you because your vast fortune puts you above the rest of us. And I believe that your father and, especially, your brother will use that fortune to get revenge on the people they mistakenly believe ruined your family. And, I also believe that unless you help us get to the bottom of this kidnapping, you will never see the sky again."

Rick smirked. "We have an outdoor yard where we exercise. I see the sky every day."

"It was a metaphor, numbnuts," Ed said.

Rick pushed back his chair and stood. "We're done here."

Ed checked his watch—10:00 a.m. "It appears that we have finished our work in this fun building."

"There is still Moira," Jay noted. "Off we go to Coffee Creek to have a talk with her?"

"Yeah," Ed said, standing. He watched the guard escort Rick back to the inner sanctum.

· · ·

Up the road at the women's facility at Coffee Creek, it did not go much better with Rick Reid's mother, Moira Simpson.

"Thank you for meeting with us, Moira," Tamryn started. "I'm Detective Gesicki with the Port Stirling PD, and I believe you know Detective Finley and Lieutenant Sonders."

Moira nodded, but did not speak. In her mid-fifties, she was a robust, tall woman with apple cheeks and clear skin, and fine features. Her thick blonde, wavy hair was neatly cut at chin length.

"We want to talk with you about…" Tamryn said.

"I know why you're here," Moira interrupted, "and I've got nothing to say to you."

"You've obviously spoken with your son, Randy. Is that correct?" Tamryn asked.

"Yes."

"We need help, Moira," Tamryn continued. "Your help. And if you agree to help us and give us information we desperately need, we're prepared to offer you help in return."

"Like what?" she smiled. "Get me out of here? Is that what you mean?"

"Perhaps."

"Here's a news flash for you, Detective; I don't want out of here. I like it. Granted, it's not the life of luxury I imagined for myself in my old age, but it's mostly pleasant. I love to read, and I can do it here all I want without being disturbed. I have very few responsibilities. I do help with food service, but it's less taxing than in my previous life because I'm not in charge. Someone else does all the shopping, cleaning, and my laundry. I'm allowed to keep my body fit, and to keep it clean, as I like. No one is interested in me, and therefore, no one bothers me. So, you three need to toddle along. We have no business to discuss."

And with that, Moira stood, went to the door, and waited for her guard.

• • •

To top everything off, they'd discovered nothing of interest or even remotely suspicious when talking to the prisoners' family members. And that was the few they had reached. Blake Bowen, Paula Davenport, Zhang Chen's California assistant, and Mrs. Peng didn't return their phone calls at all. They would have to put shoe leather on pavement to talk to them.

CHAPTER 26

6:30 p.m.

Scone appeared with two copies of the finished artist's sketch of the man Graeme Thomson saw in the car park. "Here it is," she said, handing it first to DCI MacLean while Matt peered over his shoulder. "Our artist said that Thomson's description of the man was quite detailed, and she's confident this is an accurate rendering of what he looks like."

Matt paled and grabbed hold of Stuart's arm. "That's the man who was following us."

"You're sure?" Stuart asked.

"No doubt. The mole on his face, it's just like that," he pointed at the sketch. "He was on the plane from Newark with us. I also saw him at Shetland Airport—I talked to him, for God's sake!—and he was outside our hotel in Inverness."

"Then it's official. He was clearly stalking you and Fern, and he's our guy. It's unfortunate Graeme Thomson didn't get a clear look at the woman, too." He handed his sketch to Scone and said, "Make copies of this and distribute to our team post haste. Matt, let's go."

But Matt grabbed the second sketch out of Scone's hand and was already pulling on his jacket and heading for the door.

. . .

Somewhere in Edinburgh

"I told you I was in charge, not you," the woman said, her face flushing.

"You are the boss, no question," he told her. "However, it appears now that you will have to shoulder more of the heavy lifting than I anticipated. Let me walk through with you how this has to work." He showed her the empty capsule. "It will be placed inside this. You will simply remove the cap and quickly brush it anywhere there is bare skin, replacing the cap immediately."

"What if I inhale it, too?" she asked worriedly.

"You won't. You'll be heavily covered; gloves, long sleeves, face mask, etc. And as soon as you get back to the vehicle, Nigel will be waiting with the antidote and will give you a shot. You're in no danger, love." He rubbed her neck tenderly.

She leaned into his hand and closed her eyes, enjoying his touch. "I can do it."

"Of course you can. Now, there's just one more wee detail, and it is, unfortunately, most unpleasant."

She looked at him warily. "What?"

"Mr. Horning does not yet have the full amount of the ransom money we've demanded. We must ensure that he is taking us seriously, or we might not get the full amount."

"He said he would have it by tonight."

"Yes, but I believe we must give him a further incentive." He paused and put his arm around her, whispering in her ear.

She recoiled in horror from him.

"No! Why not her?" She pointed at an unconscious Fern slumped into the far corner of the room.

"Because he will think we've already killed her and will call off the ransom exchange. It has to be you, I'm afraid. It's either this or you lose your house and your children."

She stared at him.

"Do you promise?"

"I promise."

"And we'll get all the money?"

I'll get it all, he thought, but merely nodded to her.

. . .

After re-visiting Jaguar car dealerships in the areas surrounding Edinburgh with the artist's sketch of the man of interest, Detective Constable Claire Campbell and her partner Detective Sergeant Paul Lennox went back to the dealership in east Edinburgh just as they were closing. They'd had no luck with the other two they'd checked out, and neither had Matt's and Stuart's teams; none of the sales people recognized the man in the sketch.

Campbell and Lennox spoke to the same salesman they had spoken to late yesterday. Martin Skene, with his ruddy complexion, short crewcut, and profound belly, said as he pointed to the artist's sketch, "Oh, yeah, I sold a Jag to that man about three months ago."

"Are you sure it's the same man? Take a closer look."

Skene leaned in and studied the sketch. "It's him."

"But you told us yesterday you had not done so," DC Campbell protested.

"I sold him a *green* Jag, not a *black* one," Skene said. "You asked if I'd sold any black ones."

"What shade green are your Jaguars?" she asked between clenched jaws.

"British Racing Green, kind of a forest-y green."

"Dark enough to look black in the twilight from a bit of a distance?"

"Sure."

"What can you tell us about him?" DC Campbell asked Skene. "We'll need to see your files. And we are in a hurry."

"What's the bloke done?"

Campbell shook her head. "Not at liberty to divulge that information. But he might be extremely important to a current, ongoing investigation. Get your sales file on him, please."

Walking briskly, they followed Skene into a glassed-in small office. He squeezed between a file cabinet and his desk with about an inch to spare and opened the top drawer.

"I keep the last six months' sales in the front of this cabinet. He has a Russian-sounding name, and he looked Russian to me. Spoke like a Scot, but clearly not born here, I would say. Ah, here it is. Vadim Guz. Paid by credit card."

"The total purchase price?" Campbell asked.

"Yes, 81,000 pounds. The vehicle was fourteen months old; it sold for 88,000 pounds new. I tried to sell it for that amount, but he knew his stuff, and I had to negotiate a lower price." Skene shook his head as if to acknowledge his huge failure as a salesman.

"What kind of credit card, and do you have the number in his file?"

"Yes, copy of the cc receipt. Here it is."

"Do you have an address for him?" DS Lennox asked and made a crossing-his-fingers gesture to DC Campbell.

"I think so." Skene ran his finger down the long first page of the sales document. "Yes, here it is. Number 15, Regent Terrace, Edinburgh. La-di-da, ritzy street, no?"

Campbell and Lennox made eye contact. She spoke, "Yes, it's a pricey neighborhood."

"Which, I guess, goes with the pricey — but worth it! — automobile choice," Skene said.

"Who is this guy?" DC Campbell said to no one in particular.

. . .

Campbell and Lennox took photocopies of the sales file. Skene protested, but not vigorously, when they threatened him they'd be back in a heartbeat with a search warrant that would close the dealership for twenty-four hours.

It was a hairy ride back to the police station, with Campbell — who wasn't the best of drivers in good times — taking a couple of corners on practically two wheels in her rush, and almost hitting a pedestrian. They arrived breathless at the Major Investigations room.

"We've got him! Vadim Guz!" Lennox exclaimed, waving the sales documentation in the air as he ran toward DCI MacLean's desk. Stuart and Matt had just returned to the station empty-handed.

Matt stood. "What? Calm down and tell us what's happened, please, sir. I'm sorry, I don't know your name."

"DS Paul Lennox, and this is DC Claire Campbell. We returned to the Jaguar dealerships we visited yesterday, but this time we took the artist sketch. We hit paydirt." Lennox bent over and placed his hands on his knees, breathing hard with exertion and all of the excitement.

DC Campbell took over. "The sales manager at the east Edinburgh Jaguar dealership recognized this man." She pointed to the sketch. "Yesterday, I asked him if he'd sold any black Jaguars recently. Turns out, he sold our man a British Racing Green Jag, and when we showed him the sketch, he recognized him immediately."

Matt grinned a true grin for the first time in two days. "That's superb work, you two," he said as he gave them both an exuberant hug. "We should have realized that Jaguar's British Racing Green color might look black in fading daylight."

DC Campbell grinned back. "It gets better, sir. We have the credit card he used to buy the vehicle, and we have his address. It's not far from the Holyrood car park. It all adds up."

"Excellent!" Matt said and turned to DCI MacLean. "How fast can we produce a team to raid this house?"

Patty took a hold of Matt's hand and said, "I'm in. But I'll need special authority to carry."

Stuart raised his eyebrow and glanced at Matt.

"Oh, trust me on this," Matt said. "She may look like a civilized, mature lady, but there are a lot of bad guys dead or in prison in Oregon because Detective Perkins went in first. She's on the team." Patty squeezed his hand.

"OK," Stuart acquiesced. "I'll arrange for a handgun special license for both of you just until we bring Fern to safety. But you are to think hard before firing. Am I clear?"

Matt and Patty nodded their understanding of the terms.

"We have a tactical team that is a highly specialized unit for hostage rescues, counter terrorism, and other high-risk incidents. They've been on standby since this ordeal began. We can be ready to go as soon as we tell them the plan. Cowards die many times before their deaths; The valiant never taste of death but once. Julius Caesar."

"I knew that one," Matt said, giving Stuart a slight smile. He looked over the Jaguar sales file. "15, Regent Terrace, Edinburgh—anyone in the room know this street?" He spoke loudly and looked around.

"'Course," said a female voice across the room. "We would all like to live there."

That got a round of laughter. Stuart explained. "It's a very posh neighborhood just north of Holyrood and close to Calton Hill. It's terraced with nice views to the southeast. But hold your horses, as I believe you like to say, Chief. There is a fairly significant complication."

"What?"

"At the far end of the Terrace, #1 is the home of the U.S. Consulate General and her office."

"The U.S. Consulate is on this same street?" Matt asked, a shocked look on his face.

"That's what I'm telling you. It's a very discreet street, and except for a subtle U.S.A. plaque above the door, and a smallish flag flying in the middle of the building, you would hardly know it was an official residence. The complication is that the street in front of the building is official U.S. property, and we can nae trespass. There are thigh-high black posts across the street at each end of the U.S. property."

"That could help us, couldn't it? He—or they—couldn't make a getaway in a vehicle going that direction, right?"

"I would think not," Stuart answered. "Not unless they were driving a tank." He turned to DC Campbell. "We need to be completely sure this is the right address. Please check our databases and confirm that the name, address, and credit card number all match. Be sure to look at the real estate data for this address, going back several years. Lennox, you help Claire. Use the desks at the front by Scone. And, may I add to what Chief Horning said. This is exemplary work and dogged follow-up. Thank you, both."

"Yes, sir. Thank you, sir." DC Campbell said. She and Lennox looked like they might start jumping up and down at any moment.

"You think our guy might have given a false address?" Matt asked. "I thought of that, too, but he would have had no idea three months ago when he bought the Jag that the police might be onto him. And even now, he would have no reason to think anyone saw him and the woman in that car park at twilight. Even if he did notice Graeme Thomson driving out, he wouldn't think we could identify him in any way."

"I just want to be sure before we go in there with guns blazing. Those properties on Regent Terrace are highly sought after, and you almost have to know someone who died to grab one. It would be quite shocking if anyone living there would be involved in a nasty case like this. Although, this might be a case of hiding in plain sight."

"You might be surprised," Matt said. "In my recent experience, a lot of the world's bad actors have a ton of money, and money talks. And if Graeme Thomson fingered the right guy here"—he pointed to the sketch in DS Lennox's hand—"he just paid 81,000 Euros for a car, and he's obviously a high flyer of some sort. We're going to Regent Terrace, and we're going now."

"We'll have to notify your embassy first."

"No!" Matt yelled and slammed his hand down hard on Stuart's desk. "No one can know. It has to be a complete surprise attack if we are to stand a chance to extract Fern."

"I understand your reticence, Matt, truly I do, but this could be a major cockup if the embassy doesn't know what's going on in their very street."

"I don't care. It's our only chance. I will take full responsibility and tell everyone that you tried to stop me."

The two men stared at each other for a moment, trying to read the other's thoughts.

Matt broke the silence. "Assemble your team, Stuart, and you'd better tell them it's on a volunteer basis only—this could get violent. If my wife and baby are in that house, I will stop at nothing."

Stuart breathed out loudly. "Understood. I have a private phrase for this kind of assignment—'it might be untidy.' Our unit is not afraid of an untidy operation. Nor am I, for the record."

Matt clapped him on the back.

"How big is your team?" Patty asked. "How many shooters are we talking about?"

"For this set of circumstances and this particular location, we'll take eight plus the three of us. Three of my men will go in the front door with the three of us, three will be stationed at a back entrance—I believe these homes all have extensive back gardens, with a small back road for access. Then, we'll put two of our units at each end; two just inside the embassy barriers, and two at the other end, the primary entrance and exit. Scone!" Stuart bellowed across the room, "please get us a detailed map of Regent Terrace now."

Scone acknowledged his request with a wave and moved immediately to a walk-in closet twenty feet from her desk at the front of the vast room.

"Sir," DC Campbell said, moving toward Stuart with a printout in her hand. "Vadim Guz has owned #15, Regent Terrace for nine years. He is a Russian-born businessman who emigrated to Scotland when he was thirty. He's now forty-four and has lived in Edinburgh for fourteen years. His photo matches our artist's sketch."

"It's go time," Matt said.

Stuart nodded and started to speak just as Scone let out a gut-wrenching scream from her desk. "Oh, my dear God!" she wailed. She was holding a small white box in her hands, a stricken look on her face.

Matt moved quickly to her. "What is it, Meg? What's wrong?"

Hurriedly, she put the box down on her desk and closed the lid. "I don't think you should see this, Chief." She looked up at him with a tear-streaked face.

"Step aside, Matt," Stuart said, coming up behind him. Calmly and silently, Matt elbowed him out of the way, and reached down to open the box, his hand visibly shaking. Looking away, Meg sobbed and hid her eyes.

Inside the box, a pudgy female finger, dried blood at the severed end, laid under a jagged piece of white paper with the scrawled words, "Quit messing around. Get the money."

The box fell out of Matt's hands and landed back on Meg's desk. He shrieked, covered his eyes and continued to howl. Stuart, with Patty at his side, looked inside.

"This cannot be happening," Patty said, shaking her head violently side to side. "Not to our Fern. No. Unacceptable. Just no no no." She peered more closely inside the box.

CHAPTER 27

"Matt, honey," Patty whispered, placing her hands on his shoulders as he sat gulping for air at Meg's desk. His back was turned away from the hateful box. "When you are able to, I want you to look at the finger again. Take your time. Breathe in and out, and then when you're ready, please take a second look. I'm not certain it belongs to Fern."

He wiped tears off his face, took a couple of deep breaths as suggested, and then at a painfully slow pace, wheeled the chair around to face the box. He looked beseechingly up at his dear friend, his eyes hollow and bloodshot, before he dared to look at the finger. "What do you mean?"

"What color nail polish, if any, was Fern wearing the last time you saw her?" Patty asked him. "The fingernail has a color I've never known Fern to wear. Can you look at it now?"

For a few moments, Matt kept staring at Patty, a vacant look in his eyes. "I don't know. I don't notice stuff like that."

"Think hard," she urged him. "Think about a meal you shared that last morning. She's holding her coffee cup. What does her hand look like?"

Matt thought, rubbing his hands on his thighs. "Pink. Her fingernails are painted pink. A light pink, almost blush colored." He looked up at Patty with hope in his eyes.

"Bingo," Patty said. "Fern almost always has either no nail polish on, or a light pink. Have you ever known her to wear a dark wine color, like burgundy?"

"I don't think so. Have you?"

"Never. She wouldn't have the patience to keep up with the maintenance on a darker color herself, or the time to spend at a salon. It's not like her."

Superman, who had briefly turned to mush, spun his chair around and grabbed the box, forcefully looking inside. "It's not Fern's finger! It's not!" he cried out to the room. "This finger is short and fat. My wife has long, slender fingers and soft, smooth skin. It's not her!" He jumped up and hugged Patty. "You're a genius."

"I know," Patty smiled, a smile that quickly dissipated. "Nevertheless, whomever is holding Fern is serious about the ransom. They cut off some woman's finger, and recently, by the looks of it. They aren't playing games. We need the full $2 million, and we need to raid Regent Terrace now."

Matt turned to Meg. "How did this box get here?"

Meg blew her nose on a handkerchief and straightened her skirt. In a shaky voice, she said, "It was delivered just now by an Uber courier. The young man has been here before, so I didn't question him."

"Track him down," Stuart ordered. "And send this disgusting thing to forensics and have them pull the print and compare to our database." Meg went to work.

. . .

Jay's phone vibrated on the table — Matt. He grabbed it. "Did you find her?"

"Not yet," Matt said. "But things are moving here." He updated Jay, leaving out the finger in the box episode — no need to frighten him more than he already was. "I've got a name and some background on a possible — no, make that probable — suspect, and I want you and the gang to spread it around to our prison friends. See if anyone reacts. Are you there now?"

"Yes. We just spoke with Rick and Moira Reid, and with Ray Peng. No luck with the Reids, but Tamryn did a great job talking with Peng about a witness protection program for him and his family. He's scared shitless of Zhang Chen, but he was clearly intrigued by the idea. He's off thinking about it."

"Great. I'm going to be busy for a while. We're going to raid the address we have on our suspect, and then I'm meeting someone to pick up the remaining ransom money. In the meantime, I want you to jot this down and listen carefully to me. Got something to write on?"

"Yeah. And I'm putting you on speaker so Ed and Tam can hear, too. Go ahead."

"First, it's *extremely* important that Amanda Wilson and the guards do their job for a couple of hours until I tell you the coast is clear. And by that I mean they need to be absolutely certain that none of our prisoners make a phone call. Can you guarantee that?"

"Matt, it's Ed. I already had that conversation yesterday with both Amanda and the warden. They've swept for rogue cell phones and have put a moratorium on any convict using the public phones until I say otherwise. It's a secure lockdown, I believe."

"What about other visitors today?"

"No go. Same scenario. Nobody in until we say so. They've been very cooperative."

"Terrific. OK, here's what you need to do. Our suspect's name is Vadim Guz—g-u-z. He is a Russian-born businessman who has lived in Edinburgh for the past fourteen years. He has Scottish citizenship. Apparently wealthy based on his home address and recent car purchase. He has not been on Police Scotland's radar for any reason that we know of, and I just checked his name on the Newark to Edinburgh flight passenger manifesto that Fern and I flew over on, and there is no Vadim Guz listed. But it was him I saw, so he's obviously got other IDs.

We are running hard to learn everything we can about him, but we're not going to wait. We are proceeding with a raid on his known address. I think there's a chance that he and his female accomplice might be holding Fern there, and DCI MacLean is pulling together their tactical unit. We're going in after her."

"Oh, shit," Jay said. "Is Patty with you?"

"Affirmative. She and I will lead, along with Stuart and three of his best sharpshooters and hostage negotiators."

"But you still think there might be a local connection?" Jay asked.

"I do. I think Guz is an international hit man for hire—that's where his money comes from. And I think somebody in the Oregon State Penitentiary knew of him, and he was hired from there. It just doesn't make any sense that a Russian living here would go after Fern on his own. There's no reason or logic to it."

"What's your basis for thinking that he's a hit man?" Ed asked. "I'm not saying I disagree with you."

"Gut feeling, mostly. I don't have any hard evidence yet. But Stuart tells me there were two kidnappings in this same area of Edinburgh last year that remain unsolved."

"Well, we know for a fact that two men currently residing in this building hired a hitman to kill you once upon a time."

"Exactly," said Matt. "There is a precedent for Zhang Chen to resort to any means to get rid of people in his way. So, I want you to get busy, bring everybody back in and float that we know the name. If you get a reaction, call me immediately. If I'm not killing the bastard that took my wife, I'll answer. Otherwise, leave me a voicemail. Got it?"

"If you're sure," Jay said, somewhat tentatively. "But if this is your guy, who's the woman who took Fern from the airport?"

"No idea. I admit there are holes in this, Jay, but I'm bloody desperate."

"Oh, no, you're starting to talk like them."

• • •

Jay, Ed, and Tamryn brought Amanda into the conference room, and shared the news with her, explaining what their instructions from Scotland were. She confirmed that no prisoner had made a phone call in the past twenty-four hours, and that the moratorium was still firmly in place.

"You have to be absolutely positive that no inmate can make a phone call or send a text in the next two hours," Ed reiterated.

"I am positive," Amanda said. "We know how to do this. You guys have a lot to worry about, but this is one thing you don't need to think about. It's done on our end."

"OK," Ed said. "We're going to bring all of our friends back into this room, one at a time. And if you can arrange so they see each other coming and going, that would be perfect. We want them to know something new is up, and that we're talking to all of them again."

"I get it. What order do you want them in?" she asked. "And I really hope this means you have a lead in your case."

"We do." Ed looked at Jay and Tamryn. "What do you kids think? Chen first, and Dalrymple or Peng second?"

"Definitely Chen first," Jay answered. "But I'd keep him separated from Ray Peng until Ray's had more time to think about the protection offer. So, Dalrymple second, I think."

"Agreed," Tamryn said. "I haven't had the pleasure of meeting either of those two gentlemen; should I step out during this round?"

"No," Jay said. "Three against one is more intimidating, and your presence will throw them even more off base and, hopefully, rattle them."

"He's right," Ed said. "Although nothing rattles Chen, as you will see for yourself. Try to poke him if you get a chance, Tam. We haven't been able to get much of a rise out of him…like, ever."

Tamryn rubbed her hands together and gave a villain's sound effect.

"I think she's ready," Ed said drolly.

"I believe Mr. Chen is reading in his cell," Amanda said. "Shall I fetch him now?"

"Yes," Jay said. "He'll think we are here today to make him an offer, so I think he'll come willingly."

"Be right back," she said, and went out into the hallway to speak to the guard outside their door.

Chen appeared a few minutes later. He paused briefly at the conference room door when he saw Tamryn, but gathered himself, came in and took the only available chair around the table.

"Excuse me, but I'm not currently in the market for a wife," he said and smiled his unsettling smile at Tamryn.

She smiled back. "That's a good thing because I'm not currently looking for a husband. I shot my last one a few months ago and blew his head off. I rather like being single."

Chen laughed. "Ahh, yet another cop darkens my door."

"This is my new partner, Tamryn Gesicki," Jay said. "She has been updated on your sorry situation. We're helping out Lieutenant Sonders on the kidnapping of Fern Byrne, and we have a few more questions for you."

"I told the lieutenant that I would only talk again if there was some sort of quid pro quo. Is there?"

"I'm afraid we haven't quite worked that out yet," Ed said. "But we'll put something on the table soon. We have some new information and want to get your take on it this morning."

"Where is Detective Perkins?" Chen asked.

"Why do you care?" asked Ed.

Chen shrugged. "I just like to know where all the players are. Especially the ones who hate me."

"She's gone to Scotland to help Chief Horning with a new development."

"Oh? What kind of development?"

From Chen's other side, Tamryn suddenly said, "Do you know a man named Vadim Guz?"

A man of slow, purposeful movements usually, Chen whipped around and looked at her. Then, as if he realized his speedy reaction might draw a conclusion for them, he slowly squared up and, casually looking down, examined his fingernails. "I don't believe I do."

"Look at me, Zhang," Tamryn said, using his first name and leaning toward him. "I need you to look me in the eye and tell me you've never heard the name Vadim Guz."

Again, moving slowly, he turned to face her, his eyes like lasers locked on hers. "I've never heard the name Vadim Guz," he whispered. And then he laughed.

"What's so funny?" she asked.

"You are," Chen replied. "So dramatic. Rather cute, I must say."

"Starting to miss women, are you?" Ed said. "Not surprising. I sure would if I were in here. I'm also sure that Detective Gesicki can do a whole lot better than you. Let's go back to the topic of the day, shall we? Did you hire a hitman named Vadim Guz to kidnap Fern?"

"No. But it is possible that I've heard the name in recent days."

"First you've never heard the name, and now it's possible you have. Which is it, exactly?" Jay asked.

"It probably means that I've heard the name Vadim Guz in this facility previously." He leaned back in his chair, arms relaxing on the armrests, and made a steeple of his long, slender fingers.

"From whom did you hear it?" Ed asked.

Zhang Chen sat quietly, tapping his fingers together as if listening to a song. No one moved or said anything for a full minute.

Finally, Ed stood and motioned for Amanda. "Please bring in David Dalrymple, and escort Mr. Chen back to lockup." He stepped aside, holding the door open, an undecipherable look on his face. Chen shook his head with a wry smile on his thin lips and stood while Amanda placed cuffs on him for the journey back to nowheresville.

. . .

Once Chen was out of earshot, Ed said, "He's not bluffing. He clearly knows the name."

"The question is does he personally know it, or has he just heard the name about, as he indicated," Tamryn said.

"He reacted strongly," Jay said. "He personally hired him." Jay's fist came down hard on the table. "Can someone tell me how in the hell he arranged this from here, because I would really like to understand it. I have no idea how, but he did. I'd kill him with my bare hands if I wanted to spend the rest of my life in here. Which I don't," he added quickly.

"The important thing is that he recognized the name — it was a strong reaction from the cool customer," Ed said. "We need to tell Matt right away in case he's walking into something very nasty. Let's get Dalrymple in here, and make quick work of him, and then ring Matt."

As Ed finished speaking, Amanda was at the door with a red-faced David Dalrymple.

"Why were you talking to Zhang Chen again?" he demanded, coming through the door and waving his arm at them. "I understood I was going to have a chance to discreetly ask around. What the hell?"

"Bzzt! Time's up," said Ed.

"Well, I can't just hit the showers and go, 'Anyone know what's going on in Scotland?'," Dalrymple said. "It requires subtlety."

"Even in here?" Tamryn said. She stuck out her hand. "Detective Tamryn Gesicki. I'm new since you imploded."

Dalrymple looked at her like she was from another planet. "Port Stirling PD?", he finally eked out. No handshake occurred.

"Yes," she told him.

"Why does Horning keep hiring women?" he said to no one.

"Maybe because they are better at keeping our community safe than corrupt district attorneys?" Jay offered.

Dalrymple snorted. "Sure."

Tamryn, on a roll, quickly said, "Do you know a man named Vadim Guz?"

Dalrymple immediately paled, and his right hand, laying on the table, began to shake. He quickly moved it to his lap. As with Zhang Chen, there was no doubt that he'd heard the name before.

"I don't think so," he finally got out.

"Really?" asked Jay. "You seem upset all of a sudden. Why is that?"

"I don't know, it just seems like an odd question. You startled me."

"Let's see if we can startle you into telling us the truth," Jay said. "How's this sound? Your BFF Zhang Chen wants to get even once and for all with Matt and Fern. And add another $2 million to his fortune. You helped him out before finding a hit man, right? We all know that. Did you help him out again, David? Did you find Vadim Guz? Because if you did, we need to know it now. Like yesterday, now."

"How on earth would I contact, much less even know about, an international hit man? Yes, I made a call to Michael Winston. I've admitted that. But he was a friend of mine. This is obviously something very different going on here."

"How do you know he's an international hit man? We didn't mention that—only his name."

Dalrymple stared straight ahead, not making eye contact. It appeared that he was thinking.

"Well?" nudged Jay.

"I don't have anything to do with this, but Chen mentioned the name to me last month. I think he's your guy."

"You think?" Ed asked. "As in, you're not sure?"

"Zhang Chen definitely mentioned the name Vadim Guz to me last month. He must have hired him to kidnap Fern."

"Really?" asked Ed. "Is that what you want us to believe?"

"I'm telling you the truth," Dalrymple said simply. "And likely signing my death warrant."

CHAPTER 28

After securing the warrant to search the premises, the Police Scotland tactical unit approached the northeast end of Regent Terrace. Even though it was after 7:00 p.m, the sun had not yet set. The team debated whether to wait until nightfall, but the finger in the box delivery had sealed the deal for proceeding as soon as possible. The kidnappers had proved their point, and waiting was not an option.

Officers moved into position quickly: front, back, and at each end of the street. There were lights on at #15, and the decision had been made to use a battering ram on the front door. Scone and the entire Major Investigations Team were on standby in the next street over to rush in and maintain order in the nearby homes on the terraced street once the unit had breached #15. One of their constables had been sent to wait outside the door of the U.S. Consulate to explain what was going on.

Detective Patricia Perkins, positioned immediately behind the three men as they manned the metal battering ram—which they called 'the enforcer',—placed her hand on Matt's arm, standing next to her, gun drawn.

"Are you doing alright?" she whispered to him.

Matt nodded and pinched her cheek affectionately, silently mouthing 'Thank you' to his friend. The two colleagues had been together in this situation previously, but this felt different to them, both of whom were scared to death of what they might find behind this elegant, glossy black door.

On the raised arm sign from DCI MacLean, the three polis — two of them each holding a handle, and the third pushing from behind — violently swung the heavy object against the door. Wood flew, but the door held firm. Again, they rammed it home in an attempt to smash down the door. This time it worked. The door shattered, falling into smithereens on the porch and inside on a marble floor entry.

Dropping the battering ram, the three officers, guns drawn, yelled "Armed Polis!", stepped over the door frame and hurled themselves into the foyer lit only by the remaining daylight, followed by Matt, Patty, and Stuart. On pre-assigned tasks, Matt moved steadily ahead with one of the officers, Patty and a second officer peeled off to the right, and Stuart with the third batterer covered the room to the left.

In less than ten seconds, a light switched on down the hallway in front of Matt and his teammate. Matt stepped around a center hall table, now covered in pieces of the door, and swiftly pressed his back against a wall, gathering himself. He took a deep breath, swung his body around and took steady aim, holding his gun with two hands, poised and at the ready in front of his body.

Patty and the three Police Scotland teammates rushed out of their rooms when they saw the hall light come on. Stuart and Patty, almost simultaneously mouthed 'Clear' to Matt, referring to their assigned rooms at the front of the house.

Footsteps sounded about twenty feet down the hallway — more than one person, for sure, although no one was yet visible. They waited.

One man, dressed casually in slacks and a sweater, followed by another man in jeans and a tee shirt, came around the corner into the light. The first man was a dead ringer for the artist's sketch — Vadim Guz in person. When he saw his uninvited guests and his smashed-in front door, he motioned hastily to the second man to go back. Man #2 quickly disappeared around the corner, and Matt took off running after him, while his partner sharpshooter trained his gun on Guz, shouting "Stay where you are! Put your hands in the air!"

Guz did as he was told, while Matt ran by him in pursuit of Man #2, glancing at Guz just long enough to register '*Shetland Airport man.*'

Matt's sharpshooter, followed by the other four cops inside the house, advanced down the hallway, until they had Guz surrounded.

"Are you Vadim Guz?" DCI MacLean asked, confronting him directly.

"I am. May I talk now?" Guz said in a normal voice with the hint of a Scottish accent. Stuart nodded.

"What on earth are you doing in my home?" Guz said, indignation rising. "Who are you? What is this invasion?" His face was red and there was spittle coming out of his mouth.

"We are Police Scotland, and we have reason to believe you may be harboring a kidnap victim, a citizen of the United States," Stuart said. "Our tactical unit has authority to search the premises." He waved, and two of his colleagues plus Patty took off down the hallway after Matt. The third officer doubled back to the front door and hurriedly signaled to the outside teams, and then rejoined DCI MacLean—holding his gun steadily aimed at Guz's heart.

"All clear," the officer said at his side.

"Turn around and place your hands behind your back," Stuart said to Guz.

"This is outrageous," Guz shrieked.

"Turn around before I put a wee bullet in your chest," Stuart said coolly.

"I am a Scottish citizen and I've done nothing wrong. This is my home!" Guz shouted angrily as he turned his back to Stuart.

'Then you've nothing to hide; is that correct?" Stuart asked him as he roughly handcuffed him. Not waiting for Guz's answer, he instructed his colleague to hold him in the hallway while Stuart joined the others in the house search.

He moved quickly around the corner and found himself in a well-lit dining room where Matt had restrained Man #2 in a chair at the end of the large table. "Where are the others?" Stuart asked Matt.

"Searching the rest of the house. I waited for you," Matt answered. "This guy says there isn't anyone else currently in the house, but Patty and your crew are making sure. I thought you and I could have a chat with him." He kneed him with vigor in the side, and the man let out a yelp.

"Yes, let's talk," Stuart said, approaching the man, who didn't appear to be afraid of them.

"Name, please," Stuart said.

"You tell me yours first," the man responded.

Matt kneed him again in the same spot. And, after thinking about it for a split second, he slapped him across the face for good measure.

That appeared to get the man's attention.

"Nigel Armstrong," he gasped, trying to catch his breath. "Who the fuck are you?"

"He's your worst enemy," Stuart replied, pointing at Matt. "Me, I'm just here to find a woman we believe you kidnapped."

"I didn't kidnap any woman."

"So you say, Nigel. Why did you take off running then?"

"You beat the door down and came in with pistols pointing at us. What were we supposed to do?" He had calmed down and seemed to be less nervous than he should be.

Matt held his gun to Nigel's temple and roared, "Where is she? Where are you keeping her?"

Nigel cringed and said, "We don't have a woman. Honestly, I don't know what you're talking about."

Matt pressed his gun ever harder against his head. "Tell me now where she is, or I'll ruin your wallpaper."

"I can't tell you something I don't know! Please," begged Nigel.

"Easy there," Stuart said to Matt, making a 'calm down' gesture with his gun-free hand, and giving him a dose of jurisdictional stink eye. "My colleague is generally a good guy, but, you see, Nigel, he believes you're holding his wife. Chief Horning will be much calmer if you cooperate. Now, what is the name of the man who lives here? The man in the hallway now?" Stuart asked.

"Vadim Guz."

Matt glanced at Stuart with raised eyebrows, and Stuart nodded affirmatively.

"What's your relationship to him?"

"We're friends. He invited me to dinner tonight." The dining room table was set for three, but there was no food present. A crystal candelabra with three long tapers glowed in the center of the table, and light danced off the beautifully wood-paneled walls.

"Who is joining you for dinner?" Stuart asked. "The table has three place settings."

Nigel briefly closed his eyes before saying, "I don't know who else is coming. Vadim didn't tell me."

"Is it a man or a woman?" Matt asked, nudging Nigel with the gun again.

"I don't know! I thought it was just going to be the two of us, so I have no idea."

"Have you seen a woman in this house?"

Nigel's eyes flickered briefly. He shook his head. "No, I haven't."

Matt slapped him again, and Nigel's head jerked sideways. "Nigel, old buddy, you're not doing too well here," Matt said, leaning down to a few inches in front of his face where a nasty red welt was forming. "We need honest answers to our questions. If you lie again, I will kill you. Have you seen a woman in this house in the past two days? Yes or no?"

With a menacing look, Nigel said, "Yes."

"Who is she? Describe her," Stuart demanded.

"She's an American," Nigel spit out, making the last word sound distasteful. "Friend of Vadim's. Long black hair. Middle age."

"How tall is she?" Stuart asked.

"Average."

"As tall as me?" Matt asked, standing up straight.

"No, shorter by a lot."

"Why is she here?"

"I don't know."

Matt pressed the gun harder against his temple.

"I don't know!" Nigel bawled.

"Is she joining you for dinner?"

"I don't know. I told you; I don't know who else is coming. Vadim wanted to talk to me about something, he said. That's all I know. Swear to God."

"Have you been to the Shetland Islands recently?" Matt asked.

Nigel looked puzzled. "Not since I was a lad."

"Vadim Guz was there two weeks ago," Matt told him. "Do you know why he went there?"

"I didn't know he did, but it's been several weeks since I talked to him. He called me yesterday. Said he had a project."

"Do you often do projects for him?" Stuart asked.

"Sometimes," Nigel said.

"Do those projects involve picking up ransom money in exchange for a kidnapped victim?" Stuart again.

"No way! I'm a businessman."

Matt looked him over. "You don't look like a businessman. You're dressed like a thug."

"I'm a house painter. I own my own business. I assumed Vadim wanted something painted."

"Did you put a woman's finger in a box and deliver it to the Leith police station this afternoon?" Stuart asked.

"What? No! I don't know anything about that."

Patty and the other Police Scotland detectives came into the room, with an older man in handcuffs between them. Before Matt could ask, she shook her head and said, "Nothing. The house is clear, all four stories. I'm sorry. This man was cooking in the kitchen. We will want to talk to him."

"Did you look in the basement?" Matt asked.

"Yes, thoroughly. We prodded walls in every room in the house looking for any secret doors. Searched all the closets, and the attic. I looked for any sign of Fern, clothing, jewelry…she's not here, Matt. And we didn't find any drugs, capsules or needles, or anything that looked like it could be a nerve agent. Totally clean."

Defeated and exhausted, Matt sat down in one of the dining room chairs, his gun still carefully trained on Nigel.

"Vadim Guz is the man in the hallway, according to this jerk," Matt said. "He is also the man who has been following Fern and me around Shetland and the Highlands—I recognized him."

"And, we know he owns a British Racing Green Jaguar, which was very likely the car Graeme Thomson saw in the car park, and that he matches the description of the man Thomson saw talking to a woman," Stuart added. "A woman who Thomson says looks like the woman in the airport CCTV footage who left with Fern."

"It's got to be Guz," Matt said. "But where is Fern?"

CHAPTER 29

7:50 p.m.

On the ride back to the police station, Matt's phone rang—Jay. "Can you talk?" he asked his chief.

"Yeah, good timing," Matt said. "We just wrapped up at Guz's house and are taking them in for formal questioning. Fern wasn't there."

Heartbroken, Jay said, "I'm sorry. Are you and Patty OK?"

"Yeah. It's him, though, Jay—Guz. He was the man following us in Scotland. And we're ninety-nine percent sure he was seen with the woman who abducted Fern from the bathroom. Stuart and I are prepared to turn him inside out once we get to the station."

"We're sure it's Guz, too. His name got a reaction from both Chen and Dalrymple—we just finished up with them. That's why I'm calling you."

"No shit? Tell me."

"You know how frigid and unflappable Chen is, right? Well, Tamryn caught him by surprise when she asked if he knew Vadim Guz. His head whipped around so fast, I thought it was going to fly right off his body."

"He knew the name."

"Yep. And so did Dalrymple. He turned white as a sheet, and then said he'd heard the name inside the pen. Said it must have been Zhang Chen. And Chen told us he didn't know the name personally but had heard it inside recently."

"So, they're blaming it on each other?"

"Or, someone else inside. Dalrymple said it had to be Chen, but we think he's trying to leverage it into a deal for himself. But the point is Guz's name is not unknown in this building, and we'll keep the heat turned up."

"Has anyone talked to Michael Winston yet?" Matt asked.

"No, but Sylvia is working on it, and as soon as she confirms it's Stafford Creek, Ed and I are going up there. If he's there like we think, we'll fly to Olympia and get out to the corrections center as fast as we can. Tam is staying in Salem to sweeten the pot with Ray Peng, and to talk to Alex Bowen and the Reids again." Jay looked at his watch—almost noon. "Getting late there, what's your plan?"

"Unless we can break Vadim Guz, we're developing a plan for the ransom exchange. I'm expecting a call soon to pick up the remaining cash and I'll be ready for the kidnapper's call later, if it comes. Not sure what to expect with Guz in custody, but we'll be prepared for anything. If we do get a call, I'll have no choice but to follow their demands, and hope my love is still alive and I can grab her."

Jay didn't know what to say. "You haven't been able to talk to Fern yet?"

"No." Matt cleared his throat and said, "Tell Chen and Dalrymple that if they tell us where Guz is holding Fern in the next hour, we'll work with the authorities to free them. And, if not, they can rot in hell."

• • •

Sylvia Hofstetter, Port Stirling PD's admin assistant, had a nice conversation with Washington State's Stafford Creek Corrections Center (SCCC) police and law enforcement liaison, Bob Hahn. SCCC, home to almost 2,000 male inmates, was located in Aberdeen, a small city west of Olympia, Washington's capital city.

Sylvia remembered Aberdeen as a mostly homely city but located in a beautiful part of the world near the Pacific Ocean. It had the unfortunate nickname of the 'Hellhole of the Pacific', due to its early 1900s reputation as welcoming all manner of dubious pursuits—brothels, gambling, saloons, and a vigorous murder rate. *Perfect place for a guy like Michael Winston*, she thought.

The heart and soul of the police department, Sylvia had uncovered the crucial piece of evidence in a recent case because of her dogged research that led to a childhood yearbook photo of Winston and his best friend. The shocking discovery put the case's final piece of the puzzle in place and resulted in four arrests.

Left depressed and alone now in the department's silent room in their ground floor corner of Port Stirling's city hall, Sylvia, her tears wiped away and her determination to help resurfacing, had tracked down Winston's place of incarceration. All the detectives were out in a frantic search for clues in Fern's kidnapping, and she needed to do her part.

More than just a job — which the lively seventy-something woman didn't really need — Sylvia had become close to her boss, Chief Horning, and exceptionally fond of Fern. She loved her two sons and was lucky to have them live nearby with her adored grandchildren, but she also cherished the relationships she had built with Matt and Fern, and, really, all of the people she worked with at city hall. They were a team; a team that kept their small town running smoothly.

She had hardly eaten since the news came from Scotland, and she badly wanted to stay in bed today and read a book to take her mind off what Fern must be going through, if she was even still alive. But that was not who Sylvia was, and she had risen, showered, eaten a piece of toast, and dressed in a nice camel skirt, matching camel crew-neck sweater, topped with an ivory, camel, and black silk scarf, tied artfully around her wrinkled neck. She was not up for — and it didn't feel appropriate under the circumstances — her customary rich colors of purple, red, and bright blue, but she would not look sloppy in city hall no matter what was going on in her world.

"Mr. Hahn, thank you for taking my call. We are working on a kidnapping case down in Port Stirling, and it's one of our own, so I'm doing what I can to help out, but I'm just the assistant to Chief Matt Horning."

Bob Hahn laughed. "My assistant, Joyce, is responsible for every success

I've had in this job. You don't need to explain to me. How can I help you, Sylvia?"

"Thank you. My department was instrumental in arresting a man named Michael Winston last year. I've checked with the Multnomah County courts in Portland, where he was tried and convicted, to follow where he'd been incarcerated. That led me to your facility. Do you know of him?"

"Yeah, Winston is here," he muttered, sounding disgusted. "We don't have a death row, but if we did, he'd be my choice for inmate number one. He's a bad dude."

"Yes, that's what I understand about him."

"How is he connected to your current case?"

"I'm not sure that he is, but the State Department employee who found and arrested him is the kidnapped woman we're searching for. She is also Chief Horning's wife. Winston tried to kill Matt Horning last year."

"You think he might have had her kidnapped somehow? Revenge?"

"We're talking to everyone in their past who might have a reason to do this hideous thing. Is it possible for my officers to come and interrogate him?"

"You betcha. I will personally see to it. When shall I set it up, and who will be visiting on your behalf?"

"It will be Oregon State Police Lieutenant Ed Sonders, and PSPD Detective Jay Finley. They were heavily involved in Winston's case. The two are currently in Salem at our state penitentiary, and Google Maps says it's about a four-hour drive. I will check with them now and see if they can make it this afternoon, or if it will be tomorrow. I'll call you back as soon as I can connect with them, OK?"

"Sounds like a plan, Sylvia."

"I wish I could come and talk to him myself, but I don't like to drive that far these days. And, I wouldn't know what to ask him anyway."

"Trust me, you don't want to be in the same room as Winston. I can't imagine how he could have pulled off something like this from our corrections center, but if anyone could, it would be a scumbag like him."

• • •

Vadim Guz's elderly cook knew nothing, other than three people were expected for dinner, and that he had not seen a woman matching Fern's description in the house. He had prepared roast beef with Yorkshire pudding, but now turned off his oven when Patty informed him that he would be detained for questioning at the police station.

All three of the men at the Vadim Guz residence were placed in holding cells for questioning at the police station. At Matt's request, Meg escorted Vadim Guz first into an interrogation room with a one-way mirror.

DCI MacLean told Matt, "I think it would work best if Patty and I interrogated Guz while you watch from the mirror room. As Vadim Guz is a Scottish citizen, I must conduct his interview. Does that work for you?"

"No," Matt answered brusquely. "It does not. You take the lead, but I will jump in when necessary, and I want Patty in the booth. I know I have no official jurisdiction here, and I understand it's asking a lot of you, but I've conducted hundreds of these interrogations, too. I trust you, and obviously I need you in the room with me in case he gives us a location or refers to local people and places, but I need to be in there. It's my wife, Stuart. OK with you?"

Stuart stared at him, sighed, and finally shrugged. "Your call on this one thing. But no violence, got it? It's not how we do things here. You need to understand that this is my case and my reputation on the line. I'm way out on a limb with you, Matt, and I prefer to not come crashing to the ground."

"I will behave like a perfect Scottish constable. You have my word."

"Alright then. And if he gives us the location where Fern is being held, then we'll kill him together," Stuart said.

Matt's eyes widened as he locked them on Stuart's.

"Joke, cowboy — a bad joke."

"I'm hoping a small part of you meant it. I'll go find Patty."

"She's right outside the door," Stuart said, opening it. Sure enough.

Patty took hold of Matt's arm and said, "Let's go. I'll man the booth while you two make mincemeat out of this Russian clown."

"How do you know we want you in the booth?" Stuart asked her.

"I know my guy," and she gave Matt's arm a gentle, loving squeeze.

Vadim Guz looked uncomfortable in the chair at the square table in interrogation room 1. It was hot in the room — on purpose — and he appeared to be sweating slightly. While the three cops watched him from the booth, purposefully keeping him waiting, Guz wiped sweat from above his lips a couple of times. He drummed his fingers on the arms of the chair, and shuffled it first closer to the table, and then moved it back.

"He's ready," growled Matt, and he and Stuart made their way to the room next door.

"We meet again," said Matt, pulling out a chair. Stuart sat next to him, both across the metal table from Guz.

Guz thought he had recognized Matt when he ran by him in his home, but he feigned surprise now at seeing him. "Shetland Islands airport, right? We chatted briefly." His voice was gravelly, and matched his Slavic looks.

"Yes," Matt said. "And you were on the same plane with us from the U.S. to Edinburgh." He paused. "And I saw you outside our Inverness hotel window. Sitting on a bench, apparently minding your own business. Sloppy." Again, Matt paused as though he was trying to collect his thoughts. But he really paused just for effect; he wanted his knowledge of Guz to sink in slowly prior to DCI MacLean's official interrogation.

"I've never been to Inverness — you must be mistaken. I did have recent business in New York." Guz clasped his hands and rested them on the table.

"Shall we begin at the beginning, Mr. Guz?" Stuart said. "I am Detective Chief Inspector Stuart MacLean, and I'm overseeing the Police Scotland investigation of a kidnapped American woman named Fern Byrne. My colleague is Matt Horning, and he is both a chief of police in Oregon in the U.S., and the husband of the victim. At my discretion and because of Chief Horning's professional status, he is allowed to participate in this interrogation. This interview is being recorded, and I must caution that this is not only a witness interview, but a suspect interview as well. Therefore, you've been read your rights as a potential suspect to a serious crime. Do you understand them and what I've just told you?"

"Yes. Whatever you say, DCI. Please proceed so I can return home."

"Thank you." Stuart looked down at his notes. "Are you the owner of a British Racing Green 2024 Jaguar coupe F-Type automobile?"

"Yes."

"Did you purchase it recently at the east Edinburgh dealership, and did a salesman named Martin Skene assist you?"

"Yes. Fat guy, short hair, right?"

Stuart nodded. Matt figured he didn't want to be heard on the tape agreeing with 'fat' as a descriptor. *Smart copper.*

"Did you drive that vehicle to the Holyrood car park yesterday late afternoon?"

Guz sat quietly, looking down at his hands, not immediately answering.

"Did you?" Stuart asked him again.

"I may have."

"Excuse me, but it's a 'yes' or 'no' question," Stuart said firmly. "Did you drive your Jaguar to Holyrood car park yesterday?"

"Yes."

"And did you meet a woman there and talk with her?"

"How can you possibly know this?" Guz asked, with a stricken look on his face.

"Is that a 'yes'?" Matt interrupted.

"Yes."

"Please tell us the name of that woman," Stuart said.

"I can't do that."

"You don't know her name?"

"I know her name, but I can't divulge it."

"Why not?"

Guz looked pained. "Because we don't want her husband to find out that we've been meeting. Why do you even care? I don't understand where this is going."

"Just so I get this straight for the record," said Stuart, "you did meet a woman yesterday at Holyrood and you know her, but you won't tell us her name. Is that a correct assessment?"

"Yes."

"And this is a clandestine relationship?"

"If by that you mean it's a secret relationship, yes, that's correct."

"What nationality is this secret woman?" Matt asked.

Guz thought for a moment. "Scottish, of course."

"Not American?" Matt persisted.

"No."

"Or Russian?"

"No."

"You were born in Russia," Stuart noted. "Do you still have family and contacts there?"

"I am estranged from my family. For many years. Scotland is my home."

"What was the nameless woman wearing when you met her yesterday?" Matt asked urgently, leaning forward.

"I'm not sure." Guz rubbed his jaw as if thinking hard. Matt thought, *You're stalling, you bastard.*

"Guess," he demanded.

"Well, I suppose she was wearing a dress. She usually does so."

"Not trousers and a jumper?" Stuart contradicted.

"Perhaps," Guz said. "I'm not sure."

"What color dress?" Matt asked.

"I don't remember. Maybe sort of a blue look. I'm not sure. Why is this important?"

"What color is her hair?" Matt ignored Guz's question and kept the pressure on. "And what style?"

"Brown, and short. Cropped, like. Modern."

"How old is she?"

"Younger than me," Guz smiled.

"Please be more specific," Stuart said. "For the record."

"She is thirty-six, I believe."

Matt and Stuart exchanged a glance. *He's deliberately describing a different woman than our witness saw,* Matt thought, and he could tell Stuart agreed with him.

"What kind of car was she driving?" Matt moved on.

"A white one."

"Model?"

"I'm not sure. I don't really know much about automobiles."

"You know enough to buy one of the top performance cars made," Matt prodded him.

"Well, I know what I like; that's about all."

"Do you own any other vehicles, Mr. Guz?" Matt asked. "We can easily check the records, of course."

That got the first reaction. Guz paled. It was a slight loss of color, but it was there. And his left eye twitched a small degree.

"I also have a Range Rover."

"What color is it?"

"Black."

"Is that it? Any other vehicles?"

"I have a people mover, but I rarely drive it. It's just for getting away."

"Ahh, I see. And what color is your people mover, Mr. Guz?"

He swallowed. "White."

Matt made a fist with his hand under the table in an attempt to control himself. "Where is this vehicle currently?"

"I've loaned it to a friend. I believe he and his wife were going up north for a week's tour."

You are lying, you son-of-a-bitch, Matt thought, but said out loud, "You're sure you didn't loan it to your girlfriend? So she could move people in a people mover?"

"Quite sure."

"I don't believe you," Matt said. He was growing agitated, even though he knew it was not the right approach.

"I've told the truth. That would be your problem if you choose not to believe me."

Stuart, sensing a loss of control, stepped in. "We will need the name and contact information for your friend who borrowed your vehicle."

"Of course," Guz said. "His name is Max Popov, and I have his number on my phone." He pointed to his jacket pocket. "May I?"

"It sounds like a Russian name," Stuart said, looking up from his notebook. "Is his full name Maksim Popov?"

"Yes, I suppose it is. But he goes by Max. I have his number here."

"I'll get it," Matt said to Stuart, stood, and reached into Guz's jacket, yanking out his phone.

Guz twisted away from Matt. "You're not allowed to take my phone!" he screeched. "Stop him, DCI!"

"I'm afraid he's correct, Matt. Please put Mr. Guz's phone on the table in front of him, so he can retrieve Mr. Popov's number for us."

Matt quickly scrolled through Guz's recent calls, searching for an Oregon area code — either 503 or 541. Nothing. The only U.S. recognizable area codes were 408 and 212, which he thought were the San Jose area and Manhattan.

When he was satisfied Guz had not made or received any phone calls from Oregon, he roughly placed the phone on the table close to Stuart. "You need to get a warrant for this phone."

While Stuart made a notation, Guz reached across the table for his phone. Matt grabbed his arm, and shouted angrily, "Where is she, Guz? Where are you hiding my wife?"

Guz grimaced in pain. "I truly do not know what you're talking about! Let go of me!"

CHAPTER 30

Stuart jumped out of his chair and restrained the two adversaries, glaring at Matt. "Chief Horning, if you can't control your emotions, I will have to insist that you leave the room while I continue to interview Mr. Guz."

Matt nodded at Stuart, quietly released Guz's arm, and leaned back in his chair. He waited a beat for the temperature in the room to lower, and for Guz to retrieve Max Popov's number from his phone to give to Stuart. While Stuart jotted the number in his notebook, Matt asked, "What is it you do for a living, Mr. Guz?"

"I'm a businessman."

"What kind of business?"

"I broker oil and gas leases."

"So, like, between Russian assets and the western world?" Matt asked.

"I also represent the Saudi and Kuwait governments."

"I see. Sounds lucrative. Is that why you were recently in the United States?"

"Yes. It was a business-related trip."

"Why did you go straight to the Shetland Islands after the flight from Newark instead of staying home in Edinburgh? You know, where I spotted you following us again?"

"I didn't follow you, Matt," Guz answered. "I find the U.S.A. an exhausting place, and I enjoy the lack of bustle and the serenity of Shetland. I go there often."

"It's Chief Horning to you," Matt grumbled. "So, it was just a coincidence that you were on our same flight to Edinburgh, and then we were on the same flight from Shetland back to Edinburgh. Is that what you want us to believe?"

"Coincidences happen on occasion. This was obviously one of them."

"Why did you tell me your *wife* flew back to the U.S. from Shetland?"

"Because it was easier than explaining about my girlfriend," he replied coolly.

"It seems to me," Stuart interrupted, "that there are many coincidences in your story that you want us to believe. I'm having trouble with that, Mr. Guz. The fact that Chief Horning spotted you in three different locations," he ticked off on his fingers, "and the fact that you own a white people mover, and our witness saw you talking to a woman who appeared to be driving the same vehicle soon after Mrs. Horning was abducted."

"Add to that," Matt said, "that you lied to me in Shetland," he ticked off his fingers to match Stuart, "and that I know for a fact it was you I saw in Inverness and you are lying about that as well, and that your description of your 'girlfriend' and what she was wearing are in direct opposition to what our very credible witness told us. I believe our witness."

"I believe our witness, too," Stuart said. "I will contact your friend, Max Popov about his use of your white vehicle, and then I'm terribly afraid we will have to know the name of your girlfriend. She is germane to your alibi, sir." DCI MacLean stared hard at Guz.

Vadim Guz sat motionless. His hands were clasped in his lap, and he gazed up at the mirror behind the cops. "Either arrest me or let me go. I'm finished with this interview," he said to both.

"It doesn't work that way," Stuart said. "You can refuse to answer our questions if that approach suits you, but we will keep asking them until we're satisfied. After that, we still have to interview your guest and your cook who were in the house with you. Then, and only then, if we cannae get the evidence we need to hold you, will you be released. You should settle in for a long night if you believe you are finished."

"I refuse to name my female friend," Guz stubbornly responded. "Ask your other questions."

"Why did you motion for Nigel to run?" Matt asked, changing direction.

"He was my guest. I didn't want him involved in whatever was going on."

"Is he a friend, business acquaintance, or does he do the dirty work for you? Like keeping my wife company in some hellhole so you can keep your hands clean?"

"I don't have any 'dirty work'. I'm a respectable, wealthy businessman."

"I think your wealth comes from your real business," Matt said. "International hit man for hire. Does that sound about right?"

"What sounds right is that you are a complete lunatic," Guz said, giving Matt the evil eye.

"Maybe. But I'm going out on a limb here and say that I think your man Nigel will finger you for the kidnapping and save himself. What do you think, DCI MacLean?"

Stuart nodded in agreement. "A very real possibility."

Guz shifted in his chair. "Impossible. Next question."

"Have you ever used a nerve agent on another human being?" Matt asked.

"Did you find any in my home?" Sarcastic.

"Guessing you're not stupid enough to store it in your residence," Stuart said. "Please answer Chief Horning's question."

"No. I have never injected a human being with a nerve agent."

"We didn't mention an injection," Matt jumped on him.

"Well, I can read like anyone else. I understand that Russians have used them on their enemies, and I would imagine injection is one of the delivery methods. That certainly doesn't mean I've ever done it, just because I happened to be born in Russia. I resent the implication. It's rather racist, don't you think? Although, probably not surprising since you are from Texas."

"How do you know I'm from Texas?" Matt huffed. "Did Fern tell you when she woke up from the nerve agent? Did she wake up, Guz? Tell me!" he demanded.

"You have an unmistakable Texas twang, Chief," Guz said, ignoring Matt's mention of Fern. "I deal with Texans frequently in my line of business, and your accent is impossible to miss."

"Did you cut off a woman's finger and have it delivered to the police station?"

"How dreadful. Of course not."

"You don't seem as shocked by that question as I would be under the circumstances," Matt said.

"I am trying to deliberately remain calm so that we can keep this interrogation moving along. Plus, I suppose that you in the police see all sorts of dreadful things in your chosen profession. It is obviously a shocking thing to have happen, but I didn't do it. I abhor the sight of blood."

"Do you have any phone voice scrambling technology in your home?" asked Matt.

"I don't even know what that is, so, no."

"It's a device that allows you to talk on a telephone without the other party recognizing your voice."

"Why would I ever use that?" Guz asked.

"So the police can't identify you in the act of committing a crime."

"I haven't committed a crime."

Changing direction, Matt asked, "Do you know a man named Zhang Chen?"

"No," Guz answered quickly.

"California entrepreneur of Chinese descent?" Matt tried again. "Rich like you, but currently in prison for trying to kill me last year?"

"No."

"Do you know a man named Rohn Reid?"

"I know who he is, but I don't know him personally."

"What do you know about him?"

"He's a technology genius. U.S. billionaire."

"Where does he live?"

"I don't know. Maybe Seattle? He was recently in the news involving some scandal."

"Did either one of these men arrange for you to kidnap my wife and hold her for ransom?"

Vadim Guz closed his eyes, sighed, and shook his head, as if he couldn't believe the conversation was back to that.

DCI MacLean said, "Were you in Edinburgh at Christmas-time last year?"

Guz tugged on his ear and looked at the mirror again. "I recall that I travelled to the south of France about that time."

"By air or train?" Stuart followed-up. "And, please know that we will check with the airport and ScotRail."

"Honestly, I don't remember where I was in December."

"You don't remember where you spent Christmas?" Matt asked incredulously. "Everyone knows where they spent last Christmas."

"I went to the south of France at some point; I just don't remember exactly when."

"Do you recall if you released a drugged and disoriented female member of Parliament in Waverly Station last Christmas? A woman you held hostage for ransom?" Stuart asked directly.

"I would remember that, and my answer is I did not."

"Do you recall if you released a beaten and drugged male member of Parliament last year on Guy Fawkes Day?"

"I did not."

"Have you ever climbed to Arthur's Seat?" Stuart persisted.

"Yes. Everyone has, haven't they?"

"Did you climb it last year on November 5?"

"No."

Matt jumped in. "You remember what you did on November 5 last year, but you don't recall what you did on Christmas? I find that hard to believe."

"You wouldn't understand this being an American, but Guy Fawkes Day is a big day in the U.K. I usually celebrate it in Queensferry at a big bonfire."

"Is that where you were last November 5?" Stuart asked.

"I expect so. At some point in the evening."

Stuart stood and said, "Excuse us for a moment, Mr. Guz, I need a word with my colleague."

Matt followed his lead, and they left the room, and Guz sitting there alone. Stuart closed the door firmly behind him and said, "Let's check-in with Detective Perkins in the booth."

Patty stood to greet them, and Matt reached out to her. "We're not getting anywhere, are we?"

Patty, desolate, shook her head, while Stuart said, "We are not. He will not break, Matt. And he strikes me as a pro who has been down this road previously. He says as little as possible, and he knows his rights. We need to talk to Nigel and the cook, and if they don't give us anything, we will have to let Guz go home."

Alarmed, Matt said, "You can't do that, Stuart. We'll have to go through with the ransom exchange, and he will kill Fern. I know he's involved."

"I fear he is, too, but we follow the rule of law here, and I must have evidence before I can detain him indefinitely."

"Guz knows that! He's stalling."

Patty said, "He is involved, and Stuart's correct — Guz is a pro. He's relatively undisturbed by being brought in for questioning, and he knows better than to elaborate on his answers. The less said, the better, and he gets that. It will be interesting to see the longer you can keep him in that room, if he'll start getting more agitated as we near the kidnapper's ransom deadline. Could you tell if the scrambled voice on the phone is his?"

"No," Matt said. "I even listened to him a couple of times with my eyes closed to try to detect any patterns in his speech, but I got no hits."

"The same with me," added Stuart. "The voice scrambling software is sophisticated. Hearing him in person didn't help me. And, we don't know for sure if it was even Guz talking on the phone; it may have been the woman."

Matt looked at his watch — 8:10 p.m. "I have an idea," he said. "My source for the rest of the ransom cash is going to call me soon with what time I'm to meet them. Let's keep Guz answering questions until my phone rings, and I'll take the call in the room with him. I'll indicate I have to leave to pick up the cash, and let's see how he reacts."

"I like it," Patty said. "The thought of $2 million in his hands slipping away if he can't get out of that room might make him twitchy."

"I like it, too," Stuart said. "As long as it doesn't jeopardize your pickup with the other person on the line. It's getting down to the wire here, and that full $2 million is your best chance at getting your wife back."

"It won't. My contact is solid and will know what I'm doing."

"Ok, I will use the restroom and take my time," Stuart said. "Wait for me before you go back in the room."

"I will, but I won't lose my cool again. I'm sorry."

Stuart patted Matt on the back. "Understandable, my friend."

"I might've decked him," Patty said.

・・・

Back in the interrogation room, Stuart questioned Guz on all sorts of things; his business dealings, Edinburgh knowledge, his travel particulars, and his personal life. Guz remained unflustered and answered simply without any elaboration. Matt knew his answers were rehearsed, and Guz had them down pat.

Matt felt his phone buzz in his pocket, he picked it up, and said to the room in general, "Excuse me for a minute."

It was Joe Phelps calling at 8:28 p.m. "It's on," Joe said. "Head to Waverly Station now. Her train will be there soon, and she's carrying the cash. Go to platform 6."

"Thank you so much," Matt said into his phone. "I'm at the police station now but will leave immediately. You've got the full $2 million, right?" He pretended to ignore Guz, concentrating on the phone call.

Joe, puzzled for a moment about the wrong amount, recovered quickly and said, "You can't talk right now, can you? I get it. Good luck, Matt. Please keep me updated as you can. May an angel sit on your shoulder tonight."

Matt fought back the hot tears building, and abruptly stood up. "I have to go," he said to Stuart, once again ignoring Vadim Guz. He glanced briefly at the mirror; a look that he hoped said to Patty, "I'm going now. I'm OK."

Outside on the police station steps, the evening was chilly, although there was still some daylight. He zipped his jacket, stuck his hands in his pockets, and turned left at the intersection on Constitution St. He walked briskly, eager to get out of view of the upper levels of the police station. Passing the cemetery on his right, he jogged until he reached Newkirkgate Shopping Centre, where he caught a cab for the remaining two miles to Waverly.

Once inside the vast train station, he found platform 6 and started walking down it alongside the long train. Almost immediately, he saw her, wearing the only purple jacket in a sea of black. She was carrying a suitcase that had seen better days.

Matt hurried to her side and took the suitcase from her hand. She exclaimed, "Darling! Thank you so much for being here." She kissed him on the cheek and took his arm as they turned toward the exits.

"Follow my lead," she whispered. "Are we going straight home or out to dinner?" she said, louder.

"Are you hungry?" Matt played along.

"Famished. Let's go to that French Brasserie just up the street and have a bite before we go home. Does that work for you?"

"Sounds good. Let's go."

She gently pulled on his arm, leading him in the direction she wanted to go. They went up the escalators and emerged onto the street. She hailed a waiting cab down the street, and it quickly pulled around the others and up to the curb directly in front of them.

Matt held the door open for her, placed the suitcase in after she was seated, and jumped in. "Harry, please take us to the brasserie, the long route," she said.

"Yes, ma'am." He checked the rearview mirror and eased out into traffic. After several sharp turns and one-way, narrow streets, they arrived in front of a restaurant about five minutes later.

"All clear, ma'am," Harry said.

"We'll be about thirty minutes," she said to the driver. He saluted her, and said, "Right."

"Out we go," she said to Matt.

He grabbed the suitcase and helped her out of the cab. A heavy fabric curtain hung just inside the restaurant's door. She parted it and they stepped into a warm, inviting room with small tables lined up in two rows in front of them, and a few red leather banquettes along the back wall. A black and white checkered floor, and a tin-covered bar added to the French ambience.

A man in white shirt, black vest, and black bow tie approached them with a hearty "Bon Soir, a table for two?"

"Yes, please," she said. "Might we have that booth in the back?" She pointed to an empty banquette.

"But of course, madam." He grabbed two menus from the small stand, and with a smile said, "This way, please."

Once settled in the private, comfy booth, she said, "I'm so sorry for your ordeal Chief Horning. Joe has filled me in, and it's an alarming story."

She looked identical to Joe's description, down to the pageboy that swung when she moved her head, and elegant purple and white silk scarf, tied jauntily in the French fashion. "Thank you," he said. "This is above and beyond for a stranger, and I promise you I will pay it back…and never forget your personal effort on our behalf."

She shrugged. "It's my job. And I'm happy to help out Joe. We've been friends for a long time, and he's done the same for me more than once. He's very fond of your Fern."

"They've been a good team since she went to work for the State Department. I know he's upset, too."

She put her hand over his on the table. "You will get her back. Ninety percent of the cases like this, they only want the money."

"I hope we're not in the ten percent that have other motives," Matt told her. "There could be a revenge factor at play here. Guess I'll know soon." He looked around the room. "What's the plan?"

"We will order some coffee and french fries, and then Harry will come back and pick us up once he determines that no one followed us here. We'll drop you on a small street behind the police station, and I will be taken to a safe house we use in Edinburgh on occasion. Here's my private cell number"—she scribbled on a page in her small notebook, tore it out and handed it to him—"and you are to call me if you need my help in any way, at any time. We have resources here. Do you understand?"

"Yes." Matt looked down at the white butcher-paper table covering. "Joe tells me that you've encountered nerve agents in your work."

"I have, and I won't pull any punches; it's nasty stuff. Your wife showed signs of it during her abduction, didn't she?"

"That's what they tell me. I haven't seen it in my personal experience." He hesitated. "Is it always fatal? Please tell me the truth," he pleaded.

"Not always. In several cases I've been involved in in London, the victims survived. One of them only spent one day in the hospital before he was released, although that's almost a miracle result. It depends on how strong the formula is, and whether the person who administers it wants to kill the victim or just incapacitate them. But people do recover from it, and you should hold out hope. I wouldn't tell you that if I didn't know it to be true."

Matt brightened. "Thank you again, Ms. Perry."

"Lisa, please. I've just given you over one-half million dollars. I think we're on a first-name basis for the rest of our lives," she smiled. "If I don't hear from you by tomorrow at 9:00 p.m., I will take a train back to London. But if things go awry tonight or tomorrow, you are to call me."

"Got it."

The waiter appeared, and Matt ordered two coffees and frites.

CHAPTER 31

Jay parked the rental car in the visitor's lot at the Stafford Creek Corrections Center outside Aberdeen, Washington. He and Ed had flown to Olympia and rented the car for the hour-long drive.

"Why are prisons always in the middle of frickin' nowhere?" he whined to Ed.

"Is that a hypothetical question that I don't really need to answer?" Ed replied.

"Yes."

"Anything else you want to whine about before we go in?"

Jay turned to face him. "We're going to be too late to help Matt find Fern, aren't we? What if they kill her, Ed? What will we do, how will Matt ever recover?"

"Do you remember when Matt was bleeding to death on his deck?"

"Of course."

"We both thought we'd lost him, but he turned out to be a tough SOB, didn't he? Whatever the outcome, our buddy will survive. It will be a long, hard road for Matt if Fern is already dead, but we will help him every step of the way, won't we?"

"You think Fern is dead?" Jay said with fear written all over his young face.

Ed paused, twisting his wedding ring around his finger. "I think there is a very real possibility that her kidnappers killed her with the nerve agent. We need to be prepared for that result."

Jay shook his head. "No, no. I can't accept that."

"Then let's get out of this supremely uncomfortable car and go talk to a man who may be involved in this nightmare."

• • •

Michael Winston entered the room with his hands cuffed in front of him and attached to a security chain around his waist. He still walked with a limp from the gunshot wound to his leg he received from a Portland Police officer last year at OHSU. It could have been worse; Fern had his head in her gunsight, but opted to not kill him, calling for backup to arrest him instead.

Although, looking at him now through the plexiglass protecting them from the hardened killer, Jay and Ed thought maybe Fern should have done him a favor. His blond good looks and fit physique were all but gone, replaced by sallow skin, thinning hair, and loss of muscle tone.

Ed spoke first. "Mr. Winston, we need a moment of your time."

Winston glared at Ed. "What do you fuckers want?"

"Still a pleasant disposition, I see. We have some questions for you regarding a current case. I'll start with an easy yes or no one. Did you hire someone to kidnap Fern Byrne at the Edinburgh Airport in Scotland?"

Winston threw his head back and laughed, a mean laugh. "That bitch who ruined my life? No, I didn't, but I hope whoever did kills her."

Trying to remain calm and giving Jay a hand sign over the table to do the same, Ed asked, "Have you talked to any inmate at the Oregon State Penitentiary since you've been here?"

Winston fingered the neckline of his V-neck dark blue prison tee shirt. "No."

"You're sure about that?" Jay asked. "Haven't talked to your old friend David Dalrymple?"

"I may have talked to him once or twice," Winston waffled. "We grew up together, as you know. I let him hang out with me. I was always the cool one, Davey was the nerd." He laughed again.

"When was the last time you spoke with *Davey*?" Jay asked, teeth clenched.

Winston sat back in his chair, as far as the security chain would allow, evaluating Jay. "Why don't you tell me exactly why you want to know, and I'll decide if your questions are worth answering."

"Pay attention, Winston, we already told you," Ed said. "Fern Byrne has been kidnapped in Scotland and we believe that event is likely connected to her work on the west coast. And that someone who has a reason to hate her — such as, scum like you — is involved or knows something that might help us save her life."

Winston sat staring at them, pondering what Ed had said. "Look, Lieutenant, you and I both know that I'm likely never getting out of here. So, there is no motivation for me to help the cops who put me here, now is there?"

"We might be able to make your life a little easier," Jay hurriedly said, feeling this interview was slipping away.

"Chocolates on my pillow, perhaps?" Winston stood up to leave but turned around for one last shot. "I will tell you one thing. You're off-base about Dalrymple; he doesn't have the balls to pull off a kidnapping. You should be talking to his employer."

"And who is that?" Jay asked.

"Zhang Chen, you dope."

. . .

After that short, but not sweet trip to Stafford Creek, Jay and Ed made their arduous way back to Salem.

"I'm sick of prisons," Jay said, going up the steps at OSP.

"Yes, you've made that abundantly clear," said Ed. "The good news is that if Tamryn hasn't made any progress with Ray Peng, we might as well go home. The bad news is — and it's very, very bad — we've failed to help Matt."

Accompanied by Amanda, the two cops were met by Tamryn in the visitor lobby. "Guess what?" she gleefully approached them. "Ray Peng wants to talk to me again, with Jay, too."

"What about me?" Ed said. "I'm not chicken feed."

Amanda spoke up. "I think he's afraid of you, Ed. Just a size thing." She smirked.

"Just because I'm slim doesn't mean I'm not dangerous," Jay said defensively.

"Stow it, partner," Tamryn elbowed him in the ribs. "We all know you're tough as nails. Let's go. Ed, wait for us, OK?"

"Wouldn't miss this shitshow for the world," Ed said, plopping down in a plastic chair.

• • •

Matt's body ached for a run or some sort of exercise. He stretched his neck from side to side and rolled his shoulders in an attempt to release some stress and kinks.

A dank fog had rolled in from the Firth of Forth or the North Sea, or wherever in the hell it came from in these parts. It didn't seem to understand that it was May now, and well into spring, and it chilled Matt's already cold bones even deeper.

Lisa Perry and her driver, convinced no one had followed them from Waverly or the brasserie, dropped off Matt and the suitcase behind the police station. The driver turned right off Mitchell St. and pulled the car to the curb. Lisa instructed Matt to follow the narrow road to the corner, take a right turn, and then a left. Walk straight ahead to the back entrance of the station. He did as instructed, calling Stuart while he walked with the case, telling him to meet him at the back door.

Stuart was holding open the door when Matt came around the second corner. He motioned for Matt to hurry inside, and Matt jogged the last ten yards.

"I hope that case is full of dollars," Stuart said, closing the door behind Matt.

"It is, and I have a new best friend."

"While you were gone, the analysis of the fingerprint on the, ahem, finger came back, and it's not in our database or yours. I forwarded it to Joe Phelps, and he told me they've got no record of the print either."

"So, just some poor woman off the streets?"

"We don't know, and we may never know. Also, I talked to Vadim Guz's friend Max Popov; remember, the friend who he said borrowed his white van to take a trip north?"

"Yeah, convenient. What did he say?"

"Backed Guz's story to the hilt. Also, rehearsed to the hilt, if I know my fiction," Stuart said. "And I do. Plus, there's more."

"What?"

"I ran Popov through our files, and he has a record—aggravated burglary under the Theft Act of 1968. He was a guest of Her Majesty at HM Prison Edinburgh for five years in the early 1990s."

"So, birds of a feather flock together. These are unsavory men, Stuart. We have to find that vehicle. I feel it in my bones that Fern was in the back of it when Graeme Thomson saw the woman talking to Guz."

"We've scoured the city, Matt. If it's here, it's well hidden."

"Where do people park their cars here anyway? It's not like home where almost everyone has a garage unless they live in New York."

"The majority park on the street, and the rest in private garages sprinkled around the city. The privileged few have attached garages. But you have to remember, most city dwellers in Scotland have one car, not four for each family like Americans." Stuart smirked.

"I take offense at that, DCI. We may have two or even three cars, but not four."

"How many do you have?"

"Well, three. But one of them is a pickup to pull my fishing boat."

"Ahh, yes, your fishing boat. And where do you keep that?"

Matt chagrined, said. "In my four-car garage."

"My point."

. . .

Buck Bay Chief of Police Dan McCoy looked at the clock, hit the intercom button in his office, and asked his assistant, "Is she here yet?"

"No, sir. I haven't seen her, and she hasn't called in."

"Shit. I need this like I need a hole in my head."

"What do you want me to do?"

He sighed. "Nothing, Amy. As her parole officer, Blake Bowen is my responsibility. I'll have to run out to her place and conduct an unannounced home visit. If she comes in while I'm gone, call me immediately."

"Sure thing, Chief."

McCoy walked to his car parked in the Chief's space and headed west toward the Pacific Ocean. It was a fine spring day. Temps in the upper fifties, a slight breeze, and fluffy white clouds dancing in front of the sun. He rolled down the window and took big hits of the fresh air. His nose could tell when he was getting close to the Bowen's road; briny ocean air filled the car.

He pulled up to the gate and pressed the buzzer. No answer. He held down the button and spoke into the speaker. "Blake, it's Chief Dan McCoy, and this is an unannounced parole visit. Please open the gate."

A seagull swooped in front of his windshield, and he watched it float on the wind off to the north. He waited. No answer. He tried again. "Open up, Blake. I don't want to climb over your gate."

All quiet on the western front. Shit.

Taking his gun with him, he got out of the police car and locked it. Somewhat awkwardly, he clambered over the locked gate and jogged up the hill to the house. Her car was not in the driveway where it had been when he was here previously.

So help me, Blake, if you've done a runner, I'll hunt you down and throw your ass back in the slammer so fast, it will make your head spin.

He stood silently in the parking apron for a moment, listening to the only sounds: the waves breaking on the beach below him and the squawk of a couple of seagulls meeting up.

The chief made his way to the barn/garage where the pavement ended and found the rollback door unlocked and open a crack. He peeked inside and in the dimness, saw only the small tractor they kept, and Alex's car. Blake's T-bird was nowhere to be seen.

OK, in the house I go, ready or not.

McCoy climbed the staircase leading up to the landing and the front door. First, he walked around the corner to the big deck and the sliding doors. Curtains were open, and there was no sign of Blake in the great room visible from the deck. He retreated a couple of steps and craned his neck to look at the second floor. No lights on anywhere. He tried the slider, and to his amazement, it was unlocked.

He went in, calling out "Blake? Are you here? It's Chief McCoy." He paused, half in and half out and waited for her to respond. No response, and the house felt cold and empty. "Blake? I'm coming in." And he did so.

She was not home. McCoy toured the main level and started to the back where the kitchen was behind a large counter island. He noticed a note propped up between a bottle of wine and one wine glass and picked up the paper. It read, "Sorry to miss you, Chief. I'm off to Mexico for a short spa visit, and I'll be back soon. Please don't worry about me." It was signed, "Yours forever, Blake."

McCoy threw the note on the floor. *Great, just great.*

• • •

Dan McCoy knew he needed to alert Jay, but he took some time to collect his thoughts. *This is going to look bad for me. I let a paroled felon leave town, basically let her escape.* He sat down on the Bowens' sofa to think.

There was no way to sugarcoat it. McCoy punched in Jay Finley's number, hoping to get voicemail. *No such luck.*

"Dan," Jay answered. "Hang on for a minute while I step outside."

"Hi. Where are you?" McCoy started, trying to make small talk.

"Oregon State Penitentiary. Just going back inside to talk to Ray Peng."

"Ah, a delightful young man."

"Yeah. What's up?"

"Blake Bowen didn't report in for her required parole check today, and I'm at her house now. She's not here, Jay."

Jay pressed his phone closer to his ear. "Are you telling me that Blake Bowen has done a runner? Please say it isn't so."

"It's so—she's gone and left me a sweet note. That witch knew I'd come looking for her when she didn't show at the station. Says she's off to Mexico, which means she could be anywhere by now. I'm sorry, man. I should have put a 24/7 watch on this house. I trusted her."

"You trusted a vile woman who helped her husband bury her best friend?" Jay shouted into the phone. "Excuse me while I throw up in my mouth."

"I know. I'm an idiot," lamented McCoy. "I'll head to the airport now and call out all the troops. I don't know how much of a head start she's got on me, but maybe I'll get lucky."

"You're not a lucky person, Dan. That should be obvious by now," Jay said, irate.

"I'll make it up to you, I swear."

"If it turns out that Blake is involved in Fern's kidnapping, and you let her slip through your fingers, it's Matt you'll need to make it up to — not me."

. . .

"What was that about?" Tamryn asked Jay as he came back into the visitor lobby.

"Blake Bowen has skated. Didn't turn up for her parole check-in with McCoy."

"I thought we had surveillance on her place?" Tamryn asked, eyebrows raised in disbelief.

"So did I. Unfuckingbelievable screwup."

"What now?"

"McCoy's on it, but it's my guess she's in Mexico by now."

"And she has friends there, as I recall," Tamryn noted.

"Friends who will no doubt help her get anywhere she wants to go. Including Scotland. I'm out of ideas," Jay said morosely.

"Well, the only thing I can think of is to have our chat with Ray Peng. Maybe he's got some dirt on Alex Bowen for us."

CHAPTER 32

Ray Peng was escorted into the conference room. He looked around furtively, as he entered.

"Whatcha looking for?" Tamryn asked the prisoner.

"Bugs. Tape recorders. You can't tape this conversation," Peng warned.

"We have the authority to tape conversations in here when warranted, but we won't record this one if that's your preference, Ray," Tamryn assured him. "Whatever is said in this teensy-tiny room is between the three of us. You have my word."

"OK, then," Ray said, speaking softly. "I've been thinking about your offer, and I want to make a deal."

"Excellent," Tamryn said. She reached out, and warmly touched his arm. "Thank you, Ray. You may be saving a life. Please tell us what you know about Fern's kidnapping."

"Not so fast," Ray said, drumming his fingers nervously on the arms of his chair. "I want the witness protection deal. Where will I go?"

"The program is run by the federal U.S. Marshalls Service, and it's up to them where you'll be sent, because Fern is a federal employee, and this case is an international incident," Tamryn explained. "I will work with them, and they will take into consideration your wishes, but they have strict parameters. For instance, it's likely to be far away from here, and probably a small city where you and your family can blend in without much attention or risk of being seen. They will provide you with a new identity and will protect you through any trials this case may require as long as you want."

"Can I ever go back to being me?"

"Yes, once you've testified for us if it comes to that. But if you leave the program at any time after your court appearances, you're on your own… no protection."

Jay added, "And, your information has to lead us to the head honcho in this case. Who planned it, who hired the kidnappers involved, and how did you learn this info. Will you tell us all that?"

Solemnly, Ray nodded.

"Do you know Alex Bowen?" Jay, impatient, asked.

"Yeah, he's in here. I didn't know him before when we all lived in Chinook County."

"Has he said anything about Fern or Matt?"

"Wait a minute," Ray said, making the 'time out' gesture with his hands. "I have another question first. Will my family get protection starting tomorrow?"

"We can arrange that, yes," Jay said. "Are they still living in Twisty River in your.. former home?" He started to say, "in your crappy trailer", but caught himself.

"Yeah, my wife and two kids. I love them, man, and I miss them so much."

Tamryn leaned in and said, "You made a bad mistake, Ray, but you got in with the wrong crowd. You can start over and make something of your life. We'll help you do that, won't we, Jay?"

"Yes. I will call the sheriff as soon as we're done here and make sure he gets a detail over there tonight to watch out for them. They won't know the deputies are there, but they'll keep them safe."

For the first time in a long while, Ray Peng smiled an actual smile. Tamryn thought he looked so young.

• • •

Darkness was falling in Edinburgh, and the misty fog made it even darker. Matt wiped the drippings off his face and hair as he and Stuart made their way through the police station maze to their squad room on the building's second floor. The suitcase was getting heavy.

Scone was waiting by their door, looking anxious. Detective Patty Perkins stood beside her, and blurted out, "Did you get it?"

Matt pointed to the suitcase with his free hand. "All here."

Patty hugged Scone. "Thank God," they said together.

"Where is Vadim Guz?" Matt asked.

"Still in room 1," Patty answered. "With your permission, DCI, I'd like to take a crack at him. I've been waiting for you to get back to get your approval. I have some names to run by him that you two didn't get to — David Dalrymple, Alex Bowen, and Ray Peng. I'd like to see his reaction."

Stuart, tired and grumpy, said, "Do you promise to play nice?"

Patty lowered her chin, smiled shyly, and looked up at Stuart through her eyelashes. "I'll be a real Southern belle. Promise."

"I thought you were from Oregon?"

"I am. And I have no idea how a Southern belle operates, but I'll do my best to be charming. Matt, you go to the booth and watch his eyes and for any signals of recognition."

"Go get him, Detective Perkins," Matt said. He offered up the suitcase to Meg. "Please store this with the other one. Has there been any other action since I've been gone? Any phone calls? Any more fingers delivered?"

Scone shuddered. "No action, thankfully. We're just waiting."

Matt rubbed his stubbly chin. "That's what we're doing alright, just waiting."

• • •

Patty greeted Vadim Guz. "Hello, Mr. Guz. I'm Detective Patricia Perkins, and I work with Chief Horning in Oregon. We are also good friends, and I flew over here to help him through this ordeal. I just have a few questions for you, and then I expect you'll be released soon."

"You're a good friend," he grumbled, making an effort to be as pleasant as he could.

"I'm focused on some connections in Oregon that you might have, but

I won't go over everything again that DCI MacLean and Chief Horning covered."

"Thank goodness for wee mercies. Get on with it, shall we?"

"What's your hurry? Have you somewhere to go soon?"

"Nowhere special," Guz said, eyeing her. "I would like to leave this station and go to my home. I have some repairs to do on my front door that you helped knock down."

"Yes, sorry about that. But we don't take any chances when a kidnap victim is involved. For the record, and to give you a second chance, do you have any knowledge of the whereabouts of Fern Byrne, an American citizen?"

"I do not."

"You seem like a smart man," Patty said. "You must know that if you tell us where Fern is being held now, your sentence as an accomplice to a kidnapping will be much lighter than when we find her the hard way—and we will find her, make no mistake about that. And, if any further harm comes to the victim, I will personally escort you to incarceration for the rest of your natural life. Which might not be too long once your fellow inmates learn about your crime."

"Thank you for that explicit warning, Detective Perkins, but I don't believe you have any actual jurisdiction in bonny Scotland, do you?"

Patty leaned forward as far across the table separating them as she could. "I am a bulldog, Mr. Guz, and I'm nearing the end of my storied police career. If you've taken my friend, jurisdiction won't matter a damn to me." She leaned back and consulted her notes, while Guz toyed with a button on his shirt.

"Do you know an American young man named Ray Peng?" she asked.

Guz considered her question briefly. "No, I do not."

"He lives in Oregon but is currently incarcerated at the Oregon State Penitentiary. Ring any bells?"

"No."

"Have you ever purchased a ghost gun?"

"You mean the kind you put together yourself?"

"That, or you've bought one manufactured by someone else and sold to you. Which is now illegal in the state of Oregon, by the way. So, if you did buy one recently, you should surrender it to me now. I'll let that one go."

"I do not own a ghost gun to my knowledge."
"Do you own a gun?"
"Yes, and it's properly licensed."
"Where do you keep it?"
"In a safe at my residence."
"Is it there now?"
"Yes. I rarely take it out."
"When, would you say, is the last time you've taken it out of your safe?"
"I honestly don't recall."
"So, not yesterday, I presume," Patty said.
"No, not yesterday."
"Were you at home yesterday? Except for the established period when we know you met a woman at Holyrood car park."
"Yes, I was home all day."
"What did you do up until the time you met the woman?"
"Mostly phone calls. Business. Oh, and I took a short nap in the afternoon."
"In anticipation of a potential hot date last night?"
"That's none of your business."
She shrugged. "I hope it turns out to be none of my business. For your sake. Moving on, do you know a man named David Dalrymple? Also an American."
"No."
"That was a quick answer. Do you want to think about it for a minute?"
"That won't be necessary. I don't recognize that name."
"You blinked several times when I mentioned Dalrymple; was there a reason for that?"
"No, just thinking to make sure I gave you the correct answer."
"How about a man named Alex Bowen?"
"No, I'm sorry. I don't know any of these people."
"How about a woman named Blake Bowen?"
"You just asked me that."
"No. I asked you if you knew *Alex* Bowen. Do you know a woman named *Blake* Bowen?"

"Oh. My mistake," Guz said. "But the answer is the same; no, I don't know anyone with that name."

"A few years ago, Blake Bowen was a popular rock star. Are you sure you don't know her name?"

"I don't follow pop culture, especially in the States."

Patty quietly stared at him for a minute. "Does your work ever take you to the west coast of the States? Ever been to Oregon or California? We are checking your travel records right now, but I'm curious." *Tell the truth, Vadim, or we'll nail you to the wall.*

Guz thought. "It's been a while, but, yes, I've travelled to California. Not Oregon, I don't believe."

"You didn't rent a car in California and drive up the spectacularly breathtaking southern Oregon coastline? Shame. It's really special."

"Plenty of coasts here to suit me."

"Oh? Which are your favorite places?" Patty asked. "Where should I go visit when we wrap up this case?"

He clasped his hands and leaned forward on his elbows. "Are you stalling, Detective? Trying to keep me here as long as you legally can? If so, I think it's time I called my advocate. I've answered all your questions, and those of DCI MacLean's. I've been honest and cooperative, and now I want to go home. I will give you one additional question, and then I'm leaving."

"Fair enough," she said. *He's not going to break.* "Have you killed Fern Byrne? I'm asking as her friend."

"I don't know a woman by that name, and I'm sure I would have remembered it if I had. No is my answer."

CHAPTER 33

DCI MacLean was furiously working on obtaining search warrants for Nigel Armstrong and Max Popov's residences, and an additional one for Guz's residence to include phones, computers, and any other electronic devices not covered in the first search. They had to release them for lack of evidence once the advocates arrived.

Scone had set up a cot in the small closet where they stored maps, and that now held the $2 million ransom money. Matt was beginning to look and act like a zombie, and they persuaded him to go rest up while all was quiet. He understood their logic, because he would need to be sharp later—perhaps all night.

He shared notes with Patty and Stuart and then shut the door and laid down on the cot, setting his watch alarm for thirty minutes. He didn't have to tell anyone to alert him the second the phone rang if he wasn't already awake. He called his father first to tell him he had secured all the cash and to let the Byrnes know what was going on. Ross shared that Fern's parents were resting, and that Beverly was watching out for them. He wanted to come help with the ransom exchange, but Matt firmly declined his offer, telling his dad that this one was for the pros only. Too dangerous. And besides, he didn't want to have to worry about two people he loved.

Matt stretched out as best he could on the small surface and closed his eyes. He rested his body, but his mind was a different story. Different scenarios for the ransom swap swirled in his head, and he tried to remember any experiences from his previous work in Dallas that he could draw on for what might unfold tonight.

It would help if he knew whether or not Fern was incapacitated. His beloved wife was a resourceful woman and a highly trained agent; she would know how to help herself if she was able to. But if she was drugged — or worse — Matt knew he couldn't count on her resourcefulness.

His other dilemma involved the cash drop. What would he do if they wouldn't let him see Fern until they had the money and were safely away from the drop location? He could beg and cajole all he wanted, but the stark reality was that he wasn't holding any cards, and they knew it. He would offer half the cash at the drop and promise the second half when he could see that Fern was alive, but they had no incentive to humor him by hanging around longer than necessary. It would be up to Police Scotland's hostage rescue team to secure the location in advance once they knew the parameters, and for Matt to be as calm and clever as he could be.

He did some deep breathing in an attempt to quiet his mind, and the next thing he knew, his alarm chimed. He swung his legs over the side of the cot, and rested his arms on his thighs, head between his legs as he stared at the floor. Summoning some new-found energy, he stood, shaky at first, but then strong and determined.

His phone rang. Jay.

"What's happening?" Matt said. "Other than the fact that I wish Scottie could beam you over here to help me."

"Scottie's not around, but I may have something just as good for you. Ray Peng is starting to talk."

Excited, Matt said, "What's he got to say?"

"I'll tell you, but first I have to let you know about a new wrinkle. Blake Bowen has disappeared."

. . .

Buck Bay chief of police Dan McCoy found Blake Bowen's car at the airport. He stood looking out at the bay for a moment with the magnificent bridge beyond that took Highway 101 traffic further north, the blustery wind whipping through his jacket and ruffling his hair. A large blue and white cargo ship, its deep blue hull matching the water beneath it, cruised in from the Pacific heading under the bridge.

Now what?, he asked himself. *Did she really fly to Mexico like she said in her note, or was that a ruse to throw me off track?* Somewhere in the file on the Hannah Oakley case, McCoy knew he had the name and contact for the Mexican spa Blake visited. If he could get them to confirm she was a guest currently, that would ease his mind somewhat. But first, he needed to know which flight she'd taken out of Buck Bay.

He put police tape around her vehicle, locked his squad car, and headed to the small terminal. Inside, McCoy approached the ticket counter in the center of the three counters—the only one currently in operation—flashing his badge even though he knew the customer service agent well.

"Uh-oh, must be a professional visit," she said, glancing at his badge. "How're you doing, Chief?"

"I'm OK, Glenda. How are you?"

"Doing fine. How can I help you today?"

"I need to know what flight—and it would've been either yesterday or this morning—a woman named Blake Bowen took, and where she was ultimately headed. I've verified that her car is in the parking lot. Can you check passenger manifests and see if you can find her?"

"Don't need to," said Glenda. "I know Blake, and she left on the flight to Denver late yesterday afternoon."

"Not to San Francisco?" McCoy asked, surprised at the destination.

"Nope. I remember because she often goes to SFO to connect with a flight to a spa in Mexico she likes."

"But not this time?"

"Not this time. Off to Denver instead."

"Do you have any connecting information for her?" he asked. "What was her final destination?"

"Give me a minute." She turned to her computer monitor and clicked away. "I don't see any connecting info, at least not on the same airline. Looks like Denver was her destination."

"Can you tell me if there are any flights from Denver direct to Edinburgh, Scotland?"

"I don't believe there are any nonstop Denver to Edinburgh flights. Passengers would connect through Newark or London Heathrow. The most likely routing beginning here would be Buck Bay to Denver to Dallas, and then nonstop to Edinburgh. It's a hike. Most locals would drive to Portland, and then go through Newark or JFK in New York."

"Were you on the desk when she departed?"

"Yes, I checked her in."

"What was her mood? How did she seem?"

"I'd say she was a little jittery. But then, she's always been high-strung."

"Weren't you surprised to see her?" Chief McCoy asked. "You knew she'd been in prison, right?"

Glenda looked pensive for a moment. "Well, yeah, I guess I was a little surprised. But there's been talk around town of her getting paroled, so I figured everything was A-OK with you cops and her. I didn't have any reason to stop her, did I?"

"No, I guess not," he frowned. "My bad. I should've alerted you and the bus station that Blake Bowen is not allowed to leave this area while her parole is ongoing."

"I'm sorry, Dan. I didn't think it through all the way. Just figured she was in the clear. After all, it was her husband who did the deed."

"True. But Blake played a role in it, and she is being carefully watched by law enforcement through her parole period. Or, at least, we should have been watching her. I'll have to check with TSA in Denver and see if they can tell me where she was headed."

"I hope she's not up to no good again," Glenda said, shaking her head.

"You and me both, sweetheart," Chief McCoy said.

• • •

"What do you mean, Blake Bowen has disappeared?" Matt responded to Jay into his phone. "I thought Dan McCoy was having her monitored round the clock? What the hell?"

"I thought that, too. He went out to do a house check on her yesterday as we requested, and she was home. But today was her day to come in to the station for her weekly parole check, and she didn't show up. Dan drove out there, and she's gone. She had the balls to leave her sliding door unlocked, and a note for Dan inside. Said she was going to the Mexico spa, and he was not to worry about her. Can you believe that woman?!?"

"She's a piece of work, alright. Is Dan going to track her down? I'd like to know for sure that she's not in Edinburgh by now."

"Yes. He's embarrassed and angry, and he's on it now," Jay told him.

"He should be. Why don't you put Sylvia on her trail, too. I know I'm scared, tired, and probably not myself, but, honestly, I'm sick of McCoy's mistakes. We can't count on him."

"I already mentioned it to Sylvia," Jay said with a smile in his voice that made it across the Atlantic.

"You're the man. Tell me about Ray Peng."

Jay explained the details of the witness protection deal they'd struck with Peng.

"Does he have any info for us now?"

"Some, but there's more to come soon now that we have a deal. Tamryn is working out the details with the U.S. Marshals' office now. Ray says he was at lunch about a month ago, eating at the same table with Zhang Chen, David Dalrymple, and Alex Bowen, and Dalrymple mentioned that you and Fern were on a vacation in Scotland. The four of them talked about your involvement in their respective cases, but nothing specific. Just the usual trashing of the cops. Then, a couple of days later, Ray overheard the three of them talking again about 'Scotland', and Alex said, 'I wonder if Rick Reid and his mom are involved?'. Then Chen, according to Ray, said, 'I'm certain they are.'"

"Chen said the Reids are involved? Is that what you're saying?"

"According to Ray, yeah, Chen thinks the Reids are behind Fern's kidnapping. Tamryn and I questioned Ray thoroughly, and that was his takeaway."

"Or, Chen is suspicious of everyone and everything, including his buddy Ray Peng, and he's trying to throw off all his colleagues inside while he's the one who hired Vadim Guz."

"Quick, look over there, you mean?" Jay responded.

"Exactly. Throwing shade on someone else to deflect from himself. Ray needs to start up a new conversation and, knowing what he now knows, see if he can get any more details. Have him open with the line of interrogation you and Tamryn are working. Make him sound like he knows about the ransom demand and that we have the money ready to go."

"OK, can do."

"Plus, tell Peng that I will personally chip in $100,000 to help him begin his new life if he gives us who in the state pen hired out Fern's kidnapping, and the name of the person or persons on this end who carried it out. And before you can say anything, Jay, I realize that's unethical to my professional standing, but, right now, I don't give a rip."

"I understand and will do as you ask. But I don't like it, Matt. It sets a nasty precedent." Jay let this issue drop for now. "Has the kidnapper called yet about the exchange?"

"No, but I'm expecting the call any minute. Hurry up with Ray. Tell him I approved the witness protection plan, and we just need to know the local connection. You, alone, have that talk with him, and have Tamryn get Rick Reid back in a separate room. Tell him he's a suspect, and he'd better open up before Fern gets killed."

"Do you think it's Reid?" Jay asked.

"No, I think it's Chen, but you won't get anything else out of him, so Tamryn might as well pound Rick Reid into the ground just in case."

• • •

The hours drug on, and for Matt, it felt like days. He was so helpless. Knowing that DCI MacLean and his entire unit were working tirelessly to help him find Fern, and his crew back home in Port Stirling was doing the same, dulled the pain a little, but the pain was still sharp as a knife and would not go away until he was holding his wife in his arms again.

His reality was that no one in this city had seen Fern since she left the airport, despite all their searching door-to-door around Edinburgh, and Police Scotland rounding up their usual snitches. Nobody knew anything, and after almost thirty-six hours, the only clue they had was Graeme Thomson's lead and the follow-up shoe-leather investigation that brought them to Vadim Guz.

Search warrants for Vadim Guz's residence had turned up nothing of interest, with the exception of two hypodermic needles. He explained them away by the fact that he is a type one diabetic and requires several insulin injections daily. Matt didn't believe him, of course, but couldn't prove that his well-rehearsed clarification was purely fiction. The search turned up no evidence of a nerve agent.

Nigel Armstrong's flat was mostly pathetic. A tiny kitchenette in one corner of the living area, and a bedroom about the size of a large closet with only a mattress on the floor, and a wooden crate for a nightstand holding a ten-inch lamp and a pot gravity bong.

The address Max Popov had given Stuart on the phone turned out to be false, and his last known address in his criminal file belonged to his sister, who shut the door in the polis' face. Stuart had tried to phone Max again, but his cell phone had been blocked by Popov.

There was no evidence that Fern had ever been in any of these locations.

So, that meant she was somewhere else. And Matt had no further clues as to where that might be. He had no option other than to wait for the phone call with ransom exchange instructions. He, Stuart, and the Police Scotland tactical unit had gone over their plan for tonight. Matt had deferred to them on this front because they knew their city to a T, and he didn't.

They had units standing by in four quadrants of Edinburgh and would be dispatched within thirty seconds of the kidnapper's instructions. Matt was scared to death that the kidnapper would know how Police Scotland operated and where they might position themselves, but, again, he was helpless in this situation because he didn't know the terrain. He had to trust them.

And, trust didn't come easy to Matt. He had learned how to trust when he came to Port Stirling, and discovered he could actually lean on his colleagues. That had never been the case in Dallas, just the opposite in fact. Many of the cops there had been positioning themselves for promotion, and rarely lended a hand to help out a fellow officer. Oregon was different, and it was more than a team, almost a family.

Strangely, after only thirty-six hours, he felt that trust with Stuart. It went beyond his obvious competence, to a place of honest empathy and compassion for how Matt was struggling. It's funny how life throws you curves, and how in one hour, you can build new relationships that stand the test of time. He had every confidence that Stuart knew what he was doing, and that he and his team would give it everything they had to achieve a successful result tonight.

If we all don't die of old age first waiting for the bloody phone to ring, he thought.

• • •

Somewhere in Edinburgh, 10:15 p.m.

"Wake her up, it's almost go time," he said.

"I can't!" she said frantically. "She's not waking up! And there's blood on her pants."

CHAPTER 34

Ray Peng, with Amanda, Jay, and two guards positioned outside the small conference room door, talked over the details Tamryn had negotiated with the U.S. Marshals Service in Seattle.

Peng was, understandably, fidgety and pale. Jay knew that every person, especially of the criminal variety, had a tell. And Peng's tell was that he literally couldn't sit still for ten seconds. He continually shifted in his chair and drummed his fingers on the arms nonstop. Jay sensed that he would have to put Peng at ease first before he could extract the information they needed.

"Where is Tamryn?" Peng spoke first. "Why are you here alone?"

Jay smiled what he hoped was a winning, comforting smile. "Because I have good news for you, and it's of a personal nature that Chief Horning wanted me to deliver to you in private."

"What kind of good news?"

"The kind that's going to put $100,000 in your pocket on top of what the U.S. Marshals witness security program will give you to begin anew in your life. Chief Horning has authorized me to inform you that he will give you—no strings attached—$100,000 of his own money with his thanks if you can help him save his wife. How does that sound to you?" Jay leaned back and waited, trying to strike a friendly, non-threatening pose.

Peng sat, reflecting. "That's nice of him," he finally said.

"He loves Fern so much, Ray. She's way more important to him than the money. He wants to show his appreciation for what you're about to do because he knows it's a hard decision for you. And, we both want to see a young man like you get a second chance at a good life for you and your family. We will protect you; you have my word, Tamryn's, and the U.S. Marshals. You'll never have to be afraid again. Just tell me what you've learned about Fern's kidnapping."

"Put it in writing."

"Tamryn is working on that right now and will have the official document to you soon. It's straightforward, Ray, no surprises, I promise." Jay crossed his fingers under the table and hoped that Tam was getting it done and that there were, indeed, no surprises. "Tell me who arranged Fern's kidnapping, and who the person is in Edinburgh who carried it out, and you can begin your new life."

Ray leaned across the table and whispered, "Zhang Chen hired a man named Vadim Guz to kidnap Fern. He lives in Edinburgh, but he's Russian, and an international hit man. Chen has used him before, going back several years."

"How do you positively know this? What's your evidence?"

"Chen told me himself."

"Was anyone else present at the time?"

"No. It was just him and me talking. He told me that if I was questioned, I was to say it was Rick Reid who was involved, and that Reid's old man paid for Guz because he hates Fern."

"But he told you he hired him? Is that correct?" Jay persisted.

"Yes, that's right," Peng confirmed. "And that Guz is an expert in that nerve agent shit."

"Who is the woman who physically abducted Fern in the Edinburgh Airport bathroom?"

"Chen didn't mention her. Only Vadim Guz. Guz probably hired her because he needed a female to grab her in the bathroom."

"How did you know about the female in the bathroom?" Jay said. He leaned forward.

"Chen told me the highlights of the plan, but he didn't tell me any other names associated with it. That Guz would prepare the nerve agent capsule and track the Hornings' movements until they had a public bathroom to grab Fern. Guz figured that the two of them would always be together otherwise, and that a bathroom at a restaurant or airport would be their only opportunity. And he figured that they would fly into and out of Edinburgh, so that made the most sense."

"Why did Chen do it?"

"Why does he do anything?" Peng said with a wry shake of his head. "It's all about keeping his street cred going until he can escape from here." He looked around the room. "He's still in charge, Jay, and it's important to him that everyone knows it. If he can kill Fern from inside here and make sure that people hear about it, well…it keeps everyone in line. See?"

Jay, startled, said, "Has Guz killed her?"

Peng shrugged. "That I don't know, only that she's being held somewhere in Edinburgh."

"Did Chen tell you that she would be killed? This is important, Ray, think hard."

"Not in so many words. But that's his usual outcome."

"If revenge is his motive, why the ransom demand?" Jay asked.

"Two million — why not?"

"Whose finger did Guz cut off and deliver to Police Scotland in a box?"

Peng blanched, and, reflexively, placed his own hands under the table. "I didn't hear about that. I don't know."

"How does Chen communicate with the outside world? He's not allowed a cell phone inside here, and regular mail would be too slow for his purposes."

Peng laughed, a bitter laugh. "He not only has burner phones, one of the guards also smuggled in a laptop that Chen connected to a private server he owns."

"What?"

"Yeah. I'm sure the guard's bank account is much bigger since Chen arrived."

"Does Chen have a plan to escape?"

"He's working on it."

"Do you know the details?"

"No. He's keeping that to himself…for now, anyway."

"You will also have to tell us about the guard in question, but we won't have him arrested until both you and Fern are safe. But you do know which guard, correct?"

"Yeah, I know the dude," Peng frowned.

"Do you know that Fern is pregnant? She and Chief Horning are expecting their first child."

"I haven't heard that mentioned in here," Peng said. "Even if Chen knows that, he wouldn't care. He doesn't care about anyone but himself. He doesn't like children—hates my two kids because I love them more than I love him."

"Wonderful human being, your boss."

Peng looked down at the table.

"Can you tell me if you know anything about the location where Guz is hiding Fern? I'm pleading with you." Jay was close to tears and thought it might help loosen Peng's memory if he let the tears go, but he composed himself for the sake of professionalism, deciding that it might be more important to Peng at the moment than his emotional plea.

"Chen operates on a "need to know" basis, and I don't need to know that. He told me about the kidnapping plot because he wants me to spread it around to the right people inside, but not the details. I'm sorry. And he won't tell me even if I asked now. He's not the boss for nothin'."

Jay nodded sadly, agreeing with him.

• • •

The U.S. Marshals faxed a copy of Ray Peng's agreement to the Oregon State Penitentiary's warden, as Tamryn witnessed its arrival. It was agreed that Peng would stay put for now, until Chief Horning and Police Scotland gave them the green light.

Madison, Wisconsin would be the new home for Ray and his family. For his safety, it was decided that he would need to be sent far away from Zhang Chen's mostly west-coast and China-based empire. Madison, a mid-sized city, had a decent Asian population that would allow them to blend in. Ray would be set up with employment at Trek Bicycle, whose corporation headquarters were nearby. No one outside of the very small circle of law enforcement would know his destination unless he or his family decided to share it with anyone else, which the U.S. Marshals Service vehemently encouraged him not to do.

Jay called Matt with the news. "You were right, Chen hired Vadim Guz to kidnap Fern." He filled in the details for Matt as Ray Peng had shared with him.

"Do you believe Peng?" was Matt's first question.

"I believe that's what Chen told him," Jay answered. "We have no way of knowing for sure if Chen is lying to Peng or taking him into his confidence, but Ray believed him."

"It explains why Chen told him to implicate Rohn and Rick Reid, for sure," Matt said and then hesitated.

"I feel a 'but' coming."

"But…I would still like to know where Blake Bowen is. Don't you think it's too much of a coincidence that she gets out of the slammer, goes home and then disappears? She has to know that McCoy will go to Mexico and bring her home if that's really where she is."

"Agreed, but Alex Bowen doesn't have the wherewithal to find and hire someone like Vadim Guz to do the job. That doesn't make sense."

"No, Alex doesn't have those connections, but his new good buddy, Zhang Chen does, and I don't like the timing with Blake set free."

Even though Matt couldn't see it, Jay shook his head. "But the timing of Blake's release, and her being seen in Buck Bay doesn't jive well with her being in Edinburgh. It's too tight. And besides, you saw the woman with Guz on the plane from Newark, didn't you? Surely you would have recognized Blake Bowen," Jay argued.

"Yeah, good point. I thought that woman looked vaguely familiar, but she wasn't someone I knew well enough to place. Unless she was highly disguised or had some facial surgery. Did McCoy mention how Blake looked?"

"He told me she looked older was all. I don't know, Matt, I think it's more probable that Chen, who has worked with Guz in the past, according to Ray, hired Guz, and Guz hired a local woman. Our witness reported that she was dressed in Scottish attire, and looked like a Scot, not an American. Apparently, we stand out."

"OK, then. You're probably right. I will ask DCI MacLean to send two constables back to Vadim Guz's house and question him further about his past ties to Zhang Chen. See what he has to say now. I can't leave because…"

"I know. The call," Jay filled in for him. "Wish I was there to help. It's frustrating, this stupid distance."

"You've done a lot, my friend. Paved the way for us to take these guys out after we rescue my wife. The focus now needs to be on finding the links between Vadim Guz and Chen; something we can use in court once we catch Guz tonight."

"Is the plan for the exchange solid?"

"As solid as it can be when Guz is holding all the cards," Matt said softly. "But these Police Scotland guys are giving it their all, and I don't know how I will ever be able to repay them if they help me get Fern back."

"Godspeed, Chief."

CHAPTER 35

The call came at 11:11 p.m.

This time, Meg didn't have to wildly alert Matt and Stuart; they were already huddled around her desk, along with Patty, waiting for the red light to flash.

The blood-curdling voice was, as on the previous call, disguised by voice modification software.

"I understand you have assembled the full $2 million for the ransom of your lovable wife, Chief Horning. Correct?"

"Yes, I have the money ready to deliver to you," Matt said, as calmly as he could muster. *How did they know?*, he wondered. *Vadim Guz.* "Once you let me talk to my wife, I'm prepared to bring the full amount to you wherever you say."

"Back to that non-starter are you, Chief? Not going to happen. You will do exactly as I say in the next few seconds, or you will never see her again. Here are my instructions. You and Detective Patricia Perkins—ONLY, no Police Scotland inspectors or constables—will, leaving your building five minutes after we hang up, bring the cash to a location in the heart of Edinburgh about ten minutes from you…"

Meg thrust her arm in the air, the signal that they had a trace on the call.

"Hunter's Bog."

"I know Hunter's Bog," Matt interrupted, hoping to drag out the call to give Police Scotland a chance on the trace. "It's a big place, where exactly do I go?" He talked slowly. "And, why Detective Perkins?"

"Because you might want help carrying the suitcases. Don't interrupt me again. Park your Police Scotland vehicle on Queen's Drive and take the trail that leads to the ruins of St. Anthony's Chapel—your Scottish colleagues can direct you. It's above St. Margaret's Loch, sorry about the uphill hike with suitcases, but you're young and in good shape. Take a flashlight, it's dark. Leave the cases on the ground underneath the arch overlooking the loch, and then immediately run back on the same trail to Queen's Drive, get in your vehicle and drive away. When I see you driving away, I will take your wife to another location in Hunter's Bog, and I will call you with directions to the spot to pick her up. If I see one Police Scotland officer, I will kill your wife. Do you understand my directions?"

"Yes. Please, at least tell me if she is alive."

The caller hung up.

Matt, trembling, said, "I have no choice but to trust his word, do I?"

Stuart shook his head. "Definitely an American," Stuart said. "We would never say 'flashlight', it's properly called a 'torch'."

Matt nodded at Stuart, and then, pleadingly, looked at Meg. "Did you get a trace?"

Meg said, "Again, partial, but it's in the Holyrood area. Based on the caller's instructions, it's legitimate, and they are near the ransom location." She grabbed the map of Edinburgh on her desk and unfolded it quickly, pointing her finger at a small red tourist icon that looked like a turreted castle. "It's here—St. Anthony's Chapel ruins."

Stuart placed his finger on a bordering road. "This is Queen's Drive. It's the roadway by the car park that you and I crossed on our hike yesterday. Do you remember it?"

"Yeah. We hiked the actual spot, didn't we?" Matt said, color draining from his face. "Do you think we were close to Fern?"

"No way to know that now. Maybe they picked this location because they saw us and realized that we would know it. Doesn't matter. We need to move now." Stuart pulled out his phone and pressed a button. "Send out the alert. We need a perimeter around Queen's Drive—unseen. The drop is St. Anthony's ruins, on foot." He paused and listened. "Yes, night camouflage, no lights. The only goal is to retrieve the victim and to apprehend the perpetrators, in that order. We don't care about the money. Are you assembled?" He listened. "Splendid, let's move now, and please tell everyone to do their best work tonight."

DCI MacLean turned to Matt and Patty, who were pulling on their jackets and securing their firearms. Both were grim-faced. Stuart tried to think of something reassuring to say to them, but his mind was focused on the task at hand. In truth, the outcome was far from assured, and nothing he could say now would change that fact.

"I'm in plainclothes, as you can see," Stuart said, "and I'd like to accompany you and Patty."

Matt stared into his eyes. "You heard the instructions. I can't risk it. I'm sorry, and you have to know how much I'd like you by our side. We have to do this one alone, Stuart."

"We'll be alright," Patty offered at Matt's side. "Between us, we have the wisdom that comes with age, and the quick-thinking and energy that comes with youth. We will grab our girl and return to safety. Take it to the bank, Stuart."

"I assume that means you will be successful," Stuart said to Patty.

Patty winked at him. "You catch on fast, DCI. Where's our waiting car?"

"Back stairs. Engine is running."

Patty took Matt by the arm, as Meg and a constable brought the suitcases out of the closet. "Let's go find Fern," she said to her great and good friend.

• • •

Stuart walked them to the back stairs and stuffed a flashlight in Matt's jacket pocket; his hands were full of the suitcases. "This is my lucky torch. It's shown me the way out of many dark places, including, sometimes, my dark mind. May it show you the light tonight."

Down the stairs and out to the waiting car. Matt got in on the driver's side, while Patty set the GPS to the coordinates. "I kinda remember the way," he said, "although it was daylight."

"Between the man and the machine, we'll find it. I'd say it's about two miles. Looks like only a couple of turns, and then we get on something called Easter Rd. From there, it's almost a straight shot to Queens Drive."

"I remember Easter Rd. It was slow going yesterday. I hope it doesn't make us late," he fretted.

"They will wait. It's two mil."

"Suppose so."

A silence overcame the two of them, each alone with their thoughts. Patty was remembering Matt and Fern's Port Stirling wedding, and how stunning they both looked. But, particularly, how happy they were. Nothing dared come between these two; she wouldn't allow it.

Matt was thinking more recently; the Highlands restaurant when Fern worried that they were "too happy". How did she know the misery that was about to befall them? What if her premonition came true? What if he lost her? He stepped on the gas a bit harder.

After one wrong turn, which they discovered in one block, they turned left onto Queens Drive and drove for a short distance until Patty pointed and said, "There! Pull over here." Matt didn't know how she'd spotted the trailhead sign in the thick, soupy fog that had settled over Edinburgh, but there it was—the trail to St. Anthony's Chapel ruins. He pulled off the road as far as he dared, grabbed the heaviest suitcase, gave the lighter one to Patty, and locked the car. There were no other vehicles on Queens Drive. Lighting their flashlights, they took off up the trail to the ancient ruin they couldn't yet see. Patty went first, lighting the way, while Matt struggled with the heavy cases.

The trail was packed dirt with the occasional bulky rock to avoid. Narrow in spots, they had to walk single file. On their right, the grassy hillside went sharply up from the trail. Patty tried to look upwards through the murky fog but couldn't see anything yet. It was eerie with no one else about them, and the only sound was Patty's wheezing as she plowed upward in the pitch-black night.

Eventually, they came into a flat clearing, with some grass now mixing in with the dirt trail. Suddenly, the ancient stones appeared in the mist, almost close enough for her to reach out and touch.

"Damn," she said, stepping into a mud puddle, the water seeping into her shoes. She shone the light upwards and saw the arch in the former chapel.

"That's it," said Matt, coming up behind her. He deposited the suitcases under the arch where they were protected from the damp. Both swung their lights around the area, but there was nothing to see but the ruins and each other.

Matt shouted, "Fern, are you here? Fern! Yell if you can hear me!" He and Patty stood motionless and silent for a full minute, but the only sound they heard was the dense fog dripping on the stones.

"Let's get out of here and back to the car," Patty said, taking his hand in hers. "Time for part two." In sheer terror, they went as fast as they could down the rocky trail, the light from their torches dancing around, hanging onto each other for dear life. Reaching the car, they raced back to the police station, showing their rear lights to the kidnappers to do whatever they would do next.

. . .

What the kidnappers did next was…nothing. Matt and the others sat at Meg's desk waiting for the phone to ring with the information of Fern's location, but it never rang. Matt paced and stewed as the minutes went by with zero communication.

After thirty minutes had elapsed since Matt and Patty returned, Stuart's internal phone rang. He answered the call and started to walk away from Matt, but Patty grabbed him by his arm and said emphatically, "We need to hear this, too." Stuart set his phone down on Meg's desk and pressed the speaker button. "Go ahead, Constable Brown. Chief Horning is here with me."

"I'm reporting in from the perimeter, sir, and there is nothing to report. There have been no vehicles and no people in or out. Not a single person since Chief Horning and Detective Perkins drove off. Our people are stationed at every entrance to and logical exit from Hunter's Bog, and there is no action whatsoever."

Matt was beside himself. "They should have grabbed the cash and run by now! How could you not see anyone?!?" he shouted at the phone.

"I'm sorry, sir, but no one has left the park. We are quite sure. Have the kidnappers called with the location of Mrs. Horning?"

"No," was all Matt could say.

"Again, I'm sorry, sir, but we haven't seen a solitary soul to apprehend."

"Then they're up there somewhere," Matt surmised. "Hiding. And hiding my wife."

"There's not much there, Matt," Stuart said. "Nowhere to hide that we know of. Just trails, rocks, grass, and watery bogs."

"They wouldn't have me deposit the ransom in that spot if they didn't believe they could get away with it," Matt said. "They are either hiding, or they somehow slipped through your police cordon. There is no other option, is there?"

The cops all looked at each other. "If they've picked up the ransom. No, there is no other option," Stuart finally said. "We'll have to go back to the drop and see if the ransom money is gone. They would have phoned by now if that was their intention. Do you agree, Matt?"

"They are not going to call me," Matt whispered. "They were never going to call me."

CHAPTER 36

Somewhere in Edinburgh, 11:45 p.m.

"So far, so good," she said, laughing nervously, pulling her black puffy coat tightly around her, and buttoning two more buttons against the damp cold. She patted one of the suitcases. "Just like you planned it. What do we do now?"

"Wait," he said. "We wait. They'll be swarming all around here for a while. My guess is that they won't be able to do much in the dark with this fog — thank you, weather gods — and they will leave and come back at dawn. When I'm sure they have retreated, so will we. I suspect it won't be too long."

"What about her?"

"Oh, she's likely dead by now. Too much blood."

"But we'll check on her, right?" she asked. "Remember, she knows me. I can't let her talk."

"Understood. We won't let that happen."

. . .

12:30 a.m.

Matt and Stuart raced up the trail through the oppressive fog to the ruins of St. Anthony's Chapel. Patty had elected to stay with Meg at the station in the event the kidnappers did call, although no one held out any hope by now, one hour later.

The suitcases were gone.

Matt slapped the arch wall. "Dammit! How could they get off this hill without our men seeing them? Where could they be?"

Stuart pulled out his phone. "Constable Brown," he spoke into it, "please send the forensics team up to St. Anthony's. The ransom is gone, and there is no one here. I want you to secure the ruins area immediately."

"This is a puzzle, DCI," the constable replied. "It is impossible that we have missed them leaving the park. Impossible! I would bet my career and my life on it! I will send forensics now."

"Thank you, Brown." Stuart ended the call and turned back to Matt. "Are you doing alright?"

"I haven't had a heart attack yet, so I guess I'm OK," Matt said grimly. He scanned the area. "Are there any secret tunnels or other structures around here where they could wait us out?"

"The only thing I know of are some traces of prehistoric hill forts around the Salisbury Crags," Stuart said, pointing in the opposite direction of St. Margaret's Loch below them. "But they are mostly just terraced remains. Everything else is solid basalt rock. And, as you saw, there aren't even trees in which to hide. It's just open space, and I can't imagine where they could be."

"What about any caves? Or maybe some type of outcropping, like a ledge or something they could hide under?"

Stuart thought. "I don't know of any caves, but there are several ancient wells around here. The famous one is St. Margaret's Well. It's close to Queen's Drive, and, in fact, it was moved stone-by-stone from what is now the middle of the drive to its current spot and reconstructed. It's believed to be holy, or some such nonsense, and it has historical significance. It's down by the car park."

"Could they get in it?" Matt asked.

"No. It's got a metal grate across the entrance. I believe that opening does lead to a well house of sorts, but it's been closed off for decades."

"Can you find it in this blackness and fog? Take me to it."

"I can find it. It's back the way we came, and then more to the west. It will take a little while, but I'm sure I can find it. It's about a ten-minute walk, I think."

"Lead the way." Matt looked around the ruins a last time, touched the arch wall softly, his heart breaking, and then followed Stuart down the trail.

• • •

12:48 a.m.

It took Matt and Stuart twelve minutes in the bleak fog to reach the well entrance. The path they were on led behind the monument, and they scrambled down four feet of grass to skirt the sharp-pointed iron railing protecting it from the hillside. The area leading to the arched entrance was set in old-looking cobblestones, with a curved modern stone facade surrounding the entrance. The bottom row of stones was covered in green moss and was damp to the touch. A blue plaque with white lettering commemorating the well's historical significance was placed above the midhigh point of the arch.

The vertical and horizontal metal grate that normally protected the opening from unwanted people or animals tonight lay in broken fragments on the cobblestones.

Stuart gasped, and Matt gave him the finger-to-mouth 'shhh' sign, while unholstering his gun. Stuart did the same, while also shining his torch on the metal fragments. "Blowtorch," he murmured. "When we passed here earlier, the grate was intact."

Matt whispered, "It has to be them." He leaned over the cavity and pointed his flashlight down. He saw water, but it was shallow with rocks barely under the surface. Carefully and without making a sound, he threw one leg over the font and into the opening, bracing himself with his hands at the sides of the stone arch. He lowered his foot until he felt water and then the rocky bottom. Maneuvering his other leg through the opening, he motioned 'C'mon' to Stuart.

Once inside the opening, they were met by a grotesque mask and lead pipe, covered with moss. Matt shuddered but trudged ahead. Once his eyes adjusted to the darkness, he could see a mini-vaulted roof overhead.

He took a few more steps and found himself in a tiny space, not quite a room, but a larger opening. They were clearly over a spring, as they were still standing in some water.

Holding his gun in one hand, and flashlight in the other, he took a good look around at the space. It was empty.

Behind him, Stuart said, "Hello, what's this?" He bent down and stuck a hand in the water, picking up something sitting atop a flat stone.

"What is it?" Matt whispered. "What have you found?"

"A button. Heavy duty."

"Let me see it. Maybe it belongs to my wife."

Stuart held out his hand, and Matt shone his flashlight on it. Carefully, he turned it over and considered the back side. "Looks like it might be off a jacket. It's too big and rough to be from a blouse or shirt, don't you think?"

"Yes. But it's intricate…maybe a woman's coat of some sort? I take it you don't recognize it."

"No, I don't. Fern's outerwear is all zips, no buttons that I can recall. Stick it in your pocket, will you? We probably shouldn't have touched it."

"It was underwater. Any evidence off it will have been destroyed by the spring water. But I'm taking it with us, might come in handy, you never know."

Matt clapped him on the back. "Good eye," he said. "You're like my detective, Jay Finley. He has an eagle eye for the details, too. He's a good partner, and so are you."

"Thanks. But save your compliments until we catch these bastards."

Matt nodded.

They spent several minutes examining every inch of the space but turned up nothing further of interest. There was no evidence of Fern having been here, and no signs of violence, for which Matt was hugely grateful. If the perps had hidden in this well—which the blowtorched grate pointed to—they had been fastidious to leave nothing behind, except, possibly, the button.

Turning to go back out the way they came, Matt suddenly put his hand on Stuart's back. "Hold up," Matt said. "What's that smell? Do you smell something?"

Stuart stopped and took a deep breath through his nose. "Flowery-like, you mean?"

"Yeah, sort of a floral fragrance. What is that smell?"

"I don't know. Something like jasmine or gardenia. A strong flower."

"Gardenia — that's it," Matt said. "I remember it from my childhood in Texas. Why are we smelling it here?"

"Couldn't tell you. It does seem a wee odd."

Matt looked the Inspector in the eye. "It's not a wee odd, it's fucking odd, and I smelled it yesterday, too," he said, voice cold as ice. "Near here, when we walked from the car park, down that pretty lane behind Holyrood."

"At Croft-an-Righ?"

"Yeah, where I went through that gate and looked at the garden. I walked down some steps to look at an old, interesting door, and I smelled gardenia. I remember it because I stopped to think if it smelled like Fern."

"Did it?"

"No, not at all. This smelled like a Texas night, and Fern's fragrance is modern and kinda with some roses in it. Totally different."

"So," Stuart said, "you're saying that someone wearing that strong fragrance was maybe in this space tonight, and that maybe that same person was at the Croft-An-Righ house yesterday? It is all in the neighborhood, so I suppose it's possible."

"Well, it's not a fragrance that's common in Scotland, is it?" Matt asked. "I wouldn't think so. Maybe in Paris, but not in this land. But I'm no expert on perfume."

"Me neither. My wife likes Jo Malone Orange something," Stuart said. "That's the extent of my perfume knowledge."

"I'm headed to Croft-An-Righ," Matt said. "Wanna come along?"

"Let's go, mate."

. . .

Stuart called Constable Brown again and told him about St. Margaret's Well, requesting that he get the forensics team down there as soon as they finished at the ransom drop site.

"It won't be long," Brown told him. "They are having a difficult time in the fog and the darkness. Told me they'll have better luck as soon as it's light."

"They need to do what they can now," Stuart said firmly. "I appreciate the difficulty, but we need results."

"I told them you'd say that."

"I am saying it. Tell them to quit whinging and get to work now. And I want two of your units to come with Chief Horning and me. Have them meet us in the Holyrood car park, at the eastern end where the barriers intersect with Queen's Drive. We're going to Croft-An-Righ."

"Aye. We'll be there. What's this about, sir?"

"Perfume," said Stuart.

Constable Brown had learned not to question DCI MacLean when he sounded crazy.

Stuart and Matt made their way following the footpath back to Queen's Drive and crossed it into the car park. Even with the unseen presence of Police Scotland, the area was still eerily quiet.

Stuart spoke in a low voice to Constable Brown, explaining the possibility that the kidnappers were housed at Croft-An-Righ, perhaps in a basement with an outside door off the garden. "But the old building is used as offices," Brown objected. "Wouldn't it be too busy to hide in?"

"Possibly," Stuart said. "But it could also be a case of 'hiding in plain sight', don't you imagine? Plus, the offices are likely only occupied between 10 a.m. and 4:00 p.m., and not on the weekend." He stared at the constable. "Look, Brown, this could be a major cock-up, but I believe Chief Horning is on to something and we need to see it through. I need your full commitment, because if he's right, it could get ugly fast."

"I'm with you, sir," Brown said firmly. "You ne'er lead me astray."

The units were organized, and the plan was developed. They would go in via the garden gate as Matt had done the day before. One of the units included a lockmaster with all sorts of keys and tools to open any locked gates, doors, etc., although his services were rarely required; people in Scotland didn't feel the need to constantly lock up everything like Americans did. Matt disapproved of the Scots tendency, but tonight, he might be grateful for it.

As the wind whistled through the overhanging trees, and the damnable fog continued to swirl around them, they made their way stealthily down the lane, hugging the sides. Matt and Stuart were at the front; they knew precisely where they were going.

CHAPTER 37

1:33 a.m.

With Matt and Stuart leading the way, the hostage rescue and tactical teams approached the ancient garden gate. This time, it was locked. Matt motioned for the lockmaster. While he worked on the old lock, Matt checked out their surroundings. All was dark, no lights on anywhere. This part of the city was quiet like a church on Tuesday night. For such a bustling city, Edinburgh could hold close its tragic secrets when it chose to.

It was only a matter of a couple of minutes before the lockmaster successfully cracked the lock mechanism and carefully pushed open the garden gate, turning to give Matt the thumbs up sign. As he did so, the gate squeaked, and the sound reverberated in the silent night. Matt hurriedly grabbed one of the gate's iron railings to hold it from moving further, letting out a breath as the screech stopped.

Stuart gave the signal to his men, and Matt, leading the way, advanced toward the steps he remembered. He felt his way slowly, tiptoeing across the garden lawn, until his hand landed on the stair railing. He could barely see the steps, and he couldn't remember exactly how many there were. He took four steps downward, and suddenly the 17th century door was right in front of his face. He held up his hand—STOP, it said to the troops behind him.

If the door was locked, as expected, the plan was to shoot it open rather than risk warning the kidnappers by fooling noisily with the lock. There had been a discussion around taking this action, but the pros outweighed the cons. Matt would shoot at it sideways rather than risk the bullet entering into the unknown room. It would be left to DCI MacLean to explain their actions later to Historic Scotland if the ancient room was empty of the kidnappers.

His ear to the door, Matt listened intently for thirty seconds. He heard nothing, no sounds in the stillness of the night. He held his gun in front of his body, using both hands, and aimed at the door lock. But then he hesitated; one of his hands was shaking so violently, the barrel of the gun was moving. He was terrified of what he might find inside the room, and he froze.

Stuart reached out, put his hand over Matt's shaking one, and whispered, "Do it. Be not afraid of greatness. Twelfth Night."

The simple message seemed to calm Matt. He took a deep breath, held it, and squeezed the trigger. The door lock blew apart, and the thunderous noise temporarily deafened him and those around him.

Matt pushed the busted door open, dragging the heavy old wood across the rough floor. Inside the large, stone, enclosed room, a faint light emanated from a distant corner about twenty feet from the door where the team stood immobile, weapons drawn, while they scoped out the room. A small table lamp perched on a stack of boxes, and Matt moved toward it like a moth to a flame.

Five feet away from the lamp, Matt's legs appeared to buckle, and he fell to his knees, moaning, "Oh, no. No, no no." He covered his face with his hands, and his whole body heaved in distress.

Stuart rushed to his side. "What is it, Matt? What is it?"

"Shoe," was all he could answer.

Stuart looked ahead and saw a leg wedged between two boxes, its foot wearing a pale pink and beige Nike sneaker. He rushed to it and pushed aside the boxes around the leg, Constable Brown dashing forward to help him.

Together, the two cleared the area around the body. Fern's body. She lay in a pool of dried blood, wearing the same clothes she'd been wearing in the airport CCTV footage.

Her hair was a tangled mess, and there was no color in her white bloodless face. Eyes closed, she laid perfectly still, and Stuart feared she was gone. He lifted her arm and felt for a pulse. At first, he felt nothing, but then there was a slight movement in her wrist. A very, very faint pulse. "Ambulance! Now!" he shouted, and the room came alive with action.

Matt, still on his knees, croaked, "Is she de.."

"She's alive, Matt," Stuart interrupted him. "Barely. Constable, keep Matt back while I tend to Mrs. Horning."

Stuart and one of the hostage rescue team knelt over Fern and tried to revive her, to no avail. Stuart checked her from head to toe for bullet or stab wounds but found no obvious source of her bleeding. Then, Stuart remembered; the baby. He put one hand over his eyes and lowered his head for a brief moment. After a couple of deep breaths, and shielding her body from Matt, Stuart started to pull down Fern's pants.

But he found he couldn't do it. It would have to wait for the medics. He just didn't have the stomach for it.

The ambulance, waiting in Holyrood car park, arrived in under two minutes, and the paramedics rushed into the basement room with equipment and a stretcher. Matt sat on the floor and watched, as if it were a movie happening to someone else. Stuart and Constable Brown moved to Matt's side, clearing the way for the doctors. Stuart massaged his shoulders, while Constable Brown, in a soothing voice Stuart had never heard him use before, kept repeating in Matt's ear, "She's going to be alright. You'll see. We're going to save her."

One of the medics took her blood pressure. It wasn't good. He pulled up her eyelids and listened to her lungs. "Get me the atropine and pralidoxime chloride combo in the syringe. Hurry, it's an exposure!"

After the nerve agent antidote was administered, the paramedics lifted Fern and placed her on a stretcher, moving her hastily to the ambulance. Stuart helped Matt to his feet, and the two followed the stretcher outside to the waiting ambulance. Once the stretcher was secured inside, one of the paramedics offered Matt a hand up. "Ride with us, Chief Horning. Talk to your wife."

From somewhere far away, those words woke Matt up, and he grabbed the medic's hand and pulled himself into the back of the ambulance, taking a bench seat next to Fern's head. A startlingly white sheet had been placed over her. His fingertips lightly caressed Fern's cheek, and it felt cold to his touch. The paramedic who had administered the injection sat on the other side of Fern, holding a pouch with a tube above her arm, as he yelled to the driver, "Go!"

"Will she stay with us?" Matt asked him, imploring the medic to tell him the truth.

"It's touch and go, sir. We can't do anything else until we get her to hospital."

"But the shot you gave her...that will save her, right?"

The medic looked into Matt's eyes. "It's probably too late for the antidote to work on Mrs. Horning. I'm sorry, but it needs to be administered within a few hours of her exposure. And we won't know the specific agent until we can run tests on her."

"You won't give up on my wife, on Fern, will you?"

The medic shook his head. "No, we will repeat administration of the antidote, and we have some further supportive measures we can take. We will exhaust every possible treatment. You have my word." He looked down. "There is one other thing, sir," he said haltingly. "Your baby. The baby has died, and your wife has lost a great deal of blood. It's a bad situation, and I'm so, so sorry to tell you this."

The weight of the past forty-eight hours crashed down on Matt, and the gates finally opened. He sobbed loudly and without restraint. The medic sat helplessly while the ambulance raced through the city.

They pulled up to the emergency entrance, and Matt collected himself. The medic tightened the straps holding Fern in place while Matt gently cradled her head whispering in her ear. As they started to lift her, her lips parted slightly, and she made a gurgling noise.

Matt lowered his face to her mouth. "What is it, Fern? Can you talk to me? I love you so much. Please talk to me."

She tried to form a word. "Ripple," she said, barely audible.

"What?" Matt said into her ear. "What are you telling me?"

She tried again, and again it sounded like "Ripple."

"I don't understand, sweetheart. Please say it again."

But her lips stopped moving.

CHAPTER 38

Inside the hospital, Stuart guided Matt to a private room with a sofa and two chairs, while the paramedics whisked Fern down a long hallway and through some swinging doors. The night nurse supervisor brought them strong and very sweet tea, the cure-all.

Constable Brown and the police units stayed behind to inspect the basement of the old Croft-An-Righ mansion. They had established that there were no other people in the building at present, but they found some evidence that there may have been others there at some point. Forensics went to work immediately, and they would report to DCI MacLean as soon as they could.

Patty Perkins had the presence of mind to notify Conor and Mary Byrne that their daughter had been found, and she would bring a car to pick them up and take them to the hospital. Meg, who wanted to stay at the station in case the kidnappers called so she could trace their location, arranged for an assistant to the MIT to drive Patty. Ross and Beverly Horning were also waiting at the family hotel and insisted on accompanying them. They knew their son would need comforting, too.

Amazingly, the tea did perk up Matt somewhat. Stuart noticed that he was coming around, and said, "Hospital tea is like a slap across the face, isn't it?"

Matt didn't smile, but he gave Stuart a look of recognition for the first time since they'd found Fern. Stuart, greatly relieved that Matt might rejoin the fight said, "Drink up, mate. It will put the hair back on your chest." He clinked cups with Matt's, and they both took a sip of the hot, black brew.

They continued to drink their tea, and Stuart remained silent, waiting for Matt to want to talk. He would sit by his side all night if that's what it took.

Eventually, Matt set down his cup, and said, "Were you in the ambulance with us?" he asked.

"No, the medics wouldn't let me. Only her husband was allowed."

"Fern tried to tell me something, but it didn't make any sense."

"What did she say?" Stuart asked.

"It sounded like 'ripple'."

"And that doesn't mean anything to you?"

Matt looked at Stuart. "I can't think well. But it must be a clue to who did this to her. My wife would try her hardest to tell me."

"It's early for you, Matt. Give it some time, and you will put the puzzle together." Stuart hesitated. "Do you feel up to talking?"

Matt nodded.

"The real puzzle is where in the bloody hell are the bloody kidnappers?" Stuart said, frustrated. "Here's what we know. They were at St. Anthony's Chapel ruins sometime between 11:15 p.m.—when they made the call—and 12:30 a.m. when you discovered the suitcases had been retrieved."

"Right."

"Then they were hiding in St. Margaret's Well. That grate, which we personally had seen earlier completely intact like it has been for decades, didn't blowtorch itself. That would have been sometime around midnight most likely, until we got there around 1:00 a.m. But where are they now?"

"They didn't go back to Croft-An-Righ. They left Fern there to die alone," Matt said bitterly. "Did we check Vadim Guz's house on Regent Terrace? I can't remember."

"Yes, we sent a team there immediately after your man Jay confirmed that he had been hired to do the deed. Guz wasn't home—obviously, he was busy elsewhere—and the house was all dark. My team went through the house, and no one was there."

"They must have gotten out of the park. Somehow avoided our teams."

"Constable Brown firmly believes that they didn't."

"Do you agree with him?"

"It's illogical," Stuart said, "but we all know that park so well, and how to secure it. It's just hard to see where they could have exited without being seen. Especially carrying two large suitcases."

"So, if they couldn't exit unobserved, then they're still somewhere in Hunter's Bog. Those are our two options."

They stared at each other. Stuart said, "I will put out an APB for Vadim Guz to broadcast an alert, and check with Scone to see if there is any news on the phone trace. We've also got his cell phone number and can use technology to track it. I need a warrant for that, but I think I'll choose to forego that step on this occasion."

That did get a flitting smile from Matt.

"I take it you still have no idea who the woman could be?" Stuart asked.

"Not unless I know a woman named 'Ripple', and I'm sure I don't." He frowned. "Do you think we might have missed something in that well? It is the perfect hiding place while we were racing about. Maybe there's a hidden room or tunnel behind a fake wall or something. Someplace else they could have hidden from us."

"It was an ingenious place to hide," Stuart agreed.

The door to their waiting room opened, and in rushed the families and Patty. Mary Byrne, Fern's mother, was the first to reach Matt, and she enveloped him in a clinging hug. "I knew you'd find her," she whispered in his ear. "Thank you."

Matt pulled away from her embrace. "Don't thank me, Mary. She might not make it."

"Of course she'll make it. She's my daughter. And you are Matt and Fern."

"The doctors aren't optimistic. We need to be realistic."

"They don't know her like we do, do they?" She pinched his cheek. "I want you cheery and your loving self when she wakes up. Do you understand me, young man? You're the one who can help her the most."

"I will be there for her, of course I will. But she's been through a lot, Mary, probably things you and I can't even imagine yet. The body can only take so much."

"I'm not naïve, you know. I know about the baby, my grandchild, and

I'm so very sorry. But I only want *my* baby back. And I know my daughter; she is as tough as they come. You know it, too. There will be other babies, we just need to help our Fern get through this. When can I see her?"

"The doctors are working on her now," Matt said. "Told me they'd come and get me when I could see her."

"I can wait. I feared I'd never see her again. I can wait a little while longer," Mary said.

The other parents huddled around Matt, and they all shared their love before talk turned to the kidnappers. He noted that Patty and Stuart were off in the corner, heads together. "They got away. With all the money," Matt told them.

Conor gasped. "They took your cash, and didn't let her go? That's not fair!"

"No honor among thieves," Matt said. "Welcome to my world."

Patty and Stuart joined in, and Stuart said, "While it's true we don't know where they are currently, our investigation is ongoing."

Matt caught Patty giving Stuart a subtle head nod, and the Scot put a map of Edinburgh down on the coffee table. "Have a look at our map. I'd welcome your input."

Matt, of course, understood that Stuart and Patty were trying to take the parents' thoughts off Fern, at least for a while. All four of them fell for it and converged over the map.

"This is the spot of the ransom drop," Stuart indicated, touching the St. Anthony's icon on the map. "And this is where your son realized the clue that led to us finding your daughter."

"What was the clue?" asked Conor.

Stuart looked over at Matt, who said, "When we went to the area around the car park yesterday — or whenever it was — to look at the location where our witness saw the woman matching the description of Fern's abductor, I smelled a strong smell that we've since identified as gardenia, probably perfume or body lotion," he explained. "When Stuart and I went to this place, St. Margaret's Well, I smelled the same fragrance."

Matt turned back to the map. "This is where we found Fern, the same place I'd originally smelled gardenia." He moved his finger around to all four locations: St. Andrews ruins, St. Margaret's Well, the car park, and Croft-An-Righ. "You can see the proximity of all four places. We knew we were in the right area."

"In addition," Stuart said, and he pointed to 15, Regent Terrace, "our primary suspect lives here. Also, as you can see, nearby."

"Didn't you have the area surrounded?" Conor asked.

Stuart spoke. "Yes, completely surrounded with the best teams we have. We don't understand how they could've gotten away. We're very sorry."

Patty leaned over the map, peering at it intently. "They didn't. They are still there. In the well," she said and looked at Matt. "It's the only thing that makes any sense."

"But we looked in the well," Stuart protested. "Walked all the way inside it. They weren't there. The only possible evidence we found was this button." He produced the distinctive button from his pocket.

Patty squinted at it. "I know that button. I tried on a coat in the Buck Bay department store during the January sales. It had those buttons. I remember because I thought they were hideous."

"Did you buy the coat?" Matt asked. "What's it look like?"

"No," Patty said. "It was a puffy black coat, made me look like an offensive lineman."

"Have you seen any other women wearing it around town?"

Patty thought. "No, I don't believe so."

"Do you remember the brand?"

"Yes, but it's a common one. There are probably thousands of those coats sold in the U.S." She paused. "Why don't you stay here with your family, Matt, and Stuart and I will go take another look at the well. OK with you?"

"Yep. I'm not leaving until I see my wife."

Patty stood on her toes and gave Matt a kiss on the cheek. "Chin up, Chief."

CHAPTER 39

Stuart and Patty hitched a ride with the MIT assistant back to St. Margaret's Well. "Call Constable Brown and tell him to bring a unit here right away," Stuart instructed her.

"Where will you be, sir?" she asked.

"In the well."

They walked in from Queen's Drive and found the forensic crew had cordoned off the area around St. Margaret's and were searching for evidence.

"Thank you for keeping at it," Stuart said, approaching Neil Aitken, who had done the excellent work in the car park finding the footprint and the car tread.

"It's nae a problem, DCI," Aitken said. "Chief Horning promised me a whisky, and I figure if I can find anything further here, he's probably good for a case."

That got a smile out of Stuart. "Aye, he probably is. This is Detective Patricia Perkins from the States, she's helping us. We're going back inside the well as soon as Constable Brown gets here with a tactical team." Patty and Aitken nodded at one another because Aitken's hands were nestled snugly in protective gear.

"Try not to touch anything, then," Aitken said. "We haven't worked inside yet." Stuart could tell from his voice that he disapproved of their entering a crime scene.

"Under normal circumstances, I would stay well away from your work,

Neil, but there are special circumstances in this case. Constable Brown is convinced that the kidnappers have not penetrated the wall of security around the park. We believe them to still be here somewhere, and we suspect they are the perpetrators of this damage to St. Margaret's Well. We need to make sure they aren't still in there somewhere."

"Like in a hidden room or secret shaft?"

"Yes. Matt and I looked around, but we're not sure we did it justice. Detective Perkins wants to have a look herself."

Constable Brown and a five-man team of armed officers approached the well. Patty greeted them and introduced herself. "The victim in this case, Fern Byrne is a close friend of mine, and Chief Horning and I work together. I believe and agree with you, Constable, that the kidnappers have not left the park, and DCI MacLean has agreed to humor me and help me search this place." She turned to look at the gaping opening behind her. "It's a low probability that they are still hiding in there, but I'm an experienced detective, and just long enough in the tooth to know when to call backup, just in case the odds are wrong this time. I'm grateful for your assistance if we run into trouble. I want two of you to follow us into the well, and the rest of you to surround the entrance. Understand?"

To the man on his immediate right, Constable Brown said, "I'm going in with them, and James, you come with us. The rest of you do as the detective suggested, fan out in the immediate area around the opening. Use your lanterns to create better visibility. Listen for our shouts or, God forbid, our gun shots, and take appropriate action."

"Aye, sir," said the other four men in unison. Patty noted that the team had their firearms at the ready, which helped relieve the sudden tension she was feeling.

Stuart went in first and then gave shorter-legged Patty a hand over the opening. Constable Brown and James climbed over next and took up their positions inside the well opening. As Stuart had warned Patty, it was a cold, dank, claustrophobic space, and she was uneasy. Silently, they trudged through the shallow water with the ancient stone walls closing in. After about one minute, they came to the room Matt and Stuart had found, and there the underground space opened up and came to an end.

Patty, too, smelled the faint gardenia fragrance and followed it around the space to the far wall. Without a word, she motioned to Stuart to follow and moved to the wall, beginning to touch each of the damp stones, once on each end. Stuart did the same, starting on the opposite side of the wall from where Patty was working. He pushed on each stone, willing each one to move and reveal what was behind the wall.

They worked soundlessly for a few minutes, about to give up, when Patty jumped backwards with a quiet gasp, her stone moving inward as the wall began to move with it. Instantaneously, she heard a muffled man's voice say, "Look out," accompanied by shuffling noises.

Stuart was at Patty's side in a heartbeat, and they moved in concert behind the stone wall opposite the moving wall, shielding themselves from whatever—and whoever—was on the other side. The wall continued to slowly open inward, revealing a larger space. A man's head—Vadim Guz—cautiously poked out from behind the moving wall. Patty and Stuart had seen enough, and burst through the opening, firearms in the 'shoot' position.

"Stop!" Patty shouted, and her voice reverberated around the stone space. "Hands in the air and down on your knees!"

A gunshot from within bounced off a stone next to Stuart's head, making a loud pinging sound. Involuntarily, both cops ducked at the ear-splitting noise. Stuart reacted first, pushing past Patty to knock the gun out of Guz's hand in one of the fastest, strongest moves Patty had seen in her decades on the force. She responded in kind, leaping forward and shoving her gun's barrel against Guz's temple.

Behind Guz, a woman grabbed the suitcases and attempted to run past the commotion. While Stuart subdued Vadim Guz, Patty swung her gun around, pointing it at the woman's head. "You, too, sweetie!" Patty screamed at her.

The woman dropped the suitcases, threw her hands in the air, and dropped to her knees, all in one movement. She cried, "Don't shoot! Please don't shoot me!"

Patty, momentarily distracted by one of the woman's hands that displayed a missing finger with a red-streaked bandage awkwardly wrapped around it and leaking blood, didn't look at her face at first. When she did, she said incredulously, "Paula? Paula Dalrymple?"

Trembling and cowering on the floor, the woman whispered, "Hello, Patty."

• • •

The Police Scotland tactical team arrived in the hidden room approximately thirty seconds after Guz's gunshot sounded at the well's opening.

"This is a right kerfuffle," Constable Brown said, slapping handcuffs on Guz while Stuart's gun never wavered one inch from the Russian's head. James handcuffed Paula Dalrymple as she collapsed onto the bitingly cold stone floor.

Two of the tactical team members opened the suitcases. "Whoa," one of them said as the top opened and more dollars than he would ever see again in his lifetime were stuffed inside. "Looks like the ransom is all here," was all he could get out.

Stuart, red-faced and agitated, said to his prisoner, "Vadim Guz, I am going to charge you, but before I do so I must caution you that you do not need to say anything in answer to the charge but anything you do say will be noted and may be used in evidence. Do you understand?"

"Yes," Guz barked, and Stuart continued, "The charge against you is that you did conspire to and assisted in the unlawful detainment and imprisonment of Fern Byrne, a United States citizen. You and/or an accomplice caused a nerve agent to be administered to the victim thereby causing her bodily harm and possibly death, which will result in a premeditated murder charge. You held Fern Byrne against her will and subsequently stole the sum of $2 million from her family. You are being charged with these crimes, with the possibility of additional charges being added once our investigation is complete. Do you understand the charges against you?" Stuart paused and glared at him.

"Yes," Guz replied, this time in a bit quieter tone.

"Have you anything to say?" Stuart asked.

"No."

Constable Brown made note of Guz's replies.

"Therefore, I am arresting you on these offences, and you are hereby remanded into the custody of Police Scotland," Stuart said, and turned to Constable Brown. "Get him out of my sight," Stuart said, revulsion in each word.

Brown and a team member moved quickly, and marched Vadim Guz out into the dark night.

Stuart turned to the woman and helped her to stand, while Patty held her gun trained on her.

"Your name, please," he said.

She flushed, but did not answer.

Stuart, calmly, said again, "Your name, please," and waited.

Again, she did not speak and looked at the floor.

"Do you speak English?" he asked.

"Yes," she answered.

"Your name then, please."

Silence.

"Her name is Paula Dalrymple," Patty said, her face ashen, "and she resides in Twisty River, Oregon, in the U.S."

"You know this woman?" Stuart asked Patty.

"We both are in a monthly book club in our small town. I live in Twisty River also, and I worked with Paula's husband, David Dalrymple, who was the Chinook County District Attorney for many years. He now resides in the Oregon State Penitentiary because last year, he hired a hitman to kill Chief Matt Horning."

Stuart's eyebrows raised to new levels.

Still, Paula remained quiet.

"You heard the caution I gave to your partner in crime, Vadim Guz," Stuart said to Paula. "I now give the same caution to you with a murder in the first degree addition for personally administering the nerve agent that has likely caused the death of Fern Byrne. Do you understand the charges against you?"

Paula looked up into Stuart's eyes. "You can't charge me. I'm an American citizen."

Stuart laughed at her. "Oh, but I can, ma'am," he said. "I have the power to arrest anyone I want without a warrant if I have reason to suspect that you have committed a crime, or I see a crime being committed. You have the ransom money in your possession, and there are other clues to your involvement, which I do not intend to divulge now. It is my opinion as Detective Chief Inspector that it is in the public's best interests to arrest you and remand you to Police Scotland's custody." For Patty's entertainment, Stuart sniffed in Paula's direction and looked down at her bloodied hand, clearly missing a finger.

Patty understood the additional clues to Paula's guilt, and knew that she and Stuart, like he and Matt, would be lifelong friends from here on out.

CHAPTER 40

Matt, at his mother's urging, had stretched out on the sofa in the hospital's private waiting room. Additional chairs were brought in for Conor and Mary Byrne, as the families waited for any news on Fern's status. He was asleep within a minute of Ross's turning down the room's lights.

Shortly after Matt drifted off, a doctor came by to give them a report. The four parents quietly slipped out of the room and talked to him.

"Is our daughter alive?" Conor asked anxiously as he closed the door to the waiting room behind him.

"Yes," answered the doctor, a plump woman in her fifties with one dramatic silver streak through her dark hair. "But Fern is in critical condition. We have stabilized her for the moment and continue to administer drugs to treat nerve agent exposure. However, we have, so far, been unable to identify the exact agent given to her, so we are driving in the dark with no headlights. But we are doing everything we can think of, and she is keeping with us for now."

Mary Byrne began to cry, and the doctor enveloped her in a hug. "You're her mother, aren't you?" she said, gently wiping the tears from Mary's face. "I see the resemblance. You are lovely just like your daughter."

"Thank you," Mary murmured, trying to catch her breath.

"Fern is unconscious, but she is not paralyzed at the moment. She did have a minor convulsion when she was first brought to us, but there has not been a second one." She paused, looking at all the parents. "I know you want me to say that she is out of the woods and will recover, but I can't say that yet. She has a chance, and we will continue to fight on her behalf."

"Can I see her?" Mary asked.

"It's better if you don't," the doctor said frankly. "She's hooked up to several machines, and it will upset you further. Give us another hour to see how our latest intervention goes, and then I'll come get you, OK?"

Mary nodded.

The doctor peered through the glass window in the door to the waiting room. "Please give Mr. Horning my report when he wakes up. Let him sleep for now."

• • •

Ray Peng nervously ate his dinner alone at a table in the prison dining room. He was trying to avoid everyone tonight while he waited for the agreement from the U.S. Marshals and kept his head down while he finished off his food. Just as he was about to take his last bite, David Dalrymple sat down opposite him, saying, "How are you doing, Ray?"

"OK. You?"

"Not so good."

"Sorry to hear that." Ray pretended to spear some food.

"Don't you want to know why I'm not good?" Dalrymple asked him.

"Sure. Why aren't you good?"

"Because I haven't heard from my wife as expected. You wouldn't know anything about that, would you?"

Ray looked up. "Why would I?"

"Some of us are starting to think you have new best friends."

"Like who?"

"Like the cops. Is that true?"

Ray laughed. "No."

"You're spending a lot of time with them. What about?" Dalrymple asked.

Ray shrugged. "They keep asking me questions. That's all."

"Don't answer them. Simple."

Dalrymple got up and left the room. Ray waited until his breathing returned to normal, and then he left, too.

In another part of the prison, Jay, Tamryn, and Ed waited for the dinner hour to end so they could present Ray Peng with the U.S. Marshals' agreement for his signature. Everything was ready to go; they were just waiting for Matt's final approval.

Jay paced around the small conference room as best he could in the confined space. Tamryn and Ed, more experienced at the police officer waiting game, sat at the table and went over their notes.

"What the hell is going on in Scotland?" Jay said. "Why hasn't Matt called us? Fern's dead, isn't she? The ransom exchange went bad, didn't it?"

Ed sighed. "Yes, Jay, Fern is dead, the exchange went horribly wrong, and Matt is dead, too. Or, Matt is very busy and hasn't had a chance yet to phone us."

"Or," Tamryn added, "the exchange went off without a hitch, and Matt is tending to his sick wife and arresting the bad guys, and hasn't had a chance yet to phone us. One of the two options, for sure."

Jay looked at his watch. "It's the middle of the night over there, for cryin' out loud. What's taking so long? And what are we — chopped liver? We're suffering over here, too."

"Matt will call us the minute he knows anything," Ed said. "He's our friend and we have to trust him. Sit down, Jay, you are making me nauseous."

In the end, it was Patty who called Jay and filled him in on all the action. "So, Fern is alive and, in the hospital, but in critical condition, is that correct?" Jay said into his phone for the benefit of Ed and Tamryn. "Putting you on speaker."

"Yes, that's the important news," Patty said, coming across loud and clear. "But I just talked to Beverly Horning who is at the hospital, and she said Fern's doctor cautioned that it's still touch and go, and they haven't identified the exact nerve agent exposure. Matt is sleeping in the waiting room currently, his first real sleep in over forty-eight hours. Beverly is insisting they let him sleep until he wakes up naturally."

"Where are you now?" Ed asked.

"At Police Scotland HQ. I was directly involved in the arrests with DCI

MacLean after we rescued Fern, and we've been here processing. I'll tell you the uncut version of events later. We have two people in custody, both of whom have been officially charged with Fern's kidnapping. We also recovered the full $2 million ransom."

"Patty, this is Tamryn. That's terrific news. Can you tell us if Ray Peng's intel was correct?"

"Yes, it was, and you should go ahead with his witness protection plan. Immediately, if not sooner. It was Zhang Chen who hired Vadim Guz to plan and execute Fern's kidnapping. Peng was right about their doing business together previously, notably in the U.K., but also throughout Europe and South America. Guz is Russian, and a known expert-for-hire in nerve agent assassinations. But there is another twist in this awful story, and y'all better sit down for this one."

"What?" Jay said, finally taking a seat.

"Chen hired Vadim Guz on David Dalrymple's request. Paula Dalrymple, David's wife, is the second person we arrested. Paula is the woman in the CCTV footage who abducted Fern at the Edinburgh airport. She was well-disguised, but I don't think Matt had ever met her. Paula administered the nerve agent that Guz prepared for her. And, before you ask, she won't tell us what it was. She wants Fern to die."

Ed slapped his big paw down hard on the table. "Dalrymple!" he shouted. "That mousy wife of his is the perpetrator? That's unbelievable, Patricia."

"I know. I got disoriented for a moment when I found her with Guz. I'm headed to talk to her again when I finish here. I've known her for years, and it's a shocker, for sure. If I recall, it was Fern who secured the Dalrymple house on the morning we arrested David. If my memory is correct, Fern can positively ID Paula as her abductor, and along with my evidence with her and the ransom money, we've got her cold turkey."

"If Fern makes it," Ed said.

"Yes, if she lives to testify."

"She, her weasel husband, and Chen all need to fry."

Patty said calmly, "We all know that's not going to happen, Ed. But please see to it that Chen and Dalrymple are placed into solitary confinement at once for Ray Peng's safety. It's a fucking prison, and word will get around quickly."

Tamryn hurriedly rose and was out the door without another word, heading for the warden's office.

Ed said, "I know you're in a hurry, but I just have one more question. What does $2 million look like?"

Patty laughed. "A whole lot of money."

· · ·

Back at the Royal Infirmary of Edinburgh, Matt startled himself awake from a bad dream. He looked at his watch, but Beverly put her hand on his, and said, "You've been asleep for two hours. You need ten, but it's a start." She smiled at her son. "She's still alive, and the doctors are doing everything they can."

He sat up, rubbing his eyes. "Can we see her yet?"

"Not yet, but soon, I think. Fern's doctor told Mary that they would let you and her parents go in when they finished their next intervention. They are trying other antidotes on her because they don't know exactly the agent that she was exposed to. And, she is unconscious, so you need to be prepared for that, son."

"I am. I just want to watch her breath going in and out."

Beverly, not knowing how to respond to that plea, just nodded and squeezed his hand.

· · ·

The Oregon State Penitentiary warden took haste in getting Zhang Chen and David Dalrymple moved into individual solitary confinement cells. Simultaneously, Ray Peng was whisked out the back door and into a waiting black SUV with tinted windows. The driver hit I-5 southbound, before cutting west south of Cottage Grove, driving six miles an hour over the speed limit the entire drive to Port Stirling, Oregon.

They picked up Ray's wife, two children, and his wife's mother, and immediately drove back to Eugene, where they were put on a government plane in the dark of night, non-stop to Madison, Wisconsin. The second Ray felt the airplane's wheels leave the ground, he wrote the name of the Oregon State Penitentiary guard who had been taking care of—for a healthy paycheck—Zhang Chen's every need on a piece of paper and handed it to his U.S. Marshals handler. With a sour taste in his mouth, the warden personally arrested Luiz Garcia on charges of supplying illegal contraband and, for good measure, added on a charge of conspiracy to commit a crime. Then, he fired his ass.

It would be years before Tamryn would see Ray Peng again.

• • •

Neil Aitken of Police Scotland forensics phoned DCI MacLean to inform him that they had picked up a print off a chair in the Shetland Airport waiting room that belonged to Vadim Guz. They also pulled prints off the door and an interior light switch at Croft-An-Righ, linking Paula Dalrymple and Guz to that location.

In 2014, when Historic Scotland was dissolved and its function transferred to Historic Environment Scotland in 2015, Vadim Guz, as a prominent Scottish citizen and landowner, had been somehow involved during the transition and had acquired keys to the Croft-An-Righ building and garden, which he had copied before returning them to the organization.

Over the intervening years, Guz had used the always-locked, unused old garden storage basement as his hostage hideaway. Never once, until Matt smelled a simple gardenia fragrance twice in two days, did anyone ever go near the place.

• • •

Buck Bay Police Chief Dan McCoy arrived at Rancho Miguel Splendida, Blake Bowen's favorite spa, with a local law enforcement officer who had jurisdiction. It was a toasty eight-six degrees, and McCoy was sweating in his police uniform.

The young woman at reception was not pleased to deal with the abrasive American policeman, but knew she had no options once Officer Cruz displayed his badge. Silently, she wrote Blake Bowen's suite number on a hotel notepad and handed it to Chief McCoy. With a nod of her head, she confirmed that Blake was a current guest.

McCoy and Cruz wandered through the resort's lush tropical paths until they located Blake's complex. Very old, tall, yellow trumpetbush trees overhead provided some nice shade from the brutal sun, for which the chief was grateful.

They found Blake beyond her pony wall gate in a small, enclosed courtyard. She was relaxing on a chaise behind huge sunglasses, a Robert Dugoni crime novel in hand.

"I like his books, too," Dan McCoy said. Blake, startled at his voice, flinched and dropped the book.

"What the hell?!?," she exclaimed, looking at the two cops.

"This kind of hell," McCoy said, extending his handcuffs in her direction.

CHAPTER 41

Detective Patty Perkins sat behind a plexiglass barrier, separating her from a dangerously unstable Paula Dalrymple. Her real hair, a short, dishwater blonde, was a stringy, filthy mess after days of wearing the black wig, and her fair skin was mottled with uneven red patches. She was visibly shaking, and her left leg was pumping up and down under the table. She looked vacantly at Patty, her eyes bulging.

Patty started the recorder next to her, glancing up at the window where she knew DCI MacLean was keenly watching. In a soft voice, she said, "Paula, honey, I'm here to help you. We are friends, aren't we?"

Paula nodded without speaking.

"Can you tell me what happened here? In Scotland?"

"You know."

"I think I know, but I'd like to hear your version."

"I kidnapped Fern."

"Did you expose her to a nerve agent in the bathroom at Edinburgh Airport?"

"Yes, I did. That was a first for me." She chuckled.

Patty blanched but kept going. "What was it you gave to Fern?"

"Some kind of nerve thingy. A topical application. Vadim mixed it up for me in a capsule in a special device he used. He told me to brush her skin with it. He knows what he's doing."

"Do you know the name of it?"

Paula thought. "I can't remember."

"Try hard."

Paula pounded on the table. "I told you I can't remember!"

In a soothing voice, Patty quickly said, "OK, it's OK, you can't remember. But if you think of the nerve agent name later, you'll tell me, won't you?"

Paula nodded.

"How did you protect yourself from it? Isn't it dangerous?"

"Yes, but Vadim told me what to do. I wore gloves while handling it, and gave myself an injection of the antidote that Nigel kept in the car."

"Why did you do this, Paula?"

"Because my husband, the famous district attorney, didn't save as much money as he told me," she said bitterly. "With him in prison, the kids and I were going to lose our home in less than a year. I had to do something to get some money."

"You could have gotten a job. Supported the family yourself."

Paula chuckled again. "Doing what? I have absolutely no skills. I was trained to be a wife and mother. That's it. I looked good on David's campaign trails, and I smiled for the voters. That was my job."

"And what do you think will happen to your children now?" Patty, going for the jugular.

Paula began to cry, softly at first, and then violent, hacking sobs. Patty sat still and let her go. After a few minutes, she handed her some tissues, and Paula took a stab at wiping her tears away.

Once she was composed again, she said, "Will you notify my sister for me? She's in Eugene, and the kids are with her now. She will keep them until I get home, and they can be with their cousins."

"You won't be going home for a long, long time. You've been arrested for kidnapping, Paula—kidnapping! That's not a slap on the wrist. You're going to jail, just like David."

"I can't go to jail. I have children. They need their mother."

"One could argue they need both their mother and their father. But you and David have robbed them of that comfort."

Paula rested her head on the table. "I'm so tired."

"I need to ask you about your finger. What happened?" Patty asked briskly. "Please sit up and talk to me."

Paula sat up. "Vadim chopped it off. He said it couldn't be Fern's finger because Matt would never stop looking for us, but we had to let him know we were serious. Said it was the only way to make sure we got the money."

"And you didn't question that?"

"Not really. I could understand his point. Of course, I hated to lose a finger, but I would've hated to lose my house more." She shrugged.

"Didn't it hurt?"

"Yeah. He gave me four Advil. And he wrapped it up nicely. Vadim really isn't a bad person like you think."

Patty sat up straight in her chair and cast a quick glance over her shoulder at Stuart. *Could this be a case of Stockholm Syndrome? Could Vadim have become Paula's captor, too, and she empathized with him? Enough to let him cut off her finger!*

"As soon as you are arraigned—that means you'll go to a court and be formally…"

"I know what 'arraigned' means," Paula interrupted. "I'm married to a D.A., remember?"

"Of course. As soon as you are arraigned, we'll take you to the hospital to have the doctors dress your wound."

"That would be nice. It's throbbing."

. . .

Jay, Tamryn, and Ed headed for home. Amanda, the warden, and several of the prison staff gave them a clapping ovation as they left the visitor entrance.

"Come back and visit anytime," the warden smiled. The three cops knew it was a line he'd previously used often.

"Thanks, but no thanks," Jay said, giving him a salute.

. . .

Ross and Beverly Horning had just returned from a neighborhood restaurant where they'd bought enough takeout food for ten people instead of just the five of them, when Fern's doctor entered their waiting room.

She was smiling. Matt put down his plate and rose to greet her.

"What?" he asked anxiously. "You look happy."

"I am. We've finally identified the nerve agent your wife was given. It's Sarin."

Matt's hand flew to cover his mouth. "That's deadly," he whispered.

"It can be. But we believe she was given a diluted version, somewhere below the lethal threshold. Which is why she didn't die immediately upon exposure."

"So, like a lower concentration of it?" asked Conor.

"Yes, exactly," said the doctor. "It was enough to incapacitate Fern, and may still cause her some on-going damage, but not enough to kill her outright. We will still want to monitor her for long-term neurological damage, but we have given her the appropriate antidote formula now, and I expect her to recover."

"Oh, thank God!" Mary cried, falling into Conor's arms. Matt joined them in a group hug, and the three of them jumped up and down together, crying and laughing. Not wanting to be left out, Ross and Beverly encircled the three, and all five did an impromptu dance of sorts.

The doctor said, "Your daughter is a lucky woman. She will live a wonderful life surrounded by people who love her very much. I don't get to see this every day in my work."

Matt broke the scrum and hugged the doctor. "We owe you everything. Thank you from the bottom of my heart."

"No, it's the other way around," she said, holding both of Matt's hands in hers. "If you hadn't found her when you did, she would have come to me already dead. You saved me from that awful fate which I've experienced too many times."

"Can we see her now?" Mary asked.

"Yes, let's allow her husband a few minutes alone first, and then her parents. Parents-in-law, you'll have to wait for the next round."

"As it should be," said Beverly, grinning. "But I intend to tell my daughter-in-law that we parents are growing weary of hanging out in hospitals waiting for my son and her to come back to us. This shit has got to stop!"

"Amen to that," Conor agreed.

HUNTER'S BOG

• • •

The doctor led Matt down the hallway to Fern's ICU room. The light in her room was low, except for the blinking machines. Still, Matt could see his wife's luminous face in the shadowy room. Her eyes were closed, but he could see her breathing slowly, and he was filled with relief.

Gently, he took her hand, bent down and kissed her on her warm cheek. Just like in the movies, Fern opened her eyes. "Matt."

"It's me, my love."

"What happened? I thought we were flying home? Where am I?"

"We're still in Edinburgh. A slight delay." He smiled.

She blinked, and for an instant, Matt thought she was going back to sleep. But her eyes opened once again. "Dalrymple."

And the light went off for Matt. "Oh, you were trying to say 'Dalrymple', weren't you? All I got was 'ripple'; I couldn't figure out what you were trying to tell me."

"Mrs. Dalrymple. She brushed me with something."

"Yes. And you've been very sick, but you're going to get better now."

"Promise me? Don't feel good now."

Matt squeezed her hand. "No, you don't feel good. But you will, and I will be right here until you do. You have to fight as hard as you can, Fern. Fight to be well again. I will fight alongside you. We'll eat and sleep and do what your doctors tell us to do. And then I'll take my wife home."

"Baby?"

Matt was dreading this question. He thought about stalling, but he knew his wife; she would want the truth, no matter how painful. In the end, he simply said, "Our baby didn't make it. I'm sorry, love."

Fern turned her head to the side and softly cried.

CHAPTER 42

Two days later

While Fern took her afternoon nap, Matt placed a call to Lisa Perry's private cell phone.

"Matt," she answered.

"Hi, Lisa. I wanted to give you an update and thank you for your actions," he said.

"Not necessary. My sources tell me that your wife is safe and will recover. I'm so happy for you."

"I'm happy, too," Matt said. "Did they tell you that we also recovered all the ransom money, and the kidnappers are in jail?"

"Yes, I got a full report. The cash has been returned to me, and I've read the reports on the arrests. We've been after Vadim Guz for some time, just didn't know precisely who he was. It's beginning to look like he is responsible for several assassinations in the U.K. and Germany—all by nerve agents—and at least two kidnappings of prominent politicians as well as your wife. We are in the process of trying to learn who hired him for those crimes as well. It's not logical that it would have been your guy Zhang Chen, but Guz is not talking so far. He will eventually tell us what we want to know, and he will be under lock and key in His Majesty's most secure building for a very long time. Well done, sir."

"I don't get all the credit. If ever there was a team arrest, this was it. Police Scotland stepped up big-time, and so did my local team at home in

Oregon. Detective Patricia Perkins from my home county and DCI Stuart MacLean should get a lot of the credit. It was Patty's rational thinking and Stuart's quick action that got Guz in the end."

"So I've heard. It was a brilliant operation all the way around, and I'm proud we could do our part."

"I won't forget you, Lisa. You came through at my darkest moment. Thank you from the bottom of my heart."

"You're welcome, Chief, and I hope our paths cross again."

"Under more pleasant circumstances, I hope!" he said. He hung up with a broad grin.

• • •

Patty and Ted left Edinburgh as soon as they knew Fern was out of the woods.

"Where are you off to?" Matt asked them.

"Out of this city, for starters," Patty answered. "Ted's completed his sightseeing here, and I don't have a desire to see any more of this place."

"We're going up to the northwest corner first and dink along the seaside," Ted said. "Patty is feeling a need for the serenity of an ocean to look at. Then, I want to see Loch Ness, and we'll visit Inverness, get a car and tour through the Highlands. I'm so relieved for you, Matt. Please give Fern our love, and we'll see you back home soon."

"I will, for sure. Good luck driving in the Highlands, you two. And I sincerely mean it, you'll need it!" He laughed.

• • •

The four parents stayed on another week, and Mary and Conor rarely left the hospital, sitting near their daughter's bedside as much as possible. Matt and Conor had a heart-to-heart talk one afternoon while Mary went to their hotel to retrieve some things, and while Fern was soundly sleeping.

Matt reached out to him first, telling him how sorry he was that their lines of work played a role in his daughter's near death. He promised to make it up to Conor.

"How, exactly, are you going to do that?" Conor responded.

Taken aback, Matt said honestly, "I'm not sure yet. What do you want me to do?"

"I want you to quit your job, make sure that Fern never goes back to work for the State Department, and have another baby."

Matt was speechless. "I can't promise that, Conor. Well, except for the baby part. That's my goal, too, as soon as Fern has recovered. But my community needs me, at least, for now. And you know better than anyone that Fern will do what Fern will do. I can't forbid her to do anything, much less pursue her passions."

"Then don't make promises to me that you can't keep. You asked me what I wanted, and I told you."

"OK, no promises, then. I will do my best to be more careful, and I will demand that Fern do the same…if she decides to return to her job. But there's no way that I'm going to tell her she can't do that. She is a wonderful person, Conor, and that's a tribute to you and Mary, but she deserves to live her life the way she wants to. If that means a return to her job, I will support her in every way I can. You're going to have to do that, too, or risk losing her love. I won't risk losing that love—which is the most important thing in my world—by standing in her way. I value the woman she is too much to ever do that."

Conor was quiet. "You're right, of course. I just want you both to be safe. I love you, too, Matt, and I'm sorry I said the things to you I said." He teared up.

"Don't apologize. We weren't our true selves last week. We were scared to death and lashing out however we could. I love you and Mary, too, and I can promise you that I'm doing some deep thinking these days about how to keep us safer."

"It will be better once we get home. Just try to arrest a better class of people in the future," Conor said. And there was a faint smile on his lips.

• • •

Ross and Beverly stayed close to their son and managed their lives at the hotel near the police station. They made sure that Matt got proper rest and healthy meals so that he could be the best version of himself as he helped Fern navigate her recovery. They also tried to see that Mary and Conor had everything they needed as well. Mary fondly referred to them as 'the project managers', a title which Ross and Beverly quite liked.

Unbeknownst to anyone, Ross had quietly slipped out one morning and went to the Royal Bank of Scotland. He owed the bank manager an apology.

The manager cringed when the receptionist told him there was a Ross Horning in the lobby to see him, but he boldly strode out to meet him.

"I'm here to apologize for my behavior last week. I'm sorry I took out my grief on you. That man was not who I really am," Ross told him, and then stuck out his hand to shake.

The bank manager shook his hand, and, with a smile, said, "Does your job offer in the States still stand?"

"No," Ross said. He turned and left the bank.

• • •

A fisherman in a rowboat on Loch Leven near Kinross felt the prow of his boat bump something. *Must be a submerged rock or log*, he thought. On closer inspection, it turned out to be a white Ford Transit people mover, carefully put there by Max Popov. Popov was tracked down by DCI MacLean and his team and arrested for 'art and part', which Matt learned was the same as the U.S. charge for aiding and abetting a kidnapping. They would prove in court that Popov had driven the van out of Edinburgh to Loch Leven on Guz's order.

A stakeout at Nigel Armstrong's Edinburgh flat eventually was successful in nabbing him as well. He, too, was arrested for art and part, and would be convicted for his role in driving the white van to the airport with Paula Dalrymple, and standing watch over Fern when required.

• • •

Sylvia called Matt one afternoon.

"What's the latest?" Matt asked her.

"Nothing much," Sylvia said. "I'm calling on behalf of Tamryn and the guys. We want to check on Fern. How's she doing?"

"She's doing better than her doctors expected. I think we'll be here another couple of weeks, and then come home. She misses all of you."

"And how are you faring, Chief? Starting to relax a little bit?"

"I'm fine. Anxious to get home, but I don't want to take any chances with Fern's health. Anything else I should know?" he asked.

"Well, there is one other reason I called. In today's mail, there's an envelope — looks like a greeting card — and it's addressed to Fern."

"Probably someone in town who's heard the story and is wishing her well," Matt supposed.

"It's from Rohn Reid. Has a return label with his name on it."

"That's weird. Open it."

"That's what I thought," Sylvia said. "Just a sec. It is a greeting card, "Get Well Soon" it says on the front."

"Read the inside to me. Does it say anything?"

"Yes, there's a brief handwritten note. It reads, 'Dear Fern, I've heard about your Scotland ordeal, and I want to express how sorry I, along with my Cold Rock Island employees, am about your trouble. We wish you a full recovery.' And, it's signed 'Warm Regards, Rohn Reid'. Get a load of that!" Sylvia said.

"That's very thoughtful of him. Have to say I'm surprised."

"People have different facets to them, boss," Sylvia said. "There's usually some good in them somewhere."

• • •

Three Weeks Later — Edinburgh

DCI Stuart MacLean and his wife, Madison — Mads, as Stuart called her — picked up Matt and Fern from their hotel. Fern had been released from hospital two days ago, but Matt insisted that they take it easy in a suite at The Scotsman Hotel for a few days before flying home. He wanted to be completely sure she was ready to leave her doctors. Joe Phelps called Matt to tell him that Secretary of State, Fred Leufeld, who Fern had met while on Cold Rock Island, insisted on sending his plane to Edinburgh to bring them home safely.

The MacLeans were anxious to meet Fern and were taking the Hornings out to their favorite restaurant—their neighborhood Indian—tonight.

Stuart pulled his car up to The Scotsman entrance, put on his blinkers, and they both got out and walked to the hotel's doors. The valet was there in a split second, approaching Stuart. "You can't leave your car there, son," he said.

Stuart said, "Oh, but I can," and flashed his badge.

"Oh, aye," said the long-time valet and went back into the warm hotel.

Stuart spotted them getting off the elevator, and, holding hands with Mads, went to greet them. He introduced his wife to Matt and Fern and gave Fern a quick hug.

"You look much better," Stuart said. "Although you are too thin."

Mads elbowed her husband and then grabbed Fern's hands. "You are not too thin, you are perfect! Stu wasn't lying to me when he said you are very pretty. And with what you've been through! We are so happy you've pulled through this terrible ordeal. Well done, Fern."

"Thank you both," Fern said. To Stuart, she said, "How on earth did you land this gorgeous creature?" She grinned.

"My wife is back, I think," laughed Matt.

The dinner, over the best Tandoori chicken and Dal makhani the Hornings had ever eaten, was full of camaraderie, cop jokes, and much laughter. The women shared a carafe of white wine, while Matt proudly ordered an excellent malt whisky, of which Stuart heartily approved, for the guys.

"I don't have a chance with the three of you," Mads lamented. "Three coppers." She shook her head good-naturedly.

"I might be retiring from a life of crime," Fern said. Her smile hid her on-going pain and emotional distress. She was able to function, and felt OK most of the time, but she had sustained some nerve damage, and it would last for weeks, if not months, while she continued to recover.

"Oh, do retire," urged Mads. "Then we can be great friends and talk about other things rather than horrible criminals. And Stu and I can pop over the pond and visit you in the far reaches of America. What fun!"

Stuart, abashed, said to her, "You can't invite yourself."

"Of course she can," Fern came to her defense. "Don't be so stuffy, *Stu*."

"Yeah, *Stu*," Matt joined in. "We'd love to have you come for a visit. My team wants to meet you and thank you for all you and your team did on our behalf. By the way, you never did tell me what your colleagues' nickname is for you. Spill."

Stuart clammed up, and Mads leaned in. "It's Becks," she laughed. "You know, like David Beckham, because my husband is always impeccably kitted out, too. He likes his clothes and his hair, does my guy." She gave him a playful pat on his cheek.

"Maybe it's because he has a gorgeous, posh wife, too," Matt said.

"I'm sure that's it," Stuart said, spearing a piece of chicken.

CHAPTER 43

One Month Later

Neil Aitken, Police Scotland forensic team leader, was watching a football match with his son and daughter at home when his door knocker clanged. A delivery man was on his stoop with a large box.

"I need your signature, pal," he said, holding out a pen and bill of lading.

"What's this?" Aitken said. "I didn't order anything."

"Are you sure? It's from Aberlour Distillery. Looks like a case of whisky."

Neil grinned from ear to ear and quickly signed for the delivery.

• • •

Two Months Later

Matt crept out of bed. Fern, his beloved wife, was sleeping soundly, her lips slightly parted, her chest going up and down gently. How he adored this woman. They would go on…and on and on. He hoped there were more children in their future, but now it was all about her full recovery, and he would let nothing get in the way of that.

They'd had a small, intimate gathering of their friends last night at the house to celebrate Fern's recovery. Sylvia and Sheldon, Ed and Milly, Jay, Tamryn, Patty and Ted, just home from an extended stay in Scotland where they fell in love all over again, Bernice and her husband, who Matt had never met, tough Sheriff Earl Johnson who cried like a baby when he hugged Fern within an inch of her life, Rudy, Walt, and city manager Bill Abbott.

It had been an evening filled with love and lots of booze. *No wonder Fern's sleeping like a baby*, he thought, and then, 'We are such stuff As dreams are made on, and our little life Is rounded with a sleep'. *The Tempest, dear friend, Stuart.*

He went down the stairs, pausing at the floor-to-ceiling window that looked out to the Pacific Ocean. The July sun rose over the hills behind him to the east, and sparkled off the deep blue water, his favorite view in the whole world. He went out to his deck, taking some deep breaths of the best fresh air on earth. A slight breeze ruffled his hair, but it was a mild day.

Of course, Roger was there to greet him.

"Whew!" the seal said. "That was too close for comfort."

"Don't you know it," Matt said. "I understand you met Jay while I was gone."

"Yep. Nice young man, good detective. Is our girl alright now?"

"She's getting there. But her doctor said it could be a long haul."

"How are we going to keep her busy at home?" Roger asked. *A good question*, thought Matt. "I have no idea," he told the seal. "I'd welcome any ideas you have."

"How about getting her hooked on one of those daytime soap operas?"

"This is Fern we're talking about, Roger. There's no way in hell she will watch daytime TV."

"She loves books, doesn't she?"

"Yeah. Big reader, my wife."

"So, buy her a honking huge gift card to that bookstore downtown she likes, and take her there today. That might keep her occupied until Joe Phelps can't restrain himself any longer and calls her."

"Excellent idea, Roger. I'm on it."

The seal bobbed up and down and grinned at Matt. "Tell Jay to come see me again. I like him."

"Will do. And, thanks for always being there for me, Roger."

"My pleasure, Chief. Have a good one." And he was gone.

Making coffee so it would be ready when Fern awoke, his cell phone in the pocket of his robe pinged with an incoming text message. Stuart MacLean. The text read:

> "Vadim Guz dead in his solitary cell. Wrists cut. Suicide, they say."

Matt hit reply and wrote:

> "Assist to Putin?"

Stuart responded:

> "We think alike, mate."

For the latest news on my life and my writing—and, who knows, perhaps a freebie or two—please consider signing up for my occasional newsletter at my author website:

www.kayjenningsauthor.com

ACKNOWLEDGEMENTS

I want to thank Stephanie Lane, the Public and Legal Information Officer, at the Oregon State Penitentiary, for giving me access and a tour of the spaces I needed to see to add authenticity to the scenes that take place at OSP. I may have mangled the prison's visiting hours and policies in the pursuit of moving the story forward—my fault, not Ms. Lane's. I especially want to thank her for letting me leave.

Thanks to the U.S. Marshals Service excellent website for a thorough description of how the Federal Witness Security program is run. They've protected over 19,000 witnesses and their families since the program began in 1971 without a single person being harmed or killed. I think that's a remarkable stat.

To the wonderful people in Scotland, I apologize in advance for my bastardization of your lilting language, colorful expressions, and cultural and societal norms. It was my intention to give this story some proper authenticity, and if I've botched it, the fault is all mine and I'm sorry. And the same to Police Scotland. I hope I've got your history, hierarchy, and policies correct. In real life, you most certainly would have caught the bad guys without U.S. help.

I also regret having to blowtorch your historical St. Margaret's Well, one of my personal favorite sights in Edinburgh.

I'm not an expert on nerve agents, and I sincerely hope I never am. Utilizing all the information on the internet I could find and talking to a person who is an expert (and who I will not name to spare him embarrassment if I've got it all wrong here), I've done the best I could in this fictional tale.

Thank you to William Shakespeare for his long-ago poetry, most of which is more true today than ever.

People, especially other authors, think self-publishing your novels is difficult. It is, but there are also many rewards for going the indie route. The most satisfying thing for me is working with the team of people who have stuck with me since the beginning, and I want to acknowledge their work.

Thank you to New York's own Claire Brown for your gorgeous, relevant, genre-perfect, and totally eye-catching cover designs. Next to writing good stories, the covers are what have made my work successful, and I'm grateful to you every day I sit down to write.

Thank you to my second New York City team member, Peter Senftleben, for his keen developmental editing that always improves my book, his joyful optimism, and his beyond-the-pale flexibility. He makes me believe in my characters and knows what they would or would not say just as much, if not more, than I do. Peter makes me look smarter than I am.

Thank you to Sue Trowbridge who runs my website and has improved my newsletter. She saved me from the clifftop when MailerLite made their transition!

Thank you to Stacey Ducker who has helped me a great deal with marketing tasks on which I seem to procrastinate.

Thank you to fellow Oregonian Steve Kuhn who formats all versions of my books. He does in one day what it would take me weeks to execute.

Thank you to my excellent team of BETA readers: MaryCay, Bart, Jeanette, Linda, and Peter M. I value your different perspectives, and always make edits based on your thoughts. All of you were particularly helpful on this book because I had my first bout of Covid, followed by a brain fog for a few weeks during an intense period of writing. At least, that's what I'm blaming some dumb errors on.

I also draw a great deal of support from some of the professional organizations I belong to — even though I don't usually attend meetings or conferences. Their webinars and advanced writerly education have been invaluable in improving my craft, especially during the Covid years. Special shout-outs to Willamette Writers, Sisters-in-Crime, and Mystery Writers of America.

To Killer Nashville for making *Mourning Bay* a top pick in their 2024 competition, and for Writer's Digest for naming *Phantom Cove* the award winner in the self-published e-book Mystery/Thriller category for 2024. I won! I'm not big on awards competitions, and I don't need it for personal validation, but it's particularly rewarding coming from these two excellent organizations.

Thank you especially to my husband, Steve, for his energy (enough for both of us when I'm flagging), his creativity in plotting when I'm baffled about where to go next, his brilliant marketing mind, his first reading of the manuscript, and his technological assistance. Also, most important, for his love.

www.ingramcontent.com/pod-product-compliance
Lightning Source LLC
LaVergne TN
LVHW091709070526
838199LV00050B/2321